MESH

Ken Coffman and Adina Pelle

It's tough to find something different to do. Here, two friends, Adina, an artist from Eastern Europe and Ken, an electrical engineer from rural Oregon, collect their short stories, mesh them together and talk about them. The result? An esoteric and stimulating collage of gypsies, poets, winners, losers, weird science and social commentary.

Also by Adina Pelle

Ghost Words and other Echoes…

Also by Ken Coffman

Steel Waters
Alligator Alley (with Mark Bothum)
Twisted Shadow (with Mark Bothum)
Glen Wilson's Bad Medicine
Toxic Shock Syndrome
Hartz String Theory
Endangered Species
Fairhaven
The Sandcastles of Irakkistan
Real World FPGA Design with Verilog

Mesh
©2012 Ken Coffman and Adina Pelle
All Rights Reserved

ISBN 978-0-9827734-4-4

STAIRWAY≡PRESS

SEATTLE

Cover Design by Guy Corp, www.grafixCORP.com
Front cover design by Gary Croft
Rear cover photograph by Judy Coffman

www.stairwaypress.com
1500A East College Way #554
Mount Vernon, WA 98273

Table of Contents

The Dam
Ken Coffman

"IF YOU KNOW what's good for you," Jeremy Harriss said, "you'll take your goddamned hands off me. Now."

Bruno held Jeremy's left arm on the ergonomic office chair's arm while Stewart wrapped a Velcro strap around it. Bruno and Stewart were not twins, but they were equally large and muscular. Bruno pressed on Jeremy's shoulder and walked to the other side. Soon, Jeremy's arms and legs were bound. He strained and wriggled, but could only move a small fraction of an inch. It was hopeless. He settled and relaxed his body, but the mirthless grin that spread across his face was filled with malice.

"My father will lop off your heads and mount them on a pole outside the Harriss International building. I'm not sure I'm speaking figuratively."

Behind him, the corner office door opened. Mario Cantonelli entered.

"Ah, your father," Mario said. "That's why we need to speak to you this afternoon. About your father."

He spoke in a calm, gentle voice with a melodious Italian accent. Jeremy strained to look over his shoulder.

"I apologize for restraining you. This is for your protection. During our conversation, you'll see why it is completely necessary."

"I tried to reach my father on his cell phone this morning. Do you know why he did not answer?"

"All in good time, my boy," Mario said.

"I'm not your boy," Jeremy said.

Mario stood and looked at the young man.

"You're right, of course. At nearly seventeen, you are on the cusp on manhood. I forget myself. When I look at you, sometimes I still see the youngster with skinned-up elbows and a skateboard. I apologize."

"Take these straps off me."

"Yes. We will—in a few minutes. I need to show you something and we can't have you overreacting."

"Let's finish with the talking part of this scene."

"Of course," Mario said. "You Harrisses like to get right to the point." He walked to his expansive walnut-veneer desk and looked over the panoramic New York skyline for a moment before turning a large Apple Computer monitor so Jeremy could see it. "This security video was captured," he shot a look at his watch, "just over ninety minutes ago."

The monochrome images were pale and grainy, but the picture was clear.

Jeremy's father, Edgar Harriss, with wind whipping his jacket and necktie, stood on scaffolding high above the under-construction dam. In the background, massive earth-moving equipment rumbled on rough tracks over raw, molested earth. He looked up as if knowing the camera watched, then climbed over the railing. After a few seconds, he released his grip and fell.

"My father is dead?" Jeremy threw his weight against the chair and would have tipped it over if Stewart had not placed a massive hand on his shoulder to steady him. "I need to go there. Right away."

With a remote control, Mario clicked off the video display. He backed up against the desk and let it carry some of his weight.

"You need to understand what you saw," he said. "It's not exactly as it appears."

Jeremy closed his eyes and took a deep breath.

"Okay, tell me," he said.

"This will take a little patience on your part…"

"Right. Patience and tying me to a fucking chair."

"As I said…"

"Just get on with it," Jeremy said.

"This was before you were born, but I'm sure you heard the stories. The dam in Ontario? The one grand failure in the history of the Harriss family. That was almost it—the end of the small empire your grandfather built."

"The Iroquois Falls Dam."

"Right. Seventeen workers killed when the dam collapsed. More than two-hundred killed in the downstream town. You know worker deaths are associated with every major construction project."

"Part of the cost of doing business," Jeremy said.

"Right. But, do you know how many workers were killed before this dam gave way? None. It was an amazing example of workplace safety precautions paying off."

"Then the dam failed."

"Yes, the dam failed. Here's the interesting part. Your grandfather became convinced worker deaths are an important part of a large construction project."

"Human sacrifice."

Mario sighed. "Blood. Human lives offered up to appease the old, hungry gods. Madness, right? Insanity."

"But, our projects over the next seventy years…"

"Yes. The quality and performance is unmatched. A

Harriss Construction project is a reliable project. Do you know about the skinny man with the penetrating eyes? The man your grandfather talked to after the dam gave way?"

"I heard. Woo, the scary guy with ritual scarring— hieroglyphs carved in his cheeks. So what? What does this have to do with Dad?"

"I knew your father for fifty-seven years. He had cancer. Pancreatic. Inoperable."

"So, he jumps into our biggest construction project in twenty years and kills himself."

"Yes," Mario said.

After studying Jeremy's face for nearly a minute, Mario gestured to Bruno and Stewart. They kneeled and stripped off the Velcro straps. Jeremy stood and rubbed his forearms.

"I need to get there," Jeremy said.

"The helicopter is waiting," Mario replied.

In the spacious Lockheed Martin VH-73 helicopter, Jeremy continuously thumbed messages into his smart phone. Mario briefly wondered who he was exchanging messages with, but was distracted by the construction at ground zero where an elaborate building was replacing the twin towers of the World Trade Center. It was, of course, a Harriss Construction project.

At the dam, the wind twirled and ruffled Jeremy's hair and drew tears which dribbled from under his wrap-around sunglasses. He leaned over the railing and looked down. The height was dizzying. Jeremy imagined what it would feel like to let go—to launch into the air and plunge to the earth.

"It probably doesn't hurt," he said.

Mario leaned in close. "What?" he shouted over the howling wind.

"The impact. You're dead before your nervous system has

a chance to fill your body with pain. I'll bet it doesn't hurt at all."

Jeremy looked up. From the control room on the far side of the dam, Stewart waved.

That meant the security cameras were turned off.

Jeremy gathered Mario's lapels in his fists.

"Silk—imported from Florenzia," Mario said. "What are you doing?"

Jeremy threw his body to the side to get leverage. Then he pushed. Mario's arms flailed. For several teetering moments, his body was balanced between life and death while Jeremy gripped his lapels.

"What?" Mario said with a wild look in his eyes.

"Don't worry. As I said, I don't think it hurts," Jeremy said before letting go. Mario cartwheeled into space. Leaning over, he watched until Mario's body landed on the tangle of rebar far below. "There's a reason my name is on our headquarters skyscraper and yours isn't," he muttered.

He wasn't conscious of it, but he rubbed his sore forearms as he walked along the catwalk toward Stewart. Bruno, with his arms bound behind his back, was on his knees. Blood dribbled from a head wound. Jeremy jerked his head toward the chasm. Stewart lifted Bruno and pressed him out over the side. They watched him whirl in the air for a brief few seconds.

"They can't hold off pouring the concrete much longer, sir."

"So? Tell them to pour. Once the pour gets going, get the workers back out here. We don't make money paying them for playing cards and drinking tea in the lunchroom."

Stewart lifted his radio and spoke tersely.

"I'm sorry I restrained you back at the office, Mr. Harriss. Are we good?"

Jeremy peered over the side. "Yes, we're good."

He reached out to pat Stewart on the shoulder. Stewart flinched.

Jeremy laughed. "Don't be afraid," he said.

"Where to next, Mr. Harriss?"

"I'm in the mood for a steak," Jeremy said, "a giant, bloody one. Then a bath? You can scrub my back."

With no expression visible on his face, Stewart nodded.

"Whatever you say, sir."

On the far bank, high above the artificial gorge, the thin man standing on a concrete slab watched and was pleased.

The young Harriss has much potential.

He shivered. The Canadian wind, pouring in from the north, was cold. The thin man gathered the collar of his jacket around his neck. He was no fan of the cold. The Lincoln SUV was warm and it waited.

The thin man climbed in and was whisked away.

Notes on *The Dam*

AP: I like the ambiguity surrounding the thin man. It's not his description that hooks your subconscious because he's described very sparsely.

KLC: I wanted him to seem like he was not quite of this earth. I like the juxtaposition of the gritty reality of construction project with the arcane and surreal.

AP: The story contains a dose of mysticism...am I right? It reminds me of old tales of ships sent on their maiden voyages only after a virgin was sacrificed and strapped to the bow.

KLC: Is that how the tradition started? Interesting. Here's a bit of Babylonian narrative from the third millennium BC:

> *Openings to the water I stopped;*
> *I searched for cracks and the wanting parts I fixed:*
> *Three sari of bitumen I poured over the outside;*
> *To the gods I caused oxen to be sacrificed*[1]

I was trying to create a modern myth…to bring superstition into the 21st century.

AP: How close are you to big construction projects, like the Hoover Dam or the Alaskan railway where many left their bodies and souls behind as sacrifices?

KLC: I'm fascinated by the scale of a project like the Hoover Dam, but other than taking a tour and capturing snapshots as a tourist, I have no behind the scenes knowledge.

However, here is an experience which marked me: I worked for a while in the factory where F-16 aircraft were built. The building was so long (nearly a mile) that you could see the curvature of the Earth in the overhead lighting fixtures.

AP: What's with the Italian ? Anything to do with their well known immortal art of edifice?

KLC: No. I was thinking about the innate Italian sense of style. In general, they dress very well and I wanted that flavor for the character.

---

[1] Source: Wikipedia, http://en.wikipedia.org/wiki/Ship_names

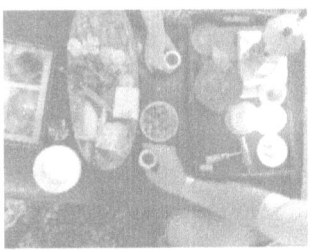

Her Secret Bordello
Adina Pelle

DEEP INSIDE, SHE craved truth in his words. There was no doubt he believed them, but they'd be quickly forgotten. Expired. Inevitably and all too soon.

"How beautiful you are. So beautiful, incredibly beautiful. I'm afraid of losing myself in your eyes."

Warmth.

She'd forgotten the feeling.

Mostly, men's words were empty, rolling over her and ending as a sad, sick mass in the pit of her stomach.

The day could have been perfect. Instead, it was full of noise and harsh colors falling from the sky; foreign sunlight painted the city and limned men's alien gestures. Piercing and stabbing—their eyes were bonded on her breast's peaks and valleys. She knew of her perfect body beneath layers of satin and cream—under blush, lipstick, mascara and carefully-arranged folds of cloth—a childlike body with young, soft bones that had been dead for years. The bones did not know how many times they'd been broken. The body had been violated, but the stain did not touch her soul. She did not see, did not hear and did not feel anything when her body was invaded.

Detached and unknowing—how often was she absent while jewels of happiness slipped through her fingers?

13

What was the depth of her despair?

She remembered only certain incursions of flesh; her body lying next to his. She did not know him and made no effort to change that situation. Their bodies were close—side-by-side. Under her skin, secrets were hidden under exhausted, shut-down senses. On the bed, threadbare sheets were scattered. From head to toe, her body hurt, but her spirit was hidden and untouched.

No one knew. No one suspected.

Nobody, nothing, no.

She created artificial boundaries…she would do anything but kiss a client on the mouth.

Shhh. Slow down. Speak slowly. I know you like me. I know you crave my aroma—that of cypress at the edge of a quiet meadow with scented hair scattered by the wind and a body made of sand twisting and conforming to yours.

The flesh remembers its long-lost innocence.

Don't say anything.

Bodies like undulating snakes. Reptilian. Cold words—language assembled from wet words as she unfolded beneath him. A predictable gush of secondhand passion and sexual instinct's fleeting moment of glory and reward.

Entwined hands, feet and whispers…everything but kisses on the mouth. A sudden, fraudulent flowering.

Above: nothing but a man's hairy, husky, meaningless body. Below: nothing but an acid taste on her tongue.

Why am I with this man?

To find peace, all questions must be suspended.

Deflected.

Evaded.

Afterward came a moment of quiet, leaky freedom. With a cigarette, she tranquilized disgust and painted over his taste with smoke and enjoyed the embrace of nicotine's small delirium.

Predictable. Each time, no different. Nearly naked, her body was dead. They had only empty names; no bodies or souls. No collective spirits. No synergy. No compassion. No love.

Only far-away sensations were left over from the barbarism of their animal coupling. Stolen pieces of remembered men were collected like trophies.

Hotel beds, fumbling illusions of love, barroom battlefields and sad, uncaring sex—everything was always the same. She raised her hands as if warding off evil.

Barely breathing, she was a soulless, mechanical doll. Instead of arms she had wings, but not for flying. Her broken wings were used for crawling around the room over cheap sheets and discarded clothing.

Trapped, she looked around with eyes filled with sadness. Nothing looked back. To God, she was invisible. Less than invisible. He was filled with love for ants and moths, but had nothing for her.

Sometimes she dreamed of the final, dying spasm of her anonymous, humiliated body followed by an eternal sleep. But, today's transaction must be consummated.

The man pulled on his clothes and left. The motel door closed with a solid finality. After a sponge bath, she arranged jars, tubes and vials of makeup on the bathroom sink. After a time, her wings changed back into hands and she reapplied her pretty mask.

Notes on *Her Secret Bordello*

KLC: I know you don't consider yourself any kind of a poet, but the delicate, beautiful phrasing of this story is a lovely example of poetic prose. This is one of my favorite AP stories. It's truly transcendent.

There is a contradiction, a cognitive dissonance between your delicate imagery and the crude topic. It's like you painted an outhouse with an artist's expensive sable brush. Is this something that came quickly with a flash of inspiration or was it something you agonized over, word-by-word?

AP: It's interesting you mention liking this story because, believe it or not, it's my favorite too. I believe it represents my real voice as a writer-painter-artist. I am and always have been moved by Charles Baudelaire and his *Les Fleurs du Mal,* so the poetry and symbolism belong to Baudelaire. I am mesmerized by the idea that in dirt and putrefaction a beautiful flower can survive, and if we look, we will find it.

In a year, I couldn't possibly write more than one or two stories like this. Not because it's hard, but because a subject like this has a very delicate exposure period. The minute the shutter is left open too long, the fragile balance between light and shadow is gone. Then what will we have? A trite story about a heart-of-gold hooker who marries Richard Gere.

KLC: Prostitutes often appear in your stories. Beyond literary exposure in books, what are your personal experiences with the 'ladies of the night' on the streets of Constanta or in the European cities where you lived? What can we point to for direct experiences with these women?

AP: I've always been intrigued by patterns in human behavior. Prostitutes lived in my apartment building when I was a college student and I observed the exchange—what women offered and what men took. It's a simple transaction—for the most part a commercial form of visceral supply and demand.

Here's what I always wondered. After the man walks away, is that the end of the exchange? Is there something the man carries away with him? Is there something he leaves behind?

KLC: Even in marriage, a man can make a woman feel like a whore. On the other hand, in other stories, you note that women often manipulate and use men. Perhaps this is a cheap thought—an unjustifiable bit of 'blaming the victim' nonsense that deserves a one-word answer, but is there any possible way can we consider this woman's 'customers' as fatal fools? Victims?

AP: This ancient transaction between a woman and a man, often following a rigorous financial negotiation, is never what it initially seems. In the end, the seduction part of the carnal bargain disappears to make room for an array of other dynamics. Everyone is the victim. After the act, no one deserves poise or dignity.

KLC: I don't want to say anything more about how I feel about this story. Let's look at what others said about it.

> ...*that cinematic quality, quick frames flickering a sad story...*
> —Sarah M.

> ...*a very vivid tale of a sad soul, old before her time...*
> —Barb N.

*How sad that she will never know the joys of love and
only feel empty inside.*
—Angela A.

*Such sadness portrayed so well. To be absent from so
much of herself and of her life is so sad. Wonderful
writing.*
—Kimber F.

You've had great response from the public about your work—
including a great quote from the legendary Tom Robbins
(Adina Pelle Rocks!). Warren Adler (author of *The War of the
Roses*) said your work is "a true exploration of a woman's
emotional and erotic life." What have these accolades meant to
you as a writer, particularly in the dark of night when you lay
awake and dream up your stories?

AP: The reader's response to my work means everything to
me. It validates me as a human and as a writer. It chases away
my inhibitions and gives me a reason to hope I might be able to
communicate the things that are important to me.

KLC: The broken wing is a powerful and sad image. The
change of her hands into wings and vice versa means there is
hope and the possibility of changing into something else.
However, this woman seems doomed. Are we misleading
ourselves if we hold out hope for your sad, beautiful, unnamed
young woman?

AP: They say hope was the cruelest gift released from
Pandora's box, yet we cannot survive without it. Everyone
gets their wings injured at some point in their life. I am a big

believer in redemption, so to answer your question, I'll throw out another:

Is there an earthly force with the power to heal broken wings?

Keptsake
Ken Coffman

SORRY, I WAS lost in thought. I'm surprised you recognize this symbol; yes, it's pagan. A girl showed it to me a long time ago and it stuck with me. Like you, she was pretty with auburn hair and brown eyes. Eyes with infinity written in them.

The first time I saw her, she knelt with a colorful, cotton peasant dress working up her thighs. Her legs were thin and covered with dust. She doodled in the dirt with a long finger. This very symbol, now that I think on it. The wind teased her hair which I noticed was braided with leaves and twigs. She said the symbol represents fate and chance romance, but she might have been mocking my nervous excitement and naked interest. When she pushed her hair back, she left dark smudges on her cheeks. It was not filth; it was charming.

I asked if she was a witch and she smiled. Could be, she said. She tugged my hand. Come, we must have wine.

I hesitated and she called me silly. As we climbed weathered stairs, the wind whirled and the long grass bowed and whispered.

Her front room was dimly lit and the air was thick with hazy perfume. She brightened the room by lighting candles in every corner—in rusty tins, stabbed into empty wine bottles and held by elaborate silver candlesticks. Flames lapped at darkness, but did not defeat it. Flickering shadows writhed on

20

the walls. Her odd dance was accented with flashing, mischievous eyes. She poured wine from an asymmetrical, black, label-less bottle, and then pulled me down to a rug woven from odd-colored yarns and decorated with strange patterns.

We live our lives in symbols, she said. I asked what our physical act symbolized and she laughed. Love and the circle of birth and death, of course, she said.

As we moved together, the walls fell away and the room moved through the candles like the solar wind flows through stars. Her stories were dreams. After my energy was tapped, she stood and, dressed only in shadows, danced again. Her body was nymphic and her hair was a silken banner. Time coalesced, evaporated and drifted into irrelevance. I was enchanted.

In the morning, the candle flames were dead. She kissed me and I clutched her body with desperation.

I love you, I said. I want to know you, to grow old with you, to possess you.

She pulled away. No, you don't, she said. You don't want to know how I pay the rent, how I look in the harsh light of the sun and that I bleed from my nethers when the moon is full. Am I boring over time? A naggart? Stupid? Am I a witch, really a witch?

She threw my shirt at me and ordered me to get dressed and leave. There was no resisting her command.

I'm sorry if I rambled. I can't help but think of fate, love, passion and chance encounters at times like this. You truly have pretty eyes. Can I hold your hand and pour you a drink from the black bottle?

Can witches read minds? I don't know. Let me show you again. Notice how the symbol seems like something solid, like a key or talisman, perhaps. Like a whispered question riding the wind.

And, when you're ready, we can go...

Notes on *Keptsake*

AP: Ken, I'm surprised—you do have a heart! What a wonderful and romantic snapshot. There's a cardiac chamber I didn't know you had.

KLC: I like to pretend I'm a cold-blooded logician and hyper-rational engineer, but all my novels are love stories. Deep inside, I am a hopeless romantic.

AP: When did you write this?

KLC: Hey, I'm old, how do you expect me to remember? Roughly, it was probably originally written in the 1980's and then cleaned up and revised a few years ago.

AP: You are generally a grammar-Nazi and punctuation-Fascist, but not in this story where there is little punctuation and the story flows without the typical structure of language. What were you trying to achieve?

KLC: Sometimes I binge on an author I stumble across. As an example, I was pulled into Charlie Huston's hyperactive world. Charlie has a quirky, minimalist approach and does not use quotation marks. It can make it hard to know who is speaking, but it also injects the words directly into your head without the barrier of interpreting punctuation. It's the kind of thing that should not work, but it does. I wanted to experiment with taking out as much punctuation as possible and see what I could do. The effect is interesting for a very short piece, but I don't think you'll see me use it often.

AP: I am reminded of Yeats:

> *When you are old and gray and full of sleep*
> *And nodding by the fire, take down this book,*
> *And slowly read, and dream of the soft look*
> *Your eyes had once, and of their shadows deep*

I have many memories like this. I won't even ask how much reality is in the story, and it doesn't matter. Memories make a nice pillow to sleep on when you are old, gray-haired and much closer to the end of your life than its beginning.

KLC: I struggle with my work. I have such respect and admiration for the written word that it offends me to take it lightly or write disposable books to be consumed quickly and tossed aside. The battle in my soul is constant, because beyond what I learned from the books in my little library and the guidance of my friends, I am an uneducated writer. Really, I have no business doing this. I have no credentials. I have no justification whatsoever for having strong opinions about how words should lay on the page.

However, don't think that will deter me. I also have a stubborn, relentless persistence. When I am cremated, don't be shocked to find bits of rusty old iron mixed with the ash and bone fragments.

AP: I like the pagan undertone of this story. As you know, I have a couple of pieces centered around gypsies and fortune tellers. You are an analytical man and I'm sure you don't believe in the paranormal, but you open yourself to fantasy, if only for an instant.

KLC: Adina, you wound me. Excuse me, I need to go off and pout for a while. You're partly right, of course. I am a hard-headed old engineer and don't believe in anything unless it can be double-blind tested in a laboratory. However, we live in an odd world—a bizarre mental construct found between our ears.

One thing I am sure of—and this is a lesson from mathematician Kurt Gödel—a closed system cannot contain enough complexity to fully describe itself. This means that anyone who claims complete certainty about anything in life is fooling himself (or herself).

To draw a correlated philosophical point, you can dispute the existence of black swans all you like and build elaborate proof and justification, but the first time you see a black swan, you need to discard your carefully constructed notions. What you *know* is not necessarily true.

You should always be open to the world delivering a surprise.

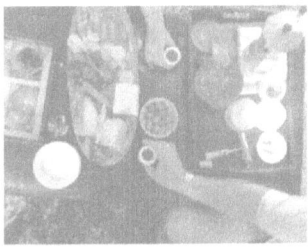

The Pursuit of Happiness
Adina Pelle

MANY AGES AGO, when the Gods roamed the earth, it was obvious that mortals needed a boost to their spirits and self-confidence or the very existence of the Gods was in jeopardy.

After much deliberation, and in an effort to avoid a plebeian revolt against the imminent law, the cluster of Gods determined that one God would be chosen to represent the celestial world as overseer of the earthly turmoil.

A rushed ruling from the newly elected God spread quickly among mortals. The decree read, in part, as follows:

> *Humans must be united by working-class enthusiasm in a democratic paradise. It is given that a stable society requires complete harmony. Each citizen of this democracy, to maintain peace and order in the earthly kingdom, can and should be happy. Therefore it is hereby directed:*
>> *Citizens shall kiss freely in public to show contentment and submission.*

I reproduced only a single passage of the new governance where the public kiss was defined as an indicator of mortal happiness. The decree also included other aspects, like banning criticism of the elected God, but we will save those elements for a future conversation.

Thus, the formal rule of kissing in public was introduced as mandatory for all mortals. To monitor the way in which the populace respected the rule and to ensure implementation of the decree, a patrol was created. Members of the patrol had freedom from dawn to sunset to identify, observe, scold and report the offenses of all who dishonored the law and refused the duty of displaying mutual affection and achieving ultimate human happiness.

The unofficial title of the new divine rule was *The Kiss Decree*. Among the populace, the seemingly simple rule generated a lot of confusion. The Happiness Enforcers often heard and dealt with excuses like the following:

> *Uh, I forgot to kiss her.*
> *Please excuse me, but I have a nasty cough.*
> *I have a toothache and cannot bear anything near my mouth.*
> *We just kissed. You were not watching carefully.*

The Happiness Enforcers, who were conscientious about the job (which included four weeks of vacation every year, medical and dental insurance and a well-funded retirement program) granted by the democratically elected God, were equipped with a number of sophisticated monitoring tools for testing the Mortal Kissing Rate (MKR). Any breach of the rule was considered treason against the supreme goal of happiness within the citizenry.

Execution of the decree was variable in different age groups and professions. In general, adolescents and young people were the most fervent supporters of kissing to show their happiness. Their lips could be heard vigorously at work in parks and alleys or other public places.

"Sorry to trouble you, but we have to kiss in the next five

seconds," a young man might say to a girl next to him.

In return, she was bound to the rule regardless of his bad breath or cold sores. Other young people turned to kissing to avoid boredom.

Now we come to the purpose my telling this tale.

Mortals between the ages of twenty-five and thirty-five had a different attitude toward the decree—a more nuanced and jaded one. It seemed they enjoyed kissing more when it was *forbidden* by their elders.

The Happiness Enforcers filled out forms capturing the date, month, year and location of the violation (or non-violation, if you will) which described situations like the following:

> *X sat on a bench in the park where words of love were exchanged with Y. Closely monitored with a calibrated instrument, the episode was fully recorded and documented. The couple did not kiss. They held hands and read each other poetry and whispered delightful words of love. There was incidental touching of private areas.*
>
> *But, they did not kiss. A citation was issued.*

Other couples obeyed the decree with great enthusiasm and gusto. Here is an example:

> *Honey, there is nothing between me and him. We were seated at the same table simply due to overcrowding at the restaurant. When the time came, we were forced to kiss to prove our happiness. You appeared at the wrong moment. Had you arrived earlier, I could have kissed you instead.*

From instrumental records and statistical analysis, we know

the decree was not properly honored by married couples. The intensity of their desire to kiss and be kissed was minimal. Married adults felt no reason to kiss in public. Many studies were funded and it was found that the desire to kiss was not present in the home either.

However, another phenomenon developed—occurring approximately four months after the decree was implemented. In spite of citations, harsh fines and prison sentences, fewer and fewer kissed in public. Tests revealed they no longer had the love inside that inspired kissing.

The democratically elected God and his counsel were left scratching their divine brows.

They observed citizens of advanced ages from sixty years and older invading the streets—enthusiastically kissing with their old, floppy lips. Otherwise, it was obvious. Humans grew less and less interested in properly manifesting their happiness. This scene displeased the Gods.

So, the divine rulers did what they always do. They wrote another decree. The democratically elected ruler worked night and day on the draft of a set of new rules to keep all mortals busy and happy.

Shortly thereafter, the first golden coins were cast.

Notes on *The Pursuit of Happiness*

KLC: This is an example of mixing a flat, toneless delivery with a completely absurd situation. The contrast is very vivid. It reminds me of Franz Kafka.

> *One morning, when Gregor Samsa woke from troubled dreams, he found himself transformed in his bed into a horrible vermin. He lay on his armour-like back, and if he lifted his head a little he could see his brown belly, slightly*

*domed and divided by arches into stiff sections. The
bedding was hardly able to cover it and seemed ready to
slide off any moment. His many legs, pitifully thin
compared with the size of the rest of him, waved about
helplessly as he looked.*
—*Metamorphosis*, Franz Kafka

There is focus and discipline required to accomplish this. In
other words, it would be easy to add florid descriptive details
to make the setting more concrete and real. As writers, we're
always reaching for the easy words. Is this discipline hard for
you to maintain or is it something that comes naturally from
the story as you initially visualized it?

AP: It is actually very hard as I am not a disciplined person.
On the contrary, I am a complete nightmare for any analytical
thinker who dares to dabble in my ideas. I am married to an
engineer whose perfectly structured analyses always come out
as QEDs. His thoughts balance beginnings with ends in perfect
symmetry. I need that kind of discipline and many times
borrow it to infuse my ideas with some logic.

KLC: When you gave me this story to look at, you knew I
would mention George Orwell, didn't you?

AP: Of course. George Orwell. I read his work when I was
very young and I remember thinking I was reading something
inappropriate considering the communist society where I grew
up. It took later years to understand my initial uncomfortable
reaction.

KLC: Well, I *am* going to mention Orwell, and not just
because of the social commentary of your absurd tale. I refuse

29

to reach for the easy reference to *Animal Farm*. I think Orwell is an excellent and underrated prose stylist. Any chance I get, I will be his cheerleader.

> *The drawing-room was a cool, light-coloured room with lime-washed walls a yard thick; it was large, but seemed smaller than it was, because of a litter of occasional tables and Benares brassware ornaments. It smelt of chintz and dying flowers. Mrs. Lackersteen was upstairs, sleeping. Outside, the servants lay silent in their quarters, their heads tethered to their wooden pillows by the death-like sleep of midday. Mr. Lackersteen, in his small wooden office down the road, was probably sleeping too. No one stirred except Elizabeth, and the chokra who pulled the punkah outside Mrs. Lackersteen's bedroom, lying on his back with one heel in the loop of the rope.*
> —*Burmese Days*, George Orwell

That snippet has nothing to do with the style or theme of your story. How do you like that as a non sequitur?

AP: As you guessed, when I wrote this story, I had *Animal Farm* on my mind. I agree, Orwell was an astute writer and his best work is far away from *Animal Farm*. However, I never had the same *forbidden* feeling while reading any of his other books as I had as a young person reading commentary about the social blueprint I was immersed in.

KLC: In this story, I'm reminded of the writers who had firsthand experience with Communism. I'm thinking of immigrants like Ayn Rand and Vladimir Nabokov, authors who wrote about the brave new world they found in the west and compared it to the brutal oppression they experienced in their old country.

> The world is going to hell, but among it all a blessed light is burning quietly for me—not from the star, which went out a long time ago, but from a new source, like a fog filled with the trembling light of stars.
> —*The Tattered Cloak*, Nina Berberova

I could be wrong, but I take your story to be an attack against the statist mentality. As a writer in the vein of the immigrants I mentioned above, give us some insight about the dark world inside the Iron Curtain and the rising welfare state here in the west.

AP: For me, it's an extraordinary paradox. Life was good in those days when I lived behind the Iron Curtain. Beyond the minor social parodies we experienced at times, life was experienced at a steady, monotonous, but safe, pace. I am speaking only from my personal perspective, of course. I read and heard firsthand accounts of abuse and suffering at the hands of the quasi-Marxists that governed most of the Eastern Bloc.

But, not me. I was an odd child, there's no doubt about that, but I grew up sheltered and dare I say it? I was happy. By the time my grandparents and parents healed from the Second World War and recovered from the gross early soviet-communist agendas—they found peace and happiness under the new system in Romania, a place completely independent from Moscow's rule.

KLC: It's clear from your story what you think about bureaucrats who crave God-like powers. Pretend you have one of these metamorphic beetles here in front of you today. What would you do with it?

AP: The only thing you can do with such beetles is have some fun. Turn them onto their backs and watch their futile legs wriggle in the air. We'll watch and see if they can flip themselves upright.

KLC: This is another story where your last line comes from of the blue sky and throws us for a loop. Abruptly, we move from love to money.

AP: The pursuit of happiness is a more pragmatic practice than we humans dare to admit. We can blame social systems, our leaders, our deity, our parents, children or spouses, but in the end, for some, being unhappy provides an ultimate satisfaction. The struggle to prove otherwise will give artists material to dwell on for centuries to come.

The Happy Halloween
Ken Coffman

CLARENCE CAREFULLY LIFTED a strip of duct tape and removed a circular section of corrugated board. The window was covered with alternating thicknesses of aluminum foil and panels made from old cardboard boxes. This insulation worked well—through the opening, cold seemed to reach through the hole to grab at him. He carefully placed the ancient glass jack-o-lantern in front of the opening and lit the candle stub by tipping in the larger taper borrowed from the fireplace mantle. The flame guttered and smoked. Wax made from pig fat did not burn very well.

"You do this every year and we never get any visitors," May said, "and how do you know it's really Halloween?"

Clarence turned. He adjusted the scarf around her neck and kissed her nose.

"Hope springs eternal," he said, "and I keep track of the days, so I know when the old holidays are."

"You're a mad fool," she said.

"Maybe so."

There was a candle in every room, but they failed to hold off the darkness. Shadows danced in every corner. Outside, the wind howled and threw icy rain against the walls.

"If a kid does come, what are you going to hand out? They won't be impressed with a dried-out biscuit or moldy potato."

33

Clarence grinned.

"Don't worry your pretty little head about it," he said, "I have resources."

"You found something at Bartertown?"

"Maybe I did."

"You're a scamp." She grinned. "If it's really a holiday, we can spare a spoon of possum stew if you want it."

Through layers of wool, she rubbed his belly. They weren't starving, but like everyone else, they were always hungry.

"What about you?" he said.

"There's enough. I'll have a spoon too."

Clarence walked to the kitchen and looked—there *were* two spoonfuls left in the bottom of the pot. Holding her hand to catch a stray drop, she held up the spoon and he opened his mouth. She fed him like a baby.

"Damn it, May, that's good."

She took her bite and tilted her head back. They savored for nearly a minute before swallowing. Clarence picked her up and kissed her neck.

"That's enough," she said, giggling.

There was a noise at the door. Clarence set her down gently and reached for the rifle leaning against the kitchen wall. May reached in her apron pocket and wrapped her fingers around the grip of her revolver. Clarence walked to the front door and pulled the hammer back on the rifle.

"Be careful," May said.

He removed the chains, lifted the wooden latch and unlocked the deadbolt. After pulling the door open a few inches and peering out, he relaxed. He threw the door open wide.

"What have we here?" he said.

It was a ghost—a three-foot-tall ghost wrapped in a ragged

sheet with crude eye holes.

"Boooo," the ghost said.

A man stood in the front yard with a double-barreled shotgun laying in the crook of his arm. He scanned left and right, and then returned his eyes to the porch.

"What did I tell you to say…"

"Trigger-tweak," the ghost said.

"Do you know what that means?" Clarence said.

"Trigger-tweak. It means you gotta give me somethin'."

Clarence laughed. "So it does," he said. "Hey, George."

"Good evening, Clar," George replied. "Bitter cold, ain't it?"

"Always," Clarence said. "Hold on a second."

He moved back into the room and opened the coat closet. Deeply hidden in the pocket of a parka was a can. He pulled a huge knife from its sheath. The knife was sharp—he was easily able to open the can. With a fork, he speared a mushy section of Bartlett pear and let the syrup drain off.

"Ready?" he said.

The ghost nodded and pulled off its hood. From underneath, a thin face was exposed. A boy. Six-years-old. Andy. Clarence slowly held out the fork and placed the pear in the kid's mouth. His cheeks bulged and a dribble of syrup ran down his chin. May, peering around Clarence, laughed.

"You like that?" Clarence said.

Andy nodded vigorously. "Yes, sir."

"Come get some," Clarence called out to George.

George looked up with a puzzled expression.

"You sure?"

"Come on," Clarence said.

He speared a pear-half and tapped the fork on the can to capture the juice.

George steadied Clarence's hand and took the pear.

"Goddamn, that's good," he said.

"What is it, Daddy? Is there more?"

"Not for now," George said. "I don't think I've had a pear since the disruption. You forget, you know."

"I know," Clarence said. "May, get in here and get some."

"I was hoping you'd say that."

She raised her head and Clarence dropped a pear-half on her tongue.

"Oh, Lord," she said. "Now you."

Clarence shrugged and peered in the can. He worked the fork and pulled out his piece.

"There's one piece left if you want to take it back to Helen. How's she been doing, by the way?"

"Same. No better, but no worse. I'm not sure she'll make it."

"You mind if I drain off the syrup first? Then you can take the can back to her."

"She'll love it, thank you."

Clarence handed the can to May who took it to the kitchen. Soon, she reappeared and handed the can back to George.

"One more time?" Clarence said to Andy.

"Trigger-tweak," Andy said.

Clarence chuckled. "Good night," he said.

He closed the door and worked at all the locks.

"You're a hopeless, sentimental old man," May said.

"That's nothing," he said. "Wait 'til you see what I have planned for Thanksgiving."

"Oh, you're such a rascal," she said. "Come to bed—let's give another try to making a baby."

He licked his fingers and pinched off the candle in the jack-o-lantern. He worked the cardboard back into place and smoothed the duct tape. Outside, the cold howled with

36

frustration.

"Sounds good to me," he said.

Notes on *The Happy Halloween*

AP: Cormac McCarthy's *The Road* was the first thing that popped in my head because of the post-apocalyptic background and the canned fruit, but obviously this is a sweet and endearing story. What was your inspiration?

KLC: I've always been obsessed with noticing how fragile our infrastructure is and how easy it would be for society to fragment without cultural glue to hold us together. We mess with traditional concepts of patriotism and family values at our own peril.

AP: Is it a coincidence that you named your main character the same as the angel Clarence in the Christmas classic *It's a Wonderful Life?*

KLC: If you believe in coincidences, then yes, the one you note is one. An amusing one, now that you mention it.

AP: Clarence and May are ageless in your story but an extremely sweet and loving couple. Is it just me or do I sense an optimistic thought? Maybe the physical world will erode, but love will still stand strong?

KLC: I make no special claim about having answers for our purpose in walking on the earth. However, in the end, what else do we have? Perhaps romance is an evolutionary trait ensuring the propagation of our species, but we should embrace our emotional rewards when we can.

AP: I like—no, I love the dynamic you created in this couple. The dialog between them is delightful.

KLC: I don't know if I have any special talent for this, but I study the way people talk and interact. I try to breathe life into my characters. I'm trying. As my wife says, I'm very trying. To me, the characters in my books and stories are alive. They are my friends. I'm reminded of *Bladerunner:*

> **Pris:** It must get lonely here, J.F.
> **J. F. Sebastian:** Mmm…not really. I make friends. They're toys. My friends are toys. I make them.[2]

AP: Beyond the sweetness the couple exudes, you add a savory touch by making the can of pears a sensory element in the story. The reader will not only enjoy that, but will go to their pantry and open a can of syrupy fruit. I know I did.

KLC: We are a decadent culture awash in complex technology, but, if necessary, we can revert to the simple pleasures of life.

AP: And of course, need I add it? Referring back to *The Road*—what a relief they didn't eat the kid. With you, Ken, I never know what to expect.

KLC: Inside, I'm smushy and gooey. I like a HEA[3] ending and that's generally what you'll get from me.

---

[2] *Bladerunner* script by Hampton Fancher and David Peoples
[3] Happy Ever After

You
Adina Pelle

I WAS TEN-YEARS-OLD. Your name was Julian. Our grandmothers exchanged recipes in the apartment complex.

Something draws my memory back to that fast-moving, nearly forgotten day...the day you grabbed my hand.

Hmmm, what a weird feeling that was.

My mind is filled with absurd details. While the train raced through the city, you dragged me down the aisle past a pile of old, shabby-looking brown suitcases. We passed a young man smelling of tobacco and a soldier with a square face—one I stared at before you and your grandmother boarded the train.

I brushed against those suitcases and my pure-white socks ended up with a stain on them—a dark patch of dirty gray. You played with my dark hair and laughed at my misery with the cruel and innocent laughter of a ten-year-old child.

That day, we were far away from the world, running into the night and searching for the edges of the most crystalline moments of childhood.

Your hair was black, wavy and smooth to the touch. Your child's body held a future man-in-the-making.

The rough soldier looked at us with tenderness—as if we were worth fighting for. In return, you made a funny face and I could not resist. I laughed.

Over the years, one thing that lingers in my mind is your

name, it echoes. I deleted all the other train stops on the map.

A dusty neon light flickered and made you look pale and feeble. Your red lips and white teeth will I remember through the years. And your name.

That train followed the same route every night for the next twenty years—awash with lights flickering in the dark and infused with memories of two ten-year-old children running and laughing in its dim light anticipating lives to come with flickering glimpses of our illusive, long-forgotten destination.

Later, the departing locomotive pulled at my soul as I waved goodbye from the platform. Through a window, the dark locks of a boy named Julian. You waved your hand and disappeared into the night. I sat on the platform and for the first time in my life wondered where everything goes.

I was fourteen-years-old and your name was Matthew.

You appeared in my dreams with the tumultuous beginning of adolescence, the beginning of life. I tried to say important things—I wanted you to look for me, to find me and tell me you understood.

I agonized in my sleep and during endless mornings and afternoons. You told me things I loved to hear. Your hair was brown—and I remember your dark, sad umber eyes haunting my dreams. You told me I was beautiful and I believed you.

After lingering dreams, I woke bathed in virginal sweat. By day, I complained about being too young to do anything important and waited for sleep and rest to come.

I forgot almost everything else about you, but your broken voice echoes in my thoughts alongside my mother's smile—the way the upper corner of her mouth slowly raised while she closed my bedroom door behind her.

I was sixteen-years-old and your name was Denis. We hid when we met because I was a minor—but, Lord; how I loved you...I wrote you poems and letters that had no beginning and no end.

Trembling, I sat on the edge of your bed with my wrinkled shirt cast aside on the floor. My shy, white breasts radiated light in the dark room under the gaze of your eyes; eyes like beacons, green and clear.

I said something about secrets but who heard? Your eyes were glued to the pink buttons of my breasts while you composed symphonies in my name. I feared my body and the way it twisted and writhed under your touch.

We did our business so quietly.

When I think of you now, your voice is lost.

I was twenty-three-years old and your name was Edward.

I stared into my wine glass and I lost myself in your black eyes. Your rough mouth smiled at me crookedly. If we had not drunk so much, maybe I'd know if I was pretty or if I loved you.

I looked beautiful, you told me—though maybe there was something you wanted from me and something I wanted from you. Everything was good with you. You were so careful with my pain.

You spoke to me with your eyes.

"So beautiful and so young."

Outside, I smelled the coming winter.

We got married and I loved you, my sad, pathetic husband, a lover steeped in sad despair and resignation. We laughed often and were serious only when arguing and shouting. I bore your child and time passed.

Over the years my eyes water and my heart hurts.

"Why, God?"

I was thirty-three years old and you did not have a name, just nicknames. I loved you because you were intelligent, spoke well and filled a gap in my life.

I said I did not know who you were, but see how it is? I remember you, no matter what your name was. You left footprints on my heart I cannot delete.

I was thirty-five years old and read your messages on my computer screen. We spoke in complicated, passionate phrases and we let our blood flow like good music.

I suggested you try loving all of me and you did, so I quit philandering and seduced you with lines, letters and verbs.

Sometimes we debated, sometimes we agreed. I loved you, you loved all of me, and my heart sang happy melodies when you looked at me.

I was ten-years-old and squinting leaky eyes along a railway going nowhere. Trains screamed by quickly; some empty and some heavy with travelers.

When I close my eyes, the chaos of my travel is finally organized.

Notes on *You*

KLC: From the Naked Man stories in *Ghost Words and other Echoes...*, you have me well-trained. The simple and casual mention of those white socks is unbearably sexy. I suppose that makes me, at least in part, a filthy old lecher.

> We passed on to a small pantry and entered the dining room, parallel to the parlor we had already admired. I noticed a white sock on the floor. With a deprecatory grunt, Mrs. Haze stooped without stopping and threw it into a closet next to the pantry.
> —Vladimir Nabokov, *Lolita*.

AP: On one hand, the white socks represent a dorky, oblivious-of-reality, awkward kid grasping at premature adulthood. On the other hand, these socks can be a seducing garment, like Salomé's last veil or Lolita—the sun-bathing girl-child.

KLC: Will you pretend this story is not largely autobiographical?

AP: Yes, I embrace that pretense. At most, I will confess to taking a wobbly walk down memory lane.

KLC: Do you think, in general, that young women enter the sexual phase of their lives too soon? Shouldn't they relax and enjoy the innocence of childhood for a few more years before it's gone forever? I suppose this is easy for me to say now as an old man—no longer a horny teenager desperate to work a girl's panties down and around her ankles.

AP: I don't think young women should always do what's expected from either the prudish or chaste ends of the spectrum. They should do what their inner voice guides them to do. The reason I say this—being fully aware of the scandal and eyebrows raised in my youth—is because I know for a fact that destiny cannot be stopped.

If tragedy brews, it will happen, sooner or later. Of course, I talk through my own prism—I was a very precocious young woman, a dreamer, but I never shied away from embracing the result of my actions. I was a common sense dreamer.

KLC: I will tell you about one of my earliest sexy experiences—this is definitely 'sexy' and not 'sexual' because it was years later before I had any firsthand experience with orgasm (how's that for a Nabokovian play on words?).

After a church service, in a dark alley, an older girl named Linda P— lifted her dress and showed me her bloomers (yes, literally, I swear this on Orwell's grave, she wore old-fashioned bloomers) and told me she wanted to cuddle me like a teddy bear. I promise you, I had no idea what she was doing.

So, tell me, what was going on?

AP: Linda was kindling something, though she might have been unsure of exactly what. We are all slaves to the flows and forces of Mother Nature. A man once told me how his mother dragged him home by one ear after catching him naked with two older girls. We're talking five- and six-year olds. I think nature owns our bodies and society our minds.

KLC: You have a son—no daughters. How do you think having a daughter would have changed your stories and your thoughts about sex?

AP: I don't think anything would change. I have only one perspective, mine, and it was built from the inside out and not so much from the outside in.

KLC: I know you spent a lot of time reading Marcel Proust and here you use seventeen words to hint at what Proust used a huge number of words to capture. À la Recherche du Temps Perdu (*Remembrance of Things Past*) is one and a half million words!

> *I sat on the platform and for the first time in my life wondered where everything goes.*

Where *does* everything go?

AP: I remember the exact moment when I realized everything has a beginning and an end and that time acts as an elastic band between everything around me.

Awareness comes when, like Marcel Proust, you wake up one morning to the smell of a freshly baked madeleine and start remembering people, places and the roles they played in your life.

KLC: From *À la Recherche du Temps Perdu*

> And so, night after night, she would be taken home in Swann's carriage; and one night, after she had got down, and while he stood at the gate and murmured "Till to-morrow, then!" she turned impulsively from him, plucked a last lingering chrysanthemum in the tiny garden which flanked the pathway from the street to her house, and as he went back to his carriage thrust it into his hand. He held it pressed to his lips during the drive home, and when, in due course, the flower withered, locked it away, like something very precious, in a secret drawer of his desk.
> —Marcel Proust, *Remembrance of Things Past, Volume One: Swann's Way*[4]

From these stories, it will be clear that I'm more verbose than you—and we're both much, much less verbose than Proust. I often puzzle over how a writer can be long-winded. It's a skill that seems to escape me. What are your thoughts? You've read very long novels and I know you love some of them more than life itself, but the longest piece I've seen from you is three-thousand words. What's going on here?

---

[4] As translated by C. K. Scott Moncrieff

AP: That's an interesting question and I think about it often. My take is that the books, the long novels by Tolstoy, Proust and Hugo, were written with a majestic beauty that enslaved my young mind and drew me to worship them. Now, as a writer, I do not have the confidence needed to deliver a long project. I feel like those shoes are too big for me to fill.

I'll get over it eventually. I want to.

KLC: As I think about *Remembrance of Things Past*, this must have been a huge influence on Kubrick's film *Eyes Wide Shut*. I say this not only as a philosophical influence, but in the way Kubrick will s-t-r-e-t-c-h a scene to capture a subtle thought or emotion. I would not describe Kubrick as a terse film maker.

As a homework assignment, before answering this question, watch the film again. Without doing any other research (by Googling Proust and Kubrick, for example, which you know will be the next thing I do), do you think Kubrick was influenced by Proust or is that the stupidest idea you've heard?

AP: I don't know. As a director and brilliant film artist, Kubrick must have read and processed the great works written before him, found inspiration in the words and naturally transferred that inspiration to his work—achieving an optimal distance between characters on the stage so the voice inflections, gazes, body movements, facial expressions and scripted lines weave a masterful and unique cosmos.

KLC: Perhaps this is a rude question a man should never ask a woman, but did you intend this story to capture all of the unnamed narrator's lovers, or just the more memorable ones?

AP: Ha! Ha! I captured my dearest moments and most-treasured mistakes...

KLC: The title is *You*, but the lovers are definitely plural. I can't imagine a tauter theme. Taken all together, the lovers are represented by the singular word. Please expand on what the title should evoke?

AP: Regardless of the title, the story is only about me. It's about the person I became after years on the crash course with the unique people I loved.

KLC: Sometimes you capture a thought in a breathtaking manner...and I'm floored by your skill and insight.

You told me I was beautiful and I believed you.

After lingering dreams, I woke...bathed in virginal sweat.

You left footprints on my heart I cannot delete.

If we had not drunk so much, maybe I'd know if I was pretty or if I loved you.

Outside, I smelled the coming winter.

AP: It all comes from the poetry I love so much—Baudelaire, Yeats, Apollinaire and Verlaine.

KLC: Imagine the young woman many years in the future as a much-older woman, let's say seventy years old. She will still want to experience love and intimacy. What will her version of *You* be like?

AP: I truly think love is ageless. Our hearts mature with age but the same coordinates guide our inner emotional compass.
  Here's something I wrote recently.

> *I love mornings when I wake and feel your tickling breath. It signals unconscious reveries of other walls surrounding different spaces—lost in time but dear to me.*
>
> *I am fully awake. You are spaced obliquely, but proportionally, in the corner of my retina, in my story in the book written while I forgot to count the days. Naked and biting my lips in the rhythm of a lost song surfacing timidly from your heart. Maybe from under the pillow.*
>
> *I know how to adore you, to forgive you, to adapt to your inaccuracies.*
>
> *I promise not to repeat my mistakes. I promise to paint your body with my tongue. I like drawing stories on your skin when we lay spread out in the morning light.*
>
> *I can tell you now—when I open wide to your traveling fingers, it's a synonym for welcoming your story. It's simply precious. And erotic. I understand what we are more every day.*
>
> *I mimic your smile in many languages. I dare you to any prejudice.*
>
> *Immersed in Zen, the smell of fresh coffee gets me out of bed.*

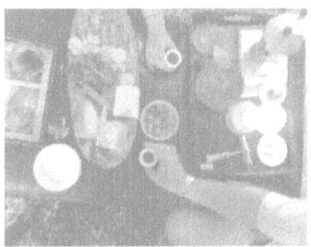

Gordy Swensen gets a Wife
Ken Coffman

THE LEXUS LS430'S bright halogen headlights and yellow fog lamps barely pierced the mist that, like smoke, filled dips in the road. Will Thomas drove too fast for the conditions—confident his heavy sedan, seatbelt, airbag, and comprehensive, no-deductable insurance policy would protect him from harm.

He lit up a fresh Camel—plucked from an engraved silver case—with the stub of a previous cigarette. Flicking the expired cigarette stub though a window gap, he idly noted orange coals scattering on the road before being eaten by the fog closing in on his tail lamps. Smoke eased from behind his teeth as he let his paunchy body settle deeply into the soft leather. The car was smooth and quiet; he imagined the tires didn't quite touch the road.

Will admired the ghostly image of his face illuminated by green dash lights; a grinning specter reflected in the windshield. His mistress, Angie, waited at his cedar cabin in the hills while his wife thought he was at a convention in Portland—his employees would cover for him if they wanted to keep their jobs. On reflection, he would prefer to be in Portland flirting with a pretty cocktail waitress named Lucy who was mesmerized by smooth talk, his wad of cash and boundless platinum credit card. She awaited his call.

He twisted the top from the Jack Daniels bottle keeping him company. After a deep draught he wiped his mouth on a monogrammed sleeve. A mangy-gray jackrabbit ran from the gloom. Will's eyes lit up. The rabbit froze in the road with eyes glowing like ghostly orbs. He eased the car over the center line and touched the gas pedal but the rabbit dashed for the roadside at the last instant. Hissing tires missed by inches. He searched the rear view mirror for the mangled body but only saw the rabbit's moony eyes staring back at him. He took a swig of whiskey. In the dash lights, a pinky diamond glittered with expensive elegance. His thoughts were bitter.

Shitty little rabbit escaped Doctor Death this time.

He loosened his silk tie and lifted the whiskey bottle in salute.

"Here's to your fucking health, wabbit."

Gordy Swensen held his .22 Marlin rifle tightly as he jumped over a log. Then, standing in silence, he listened to the subtle sounds of the night. Mice rustled in dry leaves and an owl swept by with a faint swish of wings. With the patience of a child poking a stick in an anthill, Gordy waited. After a few minutes, he whistled and his dog, Trapper, burst from the underbrush. Gordy stooped for a sloppy kiss.

"You see anything out there, Trapper?" Gordy whispered. "Any fat possums for my stew?"

He ruffled the hair between the dog's ears.

"Nothing? Then we'd better get home, old Trapper-dog."

The dog ran ahead with surprising speed along a barely visible trail.

Gordy was a half-wit, but these hills were his home. He lived in a ramshackle house at the end of a dirt road passable only by a determined driver with a four-wheel-drive truck. Gordy did not care about the road; he'd inherited a car but it was engulfed in blackberry vines. Gordy's dad was the last person to drive the car, but he'd died years earlier and was buried next to his mother on the hill beyond the outhouse. Each spring, by tradition when the flowers bloomed, Gordy placed a bouquet of daffodils and tulips on her grave—and pissed on his father's.

Gordy lived on forage and his Dad's state disability checks that still kept coming. He kept careful track of the days on a drugstore calendar. When the end of a month came around, he would hike into Rockville where Gracie Thompson would give him the check to sign. He would pick up a bag of flour, dry beans, and licorice sticks. At thirty-six, Gordy was a good kid. Everyone liked him though he never bathed and spoke only to Trapper.

Gordy ran to the top of a hill where he could see fog filling the valley floor like cotton candy. The air was cold and his old leather boots were soaked through. Trapper's fur was matted and dripping.

"Time to get home, Trapper," Gordy said after noting the angle of the moon. "We'll take the shortcut over Highway Twenty. Wanna take the shortcut?"

Trapper answered by running ahead. He disappeared into the brush.

Will hit the scan button on his radio. Trying to find a classical music station, he only heard country-western or Mexican music which faded in and out.

"Shit," he mumbled as he slapped off the radio.

Taking a swig of Jack Daniels, he stuck the bottle between his thighs. He thought about the woman waiting at the cabin. In the city, she was his administrative assistant. In the cabin, she was his slut. This was her last wild weekend—back at the office a pink slip waited.

51

"I'm gonna fuck her eyes out, and then cut her loose. Don't fuss with my coffee, baby, just hit the road."

He laughed when he pictured the look on her face. Her officemates would look the other way and pretend to work. He visualized tears running down her face and ruining her makeup. He'd already picked a replacement; a sweet young lass from the mailroom was giving him the come-on, undulating her ass under a short skirt and teasing his nose with sweet perfume as she passed.

He'd already bought her a diamond as big as a green pea. His penis swelled as he imagined her wearing that and nothing else. Will, irresistibly charming when he wanted to be, was a real bastard when he tired of a woman. He forgave himself for that; such were the rewards of hard work and success. He felt a flush of pleasure when he saw a dog appear from the brush beside the road. As the dog took a tentative step onto the pavement, Will pressed the gas pedal to the floor. The big car accelerated briskly.

Gordy moved with deceptive speed through the woods. Occasionally Trapper would stop and sniff the night air or urinate against a rock. When they came to Highway Twenty with Trapper trotting ahead, Gordy trailed in a leisurely manner. When Gordy saw headlights sweeping through the trees he felt an instant panic. Mired like a horsefly in syrup, he watched Trapper frozen in the headlights with his tongue lolling as the gray sedan poised for the strike.

In that instant, he knew Trapper was dead.

There was no time for Trapper to go forward or come back. After a stationary instant, the scene came to life and the car roared by. Gordy caught a glimpse of the man behind the wheel. Squinting eyes and mirthless smile. Trapper flew through the air in a boneless heap and dropped on the road's gravel shoulder. The sedan's taillights flashed and disappeared as the car rounded a corner. Gordy drew Trapper into his arms and held the warm body until it cooled. Through tears he rocked, kneeling with stones biting into his knees.

An unbidden thought revolved in his head.

I know where the man goes,

I know where the man goes...

Gordy walked through the woods carrying Trapper's corpse. Congealed blood was sticky on his clothes. He glided through the night feeling empty and dead. After a few miles on the deer trail, he stopped. Hidden by ferns, Gordy looked at the cedar cabin. The gray car was parked in the driveway. Like part of his body, the rifle was slung over his shoulder. He laid Trapper on the ground and fished in his pockets for loose long-rifle shells. With his attention fixed on the lights streaming from the cabin windows, his hands filled the chamber of the rifle automatically.

"Mr. Rich Man in your rich man house, I see you," Gordy said under his breath.

Tears streamed down his face as he leaned against a tree and aimed his gun.

"*You* have *things* you want from *me*."

Will, shaking with anger and breathing with ragged gasps, tried to appear cool and in control. "You'll send filthy pictures to my wife if I don't play your game. Well, I don't eat shit and I know how to deal with blackmailers."

"I just want to keep my job. You can transfer me to sales or something. I don't want to end up like Sharon Miles."

She picked up a framed photograph showing her and Will smiling and lifting champagne glasses from the deck of a rented yacht. She held it out.

"You told me you loved me," she said.

Will slapped the picture from her hand.

"Jumpin' Jehovah, buy a clue, will ya?" he said.

Will turned slowly to the bar. Picking up the bottle from the car, he tilted it to pour another drink. Leaning against a wall, he cooled his forehead with an ice cube. His expression was empty and passive, which terrified her more than his angry outburst.

"You know something, Angie? I'm not even here. I'm at a convention in Portland. I don't own this place. My lawyer bought it and even he doesn't know where it is. And you're not here, you've gone crying back to Mom and Dad in Saskatoon or Moosehead, or where ever the fuck you're from. No one knows we're here. You could disappear out here forever, real easy." His words were curt and clipped. He chuckled. "Something else occurs to me. I've never screwed a dead woman before. You know what the judge said. 'When death is inevitable, you might as well relax and enjoy it.'"

Shuffling his feet, he eased closer. Scared, she stared at the tension in his health club muscles and the vein throbbing in his forehead. Distracted by the blue and yellow light refracting from the big diamond on his pinky, the instant stretched into eternity.

"Goodbye bitch," he said calmly.

Gordy focused on the scene fifty yards away. The rich people were fighting.

They must have bad toothaches.

Gordy flashed on his father reeking of moonshine bought from the Indians up river—staggering and falling to the floor.

"A little more medicine for my toothache," he said before passing out.

Gordy took note of the wind coming from his left. He let his breath out slowly as he gently squeezed the trigger. As the rich man tore off the pretty lady's shirt, he fired the gun between heartbeats like his Daddy taught him. The gun cracked flatly in the night.

Will stood for an instant looking from the rags of the silk blouse in his hands to the little hole in his woolen pant leg.

"What the hell?" he whispered as his leg crumpled.

He had not fully comprehended the scene when the second shot shattered his elbow. Angie moved in belated self-preservation. Her hand fell to something on the table and she instinctively thrust it into his face as he fell. She should have closed her eyes but it was too late—she glimpsed the shard of bloody photo frame glass jammed in his eye socket. After falling backward on the couch, she did not notice the cold air on her chest, the wind ruffling her hair or the shreds of silk hanging from her shoulders. She did not notice the big clock chiming in the hall. She did not notice Gordy's gentle hand wiping tears from her face. Her eyes were open but she did not see.

Gordy wrapped a blanket around the lady's shoulders. He dragged the rich man out, found a shovel, and spent an hour digging a hole deep enough that the coyotes could not dig it up. He laid the man in the hole, and then laid Trapper's body on top—with the man's arms wrapped around. He stood for a minute whispering to the pair.

"You two have a good sleep. I'm gonna take care of the girl. She can wear Mom's clothes and I'll paint her face with Mom's stuff. I know we'll be happy. I hope you'll be happy too."

He shoveled dirt into the hole. After scattering pine needles around, there was no sign the hole ever existed.

Back in the cabin, he found the girl exactly as he left her.

He took one of her hands and lifted it. It stayed suspended in air then slowly returned to her lap. Her eyes were open but focused on infinity. He smoothed back her hair.

"Don't worry, pretty lady, Gordy will take care of you," he whispered.

He gathered her limp body in his arms and carried her into the night.

Notes on *Gordy Swensen gets a Wife*

AP: This is a gripping tale. In Gordy, I see a little of Lenny from Steinbeck's *Of Mice and Men*. The juxtaposition with the rich man's manners makes for a memorable character study. What inspired this story?

KLC: Like a lot of writers, Stephen King was an inspiration to me—not only his amazing commercial success, but I think his string of books in the 1970s including *Salem's Lot*, *The Shining*, *The Stand* and my favorite SK novel, *The Dead Zone* were as good as commercial writing gets. I studied his books and tried to figure out his style and how he applied his craft. *Gordy Swenson gets a Wife* is one of my earliest short stories and can safely be considered a tribute to Stephen King.

AP: Revenge and vengeance are wreaked at the end of this story. In the real world, do you believe in the eye-for-an-eye retribution for criminals?

KLC: I am not so naïve to believe that justice is always served in real life. Sometimes the bad guys win; they get away with their crimes and thrive. In our storybook worlds, we get to play God and make sure the proper fruits of evil are delivered.

AP: Does the fact that Gordy is retarded change the weight of the story?

KLC: First of all, you can't say retarded anymore, Adina. You're supposed to say something like developmentally disabled. Perhaps a person of more normal aptitude would take his vengeance in a more creative way—perhaps by leaving Will blinded and gelded—but alive.

AP: Will is not only a rich man, but a bastard. Do you associate wealth with a low end morals and ethics? Would Will have thought in the same manner had he not been wealthy and powerful?

KLC: Generally, taking a lesson from *The Bell Curve*[5], I associate low morals with stupidity and stupidity with poverty. That said, there are rich people who are corrupt and sleazy and there are poor, unsophisticated people who are wholesome. I suppose I would use whatever theme supports the story I want to tell.

In addition, perhaps my thoughts have changed. I wrote this story when I was very young. I'm not a wealthy person, but I make enough money that I'm able to fake it for short periods of time. Perhaps I have more respect for the wealthy now.

AP: Did you write this story hoping to get the reader's sympathy for the underdog?

KLC: Sympathy is not the right word. I hope to get the reader

---

[5] *The Bell Curve—Intelligence and Class Structure in American Life,*
Richard J. Herrnstein and Charles Murray, Simon and Schuster, 1994

inside Gordy's head and share a piece of his life. Empathy? Why do people read? To enjoy a flight of fancy? This story is a bit of distraction from the real world. Entertainment, that's all.

AP: I like the cinematic quality of the scenes; I can almost envision a camera jumping from one scene to the next. It builds momentum and stimulates the reader toward the conclusion. This a skill few writers master. Does it come easy to you?

KLC: You're too kind to an old man, Adina. However, in a self-indulgent book like this, I suppose this is no place for false modesty. I have always had a vivid imagination and there is a lot more going on inside my head than you'll ever see expressed in the physical world. To me, these stories are more real than the outside world and I put myself into them and bring them to life the best that I can. I was a bad writer for a lot longer that I should have been—perhaps I'm too stubborn to embrace lessons that others absorb easily, but eventually I figure things out.

After the novels I've written and the books I've studied and edited and published and the story contests I've hosted and all the books I've lost myself in and loved, I feel some sense of power over the written word—a certain sense of mastery. I struggle with passages and themes like everyone else, but I'm confident.

If I can visualize a scene, I can capture it on the page. This comes from doing it over and over and fumbling with stories and paragraphs and words that don't work and making lots of mistakes and relentlessly fighting through all the barriers.

If you bang your head against a door long enough, believe me, it will eventually open.

Summer Every Thursday
Adina Pelle

It's been my good fortune to enjoy a flyspeck of international acclaim, to hang with some big-time artists and performers whose work I admire, to track orangutans in Sumatra, raft Africa's wildest rivers, et cetera, et cetera. But overall, nothing has ever thrilled me more than watching a woman step out of her underpants.
—Tom Robbins

BEKIM IS NOT an Islamic fundamentalist. He is not a terrorist or a celebrity. He is an ordinary man who makes a living by performing daily an ordinary job—one wrongly categorized as appalling and disgraceful.

He is a garbage collector on a sanitation truck.

Few from Bekim's far away homeland could boast of such a respectable and stable job, so Bekim feels no shred of humiliation for collecting garbage in America.

Bekim is a short man—bony, olive-skinned with prominent cheekbones and dark, slitty eyes, a big nose and a shy smile under a well-groomed, dignified mustache. He came to America to gather money so he could make an offer of marriage back in his village. In Gulpazar, his native hamlet hidden at the foot of snow-capped mountains, the custom

59

prevails. The bride must be purchased from her father with a respectable dowry. This is why there are so many unmarried girls and so very few young men in the village—most of the bachelors had left for foreign lands to gather money to come back and win their brides.

Bekim followed the custom and promised Aisha he would return as soon as he put enough money aside to pay for the wedding.

Bekim's work is simple. Each morning except Sunday, at six in the morning, he leans from the side of the green and white truck to empty garbage bins left at the end of driveways by busy people who were mostly still in their beds at that hour. Bekim picks up the waste containers, then lowers them to the carrier which automatically empties them. The contents disappear in gnawing jaws of steel where they are ground up and compacted.

When the metal beast's belly is full, the garbage is unloaded at the station—sorted, processed, and incinerated.

Bekim works his shift with Sabri, the truck driver. Sabri's family back home waits by the mailbox for the money he sends home on payday.

Their route is precisely controlled and rigorously calculated. They navigate their route twice a week—on the suburban streets assigned to them.

Sabri is so used to the route that he knows exactly when they will finish the job. At noon on Mondays and Thursdays, for example, they stop at the end of the same street—a dead-end lane by a fenced park where neighbors walk their dogs. The last house has been serviced, so they pull off their overalls and wash their hands and faces with clean water from a plastic drum. Then they spread a mat from the truck's cab and pray. After offering their sincere devotion to their deity, they put out food packages and eat together, as is appropriate.

In the final house on the route lives Mrs. Thiess, a woman about forty-five years old with weak and wilted dull-gray-blond hair—wearing a pair of thick spectacles. She is widowed and lives alone with two cats, which share the three rooms of her home. A tiny courtyard surrounded by professionally trimmed hedges is visible in the back. The house is like all the other houses in the neighborhood.

Every Monday and Thursday, the woman sits on her porch and watches the two men. She does not supervise or look for their mistakes, but instead, seeks their company. The company her cats provide does not satisfy; she was lonely. They exchanged a few words each time—general observations about the weather.

Bekim missed the sun. The relentless burning sun of his native land parched the dirt streets in his village, ripened the pomegranates and dried the figs.

One Monday, Mrs. Thiess invited them to join her for a cup of hot tea. The day was cold and cloudy. Bekim's skin felt tight and tingly and frozen. He accepted.

"Go in by yourself—you are younger and have no family," his partner whispered.

Bekim was baffled by Sabri's suggestion, but he did not want to refuse the kind invitation, so he crossed her threshold to follow the woman inside. He found it strange that he knew her as a round figure muffled in thick sweaters, yet today, though it was bitterly cold, Mrs. Thiess wore a thin silk gown with large floral printed poppies on a blue background. From underneath, bare legs were visible. Bekim entered the kitchen where a whistling kettle and a plate of chocolate cookies waited for him.

"This year, summer does not want to come," said Mrs. Thiess.

Bekim agreed. "Right," he said. He sipped from a cup of

boiling-hot tea, burning his lips. "In my country, it's always hot. The sun shines all the time. I think it's a great place to live. Yes, it's great, but here it is different."

After this brief dialogue, there was an awkward silence in the room. The woman watched him with a mouth curved in a mysterious smile. More confused, he silently admired the geometric design of the kitchen floor tiles, not knowing what else to say. After finishing his cookie and emptying his cup of tea, he rose and prepared to leave, but Mrs. Thiess made a step toward him. Raising her arms, she threw them around his neck.

Her face was flushed with a crimson glow. She bit her pale lips.

"I want to enjoy summer in November," she said.

They made love on the kitchen table, and then went into her bedroom to make love again. Since her husband died, no other man had wrinkled her sheets. After finishing, Bekim dressed quickly and peeked through the curtains at the garbage truck.

From the behind the steering wheel of the garbage truck, Sabri gestured.

Hurry up.

Bekim walked through the house, then stood on the porch and looked back at the woman. She looked into his face with fond kindness.

"For us," he said, "Thursdays will always be summer."

Bekim the garbage collector was neither a smooth talker nor a meteorologist, but about Thursdays, he was right. On the following Thursday, warm air blew in from the mountains. Clouds in the sky washed away and the sun melted the ice.

Every Thursday, she waited for him in the kitchen with a whistling kettle and a plate of chocolate cookies. After emptying her trash bin, he came into the house for a cup of tea. After a cookie, he enjoyed the sight of her dressing gown sliding from her shoulders and falling onto the gleaming tiles of the kitchen floor.

Sabri laughed at him, but Bekim knew he did nothing wrong. Quite the contrary. When he was just a boy, an old dervish told him:

> The sin Allah finds hardest to forgive is a man refusing a woman's invitation into her bed.

Whether this rule applied to men and women all around the world, Bekim did not know.

But he knew summer every Thursday was good.

Notes on *Summer Every Thursday*

KLC: I've described your short stories as a mix of character study, memoir, parable, fable, morality tale and essay. Sometimes, the story starts as one thing and ends as another. As an example, this one starts as a character study and ends as a parable. How conscious are you about the landscape a story covers while they are being composed?

AP: I start with a particular story arc in mind, but almost every time—once the words are in front of me—the story shifts and I gravitate toward a different ending.

However, this particular story is exactly how I heard it some years ago while in Dusseldorf.

KLC: In this story, you give us enough history and description to feel like we know the characters. You don't always do that. Generally, people like to read about people and in this one, you cater to that. What is it about these characters that earned, in your mind, additional introduction and description?

AP: It was extremely important that both characters were well-anchored. They are, each of them, not only at completely different ends of their town's social spectrum, but also have a solid presence in their ethnicity.

KLC: The main characters are Muslim, but you make it clear they are not radicals. What can you say about your interaction with the Muslim community, both here and in Eastern Europe? While we're discussing this, you let it slip that Bekim is a Sufi Muslim when you mention the dervish. This sect is a more inward-looking religion. Are you just toying with these details or is there a larger meaning you hope to convey?

AP: I am very familiar with the Muslim community. It was important to me not to lead the reader in the expected direction when this community is brought up. I grew up in a region which, for centuries, belonged to the Ottoman empire. It was freed mid-nineteenth century. The current population is a mix of two cultures.

As an additional linkage in this story, my first romantic crush was on a Turkish boy.

KLC: I'm curious about Bekim. Will his casual 'relationship' with Mrs. Thiess lead him to change his plan for going back to his home country to take a bride?

AP: No, I don't think it will. The fact that both were there at the right time for each other attracted me to this story, but it was not intended to be a permanent realignment of their fates.

KLC: Opening with a quote from Tom Robbins (the popular contemporary author of *Another Roadside Attraction*, *Still Life with Woodpecker*, *Even Cowgirls get the Blues* and other New York Times bestsellers) is an interesting choice since you generally favor quotes from the literary classics. Doesn't this reveal a bit of curious schizophrenia about your reading habits?

AP: I *am* a schizophrenic reader, you got that right. I'll switch between Turgenev and knock-knock jokes on a daily basis. I really enjoy the serio-comic novels Tom Robbins writes. They have a social theme and a philosophical undercurrent. Sound familiar?

KLC: We're not supposed to discuss religion or politics in polite company, but I want to press you a little bit. I know you are not a particularly religious person, but it appears you are comfortable with whatever approach people take to get them through their long, dark nights. You're not attacking and you're not mocking.

Beyond 'Ken, you are stupid,' what can you say about this?

AP: With no shadow of doubt, I respect the spiritual cover that shelters our dreams, fears and beliefs. In one way or another, there's a personal-spiritual dimension every person must live with.

Games of Chance
Ken Coffman

ROGER WINDSOR STRAIGHTENED and adjusted his necktie in the mirror until it was perfect. He ran fingers over his chin to make sure he did not need to shave again. His chin was smooth. He walked to the window and looked out over the pool.

One of the tourist barges drifted on the fake stretch of Nile River. He winced at the pretentiousness of it. The barge was full.

They must feel they're getting their money's worth for the ride around the hotel in a glorified ditch.

Roger was the General Manager of the Cairo Resort-Hotel in Las Vegas. He was paid very well for his service but he still felt uncomfortable with the generic tackiness of his hotel.

Tut's Hut Bar.

Ouch.

From the twenty-eighth floor he could see the back of the concrete replica of the Great Sphinx of Giza. He fought to have the sphinx built like the actual one, broken-off nose and all, but he was overruled.

"The Sphinx must have a nose job," Werner Anders had said. "People want to see beautiful things, not broken things."

When you put up two-hundred-and-seventy million dollars to build a casino shaped like a pyramid, you get your way, even if you

66

have no style.

Life is a bitch.

Roger looked at his watch.

Time to go.

It would not do to keep the boss waiting.

He rang the bell at three o'clock, right on time. The man answering the door nodded and stepped aside. He showed no emotion while leaning out and scanning the corridor before shutting the door. The man's suit was beautifully tailored—designed to hide the gun under his coat. These valet-bodyguards always made Roger nervous. Werner sat on a front-room couch rubbing his hair with a towel, obviously just out of the shower. He wore one of the hotel bathrobes.

"Ah, Roger Dodger, so nice of you to make it." He gestured at an easy chair. "Care for a drink? No, you wouldn't, not on company time, right?"

Roger nodded, distracted by a bare foot sticking out of rumpled bedding in the master bedroom. Werner followed Roger's glance and nodded at the bodyguard who eased the door shut.

"Thank you, Oliver," Werner said. "We'll be okay on our own, I think."

Oliver nodded and walked to the study door. He gave Roger an impassive fish-eyed look as he pulled the door shut.

"I believe Oliver could eat beer bottles and shit diamonds," Werner chuckled. "Funny, eh?"

"Yes, sir, very funny." Roger tried to look amused. "What's on your mind, Werner? I know you didn't call me in here to talk about Oliver's bowels."

"That's one of things I like about you—you get to the point. That and you don't steal from me. That's right isn't it? You don't steal from me?"

"I'm no thief, boss."

Werner sat for a moment looking at him.

"I believe you and I'm almost never wrong. It's the *almost* that sometimes gets me in trouble. Like the time I was *almost* positive my second wife wouldn't be home for one more day. Cost me four-million and a chateau to settle that little mess. I think the bitch is staying here at the hotel right now— gambling with my money, but never mind."

Werner leaned over. His robe parted to give Roger a look at the purple veins in his scrawny, but well-tanned legs. Werner opened a leather briefcase, pulled out a sheaf of computer paper, and tossed the bundle across the coffee table.

"You know the game," Werner continued. "Mister and Missus Buttfuck come here to look at my concrete pyramid and put their money in the slot machines. In return, I take one-point-three percent off the top and stick it in my pocket. The problem is, I have never gotten one-point-three percent out of this operation. I only get one-point-oh-two percent."

He grinned. Roger admired his dental work. Werner continued.

"How am I supposed to pay Clarisse's phone bill if I'm expecting four-hundred-and-seventy-three-thousand for the quarter and I'm only getting three-hundred and seventy-one thousand and change? If I didn't love you so much, I'd think of you as skimming some of my cream. Then I'd have to fuck you up."

"I'm aware of the numbers and I'm looking into it. I'm as mystified as you are, boss."

"Well, Roger, I want you to know that it's time to stop looking into it. It's time to fix the fucking problem. We have to make our nut. You don't know how pissed off I'm going to be if the finance company repossesses my Toyota."

Werner's laughter echoed in Roger's ears as he left the

room and made his way to the elevator. He mopped his forehead with a handkerchief.

In a private conference room, Roger stood at the head of the monstrous walnut-veneer table. The leaders of the various casino operations were gathered and looking nervous.

"What have you got, Sally?" Roger asked.

Sally was in charge of accounting.

"I don't really have an answer yet. It looks like all groups are coming up a little short. Our grosses are okay, but our margins in every area are light. Accounts are being paid on time, receipts are looking good, we just can't seem to turn enough profit." She waved at a stack of paper. "In every area, it's the same problem."

"Does it look like someone tapped us?"

"No, I don't see any sign of that."

"Well, there must be an answer. Burt, what is your story?"

"I don't really see any specific problem. Our food ratio is good, we're getting plenty of traffic and all the books balance. I just can't quite meet my operating profit goal. I can't explain it."

An exasperated look passed over Roger's face.

"Gordon, what's happening with attractions?"

Gordon pulled up a screen on his laptop computer. "It's about the same," he mumbled. "We are on-target for revenue, but the expenses eat us up. I've never seen anything like it."

Everyone around the table nodded.

"Does everyone here like their job?"

They all nodded gravely.

"Get your numbers up or start practicing 'would you like fries with that, sir?'"

They shared a puzzled look.

"Repeat after me, dammit. Would you like fries with that,

sir?"

In unison they repeated the words.

"We have to get to the bottom of this."

They started to repeat these words too.

"No, you idiots. Please go back to work and get this figured out."

The Cairo had an entire basement floor dedicated to computer and surveillance operations. Roger ran his security card through the reader and entered the computer room. He took a chair next to the Chief Programmer, Bill Evans. Bill ate a Hostess cherry pie and sipped a Mountain Dew while scrolling through lines of computer code on his workstation. Roger tapped him on the shoulder.

"Hey Roger," Bill said. "What do you say?"

"I say, what the hell have you found?"

"This is kind of interesting." He used his mouse to open some windows on the computer. A 3-D image appeared. "This is a histogram of slot machine payouts. The x axis is time, the y axis is gross revenue and the z axis contour is net revenue. See how the curve comes out?"

"I see it but I don't know what it means. Is someone tapping in and stealing from the casino?"

"No, no, no. That's impossible. This is something different. I haven't quite put my finger on it yet. Give me another day and I'll figure it out."

"For all of our sakes, I hope so. Cherry pies on me for the whole staff for a year if you come up with a solution. Okay?"

"Cool." Bill returned his attention to the terminal.

Roger checked his email at the computer in his office. The usual crap—game machine vendors and a Chamber of Commerce membership renewal request. There was a message from a Doctor Adell.

Perhaps you remember me. We met briefly during our conference on fertility last year. Something curious happened to some of our couples who attended a fertility workshop. I thought you might be interested. Of the 115 infertile couples that were present at the conference (guests in the hotel), 73 (an incredible 63.5%) are now expecting babies. There were seven couples who stayed at the Excalibur, none of those couples are pregnant. We have looked for some aspect of the therapy which could explain this (and make me a wealthy man), but there are no indicators. We continue our research, but for now you could truthfully state that your hotel appears to have some rather amazing medicinal character. If you do use this to promote your hotel (Like the 'Love Boat' or something), I would appreciate it if you would spell my name right, Adell, with 2 L's.

Roger was lost in thought when the phone rang. It was Bill Evans from the computer room.

"Hey, Roger, I know *what* is going on. I don't know *why*, but I can tell you what."

"I'll be right down," Roger said.

"Look at the histogram. It plots the distribution of our random numbers." Bill pointed at a series of graphs on the computer screen. He continued, "All of our machines are linked together with a local area network. All of the games use random numbers generated by the main server to calculate the next game result. The mainframe array uses a seed number to calculate a new random number which is distributed to each of the machines. See what's going on?"

"No, I just see gibberish. I use computers, but I don't know how they work."

"It's here as plain as day. This is a distribution of our random numbers. See this curve? Our random numbers are not random."

"Someone changes the numbers and siphons off our cash?"

"No, no. Look, the numbers are not random. What's happening is that the customers win more often than they should. Not just some customers, all customers. This is a lucky place for gamblers."

"Fix it."

"It's not a software or hardware problem. How can I fix it?"

"The computers are screwing up and you can't fix it? Do I need to hire someone who can?"

Bill grumbled. "The computers are fine. I checked data from the day we opened. The algorithms and hardware are perfect. About the best I can do is import random numbers from the Excalibur. That will get us going until we track down the anomaly."

"Hell yes. Do it."

"Yes sir, boss-man," Bill said. "Fucking bean counter," he muttered as Roger walked away.

"Goddamned propeller-head," Roger complained as he walked out the door.

Roger walked through the casino. From the atrium he could see thirty floors to the top floor of the hotel and the one-hundred-and-twenty-foot concrete obelisk towering over the mini-shopping mall. Roger was proud of his tacky masterpiece with its fake sphinx and the world's brightest light beam shooting from the pinnacle. The hotel even contained a replica of King Tut's tomb which was designed with the exact dimensions of the real thing.

Maybe we made it too close to the real thing and we are cursed.

Roger laughed bitterly.

We could make a commercial.

Attention everyone. The Cairo Resort is under the influence of pyramid power. Come break the bank at the Cairo.

He wiped tears from his eyes.

Christ, I'm such an ass.

He stopped at the Obelisk bar and sipped a double-shot of Old No. 7 Black Label Jack Daniels—feeling like he needed something more, perhaps just some sleep. He sat and watched his reflection in the bar mirror.

He remembered what Werner had said.

Betty, Werner's second ex-wife, had a room at the hotel.

Wouldn't that frost the boss's ass if I got it on with her?

Roger pulled a quarter from his pocket.

Tails I get some sleep, heads I call Betty.

The coin rolled off the bar, hit the floor, and rolled under the bar's footrail. He got on his hands and knees to fish it out.

Heads.

While searching, he spotted a ten-dollar casino chip—he stretched his hand and picked it up.

He asked the bartender for a house phone. A couple of calls later, he had Betty on the line.

"Shit, honey," Betty said. "I was sitting here in my nightgown having a drink and feeling sorry for myself. Come up."

He asked the bartender for a bottle of Cognac. The bartender winked as he handed it over. Roger stopped at Sobek's Sundries, the gift shop, and bought some flowers. He found himself whistling as he walked down the hall to her room.

He was feeling very lucky this night.

Notes on *Games of Chance*

AP: An excellent story, Ken, I felt as if I was watching a gangster movie from the 1930s. The pace, the lingo, the subject. Did you watch a lot of those movies?

KLC: No.

AP: Roger is a character the reader can very easily visualize. I know when I write a story, I have many doubts about how detailed I should be when describing my characters. Do you find yourself in the same dilemma or do characters come easy on your pages? You have some memorable ones, including my favorite, Glen Wilson[6].

KLC: Generally I love my characters and feel an obligation to capture them just right. In contrast, I am not verbose. Like a software project, I've been trained to try to achieve the elegance of putting in just enough to get the job done. There should be no fat. I feel an obligation not to waste the reader's time. I did a poor job of breathing life into Roger, probably because I don't like him much. He's a soulless, all-business kind of guy. We'd never be friends.

AP: Roger is a lady's man. He's an honest right hand for his boss, but his loyalty ends when women are involved. He goes after his boss's ex-wife. Is that a passive-aggressive sign of rebellion?

KLC: Are you sure you wouldn't make a good therapist?

---

[6] The central character in The Continuing Adventures of Glen Wilson which starts with a novel called *Steel Waters*.

You're exactly right—Roger is both boss and slavish servant. Like anyone in a corporate middle-management position, that role drives them mad.

AP: There are several stories buried within the main one. Do you envision a follow up?

KLC: No. I said everything I wanted to say about the Cairo Resort-Casino and its operation. Of course, themes of luck, free will and the mix of technology and magic are recurring topics in all of my work. These thoughts move and challenge me. I will return to that well over and over.

AP: It's clear you're riffing on the Luxor Hotel in Las Vegas. Why make up a place and not just use the Luxor as the setting?

KLC: It's a cheap cop-out. I wanted to make up features that are not part of the Luxor complex. If the hotel-casino was called the Luxor, then people would naturally expect the details to be exact and accurate. I didn't want to be trapped in that box. I'm a story-teller, not a reporter.

The inspiration for this story was the urban legends about razors staying sharper when they are stored in pyramidal structures. That's why, early in the story, Roger does not need to freshen his shave. This is a case where we've built a fake—a replica of something—and accidentally captured some of its magical properties. As technically advanced as we are, we're often messing with things we don't fully understand. That's what I was getting at.

AP: How much do you know about gambling? I couldn't help but smile at the winning theory you had Roger scratching his head at. Is that something you thought about?

KLC: Because I'm moderately good at math, I don't spend a lot of my money when the odds are against me. I'm not a purist—I've been to Vegas and casinos, but I'll generally plunk down twenty dollars, play one hand of blackjack, and then, win or lose, walk away.

I was more interested in the computerized random number generator and what "pyramid power" might do to our algorithms.

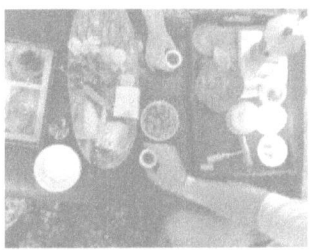

Marjorie and the Master
Adina Pelle

IN HIS COLD, quiet office, the expert writer and master of romance novels gingerly moused his cursor over brightly-colored rectangles denoted with XXX and warnings like "Access denied to persons under 18 years old." His writing style was obsolete—he affected a visually descriptive style ala Honoré de Balzac and slavishly copied this author's unhealthy work habits and asocial behavior. In a contrary salute to modernity, his texts were edited on a personal computer with a powerful Intel Core TM i7 processor, video card with expanded memory and a 500 trigabyte Envy GTX260 hard drive paid for with a malnourished credit card.

Of late, the master of letters was trapped in an inspirational crisis. Now and then, he'd capture an anemic poem or two, but the muse had abandoned his cortex, so he sought a more visceral satisfaction via the Internet—specifically in the vast range and quantity of made-to-order, less-than-virtuous online entertainers. With practiced rapidity, he clicked through the profiles of silicone-inflated sirens while heroically resisting the temptations of alluring, suggestive nymphomaniac housewives to land on a site called The Hot Nymphet.

All creative types—including our accomplished master of prose—stop for inspirational breaks in this virtual version of the carnal Eden.

Don't they?

The nubile clusters of demoiselles were cram-packed with nude temptresses, bleach-blondes with brown-toned, exotic skin bearing freckles, or not, and vast expanses of naturally rosy epidermis in Asian or Caucasian hues—sweet, naïve, and highly-perverted. By the score, they were uninhibited, leather-laced maidens of chains and whips.

Our uninspired explorer looked at all of them. Like a starving Casanova, he felt their nipples and images of digitally-manipulated, photogenic golden skin, and studied their pubescent personalities as described in a set of informative questions and answers.

He devoured the captions.

Punish me, I've been bad.
I'm tight and wet and ready.
I'm afraid and alone. Come, and keep me company.

Suddenly, his attention was captured by the perverse monologue of a young and immature, but brave, outgoing and determined mistress dressed in flannel leggings and a multicolored bandana. With reddish hair and ivory skin, her body was fit and toned—shaped like slender Artemis chasing deer through mythical gullies.

Marjorie.

This teenager was known to all who wanted a disengaged tantric orgasm via a web-cam or a revival of their sacral chakra (the obvious therapy for a lazy prostate). She solved life's big problems with creative sexual routines and rituals.

The Master, undergoing unperipheral excitation and cortical spasm, glued his eyes to the web-cam. Marjorie, his poetic dream, owned the screen wearing the cheerleader's uniform: short skirt, saucy bow tie with stars and a bra made of fringed gold epaulets.

"Hello, stranger," the charismatic creature said in warm greeting. "How are you?"

The Master swallowed with a dry throat. He gathered his courage, and replied.

"I'm well. And you?"

"I hurt myself while practicing the splits," replied the adolescent. "Do you want to see?"

Without waiting for his response, she lifted her short skirt to reveal a curvy-round, perky posterior.

Our fan of the Muse of barely-pubertal charm wiped his glasses and took a long look at her buttocks. There was no sign of any bruising.

"Come and kiss my injury," the girl urged.

The Master puckered his thick lips on the eye of the camera.

"Wow, that feels so good," Marjorie muttered immodestly.

The Master Faust advanced his exploration and inspected her nipples, her breasts, thighs and navel—adorned with a sparkling ring. In his blood, he felt a raging turbulence. A torrent of arterial hormones. But, in the middle of his youthful exult of syncopated breathing, a popup display appeared. The nymph was hidden behind a blinking message on the silver screen bearing a Mephistophelian demand.

To continue the conversation, please go to http://www.Nymphete.com and open an account.

"Of course," meditates our Faust. "If I had any money, I could have it all."

So, he continued his clicking to find more free samples.

79

His concupiscent muse reappeared in a different body, this time in Eve's costume with a tiny patch of green fabric where the fig leaf historically reigned.

"Do you wish to restore your youth and ejaculate like an eighteen-year-old?"

"Yes, yes, yes," the Master feverishly responded while clicking feverishly.

He had a difficult time controlling the pace of the unrestrained castanets beating in his chest.

"Okay, daddy, watch me carefully…"

The nymphet snaked her hips while gently pulling the string holding the leaf attached so strategically over her pelvis. Faust, with a wistful and petulant expression, stared at her fabric-covered pubic mound, the heart-shaped slice of pelvic heaven, and drowned a sigh. His fingers worked at the damp, sweaty keyboard. Unlike his literary counterpart, Goethe, the internet Master was not visiting Purgatory. Instead, he stood at the gates of Interactive Heaven until he was stopped in his tracks by a banal, but fatal myocardial event.

The blinking popup screen that masked the glorious unveiling of the promised valley was wasted on his dead eyes.

And what of Marjorie, the nubile cheerleader?

She married her wealthy Internet guru—the entrepreneurial Nymphete webmaster—and now manages the nuns and schoolteacher division of his thriving online entertainment agency.

Notes on *Marjorie and the Master*

KLC: I'm tamping the tobacco in my Freudian pipe and peering at you over the top of my glasses. What's going on here, Adina?

AP: Oh, Ken, many times a cigar is just a cigar and even the Machiavellian prince of psychoanalysis, Freud, knew that when he futilely foisted his sexual interpretations on hysterical, bored housewives at the turn of the century. Sex kills boredom, sells books and expensive drinks in cocktail lounges and turns paupers into kings and kings into paupers.

KLC: No, really. Let's dig deep and be brutally honest. What's going on?

AP: Let's steal a thought from an old Hollywood actor:

> *I can remember when the air was clean and sex was dirty.*
> —George Burns

There is a whole new world behind the pixilated silver screen. It relieves the embarrassment of airing your neurosis in front of a stranger, who, if a follower of Freud, will write five pages of psychoanalysis to basically conclude you need to get laid.

KLC: Okay, if that's the way you want to play it. In response to your comment, I can't help but think of Alice Harford's (played by Nicole Kidman) terminal (and redemptive) line in Stanley Kubrick's *Eyes Wide Shut:*

> *You know, there is something very important we need to do as soon as possible. Fuck.*

If we stick with EWS for a minute, here is a wise bit of analysis from a reviewer:

That is why the film's recurrent motif is of the Christmas tree. For desire is like Christmas: it always promises more than it delivers.[7]

Well, never mind that, let's talk a little about Balzac. He was obsessed with capturing the small details of the normal human experience. This was different for the time and was a sort of reinvention of the novel and an influence on Dickens and others, like Henry Miller—and Adina Pelle?

"Well," he went on, "when folk of that kind get a notion into their heads, they cannot drop it. They must drink the water from some particular spring—it is stagnant as often as not; but they will sell their wives and families, they will sell their own souls to the devil to get it. For some this spring is play, or the stock-exchange, or music, or a collection of pictures or insects; for others it is some woman who can give them the dainties they like."
—Honoré de Balzac, *Father Goriot*

AP: Yes, Balzac, he was the first writer who puzzled me a little bit. I was about fourteen-years-old when I first read his work. I remember being confused, yet very excited when I read about a young lady who failed to get pregnant after three years of marriage[8]. It turned out her husband was having anal

---

[7] EYES WIDE SHUT, What the critics failed to see in Kubrick's last film. by Lee Siegel.
http://www.indelibleinc.com/kubrick/films/ews/reviews/harpers.html

[8] Now then, Imbert de Bastarnay, an old soldier, ignorant of the tricks of love, entered into the sweet garden of Venus as he would into a place taken by assault, without giving any heed to the cries of

sex with her and the poor demoiselle had no clue what goes where and why. Of course, it took me years to laugh at it without the odd feeling that I didn't understand the whole picture. Which I didn't.

KLC: A sex-infused story like *Marjorie and the Master* naturally makes me think of other sexy writers like Henry Miller.

> **George Wickes:** Didn't you say somewhere, "I am for obscenity and against pornography"?

> **Henry Miller:** Well, it's very simple. The obscene would be the forthright, and pornography would be the roundabout. I believe in saying the truth, coming out with it cold, shocking if necessary, not disguising it. In other words, obscenity is a cleansing process, whereas pornography only adds to the murk.[9]

Do you have any comments about the indistinct line Miller draws between obscenity and pornography?

---

the poor inhabitants in tears, and placed a child as he would an arrow in the dark. Although the gentle Bertha was not used to such treatment (poor child, she was but fifteen), she believed in her virgin faith, that the happiness of becoming a mother demanded this terrible, dreadful bruising and nasty business; so during his painful task she would pray to God to assist her, and recite *Aves* to our Lady, esteeming her lucky, in only having the Holy Ghost to endure.
—*How Bertha Remained a Maiden in the Married State*, from *Droll Stories* by Honore de Balzac

[9] *The Art of Fiction* No. 28, Issue 28, Summer-Fall 1962, as found at: http://www.doctorhugo.org/henry/books.html

AP: I believe in the truth and honesty of the moment. There are times when reality is visceral, or obscene if you will, and I totally back up the concept that pornography murks the lenses. But, pornography is a necessary crutch for passing through reality to fantasy and back for many folks.

KLC: Miller is more direct and explicit than either of us care to be. I like indirection and mystery.

> *I shoot hot bolts into you, Tania, I make your ovaries incandescent.*
> —Henry Miller, *The Tropic of Cancer*

AP: If you pay attention, later in this collection you'll note I used ovaries as a neuralgic house d'climax in *Farewell, Fair Cruelty*.

KLC: We're not illegally importing Henry Miller books from Paris. That was so very few years ago! Now we're downloading the most explicit videos from Hong Kong and Kiev. Where is all this going?

AP: The cover of anonymity enables the Internet to be a well-disguised Freudian therapy. To paraphrase Kurt Vonnegut, be careful what you download.

KLC: I often think women would like to make men obsolete and replace the messy toil and trouble of relationships with artificially inseminated, made-to-order children and cozy lesbian relationships in plush, color-coordinated condos. At the same time, perhaps men would like to replace women with fully-articulated Japanese robots. I wonder what H. G. Wells would make of the odd advances of technology?

AP: Your thought is just the tip of the iceberg. The concept of men and women living with or without each other is fun to explore but everyone knows it's a self-imploding subject—a pathway ending in the same dismal (or hopeful) place it started.

The Talent Scout
Ken Coffman

IN HIS OFFICE on the 145th floor of Dubai's Burj Khalifa, the second-tallest building in the world, George Spallon leaned back in his chair and scratched his nose with a PDA stylus in his right hand—at the same time, he typed a text message with his left hand. There was a tap at the door.

"Open," George said with a disconnected tone.

The door recognized his voice command and slid open smoothly and quietly.

Don Blankenship poked his head in. "Got a minute, boss?" he said.

George waved the stylus in the air like a conductor's baton. "Come in."

The wind off the desert was brisk and the building swayed. Both men were used to it and paid the building's flex no mind. George's left hand continued working on the keyboard as if his digits were not part of his body.

"What's up?" he said.

"I want to talk about one of our engineers."

"An engineer? What the fuck? We have a lot of engineers. How many? Forty thousand?"

"Forty-seven thousand and change if you count the Finns we just bought."

"If you add up all the layers, I must have sixty-thousand

people reporting to me, and you want to talk about one engineer. This must be good; you pique my interest. *Which* engineer?"

"Anand Ravishunkar. He's in our logic synthesis group."

"Remind me. What's our latest lithography?"

"Nine-hundred and ninety picometers."

"Yeah, I remember, we wanted to beat Intel and Samsung to sub-nanometer. This stuff is getting unbelievably small. A handful of atoms between insulators. I sure hope that gamma ray imaging works. We're getting into spooky territory."

Don dropped into George's guest chair.

"Where's Engleberry?" Don said. "We might want to pull him into this conversation."

"He's in China. Bayan Obo. Working on the lanthanum contract."

"He has a hundred people working on that. Why did he need to go?"

"It's tricky. He didn't trust the team to balance the lock-in price and the length of the contract. If the anti-grav technology works, we have a competitive advantage if we lock down a long-term supply of lanthanum and neodymium-mischmetals."

"Ah," Don said.

He dropped his head into his hands and rubbed his temples. George's his left hand tap-tapped on the rubber, ergonometric keyboard built into the desktop.

"Ravishunkar."

Don looked up. "Right. Sorry. Sleep. Not much. Here's the deal. Anand synthesizes logic for the multiply-accumulator section of the new MasterMind chip. He's part of team, a couple of hundred engineers and he has a little piece of the design. S-cobordism and co-homology algorithms. Bordism groups in stable vector bundles."

George stopped typing and looked at Don intently.

"You're mistaken if you think I understood any part of that."

"Sorry. It sounds more complex than it really is."

George's left hand started typing again.

"Keep talking," he said.

"We lease this software from Synaptor, but there was a mix-up in accounting and we didn't pay the bill."

"You have a budgeting problem? Move money from your entertainment reserve."

"We already took care of the billing. What I'm telling you—the software was disabled. It was not working."

"Okay. We lost a couple of days in the dev schedule? Do the daisy chain from Los Altos to Seoul to Bangalore to Montenegro and catch up. You don't need me to tell you how to put the global resource team to work. I'm getting bored."

"The software was disabled, but an output file was created. It looked like garbage. Just a bunch of random crap."

"So?"

"The file was accidently ported to a prototype hardware platform. The build, download and test cycles are all automated. They took off and ran on their own."

"Ah. Are we finally getting to the point of your visit?"

"Yes. The file worked. In fact it worked great. Better than great. I almost hate to say this next part, but the data is live on the sub-secure network. You can look for yourself. Before the logic inputs are settled—just a tiny fraction of a nanosecond prior—the output goes valid. It looks like our propagation delay from input to output is negative. The answer appears at the output before the question is fully settled."

George stopped typing and leaned forward in his chair.

"Which is, of course…"

Don finished the sentence. "Right. Impossible."

"You're right, Don, that is interesting. If I'm with you, we have an employee who can visualize circuit operation and create a file which runs faster than the speed of light on our picometer platform."

"That's the theory that best matches the documented facts."

George considered the information for a moment before speaking.

"So, what does this Anand want?"

"I wanted to make sure this was handled with extraordinary delicacy. You can ask him yourself. I told him to come up at three o'clock, so he should be outside. Do you want me to stay, or do you prefer to talk to him privately?"

Deep in thought, George held his fingers and thumbs before his face and wiggled them. It was as if he'd never seen them before. "Is there anything else I should know?"

Don shrugged. "I think you have the relevant facts."

"Okay, your call. You want to stay, you stay. If you have better things to do? That's fine. Go. See if he's in the reception area. If so, please send him in."

Outside, Anand perched on the edge of a leather chair thumbing furiously on his iComm peapod with his head three inches from the display. Don stood for a moment watching. The young man was small, delicate and very slender. Nearly a waif. He wore black jeans, dainty black sneakers and a black t-shirt with a washed-out, blotchy-bleached Rorschach pattern on the side. Don waited a half-minute before touching Anand's shoulder.

"A second, just a second," Anand mumbled before tapping the send button on the touchscreen with a stiff index finger. "They don't know who they are messing with."

"Are you arguing with someone in a political chat room?" Don said.

Anand flushed. "Uh." He looked at his shoes. "The Kitsune

Tanuki of Osaka. Japanese. The fabulous adventures of a supernatural, raccoon-type creature."

"I know what a Tanuki is," Don said with a dry tone. "Mr. Spallon will see you now."

"What's this about? Am I in trouble?"

"No," Don said. "You're not in trouble. I don't want to speak for Mr. Spallon, but it's quite the opposite, I think."

The henna-haired receptionist sat behind a long counter. Under the counter, a giant, curved electronic display showed roiling, live-action sea water being sliced by the hull of a sailing ship. The sound of the water filled the room with a barely-audible hiss. The receptionist wore elaborate eye-makeup and peach-colored lipstick. She had perfect ivory skin that looked synthetic.

Could it be? Don thought. *Is she artificial?*

Don made eye-contact—she smiled and pressed a button. George's door smoothly slid open. With his iComm dangling from a wrist strap, Anand walked through the door.

Inside, Anand walked directly to the wide expanse of crystal windows and looked out over the city. Dubai was engulfed in a greasy-looking smog. The city crowded the washed-out blue water of the Persian Gulf. He pressed the side of his head against the glass.

"I can't quite see my apartment," he said.

"Where do you live?"

"Fourth floor of the complex on 27B Street."

"Nice place?"

Anand shrugged. "Better than the flat on Third Cross Road in Bangalore where I lived as a student."

"When you're done looking, take a seat."

Anand nodded. He studied the landscape. "I see Palm Island. It looks spectacular from here. Fronds made from sand bars. You probably live out there."

"I live in this building like all the other company executives."

George patiently waited while Anand pointed out the sights and marked them with his finger—leaving oily splotches on the glass. George opened a desk drawer, pulled out a spray bottle of window cleaner and a soft cloth, and proffered them.

"Would you mind cleaning up your mess?" he said.

Anand glanced at the bottle. He turned and walked around the desk and perched on the edge of the guest chair.

Sighing, George got up and sprayed the window and scrubbed the glass until it gleamed to his satisfaction. He returned the bottle and cloth to their places in the desk drawer.

"Do you have children, Anand?" George said.

"Three and another coming. My wife is very fertile."

"Good. Would you like to live in the tower? There are very nice apartments available. Just decide if you prefer a western or eastern view."

"That sounds okay," Anand said. "Can we get a view of the Dubai Fountain?"

"Yes," George said.

Anand glanced at the display on his iComm.

"I should get back to work. My boss watches over us very carefully."

"We have almost three thousand employees in this building…and they all report to me. If your supervisor has any questions he can speak with me directly."

"She. The lab manager is a woman. Cheng Mao Ying. We call her Chairman Mao."

A brief hint of smile flitted across George's lips.

"Whatever," he said. "You grasp my point. I'm going to be very straight-forward with you, Anand. As a company, we cherish—recognize and reward—unique talent like yours.

Skill and intellect are our most valued assets. You can leave the company right now, today, no problem. However, if we invest in your well-being and your family's well-being, you will not resign to work for World Dynamics or Shenzhen Happy Panda Technology. Simply put, it will not happen. You'll work hard, harder than you ever thought you could, but we will reward you for your effort; grant you company stock and pay you a percentage of your division's profits. Shall we shake hands on our understanding?"

Anand shook his head. "I don't like casual contact with others."

"Fine. Nod your head if you agree."

Anand shrugged and then dipped his chin. "Can you get me a tin of Jasmine Tusli Tea from Tamil Nadu? It's been devilishly difficult to import."

Without losing eye-contact with Anand, George reached out with his left hand and started typing on the ergonomic keypad.

"Consider it done," he said. "Now it's time for you to get back to work."

Notes on *The Talent Scout*

AP: This is another one of your abstract engineering stories. You call it *nerd-porn*. That's funny.

I am curious why you chose the Middle East for a setting—as opposed to China, for example?

KLC: I simply wanted an exotic location. Right now, the Burj Khalifa is the tallest building in the world; the second-tallest in the time frame of the story. If I was young, I would be tempted to move to a place with lots of economic activity and potential where money is being spent to create the future. This used to be Seattle or Silicon Valley or Boston. Now it's Bangalore, Singapore or Dubai.

AP: This story has layers of paradoxes and truths illustrated by the way bright minds are rewarded and the super-tight grip corporations hold on intellectual property. What are you exposing to the light? For myself, thinking about this aspect of modern life leaves me feeling bittersweet.

KLC: I wasn't trying to capture a moral tone. I was thinking about talent, human nature and engineering management.

It's also fun to play with Quantum Mechanics. Semiconductor processes approach line spacing that are tiny wavelengths apart. That's far stranger than anything I could dream up. Perhaps we *will* get to a point where we can manipulate physical processes with our minds.

AP: The Marxist reference is brilliant...

> The lab manager is a woman. Cheng Mao Ying. We call her Chairman Mao.

Please comment.

KLC: You're too kind, Adina. Engineering humor is dry and indirect. This is just a bit of random silliness.

With this passage, I was also commenting on the nature of talent. The lab manager is a dictatorial woman in a Middle Eastern location working for a multi-national company. That's the way merit-based companies operate. It doesn't matter what you look like, where you come from or what your ethnic background is. What matters are your skills and intellect and what you can do.

AP: The way you end the story allows the reader room to take things in a variety of directions. Are you being lazy? If you had to add another page to the story, how would you end it, or rather, how would you change the ending if you were forced to write one more page?

KLC: I don't think I'm being lazy. I worked this thing over quite a bit and it lays out much the way I wanted it. Once I make my point, it's time for the story to end. Isn't that how you do things?

If I was forced to add a page? I'd probably follow Anand home and let him play with his kids. He can tell his wife they are moving to the tower. Now that I think about it, I'll bet she also has an odd personality and skewed worldview.

I was going after observation and commentary on engineering management. The interesting part to me is the way George, the supreme, all-powerful leader, both rules over and caters to his talent.

Who got up to wash the window?

A Rebel Heroine
Adina Pelle

"I WONDER IF any writer would want to write about my life?" she whispered to herself while sitting alone and sipping a drink at a cocktail bar table.

The idea made her laugh.

A lonely girl in a bar early on a Friday evening—dizzy and blabbering nonsense.

Stop kidding yourself. You're a colorless woman who knows nothing outside of work. You're not currently involved in a dramatic love affair and there are no diamonds or daring deeds or daggers— only dandelions and dust. A writer would need imagination galore just to fill a few anemic pages.

If only I could buy some natural charisma—the real, internal kind, not the false stuff made of rust and cardboard and grease.

Unconsciously, she pulled back her shoulders so her breasts fought against the fabric of her gauzy blouse. Sipping from her glass, she tried to look mysterious; batting her eyelashes at the young waiter the way she imagined a heroine in a book would.

Maybe I need more mascara to achieve the proper melancholic, overdramatic effect.

In her mind, her private universe, she visualized a solar wind burning so brightly that people looked to the sky with fear and hid in shadows.

95

She ordered a refill of her gin and tonic and with dreamy eyes allowed herself to be spoiled by a fantasy: the warm feeling of being special and surrounded by light while safe in the cozy cocoon of confidence known only to the extraordinary.

The curtain fell over the remainder of the night.

I wonder how many heroines must endure a massive hangover such as this.

She tried to imagine a romantic slant to her rude awakening. Instead, she entered the scene coughing, with disheveled hair, makeup running down her cheeks and an empty bed still holding the shape and warmth of a missing man.

She imagined what the utterly-disappointed writer would say about her.

"What a sad, hopeless character I chose."

Damn it. I need coffee or I'll go crazy.

She knew of no heroine in any popular novel who smoked in the morning on an empty stomach. Breakfast is the most important meal of the day, everyone knew that. She should have a glass of fresh-squeezed orange juice instead of yesterday's stale, leftover coffee. And, perhaps some exotic fruit she would peel with ethereal fingers.

But none of that happened.

Will the writer still notice me when I am out of bed and dressed?

What if the writer could read her mind?

That would be all right, though she'd have to neatly arrange her private thoughts. Lay them out in an orderly fashion on shelves in the wardrobe. Then, scatter cinnamon and clove scented potpourri on the shelves to make them smell nice. She should think only in pretty metaphors and toss away words like *son of a bitch* and *fuck* and *loser*.

Maybe the clever writer would edit her thoughts.

You know, when you're under a magnifying glass, time goes by slowly. It crawls and you accomplish nothing. Nothing remarkable, anyway. Nothing that deserves immortality as captured in words on a page in a timeless novel.

Finally, our heroine, annoyed and fed up with the self-inflicted pressure, crept out the back door. She walked down the backstairs of her story and slammed the garden gate in the author's face.

Notes on *A Rebel Heroine*

KLC: As a writer, do you rise above real life scenes and imagine what they look like to an omniscient observer? Is this an experience that happens to you often as you live your day-to-day life?

AP: I definitely rise above reality. Doesn't everyone?

The truth is, ever since I was a child, I preferred fantasy to reality. My mind followed the Flaubertian pattern and I was mesmerized with Emma Bovary and lived her delusion as if it was mine. Even now, in my middle age, I live with the hope of being part of the universal human condition every time I read or write. This way, especially as a writer, I become a translator of different perceptions of reality.

George Bernard Shaw once said:

> *Imagination is the beginning of creation. You imagine what you desire, you will what you imagine, and at last you create what you will.*

KLC: Often, your characters seem like sexy, sensual creatures. You certainly do not run from frank sexuality. Where does your courage to be so bold come from?

AP: I was never a fan of mainstream romantic literature, but I always believed in love. Love and sometimes lust, as interchangeable as they often are, fueled every great story ever told, and mine alongside with them.

We are all, sexually-speaking, competing for the same seat on the bus, but that's what makes life interesting—the individual's tightly-held conceit that we are all sexual gods. I like writing about seduction as frankly as I possibly can because I see it as a way of enticing someone into thinking about what they secretly desire.

KLC: There is a lilting and playful quality to passages like this one, which seems like a tribute to Vladimir Nabokov as we trip through the 'd' words:

> *You're not currently involved in a dramatic love affair and there are no diamonds or daring deeds or daggers—only dandelions and dust.*

How do other authors enrich and manifest themselves in your work?

AP: Oh, I am a big fan of Nabokov and most likely some of his technique subconsciously crossed over in my own craft without me even realizing it.

KLC: A story like *A Rebel Heroine* mixes gritty, mundane details with the absurdity of a Kafka-esque tale. There is poetry in the mix of the fantastic internal landscape with the heroine's plain life. Please comment on how you mix the lyrical poetry of some of the passages with earthy reality.

AP: I always had a hard time dividing poetry and belletristic work. In my mind, Baudelaire and Zola, or Kafka and Ezra Pound, Balzac and Chaucer and so forth, all *belong* together.

KLC: The abrupt ending where the lady slams the door in the author's face is a perfect coda to the story's tempo and is a bit like slamming the door in the reader's face too. How do you compose instances of rhythm in your writing?

AP: I am a rather selfish writer. I write each story to satisfy my own frame of mind. Some stories move at a fast pace with abrupt endings while others delve deeper in the mind of the character. Not me, the character.

I set aside my personal attachments and thoughts before I begin writing. It's like emptying your pockets before swimming across a river.

Deep Purple
Ken Coffman

NICK, WITH THE collar of his long black coat pulled over his ears, worked his way through a group of onlookers. He lifted a sagging strip of yellow crime scene tape and dipped underneath. Once inside the line, he shook rain off his sodden hat and made eye contact with a female bicycle cop wearing an aerodynamic helmet. The cop nodded in greeting and gestured toward a lump covered by a wool blanket. The heap lay at the foot of a massive round concrete support for the freeway overpass. Far overhead, tires hissed on wet pavement.

"Another one?" Nick said.

"Yeah, same thing. The M-E made us pile up sandbags to keep the vic from washing away. They should pay us more if they expect us to do manual labor. Look at my uniform."

Nick glanced at the cop's dirty hands and muddy shoes.

"Put the cleaner's bill in an expense report and the shift Sarge will sign off on it."

"My point is...the city engineers should do the sandbagging."

"You want to get off bike patrol? Into a squad car in a better neighborhood?"

"Yeah. You bet."

"Then stow the bitching. Any witnesses?"

After a flash of annoyance washed over her face, the cop

100

pointed at a hunched figure handcuffed to a parking meter.

"We caught the tagger. He might've seen something."

"Tagger?"

The cop tugged Nick's arm and pointed at a garish purple lightning bolt spray painted on the concrete above the victim's body. Nick studied the graffiti tag, and then glanced back at the artist who seemed to be talking to the parking meter.

"What'd he say?" Nick asked.

"Maybe you'll have better luck. Except for wanting a buck for a cup of chili at Wendy's, I couldn't understand him. I had to cuff him to keep him from wandering off."

"Did you give him the dollar?"

"No. Can I expense that too?"

Nick studied the officer's face and did not respond. He waved the cop back toward the crime scene tape and turned. A stream of muddy water cascaded around the sandbags. Nick skipped over the burbling water and, studying the pavement, walked to the body. Water, stained a vivid violet as if dyed, painted a path to a storm drain. A man, wearing a navy-blue jacket, leaned against the concrete pillar and tapped notes into a touch screen computer. The left side of his jacket said 'Medical' in white silk-screened letters. The right side said 'Examiner'.

"Hey, Bill," Nick said. "What do you think?"

"I think I shoulda' stayed on Dad's pig farm in Iowa." Nick, expressionless, stared until Bill spoke again. "Potassium phosphate."

"I'm a cop, not one of your egghead grad students."

Bill sighed and flicked a drop of water off the end of his nose.

"That's what's left—a kind of salt. The body is completely dehydrated. Somehow, the calcium gets consumed and the remainder is a variety of salts, mostly Potassium phosphate.

Dissolves real easy in water. If we didn't block the water, there'd be nothing left to shovel in a bag. Bones, teeth, fat, skin. Everything. Powder."

"What about the smell? It stinks to high heaven."

Bill shrugged. "Sulphur."

Nick scowled. He took a few steps back and studied the graffiti. A purple lightning bolt coming from a dark cloud. The cloud was drawn angry.

"What can cause this?" Nick said.

"I tag 'em and bag 'em," Bill said. "*How* is not my department. Still, I was up until midnight for a week making a few calls and running a research engine. Far as I can tell, *nothing* can cause this."

"So, it can't happen?"

Bill shrugged. "But it does," he said. "I know the punch line."

"What do we know about the victim?"

"The clothes are intact and there was I-D in the wallet. Eugene Bailey. The Barney Jake ran it through the computer. Lots of priors. The D-A messed up and Eugene walked on a murder-rape charge. No one will miss this slimeball. Know your Bible, Nick?"

"No."

"It's like God woke up. All seven victims were guilty of rape and murder and walked due to technicalities. Like Lot's wife, Nick. They were turned into pillars, get it?"

"Nonsense."

"The Bible Belt fundamentalists on the radio are frothing at the mouth." Bill leaned close and whispered. "You didn't hear this from me…"

"What?"

"There are more. Three in Detroit, one in Pittsburgh and you wouldn't believe the rumors coming out of Las Vegas."

Bill grinned. "Funny, eh? Like God punched the time clock and is back on duty." Nick blinked and brushed damp hair off his forehead. "You know," Bill continued, "for as long as I've known you, how long? Six years? I don't think I've ever seen you crack a smile. You shouldn't be so serious all the time."

"Guess I'll interview the witness," Nick said.

"Good luck with that," Bill commented.

Nick walked to the scrawny man handcuffed to the parking meter. Rain dripped from the man's scraggly gray beard and his eyes flicked from side-to-side as if he was watching for attack.

"For a dollar, I can get a cup of chili at Wendy's," he said. "One cup a day can keep a man alive."

Nick sighed and pulled an aluminum-foil-wrapped package from his raincoat pocket. "How about half a pastrami bagel now and I'll buy you a cup of chili later?"

"They'll give out extra crackers if *you* buy it. Two packages, four crackers, that's all they'll give me."

"And a handful of crackers…"

The man took the mashed sandwich and held it up so he could look at it sideways.

"What I gotta do? I ain't faggin', not for no one."

Nick hooked a thumb over his shoulder.

"Just tell me what happened to the man."

The gaunt man laughed and a chunk of bagel fell from his mouth and lodged in his beard. "They didn't have the right paint. At the hardware store. Not yellow enough."

"You got anything to add to your picture? A cloud formed and a purple-yellow lightning bolt came out and hit him?"

"He tried to run, but the cloud followed him. Fast. Before I painted, I touched him. He fell to pieces. Purple dust."

"After the lightning bolt hit him, he was standing up?"

The vagrant stood up—ramrod straight. "Like this," he

103

said. "Dollar, dollar, dollar, can I have my chili now?"

"How'd you get up there to paint that thing?"

The tagger grinned. His front teeth were brown.

"We have skills," he said.

Nick waved to the bicycle cop.

"Uncuff him."

The Wendy's restaurant was uphill a few blocks.

"Come on," Nick said.

He didn't wait, he started up the street and the bum followed.

Nick was bone tired; tired to his very soul. His secret weighed heavily on him. He'd gotten away with his crime—the dead girl was long forgotten by nearly everyone. When the hair on his arms prickled with electricity he was unsurprised. The bum stopped, pointed and laughed.

Nick turned. Indeed, the boiling purple cloud looked angry. Very angry. The misty air was saturated with the overwhelming odor of rotten eggs. He spread his arms and raised his face to the sky.

"It was an accident," he shouted.

But he knew that was a lie. And so did God.

Notes on *Deep Purple*

AP: Ken, this has got to be one of your most eerie pieces. I want to say morbid but I won't, simply because it unfolds with so much gritty realism. It almost reads like a documentary. You don't think of it as fiction until the end when you shake off the lingering purple dust and sulfur odor and come back to reality. Where did this story come from—which corner of your subconscious hid a cosmic vigilante?

KLC: This story was born in a dream. Often my dreams are very vivid and sometimes I dream in movies or stories. In this case, I had a setting—under the viaduct in downtown Seattle—and I had a character raising his arms to the sky and confessing his sin.

AP: There are powerful biblical similes and metaphors. How familiar are you with the bible?

KLC: I haven't spent years studying it, but I have some copies, both paper and electronic, and I read and study them in bits and pieces. It's an interesting historical document filled with humanity and adventure.

You're right, this is a biblical tale of vengeance, justice and surreal miracle. I intended to leave the reader wondering what would happen if God woke up from a long nap and took a more active interest in the affairs of our fellow men.

AP: On a personal note, I couldn't stop smiling when I read about the sulfur stench. I had an evil boss some years ago and I swear I smelled sulfur every time he was around.

KLC: The smell of brimstone seems to follow along with ugly souls.

AP: There's the same theme I came across in a couple of your stories, that of revenge, especially when the mainstream justice system fails. Is this something you often think about?

KLC: Sure, justice and karma and the stains left by our crimes and errors. There are plenty of examples of evil that is not balanced in this world, so I think there's always hope for balance in the next.

AP: A talented director finds inspiration in the optimal distance between two characters on stage so the voice inflections, gazes, body movements, facial expressions and text lines weave a unique cosmos. On the other hand, a writer needs to achieve the same effect through words used just the right way, whether in dialog or setting. You captured the whole gist of the story brilliantly. How long did it take you to achieve this balance? And was it hard work? I am asking because I don't think I ever had the patience to go into so much detail in any of my stories and of course, now I wonder if I should address this void in my character.

KLC: I've written a lot over the last twenty years. Now, in some ways it comes easy, but at the same time, it can be agonizing, gut-wrenching and murderously hard. I spent about ten hours going over and over this piece to try to capture a mood and setting and to breathe life into the characters. I desperately want them to live and not lay dead on the page.

It takes a persistent stubbornness to achieve anything transcendent and it's maddening when the words don't cooperate. I don't recommend the writing life for the faint of heart.

AP: The scrawny man is the usual suspect. You obviously tried to make a point. What is that point?

KLC: You're not the first person to suggest the bum is the agent of vengeance. That mystifies me. Clearly, I blew it. If I did my job properly, it should be evident the bum is an innocent bystander. He's not God, he's a witness to a strange miracle.

AP: I know this is fiction, but I wonder if by capturing the words of the story you didn't play the game I often play. If you make the story believable, then it shares a piece of our reality.

KLC: We're dabbling in the world of the mind. If it's real in our thoughts then it's real enough. Think about what you know, what makes you interact with the world in a certain way and how you will react in a given situation. Much of what we do is based on art and culture and the summation of our mindset. These things are not fully of the physical world.

The Man with a Guitar
Adina Pelle

WHILE DESCENDING THE subway stairs, I heard the train pull away from the station. I turned the corner and saw it leave the platform and watched its receding lights—dim, bleak glows—disappear into the tunnel. I was running late for work—all because this morning I stopped for a cup of coffee on my way to work.

Coffee which I usually enjoy at home before leaving.

On the platform, there were a scattered few people; they duplicated my enthusiasm on their faces—as if listening to a pitch on aluminum siding from a persistent salesman. I shared the desolate face of those on their way to work. Waiting, I sat in a modern, uncomfortable seat and opened my newspaper.

I read an interesting article about bizarre objects found in Mexico—speculated to be of space-alien origin. A man spoke, but I did not immediately recognize that he was speaking to me. He touched my shoulder and repeated his question in a repetitive way, stretching every word.

"Train to University? From here you take?"

I peeked over the newspaper.

"Yes," I said.

He sat down, leaving a polite gap between us.

After adjusting the fold of the newspaper, I returned my attention to the article.

"How many stations to Union Square?"

I thought for a moment before answering.

"Four."

Using my peripheral vision, I discreetly examined the man. He held a guitar case on his knees and wore a black pouch around his waist. About thirty years old? The expression on his face was older than that.

A foreign tourist for sure.

From where?

He had an olive complexion—his long, thin fingers drummed on the plastic seat producing an odd polyrhythmic rhythm.

I could not focus on my newspaper so I closed it.

"Are you a musician?" I asked.

He looked at me with a dazed expression.

"Yes," he said after a moment of thought. "I am a teacher of music."

"Well, it means that we're colleagues." I introduced myself. "I'm a teacher too. John, professor of mathematics." I stretched out my hand. He slowly reached out to shake my hand, but did not offer his name. It bothered me for an instant, but I knew many artists were unconventional characters. "At which school do you teach?"

"I am a private tutor," he said. "I do not work for a public school."

"I see."

After that, I couldn't think of anything else to say. With his long fingers, he tapped on the plastic seat, and then stopped.

"You?" he asked with a polite tone.

"I teach math at The Industrial School."

He shook his head in sympathy.

"It's a long way to get there."

"I thought so at first, but I've had twenty years to get used to it. It no longer bothers me. I wanted to sell our condominium and move closer, but my wife did not agree. We like our home because it is quieter than downtown—at our age, we need peace and quiet."

My inevitable habit of engaging in conversation with strangers whenever opportunity presented made me angry with myself. I wanted to apologize for prying, but kept silent instead. Time dilated.

"Do you have children?"

He surprised me with the question. He wouldn't meet my eyes. He stared at the platform's gray marble tiles.

"Yes," I said. "We have a boy and a girl."

"All grown up?"

"The girl will be nineteen this year—the boy is fourteen."

He did not respond. Ten minutes passed in silence. In anticipation of the coming train, the platform filled with people. The guitar man sighed with sadness as if the weight of the world rested on his shoulders. Beads of sweat dotted his temples and forehead.

"It's so hot," he said.

It was a frigid November day. I couldn't think of anything to say. The train roared up and stopped. I got up and climbed into the carriage. Through the closing doors, I watched the man with the olive skin. He did not move. Holding the guitar case across his lap, he dabbed his forehead with a handkerchief. The image of his lonely figure haunted my thoughts during the journey through the underground city. Then my busy school day started and I forgot about him.

The next day after I drank my coffee, I went downstairs to get the newspaper from the sidewalk vendor and sat on the bench in front of the condo building to read it. The title screamed at me in big, bold letters.

Terrorist Attack—Subway

It commanded my attention. The attack took place between the Union and 34th stations and the massive blast destroyed part of a commercial complex.

Seven people died, twenty-seven were wounded and many more were missing. A cold sweat ran down my face. Below the fold was a fuzzy image taken from a security camera.

I recognized the sad expression on face of the man with the guitar.

Notes on *The Man with a Guitar*

KLC: In *Summer Every Thursday,* you bend over backwards to be fair to the Muslim community, but I think it's safe to say, though you are not specific, that the man with the guitar is a Middle Eastern terrorist. True?

AP: I did not have a specific ethnicity in mind. However, the story was sparked by something I read in a newspaper. The thought of being at the wrong place at the wrong time motivated me to write this story.

KLC: I want to mine your experience growing up with much more exposure to Muslim religion and culture than many of us. If the question is 'how do we protect ourselves from religious extremists?', what is your answer?

AP: How do you protect yourself from people like Timothy McVeigh? You can't.

KLC: The terrorist made a moral choice to spare the math teacher, but still murdered other innocents. What point were you making with that moral choice?

AP: I don't think the bomber rationalized the sparing or the sacrifice of anyone. What I tried to convey is the possibility of regular people being monsters. Any villain is somebody's son or daughter.

KLC: In your previous book *Ghost Words and other Echoes...* there is a memorable story about a bombing called *The Wedding Ring*. Clearly, the randomness and brutality of this kind of violence is on your mind. What can you say about your direct personal experience or the experience of your family and friends?

AP: I traveled in Israel and the Middle East when I was younger and I remember the casual approach to extreme actions. It's almost as if people quietly accept tragedies like these and continue with their lives as if nothing happened.

KLC: This story drifts along without much color or depth; then comes the shocking twist of the ending and we are forced to think back to the details of the interaction between the two characters—seeking clues. What is the lingering feeling or thought you hope to leave us with?

AP: The thought of an ambiguous life is terrifying to me. Everybody should have intimate communication with his or her conscience.

KLC: Burton Cummings expressed his thoughts as so:

And I stood cryin' while the two tall sisters fell down...

—Burton Cummings, *Look Out Charlie (There's a New Bartender in Town)* from *Above the Ground*

Where were you on 9-11 and how did the events of that day affect you?

AP: I was working at Travelers Insurance and just starting my day when the news came through. I was as affected as everybody else. Two of my colleagues were on their way to Hartford from Philadelphia and became caught in the New York City gridlock.

Chic Mohammed
Ken Coffman

THE BOEING 777 had seen better days. Donated by Anchorage Airlines, it looked as if it was ready for the one-way trip to the Arizona boneyard where old airplanes went to die. Charlie Pearson, wearing a flowing white cotton dishdasha robe and matching taqiyah cap, was perched on the captain's seat. He coughed into a handkerchief and examined the deposited pink glob. Kip Stanton looked on with concern.

"You sure you're up to this?" Kip said.

Charlie shrugged and twisted the cap off his Oxycontin bottle. He tossed back a pill and washed it down with a swig from a plastic water bottle, and then pressed an oxygen mask to his face and took a deep breath.

"As long as I don't run out of my little friends, I'll make it," Charlie said. He flicked switches and looked over the computerized displays. "Plane flies itself anyway, so what are you worried about?"

"I'm not worried, but this plan..."

"We've been all over it, backwards and forwards and up its ass. It sucks, but everything else sucks too. That terrorist is acquitted and gets a taxpayer-paid flight to Syria? That sucks. I know you pulled strings at the Department of Justice and the State Department and I appreciate it. I said I'd fly this bird and I damned well *will* fly it. The time for second thoughts is long

114

past." He fingered his upper lip. "How's my mustache?"

"You look like you just wandered in from the desert."

"Fuck you too. Speaking of the time? It's time for you to move your ass out of here...I see the motorcade."

Kip leaned down to look through the side window.

"You're right. Look, Charlie. America will never forget this day."

"Yeah, whatever. Get out of here." Charlie put his hand on Kip's shoulder. "Tip a glass for me at McMahan's, that's all I ask."

"A round for the house in your name," Kip said.

"No need to go crazy," Charlie said, laughing. His laughter devolved into a coughing fit. "Go," he wheezed.

Flassid 'Chic' Mohammed, carrying a leather sports bag over his shoulder, walked up three steps, then turned to address the press corps gathered on the runway. As the crowd shivered in the brisk wind, they raised their cameras and digital recorders. Chic started his seventh impromptu speech of the day.

"Infidels, I am the Messenger of Allah. May Allah bless us and grant all his followers peace. I am ordered to complete that in which there is obedience to Allah and to abandon that in which there is disobedience to Allah. Allah—blessed is his name—came to the den of swine—Satan's courtroom—and rubbed defeat and shame on the heads of my enemies. I shall never swear to a thing I know is wicked or swear to a lie I know is a lie and Allah will deliver me from the evil grasp of the overturner and corrupter of hearts."

Paul Chambers closed his notepad and slipped it in his jacket pocket. He tugged the collar of his camera man, Jin Lee.

"Christ on a cracker, isn't this the same speech he gave at the courthouse?" Paul said. Jin shrugged. "Screw it—we'll piece the story together from what we have. I need a drink."

"I know a place nearby," Jin said.

Paul grinned. "You always do," he said.

Charlie, with his dishdasha flapping in the wind, stood at the top of the stairs and watched the cleric-terrorist preach to the small crowd of reporters. He caught only scattered words and phrases.

"Innocence…Islamic revolution…a word would be enough for any people with lofty morals, but with you, words do not help, so you'll submit to the flaming sword of Allah."

With that, Chic Mohammed turned and climbed the remaining stairs to the aircraft passenger hatch.

Charlie gritted his teeth and bowed his head.

"Welcome aboard, brother," he said.

"I piss on these Jew-pigs," Chic said. "Get this jet in the air."

"Right away," Charlie said. "I'll let you know when we're on approach to Havana."

Chic tossed his bag on an empty seat and looked over the empty passenger compartment.

"Is there any ginger ale? I got a taste for it in prison."

"No," Charlie said. "Take any seat you like."

Through the headset, Charlie got clearance from Reagan National ground control and taxied to the end of the runway. He checked the controls and gauges one last time before pressing the toggle switch that engaged the autopilot. He leaned back and watched as the ground sped by. The plane lifted off. He checked the GPS coordinates for their destination. He remembered what Kip said after Charlie suggested the plane go down at the site of TWA Flight 800, the 747 that mysteriously crashed after taking off from Kennedy Airport 1996.

"The conspiracy crowd will go batshit when they find out you crashed there," Kip had said.

"Let 'em," Charlie muttered.

It was a mistake to remove Flassid 'Chic' Mohammed from military tribunal in the Guantanamo Bay detention camp and give him a civilian trial. Acting as his own attorney, he lectured the court and listed a series of violations of his civil rights.

He was denied timely access to an attorney.

He was never read his Miranda rights.

The jury was not composed of his peers.

Then the current administration ruled that waterboarding was torture and the mainstream press flooded the airwaves and newspapers with hostile stories about administration policies. That was enough. After an hour the judge rapped his gavel.

"Case dismissed," he said.

Raúl Castro extended an invitation; Chic Mohammed would be a welcome guest of Cuba while a flight to Syria was arranged. While union-organized student rioters mobbed the National Mall, quick preparations were made to whisk Chic out of the country. Charlie, a former Marine and retired commercial airline pilot was in his terminal stage of lung cancer. He volunteered. Sympathetic clerks at the Justice Department pulled strings. A hasty plan was set in motion. The plane would be programmed to crash into the ocean. Though delayed, cruel justice would be served.

Charlie watched the colorful flight computer display until the estimated time to arrival was twenty minutes. He pulled a cigarette from his jacket pocket. A Camel, unfiltered. It was twisted and crooked—he straightened it out and stared at it for a few moments before lighting it with a battered Zippo. He filled his corrupt lungs with acrid smoke—and, while holding the cigarette as far away as possible—followed up with a breath of oxygen. It was enough. He stubbed out the cigarette and unstrapped his safety belt, took off the taqiyah cap and peeled off the fake mustache—and threw them aside. It was time for the part of the plan no one else knew about. With a twisted grin on his face he dry-swallowed a final pill and worked the utility knife from his pants pocket. He tested the short, razor-sharp blade with his thumb.

"Let's roll, Chic Mohammed," he muttered.

Notes on *Chic Mohammed*

AP: Was the subject of this story inspired by the headlines?

KLC: Yes. It irritated me when the Obama administration decided to try the terrorists housed in Guantanamo Bay in civilian courts. They've backed off on that now, but nonetheless, what possible benefit to the American public would come from this nonsense? So, I wrote a little story to create a bit of virtual justice.

AP: There is a universal destructiveness to fanaticism stemming from religious dogma taken out of context or twisted to justify an evil action. The story is tailored for Chic Mohamed but did you think beyond it?

KLC: I've always been against zealotry when imposed by others. If you want to act a certain way and argue for a philosophy, that's fine. But to use the power of government or the mob to work your will against others? I will fight against this until I take my last breath.

AP: I sense your complete detachment as a writer from the action. You do not condemn it nor approve it. Was it hard to stay impartial?

KLC: Oh, Adina, have I fooled you? I am hardly impartial—quite the opposite. Because of my technical training, I tend to be analytical about things, but like everyone else, I have a worldview, philosophy and biases. Humans make very flawed computers—even the most deranged and disconnected person thinks he (or she) is operating logically and with consistency.

AP: We touched on this earlier, but I want to revisit the question. What do you really think? Do you believe in eye-for-an-eye justice?

KLC: I believe in deterrence. For evil acts, there must be consequences. I believe in karma and sometimes we humans have to be agents of karma. I don't believe in letting just deserts wait until the balance sheet is reconciled in the next world.

AP: I enjoyed the aviation aspect of your tale.

> *Through the headset, Charlie got clearance from Reagan National ground control and taxied to the end of the runway. He checked the controls and gauges one last time before pressing the toggle switch that engaged the autopilot. He leaned back and watched as the ground sped by. The plane lifted off. He checked the GPS coordinates for their destination. He remembered what Kip said after Charlie suggested the plane go down at the site of TWA Flight 800, the 747 that mysteriously crashed after taking off from Kennedy Airport 1996.*

KLC: I try to ground my work with as much hard reality as I can. I threw in a reference to the Flight 800 conspiracy as a bit of whimsy. I know people who work at Boeing and we talk about things over beers or at lunch.

Anyone who believes frayed wiring set off that fuel tank explosion? What can I say? It seems highly implausible. Insiders I've talked to claim Boeing rolled with that absurd explanation for calculated and cynical political reasons.

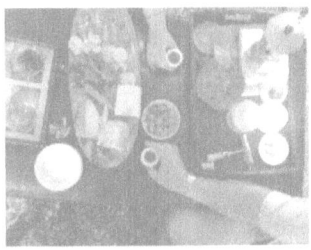

The Fist
Adina Pelle

I SHOULD HAVE killed you. I should have acted on my instinct before waking up.

Between vodka shots, the thought that I missed my chance upsets me. You sat at one of the two empty tables behind me.

You. Young, ignorant and illiterate with large, fleshy hands and legs like sturdy pillars that secured your drunken clumsiness to the floor. Like a bouncer who belches with callous disregard for propriety, like one who laughs out loud and never hesitates to fill a room with noise.

You are the male half of an annoying couple…a couple I studied for an hour while you plumbed lower and lower depths of human degradation and stupidity.

Your wife has oily, yellow-dyed hair pulled back in a sloppy ponytail. Her blonde hair looks sickly against the brown and gray stripe growing out on her head. Low-rider jeans are unsuited for her inflated belly where new life is forming; rolls of blubber unfold over her leather belt and turquoise buckle.

For sport, you turn toward her with a sudden motion. Instantaneously, from hard-learned habit, her hands fly up to cover her face. She knew the next step of that brutal dance. You gently move her trembling hands out of the way and your powerful fist strikes her face full of tears.

Did you pull the blow?

121

It doesn't matter; it was strong enough to send her to the floor. I know your human species. You are subhuman—a drunkard piece of shit.

Sitting at my table, I thought for a while about drinking the emotions of others—it was a reliable and seductive way of entertaining myself. But now, I stare with a paralyzed soul at the sight before my eyes.

What kind of man beats a woman?

With lightning speed, my bare hands find their way to your neck and soon you are unconscious—a flabby punching bag for my fists. My fists are like pistons; relentless and untiring.

I soon feel lighter than air as a peaceful wave of silence surrounds me.

Walking out of the bar, I saw a very familiar looking man lying limply against a fence. I bent over and touched his shoulder. He lifted his head. I stared down at myself.

With an indecipherable mumble, he raised his flushed, sleepy face—looking confused as he rotated his eyes in a loopy orbit. With considerable effort, he released a muddled sentence in a hoarse voice.

"My stomach is killing me."

I knew this. An acute loss of clarity comes through the stomach, especially after a fiery swig of vodka.

Next, he raised his trembling hands to his temples. His shirt was covered with blood. His fists were raw meat.

Who had he been beating?

He leaned against a rusty fence next to the bar.

"I'll help you get up, but you should go home," I said in a stern voice while looking down at him with pity.

I tried to pull his arms around my neck, but they fell limply back to his body. He was in the mood for arguing, though his articulation was labored.

"Don't try to lift me. If I stand, I get dizzy. I had a few glasses of vodka, but my stomach pain doesn't come from the vodka, it's from the fight."

I was cool.

"What fight? Shouldn't you go to the hospital?"

He seemed dismayed by my proposal.

"No, no, I don't need medical treatment. There's nothing wrong with me, except this terrible stomach pain. I got a fist in the stomach. He rammed his fist in my belly…"

The fist, a standard deviation of space.

The streets appeared to narrow as I felt an impulse travel through my body—a vibration from my heels to the top of my head.

"You should go to the hospital," I insisted.

"No, let me tell you the story. After I punched his face, the scum hit my left shoulder, then my right. I got dizzy and fell to the floor. After a few hours, I woke up near this fence. I do not remember anything else."

I decided to walk away and leave the man wearing my face lying injured against the rusty fence between the two rulers of his life, the fist and the vodka bottle.

My mind was filled with a dense fog of unresolved thoughts. I tried to make sense of the world, but nothing came through.

I decide to walk home for food. My house is full of light as I step in. A familiar voice resonates and calls my name. It's my wife holding a glass of ice water. She wraps ice in a towel and swathes the bundle around my fist.

My fist is bloody and the pain in the pit of my stomach makes me cringe.

What happened to me? Where have I been and why do I hurt so bad?

Thoughts circled in my head only to settle when my wife's voice pierced the vast unknown between my past and present.

"George, do you hear me? All night you were drinking in the bar and now you complain that your stomach hurts."

Flabbergasted, my head weighed a ton. I try to fathom what happened.

"Take off your shirt; it's covered with rust stains."

My wife's words boomerang in my head and bounce off my cortex—waking a thought that had been dormant.

I should have killed you. I should have acted on my instinct before waking up.

Notes on *The Fist*

KLC: How much of this story should we attribute to the madness of alcohol and how much to objective reality with straight facts we can trust?

AP: That's an interesting question. I guess I'd assign a little to each. On one hand, everyone knows nothing anyone says in a bar is true and on the other hand I am reminded of some famous drunks:

> *Always do sober what you said you'd do drunk. That will teach you to keep your mouth shut.*
> —Ernest Hemingway

or my favorite of all:

> *It is time to get drunk! So as not to be the martyred slaves of Time, get drunk; get drunk without stopping! On wine, on poetry, or on virtue, as you wish."*
> —Charles Baudelaire

KLC: You toss a lot into the mix. A woman being physically abused. The destructive power of alcoholism. The disconnect between what a man thinks and what is real. Let's not tease; name the themes you hope the reader takes away from this story.

AP: One of the things I love to do—I've been doing since a kid—is watch people. I look around and take account of human behavior. A bar or restaurant is a voyeur's paradise because of the plethora of life styles and personal dramas on display.

I tried to capture a scene that is too common in some bars—that of abuse under the shroud of alcohol and a response to a situation that might not happen if the parties are sober.

Secondarily, I wanted to explore the dysfunction of a hopeless couple.

KLC: This story circles back on itself, as if the protagonist is trapped in a destructive cycle or loop. What inspired you to use this circular story form?

AP: Life has a tendency of repeating itself—we loop through the same mistakes over and over again.

> *This life as you now live it and have lived it, you will have to live once more and innumerable times more; and there will be nothing new in it, but every pain and every joy and every thought and sigh and everything immeasurably small or great in your life must return to you—all in the same succession and sequence—even this spider and this moonlight between the trees, and even this moment and I myself.*

125

Mesh

The eternal hourglass of existence is turned over and over, and you with it, a grain of dust.
—Friedrich Nietzsche

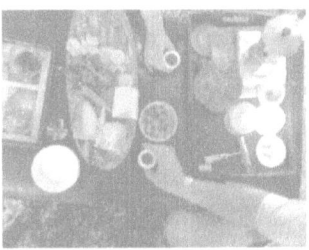

The Rookie
Ken Coffman

THE LONG HALLWAY was illuminated by flickering fluorescent lamps. Oren Kahler's footsteps were inaudible, masked by the background noise of the air conditioning system. The industrial tile floor gleamed. The hallway was rarely used but it was still routinely polished by the nocturnal janitorial staff.

Damned waste of money.

He made a mental note to check on canceling the cleaning service. He wouldn't be too hasty in case the service company was owned by a Director's brother or something. Oren was still embarrassed over an incident that involved the lucrative photocopy machine maintenance contract. It turned out the CFO's wife's cousin held that contract. A man had to use caution when affecting the plunder of others.

Traveling down the endless hallway, the doors he passed had numbers and descriptions that could only be invented by the Government. For example, room D1766 held the title: Logistics Center Storage Center 33. It was probably used to store last year's obsolete procurement forms and might soon be used to store this year's obsolete procurement forms. The building was owned by the U.S. Government but was leased to the International Dynamics Corporation for a dollar per year. A subtlety in the contract held Uncle Sam responsible for the

127

utility bills—water, sewer and garbage. When added to the equation, it worked out that IDC was actually paid about $16,000 per year for the privilege of using the building. Oren was particularly proud of this maneuver. It was directly responsible for his promotion from Associate Director to Assistant Director. A minor title change perhaps, but worth $22,000 per year—and a reserved parking space for his company sedan.

Oren looked again at the pink telephone message slip. It simply said "Meet me in D1881, Surplus Equipment Room 52, at 1400 hours. Tell no one. Walt Brunner."

Oren wondered what lame-assed Brunner wanted and why the meeting was such a secret. The message slip had been sealed in an envelope and slipped into Oren's mail slot. Oren entered Room 52. It was filled with old metal desks and filing cabinets. IDC laid off twenty-percent of the Engineering staff the previous year. This left a lot of extra space which had been remodeled to make bigger offices for Management as rewards for cutting cost in such an effective manner. The old furniture couldn't be sold because it still belonged to the U.S. Government. In his spare time, Oren looked for a profitable way to get around this minor detail.

One of the desks had been dragged to the center of the room. Walt Brunner sat behind it with a strained look on his face. Walt was the Lead Engineer on one of the reorganized projects. The project was too lucrative to cancel completely so the hardware design was shipped out to a joint venture company in Belarus while the software would be bid out to the Soviets and an Indian company in Mumbai. Walt was a round little guy with gray hair that stood straight up when he was concentrating. He wore a wispy goatee and mustache. With a red face, he sweated profusely in spite of the cool of the room. He wiped his face with a handkerchief. Oren flopped into a folding metal chair set up in front of the desk.

"What do you want, Walt? I have a meeting at two-thirty," Oren said.

"I want to know why you axed the V-R project when the projections showed we could make a lot of money on it."

"Now, Walt, the management team has been all through this with you. We agreed the project would make money but not until 2018. 2018 dollars don't do us any good. This year's bonus is calculated using this year's dollars. Besides, the company will make a lot more money if we farm the work out."

"We showed we could be competitive even if you don't count social costs; the costs of unemployment insurance, welfare and food stamps. Why is it company policy to turn taxpayers into welfare cases? The people laid off were hard-working and talented. The company had a lot of investment in them—investment in training and work experience. The situation doesn't make sense."

"Look, Walt, the bean counters have been over this again and again. The company exists to make money for the shareholders and we're going to make more money sooner if we ship the design and manufacturing overseas. It shouldn't take a brain scientist to figure this stuff out. If all you want to do is rehash old news, then please excuse me, I've got work to do."

"You're not going anywhere, Mr. Oren Kahler. You stay right where you are until I say otherwise."

Walt pulled an old Colt .45 automatic from the desk drawer. He pointed it loosely in Oren's direction. Oren leaned over slowly until he could see that the safety was off and that the hammer was cocked. The blue finish on the gun was worn off in places. It gleamed with dull menace in the harsh light. The gun shook as Walt used his hand to mop sweat from his forehead.

"You bastards don't understand what you are doing to decent people—people who trusted the company to take care of them, not lay them off or buy them out with crappy early-retirement deals. This country used to be the best in the world at manufacturing and design until the MBAs and lawyers took over. Now we shuffle paper and export jobs so you can support your stock options, bonuses and golden goddamned parachutes. Fuck you, Kahler, fuck you all."

"Walt, Walt. I hear what you're saying and I understand why you're a little disturbed, but things will turn around—this recession can't last forever. With the situation in Iran and North Korea, defense spending is picking up. Things are going to be tough for a while, sure, but all good things come to those who wait. When things get better all your friends will be recalled and everything will be fine. You just need to have a little faith in the system, that's all. And look, Walt, you still have your job, don't you?" Oren felt a little twinge as he said this because he knew Walt's name was on the latest draft of the next layoff list.

Walt's voice cracked as he quietly spoke. The gun wavered between the floor and the ceiling. Oren's eyes tracked it carefully.

"You know how many people laid off in the last three years have been recalled? Do you? None. Not a single one. We lay off people to save on payroll but do you know how much we've saved? In three years we got rid of thirty-seven percent of our people but payroll costs only went down eight percent. We save a little money and the fucking directors give themselves another raise and fat bonus. Goddamn you all to hell."

Tears ran down Walt's face. He lowered the gun until it rested on the desktop. He buried his head in his arms. Oren reached over slowly and carefully took the gun.

"Take it easy, Walt."

Oren opened the storeroom door and looked both ways down the hall. No one was in sight. He shut the door quietly, then folded up his chair and placed it on a stack with other chairs. Shredding a tissue, he wadded up two balls and carefully pressed them into his ears. Watching, he stood before the sobbing engineer for a moment. Lifting Walt's head gently, he placed the gun in the soft spot under the chin and pulled the trigger twice. The roar was loud in the room and a crimson spray covered the old furniture behind the body.

Oren engaged the safety and rubbed the gun down with another tissue from his pocket. He pressed the gun into Walt's hand—making sure to get a thumb print on the trigger. After switching off the safety, he threw the gun onto the floor. He wiped down the areas on the folding chair and the doorknob that he might have touched. He was careful not to get any of Walt's blood on his shoes or slacks.

He was familiar with the gun—the trigger was a little touchy. Old Colts had a problem with firing twice on a single trigger pull. He didn't expect the cops to think anything of it. Taking a last slow look around the room, he removed the tissue from his ears. Everything looked okay except for the corpse. Walt was undeniably dead and definitely not okay. Oren opened the door with a tissue on the knob and again made sure the hallway was clear.

Fucking rookie.

After easing the door shut, he rolled up the tissue fragments with the pink message slip and slipped them into his coat pocket. They would later find a home in the secret document burn bag. Taking a quick look at his watch, he walked briskly down the hallway.

He had to hurry. He was running a little late for his 2:30

meeting.

Notes on *The Rookie*

AP: Oy, this one hurts. The beginning made me think of movies like *About Schmidt* or *Glengarry Glen Ross* but the finale took me into Quinton Tarantino's universe.

Introduce me to your thoughts, what triggered this?

KLC: As an engineering manager at a couple of aerospace companies, I had the pleasure of laying off employees, which is no fun. Then, twice, it was my turn to be laid off.

I have a cynical sense of what it takes to succeed in the modern business environment—and it's not that different from our cave man days. What's the easiest way to get a mammoth shank? Hide behind a bush and kill the successful hunter with a rock, then steal his meat.

AP: You take a shot at the government and its archaic thinking. Tell me what you really think about it.

> There is no nonsense so arrant that it cannot be made the creed of the vast majority by adequate governmental action.
> —Bertrand Russell

KLC: I have a low tolerance for nonsense and bullshit—all of which abound in the government. It surprises me when people have supreme confidence in government bureaucrats and their programs. I know there are good, smart, hard-working people who have G-jobs, but my direct experience is with things worse than laziness and incompetence: the destructive power of self-perpetuating, wrong-headed, soul-killing ugly evil that turns common sense on its head.

I'm no anarchist; I know there are functions that must be done by the collective, but the role of government should be minimized and hacked back whenever it inevitably tries to grow out of control—which is central to its nature.

AP: Why the gruesome ending? Walt could have easily walked into oblivion to start his golden age of coupon clipping and four o'clock buffet dinners. Walt seemed like a decent fellow. Why did he have to die?

KLC: I think people underestimate how ruthless successful people can be. There's a reason certain people do well in clawing their way up the bureaucratic food chain. Can we consider *The Rookie* to be a cautionary tale?

Be wary if you ever find yourself between an ambitious wannabe executive and something he (or she) wants. For the record, I want to mention I wrote this story long before a friend gave me *Snakes in Suits*[10].

AP: Let's look at what Michael Moore has to say:

> *One of the most ironic things about capitalism is that the capitalist will sell you the rope to hang himself with. Actually they will give you the money to make a movie that makes them look bad, if they believe they can make money off it.*
> —Michael Moore

---

[10] *Snakes in Suits, When Psychopaths go to Work*, Paul Babiak and Robert D. Hare, HarperBusiness, 2006.

I am no fan of Michael Moore but I listen to what he has to say. You?

KLC: If he accidently stumbled across a truth or said something original or interesting, it would be wasted on me. You know he's paraphrasing Lenin, right?

> *The Capitalists will sell us the rope with which we will hang them.*
> —Vladimir Ilyich Lenin

AP: You don't like Michael Moore? Then how about P.J. O'Rourke?

> *Anyway, no drug, not even alcohol, causes the fundamental ills of society. If we're looking for the source of our troubles, we shouldn't test people for drugs, we should test them for stupidity, ignorance and greed.*
> —P.J. O'Rourke

KLC: That's more like it. I love P.J. and met him briefly at a reception once. Like me, he's a libertarian. Books like *Eat the Rich* and *Holidays in Hell* were big influences on me.

I wonder if he'd like our book? I'll send him a copy and find out.

Let's end this with another quote from P.J.

> *Every government is a parliament of whores. The trouble is, in a democracy, the whores are us.*
> —P. J. O'Rourke

The Bright Light of Being
Adina Pelle

TRANSFORMED INTO A bar, the old cellar's brick walls and round, gothic arches attracted a certain type of dubious customer.

Some gathered to listen to jazz musicians playing rambling, hour-long songs, others to listen to poets shouting free verses laced with profanity. The reek of misery was overwhelming.

From the beginning, customers included tattooed rockers, hefty bikers and zoned-out hippies. The police owned the streets, but left the bar's customers alone in this hidden sanctuary—enjoying endless cups of muddy coffee, thick, acrid smoke that caressed the low ceiling and their cursing, laughing and rattling of chains. On every finger, it seemed there was a gleaming ring bearing a skull, crossbones and ruby-red eyes.

And, in the shadows, a strutting, doe-eyed array of accommodating young girls—this place of perdition attracted clueless students and other lost souls—along with young, right-wing extremists and would-be writers with romantic ideas about finding literary inspiration in a wine bottle. It was a motley and loud bunch of characters who thought of this seedy dungeon as the neuralgic center of the city. The older denizens held court at key tables and shot disapproving looks at the youths who waxed eloquent about anarchic plans to overthrow society's social order.

Julian, a handsome young man bearing a coincidental resemblance to a popular rock singer, was one of the young customers. Of financial necessity, he lived an austere, frugal life and enjoyed episodes of low-budget debauchery by taking advantage of his witless entourage.

He had one affectation, an expensive Rolex watch which awed a certain type of impressionable girl. When the time between welfare payments, his wife's paycheck and cash contributions supplied by parents stretched too long, he used the watch as a security deposit for his rolling bar tab. The watch was not an indicator of underlying wealth—it was stolen from the wrist of a banker, but dropped on the sidewalk during the fleet-footed thief's daring escape. Julian was at the right place at the right time. All he had to do was lean over, pick it up and slip it in his jacket pocket. He knew, as long as he had the watch, he would never starve, so he always redeemed it when he had cash. He valued it as much as life itself.

Although deeply confused, he was ungovernable. Harsh, acidic rejoinders were inevitable when he felt attacked. He drank, laughed, smoked and engaged in endless monologues about the future of art, mankind and the world. Deep inside, he wished for a simple life—with enough money to make every passing day a Xerox copy of the one before. Unfortunately, he had a self-defeating attitude that poisoned his thoughts. His mind seethed with twisted, self-obsessed ideas about love. His destructive behavior rode a wave of alcohol, drugs and a weakness for sex with beautiful young girls.

Beyond drugs, he was a relentless consumer of alcohol—in any form. Wherever he was you would inevitably find a cup, a glass, a jar or a bottle.

When his wife met him at the bar after a long day at her

job as a clerk's assistant at a boutique, she craved peace. He wanted to talk.

"Do you have money?" he said. "I need another drink. There's nothing else to do."

Though it was May and the sun had shaken off its winter hibernation, his wife was dressed in a long, purple-wool dress and green boots. Lots of junk-jewelry trinkets were strung around her slender neck. Her makeup was smudged—with tear-tracked rivulets on her cheeks like rain on a dirty window.

Lately he fought to suppress an urge to break her—to smash her like a glass.

"Your life revolves around drinking," she said. "Do you ever think about me? I wasted my youth on you. My best years are lost and now I'm old. Ancient. Thirty."

She took out her makeup kit and worked on her face with trembling hands. It was hopeless. Her breathing dissolved into hiccups as tears took over. She sat like a mad dog alternately crying and growling. Her fists tugged at her ravaged hair and her mouth was turned down at the corners as if gravity weighed more on her face than it did the rest of the world.

Her best features were big, white breasts framed by the purple dress like loaves at the bakery. He stared at her chest and felt a stirring.

"You still look good, baby."

"Shut up. Do you think of what I do for us? For you? For you, so you can drink all day and do nothing? So you can stay home and work on your paltry poems which never brought us anything—not even a penny."

Julian watched his wife speak and tried to comprehend her words. He couldn't understand her; she seemed like a desperate soul ready to seize any lifeline. A mentally-unbalanced woman, one who offers herself unconditionally, but only to steal a man's energy. Her lush body a tool used to dominate a man and trample him under her feet.

Outside, there was a clicking noise on the stairway from the metal tip of an umbrella on concrete. Through the cellar doorway came a man; a jarring, out-of-place figure wearing a black overcoat and wide-brimmed hat which he carefully removed and placed on the table.

The man had an ominous air about him, as if danger flowed in his veins. It is said that eyes are the windows to the soul; however, this man's dark eyes were more like gateways to hell.

The waitress approached. It was her job. She had to.

"Young lady, bring me a white Russian," the stranger said. "Dust off your bottle of Akvinta and use Tia Maria, not Kahlua. One ice cube. Please."

After ordering, he studied the other customers in the room before addressing Julian.

"You live here?" he said.

"Yes," confirmed Julian with a merry twinkle in his eyes.

His wife, blinking as if trying to melt her tears, remained quiet in her corner.

The waitress placed the man's drink on the table. He eyed it suspiciously and smelled it. He shrugged. His voice was raspy and faint, but hypnotic.

"Okay," the stranger said. "Let's drink."

Julian thought the idea was outstanding.

"Let's," he said.

They raised their drinks.

The man seemed far away—with a face obscured by darkness and clouds.

"We live with the deepest inversion of values. All you people, without exception, worship things with no worth...even those who preach about tacit dissent."

The stranger lived in sophisms—there was no doubt where his psychic strength was stored. Anyone like him arriving at a clear understanding of human nature, was unpredictable and dangerous. He spoke while watching from his peripheral vision; he didn't look directly at Julian.

"Let's play a game," the man said. "A speculative game."

"What kind of game?"

"The game goes like this. Let's imagine a time ten years from now. You've been married another ten years. You are bored and disconnected—with a nonexistent sex life. You suspect she is unfaithful. You are cheating on her. What motivates you to love and trust your wife? What's to keep her from not sleeping with someone else?"

Julian knew his wife cheated on him; it was his idea. He hoped the boutique owner would give her a better job with more money. They needed money. Besides, the shop owner was old and fat, so Julian didn't care if his wife slept with him.

Money to spend on alcohol, rent and bills. Money was important for living. His wife's honor was expendable.

"I don't see the point of this game," Julian said. "Ten years is a long time. Maybe I won't be alive in ten years. This game is stupid and proves nothing."

"It *sounds* stupid, but the point is that life throws out surprises every day. How do we respond to them? By seeking affection? Craving change? Do we show sympathy for the extraordinary? Out of simple inertia, does something make us go wrong and violate our vows and walk a crooked path?"

Julian thought about the stranger's words.

"There's an immoral being in each one of us. Why don't we release it?"

The response was unexpected.

"Surprisingly, due to apathy and not fear. Successful criminals win out over fear and become monsters, bigger than anything. The final colors defining you as a frail human invade and take over so you start drinking every night and lying to yourself about it in the morning."

Julian's thoughts were tangled and heavy from alcohol. He didn't know what to think next.

He snapped out of his wine-induced haze and looked around. Protected by thick smoke were married politicians, law students and sculptors in their golden ages devising secret alliances with friendly journalists—and confusing waitresses with bizarre drink orders.

Looking at the glowing end of his cigarette, Julian recognized the man's hallucinatory spectacle. Julian knew that, despite his extraordinary intelligence, he lived an anonymous, generic and desperate life.

The scary and revolting thought—that things happen even if nothing happens made him recognize how close to the edge he was. He was one step away from the eternal misdeed—the biggest transgression of humanity—an average existence. It would swallow him if he didn't stop in time. He would be one of the regulars in the crowd every night, shredding his public image beside young politicians of various parties, teachers, persecuted rebels and journalists who lived off documenting human misery. The cellar would always exist as a complete synthesis of wasted energy.

Maybe destiny is a wine—you fill a glass, drink it down and then another, until you are drunk and fall asleep in a ditch. If you look down from afar you see the ditch is merely a lifeline in the palm of someone greater—a nameless being you never knew.

"Everything can be restarted," he whispered. "Like a shoestring, life has two ends. You can start from either end."

He rose to his feet and flipped over the table.

His wife looked up at him with wonder.

"Alienation settled over us like bitter dust. Let's open our hearts and restart our history. Let's build a new life—stronger and better."

He extended his hand. She took it. Hand in hand, they stood over the man-in-black—looking down on him. Julian pulled the heavy Rolex from his pocket and stared at it for a brief moment before placing it on the table.

"You can have your fucking watch back," Julian said.

They walked toward the door; their boots crunched on broken glass spread across the floor.

The stranger slid the watch onto his wrist and laughed, and then raised his index finger into the air.

"I'll take another drink, please," he said.

Notes on *The Bright Light of Being*

KLC: What is your experience with bars; particularly the contrast between a European bar and an American one? I've had vivid and memorable experiences in European bars (for example, Germans in Munich packed in so tight I couldn't breathe—raising their mugs and bellowing a patriotic song at the top of their lungs), but never anything that memorable over here.

A lot of American culture came from Europe, but, as far as I know, this aspect did not survive the journey over the Atlantic.

AP: I am familiar with the old fashioned English style pubs—smoky and noisy. In college we gathered in places like that and planned the future of the world. You are right, I haven't seen very many American bars to remind me of the European ones, but then again, the older I got the less I frequented bars.

KLC: I don't mean to belabor the bar setting and image, but my father was a barfly and my wife's father a somewhat lesser species of barfly. There is an unpleasant autobiographical Charles Bukowsky film called *Barfly* (with Mickey Rourke) which captures the seedy, loserville image I have of an American bar. When I give up on life and my ambitions, I'll probably spend a lot more time in bars. The redemptive loser in your story achieves wisdom and clarity in a bar, but that's the opposite of a place I'd expect to find it. What's the bottom-line reason you set this story in a bar? Was it a European reason or an American reason?

AP: Without a doubt, I had the old college waterhole in mind where the fate of the world was argued back and forth and where revolutionary thinking was fostered. Julian is young and naïve about life and its meaning. His conscience or subconscious gatekeeper walks in and shows him a potential future he cannot cope with.

KLC: Many times in your work, I feel like you are working on a troubled truce with your demons. And, let's be honest— you'd look good in the purple dress worn by your unnamed, long-suffering wife-character. What is the nature of the demon you wrestled when writing this story?

AP: I struggle with mediocrity, fighting against it all my life. In my youth, the idea of an average existence constrained by average ambitions terrified me.

KLC: To me, this is a scary story. As I read it, I was worried about the fate of the wife and Julian and it seemed like things could go seriously astray when the mysterious man-in-black appears. However, you relented and gave us a fairytale ending.

Was there a temptation to write a dark and relentless tale? What made you decide to give the reader a break?

AP: No, I never thought about ending this story in darkness. I started it in an ambiguous light and worked toward clarity.

KLC: Beyond the obvious implications of fleeting time and materialism, what should the reader take away when thinking about the Rolex?

AP: I used the Rolex to anchor the story in material realism. Everything else in the story is intended to be fleeting and interchangeable.

KLC: Suppose I suggest we change the name to *The Bitter Wine of Destiny?* What would you say?

AP: Oh, Ken, have I ever doubted you? If you want to change the name, that's fine.

KLC: Ah, I was just kidding to see what you'd say. However, I do think *The Bitter Wine of Destiny* has a nice resonance. We'll see what ends up being used in the book.

.

If it Wasn't for Free Will…
Ken Coffman

THE WINDOW WAS rolled down, but it was no comfort. The air conditioner was broken. I could imagine the repairman grinning at me.

"Looks very serious, Meester."

Maybe he will make enough money to buy himself another gold tooth. I fanned myself with a newspaper, but it barely stirred the dead city air. I waited for the traffic light to turn green. Fire trucks have strobe lights that turn traffic signals green for them; my car had some way of ensuring the lights turned red. I could see a white limousine approaching; he sailed right through the intersection. The car was spotless. The driver wore dark sunglasses which swept sightless over me. I'm used to it; people don't look *at* me—they look *through* me.

Maybe I should explain a few things. I've always been unlucky. Unlucky in love—I'd still be a virgin if my fat cousin Clara hadn't felt sorry for me two summers ago. Unlucky with money—if I bet on a horse it would fall dead on the backstretch. Unlucky in health—I could catch a cold by reading about symptoms in a newspaper. I was a born loser. Seeing this dude in the white Cadillac make the traffic light filled me with rage.

I drove my car across two lanes of traffic, leaving an old

lady mouthing bad words and waving an arthritic middle finger at my blue smoke. I tried to catch the man in the white car but I got stuck behind a street sweeper.

For the next week I was haunted by images of that guy at every turn. I even dreamed about him drifting through a crowd looking cucumber-cool while I followed, trying to look debonair with cracked-lens sunglasses sliding down my oily nose.

The following week, while being insulted by a sales clerk—I saw the lucky bastard gliding up an escalator. I hated him for being able to wear white. My attempt would cause a chocolate doughnut to hurtle from unknown regions of outer space on a collision course with my shirt. I'll never forget the platter of spaghetti that once did a beautiful three point landing on my white trousers.

I abandoned the sales clerk and followed the man in white. I lost him when I tangled with an old woman carrying a shopping bag filled with china teacups and a treacherous display of German crystal figurines—and a humorless store manager.

A serious obsession took hold. Every guy with a girl on his arm symbolized the distance between me and that damned perfect man in white. I could not sleep without some new torture waiting for me. For example, trying to be charming with a green stump of broccoli in my teeth while the man in white simultaneously ate, drank and romanced a stunning babe. This vision made me so upset that I spilled wine on the lumberjack sitting at the adjoining table. I woke just before he killed me.

While waiting at the bus station for a friend who never showed, I saw the man in white. I would not lose him this time. I don't know where this obsession came from; maybe I hoped his good fortune would rub off. I almost caught him when he plowed into a lovely woman in a black minidress. He knocked an armload of her packages to the floor. I was shocked—how could this happen to Mr. Perfecto? I turned back to my bench to find a surly bum had claimed my newspaper. Depressed, I turned to leave the station and caught sight of the man in white chatting cheerfully with the lady as he picked up her packages. She smiled at him in such a way that my knees got weak from twenty feet away. I could see her press paper into his hand, probably a telephone number, home address, hell, probably taxi fare too. As she walked away I tore my eyes from her retreating rear and grabbed the man's arm.

"I've been looking for you," I said.

He turned his glasses on me. My dual sweating images stared back from the mirrored lens. Smiling, he lifted the glasses and his eyes devoured me. The bus station made a disorienting ninety-degree shift. The rumble of busses passed through me and the overhead lights shifted in strange constellations. When he spoke, I swear his voice did not travel through the air between us; his words appeared directly in my brain.

"This looks glorious to you doesn't it? So precious. You will learn soon enough that free will is to be valued above good fortune. The lovely element of chance, the anticipation of the unknown. Such sweet prizes. You'll learn."

The words were mixed with bitter laughter. His eyes held me frozen in time and space.

"Take them," he said, "you've earned them."

He pressed the glasses into my hand. For an instant I swear his teeth turned yellow, and did an old tomato sauce stain appear on his jacket? I watched him stroll away. He laughed as he stopped to scrape dog shit off of one of his shoes. I lifted the glasses to my nose. I took a step backwards and felt two soft, warm objects stab into my back. When I turned around the first thing I noticed was how extraordinary and large her breasts were.

"Well, excuse me," she said. "My name is Lisa, what's yours?"

As I took her hand I almost didn't notice the glazed look in her eye. I almost didn't notice the invisible strings binding her to me. I almost didn't notice she had no chance, no choice. And that's how it's been. The dice fall my way. The deck is stacked in my favor. Heads I win, tails you lose. A life of dull fortune.

My only hope is that my savior is out there—chasing me in my white suit. Out there with a jelly doughnut target on his new shirt—tired of being at the end of the cosmic garbage chute.

He is out there and if I have any luck left at all, someday, he'll find me.

Notes on *If it Wasn't for Free Will…*

AP: Let's start by talking about the title. What was your thought?

KLC: You've heard the expression…

If it wasn't for bad luck, I'd have no luck at all?

As usual, when I picked the silly, longwinded title, I was just playing around.

AP: How about a quote?

We must believe in luck. For how else can we explain the success of those we don't like?
—Jean Cocteau

Do you believe in luck, Ken?

KLC: I'm one of the most fortunate guys who ever lived, so I'd be a horrible ingrate if I didn't believe in luck. However, it's clear the underlying universal engine runs on randomness and disorder. It's human nature to seek (and find) patterns. We have a basic need to believe everything happens for a reason. I don't think the human mind is capable fully embracing chaos. I've argued with my son and others about free will. Many don't believe it really exists—they believe we're meat machines and free will is an illusion.

I don't buy it. We might not have as many choices as I'd like, but we control our behavior. We make choices and to a certain extent, we can choose the world we live in.

AP: This is fine parable with a cosmic (and comic) center of gravity. I belong to an over-achieving group that constantly questions life and destiny. Some people describe their misfortune as luck when they've simply acted less sensibly than others. Where do you stand on this issue? In other words, are you confident in enjoying the fruits of your hard work without calling it luck?

KLC: I work hard and make positive and productive choices. I don't have the deep-set urge to self-destruction others seem to have. On the other hand, there are random elements that worked for and against me over the years. Call it luck or call it something else, I don't care, but you'd be foolish to ignore the fact that when you flip a coin, sometimes the result is positive and sometimes the result is negative.

AP: *If it Wasn't for Free Will* is a funny piece.

Ken Coffman and Adina Pelle

*The wit makes fun of other persons; the satirist makes
fun of the world; the humorist makes fun of himself.*
—James Thurber

This story holds nuances of satire and self-deprecating humor.

KLC: Sometimes it's not easy, but I try not to take myself too
seriously. If you think about it, we're all absurd, silly creatures
running in tight little circles doing things we consider
important, but which are truly irrelevant from a larger, more-
universal point of view.

AP: Humor is a way for people deal to with the irony of
human aspiration. Do you see irony as an effective weapon
against life's incongruity? If nothing else, it's a sure cure for
monotony.

KLC: On occasion, my sense of humor gets frayed around the
edges—which is not good for my blood pressure.

AP: What defines a loser, Ken? Do you believe in the concept?

KLC: That's a great question, Adina. As an engineer, whether
it's appropriate or not, I tend to think of things in analytical
terms. How is a man's life to be measured? Is it an integration
of everything summed together or is it the end point? There's
no definitive answer, but it's fun to think of these things. If
you lead a good, charmed life that ends with a horrible
industrial accident, is that a good life? If you do horrible things,
but also do transcendent things, can the net result be positive?
Does the sequence matter?

There are people who do everything just right, but things
do not fall their way. They lead an old woman across the street

149

and are crushed by a bus as a reward for their good deed.

I'll answer your question clearly, Adina. Do I believe some people, through no fault of their own, are losers?

Yes, I do.

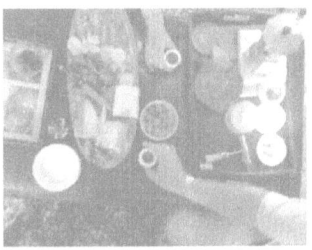

The Attic in my Grandmother's House
Adina Pelle

THE NARROW STAIRCASE ascending to the attic fascinated me throughout my childhood. At the end of the stairs, there was a small door. Thinking of what might be hidden behind that door fueled my imagination with mystery, fantasy and images of spooky ghosts.

After grandmother died, the house sat empty for a while; it later sold at a ridiculously low price, making it easy for me to redeem later at an even sillier low price.

This cottage was hidden among dunes and overlooked the sea. Harsh weather, time and strong winds added to its wrinkles, as they do an old sailor's creased face.

At night, while sitting in darkness by the seaward window, I watched the restless silver shuffle of waves in moonlight. I listened to lost thoughts and bathed in foggy memories while the gentle, soft wind massaged the old house. The house barely complained—merely emitting a few feeble creaks and groans.

The staircase leading to the attic's little door held me in the same childhood spell. Today however, I gathered my courage and stood before the mysterious door—armed with a flashlight. I climbed the old wooden stairs; the narrow steps squeaked under my feet. My timid fingers touched the rusty key in my skirt pocket. When I reached the top of the stairs, I slipped the key in the old lock. The rasp of the stubborn lock grated on my spine. I pushed the door open with my foot and walked through a forest of hanging spider web threads.

The attic was cavernous—stretching over the entire top of the house. The wood beams were blackened by the relentless passage of time. It looked like a church tower. At the far end, I saw a round, dirty window. Through it, the incurious, pale light seemed too shy to make itself boldly known in the dusty room. The space was filled with old trunks, filing cabinets, a huge, oval man's height mirror, incomprehensible, deteriorating yellow magazines, a baby stroller with large wheels and a gramophone with a disc under its twisted arm. I turned its handle several times and the disc began to rotate. From its black hole funnel, a somber voice fractured the eerie silence with Portuguese words I recognized: Edith Piaf, *La Mer*.

Qu'on voit danser le long des golfes clairs
A des reflets d'argent
La mer, des reflets changeants sous la pluie[11]

(That one seen dancing along the clear gulfs
Has silver reflections
The sea, changing reflections under the rain)

I lifted the hem of my skirt above the dirt and dust and pushed a wooden trunk toward the obscured window in the corner. From behind the trunk, a picture fell over. My attention was drawn to a portrait—a finely detailed woman's face expertly drawn with a charcoal pencil.

I was amazed. The woman in the drawing looked happy and filled with eager anticipation. Her eyes were focused on the faraway distance. A melancholy beauty hid under her

---

[11] *La Mer*, Charles Trenet and Leo Chauliac

happiness. Her eyes were filled with a certainty about the way of the world and the life that stretched before her.

Was I imagining this?

She looked very much like me.

In a fever, I looked in the other trunks with the hope of discovering more about the beautiful young woman in the drawing. There was nothing to be found.

Exhausted, I sat on my haunches and rested. An image caught my eye. The room filled with color and light. I brushed cobwebs and dust from the large, oval mirror and saw a shadowy silhouette. She was here. With me. But, after a few seconds, the woman's outline faded and she disappeared in the loft's dusty light.

The room quickly returned to lonely cobwebs and forgotten memories. All hope dissipated.

I walked to the small window and stared at the sea lapping at wet sand and listened to the breaking of the murmuring waves.

They whispered a name I could not understand.

Mine.

Notes on *The Attic in my Grandmother's House*

KLC: This is one of your rare stories written in a first-person perspective. This hints at it being more of a memoir than a fantasy tale. What led you to the decision to take this POV?

AP: I took the first person approach because there is a lot of biographical material in it. My grandmother didn't live in a house by the sea but the attic in her house fascinated me. As a kid, I would spend hours going through boxes full of old photos, wooden chests with broken locks, piles of old clothes. At the same time I was terrified by spiders and mice.

KLC: This question also relates to many of the intimate tales in *Ghost Words and other Echoes*... How much of your work should we interpret as autobiographical?

AP: Most of it is—at least—inspired by true events. I intend to leave every reader completely confused, puzzled and not knowing what to believe. Sometimes, even I have a hard time deciphering the truth in my stories when my imagination and intellect clash.

KLC: Music is an important part of your life and appears in the corners and the underlying fabric of many of your stories. If we were forced to pick three songs to decorate the soundtrack of your life's story, what should we pick?

AP: Edward Elgar's *Cello Concerto in E minor, Op. 85*, Samuel Barber's *Adagio for Strings* and Edith Piaf's *Je ne Regret Rien*.

KLC: There is a human comfort taken from looking at our place in our ancestral lineage and the rippling waves of history. As Mark Twain said:

> *History doesn't repeat itself, but it rhymes.*

If you could send a telegram into the future? Let's say, to a great granddaughter struggling with heartbreak or existential despair. What would you say to her?

AP: It's funny that you mention that idea. When I was fourteen, I wrote myself a letter to open when I turned thirty (thirty seems very old to a kid). I completely forgot about it until a couple of years ago when I got a call from my mother telling me that my father, while gardening, dug out my time capsule hidden in the back yard. I had her open the letter and read it to me. Of course, I had not achieved any of the socio-economic and professional goals I set for myself, but what got my attention was one sentence where I, as a fourteen-year-old kid, hoped for the later adult I would become to be proud of myself and my life. I am happy to admit—as a forty-some adult, I fulfilled my teenage prophesy. So I guess this would be my message to everyone: live a life your childhood self would be proud of.

KLC: This is a grayscale ghost story. It reads as if the words are washed out and faint. There must be a huge temptation to overwrite a piece like this, but the effect would be like putting a clown's nose on Mona Lisa. How do you know when to lift your fingers from the keyboard and let a story be what it is?

AP: I am still not sure of what will come from my pen, or rather, my keyboard. I rarely end my stories where I initially planned. I am a bewildered reader and writer—all at the same time.

Twins
Ken Coffman

THE ROOM SMELLED of dust and feces. In the dark, rays of light streamed through tears and seams of the aluminum foil that covered the windows. Sunbeams pierced the gloom like searchlights. Gabe, with a sawed-off shotgun lying across his lap, sat on a folding chair spooning cold chili from a tin. With filthy fingers, he wiped the inside of the can to get the last of the sauce and grease. A rat rustled in discarded cans in the kitchen. Beyond caring, Gabe rolled the can across the floor to join the others. After two days of staring at the last can with his empty belly gnawing on itself, he'd finally opened it. The pantry was empty.

It was his third week locked up in the house. The power and water had been cut off two weeks earlier. Out of habit, he stored his improvised chamber pot, a five-gallon bucket, in the useless bathroom. Harry, his toy terrier, did not smell much. His body was wrapped securely in black plastic and sealed with duct tape.

Sorry, Harry. I couldn't feed you. It's better this way.

Despair pressed on his shoulders while he watched the sidewalk in front of his little house. Movement caught his peripheral vision. He shuffled across the floor to get a better view. Two boys. Twins. Dressed in Boy Scout uniforms. Gabe's heart flopped in his chest like a dying fish. The boys walked down the sidewalk and stopped in front of his house. They turned and looked. Margie's overturned tricycle blocked the concrete walkway. One of the boys rotated it onto its wheels and rolled it onto the overgrown lawn.

Gabe, with clenched teeth and a death grip on his shotgun, tried to tamp down Margie's memory. What happened to her was not right.

I'm so sorry, baby.

The boys stood and watched. A breeze ruffled their blond hair.

Please keep walking. Don't come here.

With a hand in his jacket pocket he fingered the remaining shells. Three in the pocket and two in the gun. Five.

Not nearly enough.

In lockstep, the boys walked toward his door.

Finally, it was almost over. Calmness spread through his body. He visualized the movements. Fire both barrels, break open the gun, reload and fire again. That left only the last cartridge reserved for himself. He pointed the gun at the door at the height of their heads and waited. At the knock, he fired. Without thinking, he reloaded.

He pushed the door open. Both boys were dead. After kicking their bodies out of the way, he walked toward the street.

The noon sun blinded him. His eyes streamed with tears. While standing at the end of his sidewalk, he looked up the street. Two boys, Boy Scouts, approached. Gabe's face twisted in horror. He took careful aim and killed them. One cartridge was left. It was time. With practiced quickness, he ejected the spent cartridges and loaded the last shell. He rotated the gun toward his head. There was movement to his right. Two Boy Scouts. One grabbed the gun and discharged it into the ground. The other grinned and his black teeth, sharpened like pencils, gleamed.

No. Oh, God, no.

There was no use running. He walked to the curb and sat down.

Up the street, a pod hovered and landed. A ramp extended and identical Boy Scouts marched out, in scores, two-by-two. Scorched and smoking from their entry into the Earth's atmosphere, three more pods landed to his right. Soon, they disgorged their Boy Scouts too.

It was no use running. There was nowhere to go.

Notes on *Twins*

AP: I am not a big fan of sci-fi books or horror and didn't picture you knee deep in the genre.

KLC: The inspiration of this story was the love of film. I've always avoided buying a video camera because I knew I'd immediately start making short films and spend all of my time living with a camera between me and the world. How do you make an interesting bit of film with no budget? By doing little things in your neighborhood like *Twins*, that's how. I had a friend with young twins—blonde, handsome boys. Instead of making a film, I wrote this short story.

In my youth, I was an insatiable science fiction reader and my inspiration was Stephen King. Why dream of success unless you dream of reaching the very top? Of course, reality beat the life out of most of my aspirations. Now I'm satisfied with a quirky twist of phrase, a story captured on paper to the best of my ability and a book sale here and there.

AP: *Twins* represents two stories in one. I was fooled by the beginning. It sounded like a cliché—a post-apocalyptic setting with Gabe as the aggressor but then I was jolted back in my seat . Boy Scouts? Oh, the horror…

Well done.

KLC: Obviously, that was my point—to turn what you think on its head and to play with what you know about things. Have you noticed that about life? Things you take for granted are often simply untrue.

AP: I was wondering why did he kill the dog and not eat him?

KLC: He couldn't bring himself to eat his last and only friend.

AP: Why the plot change? Clones descending in a flying object from Mars. I would have never thought that up. Is this a genre you'd like to pursue?

KLC: Many of these stories are experiments to see what I can do; to see what I can lead the reader to think and feel. I wanted something far removed from the reader's expectation.

There is probably at least one horror tale in me. It would be fun to play with the sacred conventions of that genre.

AP: The descriptions are very vivid. You are a master in that respect. I could draw Gabe easily or pick him up from a police line-up, based on your well-crafted sketching.

KLC: It's easy to heap on the words; you'd know a character very well if I piled on page after page of description. You'd be bored beyond tears, but you'd know the character. How do you pare things down to their essence? I pore over the words to make them as efficient as possible.

AP: There are also dynamic elements to your writing.

In lockstep, the boys walked toward his door.

All in all I can learn a lot from a writer like you.

KLC: I invite the picture into my mind, then describe it on paper the best that I can.

The Light Journey into Night
Adina Pelle

AS HE DROVE home, darkness fell. An annoying rain, like spit from the mouth of an enthusiastic talker, sprayed on his ancient Honda's windshield while nearly-useless wipers struggled to keep up. The headlights were in no better shape—fighting with their last spark to shed light on the dark road as he traveled through the mysterious night.

Fortunately, he knew the smallest detail of the twenty miles between his parent's house and his own. After all, he'd made this hometown journey hundreds of times.

His father lived alone. Two weeks prior, on his last visit, they'd visited his mother's grave. Afterward, they talked, sipped glasses of brandy and recalled for the thousandth time funny little events from his childhood mixed with the great events of their family history.

This time he'd helped his old father prepare for the holidays. It was the day before Christmas Eve. He would have left earlier to avoid driving at night, but wanted to make sure everything was in order for his father.

Holidays were not the same as when he was a child. Carolers were no more, but decorating a Christmas tree brought a festive feel to the house. As a child, he went to the edge of the forest to steal a few branches of fir. They would decorate them with cheap paper ornaments and adorn them

161

with 'silver' packages of cheap candy.

What a time.

The road was not busy. He turned a corner and saw a bundle in the middle of the road. Instinctively, he rotated the steering wheel to the left, but it was too late. Both right-side wheels passed over it.

He slowed down and tried to think.

What the hell was that?

He gave up and accelerated.

What could it have been? Maybe a dog, nothing more than a dog? Perhaps a dog, already dead, run over by someone else before him.

He recalled an event in his village when he was a child. A drunkard was run over by a tractor. Ironically, the tractor was driven by another drunkard. After an investigation, the driver was sentenced to many years in jail, but there was a rumor which suggested the accident's author was actually a renowned politician, inebriated, driving in his Mercedes.

Did he pay the tractor driver hard cash money to escape the charges?

What if I ran over a drunkard too?

Or, God forbid, a sick person, fallen in the middle of the road?

I am no coward. I will return and see what it was.

He'd do jail time if necessary, but, after all, what was someone doing on the road at night?

Maybe I will be found innocent.

But he'd left the accident scene. In itself, that was a crime.

What would Mildred say?

She tormented him constantly about how he was careless, how he was always dreaming, how he was an absent-minded poet. She rarely let him drive without her accompaniment, always with acute observations—always right and always careful. It was annoying, but useful.

Generally, her assistance was helpful.

She will never forgive me.

He needed to know what the bundle was. He pulled over, pressed his palms to his temples and let his thoughts roam free. The pressure building up in his head left him dizzy. He could continue driving as if nothing had happened—let go of guilt and see if anything happened.

Then what?

Maybe he would hear an announcement on the radio as he approached the city. The police were relentless in hit and run accidents. They would search for the car.

Should I hide the car?

Although he struggled to gather the money to buy it a couple of years prior, he was prepared to give it up to a junk yard.

I must return.

He looked left and then right before turning the car around. He traveled ten miles when an ambulance—with lights flashing and a deafening siren—passed him. He felt a sick feeling fly through his weakened body.

Oh, no.

So soon?

Traveling in the wake of the ambulance, he stepped on the gas pedal and picked up speed. Before he knew it, he passed by the place where his run-over victim was visible in the middle of the road. He grasped at calm and pulled over on the right side of the road next to his sad victim. It looked like a bundle of dead blankets.

It was totally inert.

No cars were coming. The ambulance was gone. He took a lantern from the car and approached the lifeless object and examined it front to back.

In the beam of the bright flashlight—whaaaat?

A bag of potatoes.

A bag of potatoes that fell from a passing truck?

Ha. Ha, ha, ha.

Oh, what a relief.

Potaaaaatoes.

How beautiful life can be. I exist, God. Happiness is alive.

While straining under the heavy weight, he carried the bag of mashed potatoes to his car.

The car's engine rumbled with reassurance.

Mildred would be waiting for him at home.

Oh, God! Thank you.

Monday I'll go to the Cathedral and pray one-hundred prayers. Then I'll give this old car away. Old girl, you've lived your life. You've been good, but there's not much more you can do for me now.

As his heart returned to its normal pace, he noticed the rain had stopped. Clouds only covered half of the sky. He had tears in his eyes—he was drunk with happiness. It was after midnight.

Tomorrow is Christmas.

It would be his happiest Christmas since he was a child.

Over the hill, the great city's lights sparkled with colorful invitation. As he drove home, trees on the side of the road were covered with multicolored lights and decorated with large and small globes. A large star reigned in the middle of the new roundabout junction.

What's this new fashion with these roundabouts?

This was not a busy intersection.

Flickering lights everywhere glinted in the tears of joy in his eyes.

With careless speed, he swerved into the roundabout. Immediately, big, bright lights from an approaching truck blinded him. In the windshield, the truck driver's mouth hung open like a cavern. This should have triggered common sense, but instead he ignored his instinct—he didn't slam the brakes.

Instead, he accelerated.

He felt nothing.

He floated in a blinding light, like an outdoor movie in slow motion—gliding in airborne color.

He entered the eternal light followed by an infinite darkness...

Notes on *The Light Journey into Night*

KLC: This story takes us on a rollercoaster ride of emotional states—from boredom to despair to joy. I don't want to build it up too much as this story is more of an experimental sketch than an epic tale, but I am curious about the range of emotions and what you were thinking when you dragged us along on this ride.

AP: This is a story about destiny and the futility of fighting against it. We struggle to do the right thing and agonize over our transgressions, but in the end, even when we follow the light, it all ends in darkness.

KLC: This story has some playful descriptions.

> *...like spit from the mouth of an enthusiastic talker...*
> *headlights...fighting with their last spark...*
> *...the great city's lights sparkled with colorful invitation...*

You strike me a dead-serious, thoughtful person. Where do these bits of whimsy come from?

AP: Me, serious? Oh my. Most of the time I am a buffoon. I always liked—gravitated toward and tried to be—the funny person. I bought a joke book hoping to find useful material. If that's not funny, then I don't know what funny is.

KLC: In your stories, I always wonder how much is made up and how much is autobiographical. For example, are you a helpful backseat driver or are you an unredeemable pain in the ass?

AP: I am, without a doubt, a useless copilot. I could not navigate a map if my life depended on it. That alone makes me a pain in the ass backseat driver.

KLC: I assume the point of this story is how you can do everything right, but fate can deal you a bad card anyway. The driver tried to avoid the bundle in the road. Though it took some time, he decided to do the right thing and return to the scene of his crime. The scare was for naught. It's Christmas Eve and all is well, but he finds himself at the wrong place at the wrong time and pays the ultimate price.

AP: That's it exactly. The supreme irony of life is that hardly anyone gets out of it alive. Can I insert a quote?

> *Life is pleasant. Death is peaceful. It's the transition that's troublesome.*
> —Isaac Asimov

KLC: It's your book—you can do what you like. Why does the driver accelerate?

AP: For the same reason he stepped on the gas after he thought he hit somebody on the road. There are two kinds of light— the glow that illuminates, and the glare that obscures.

Feinstein's Weapon
Ken Coffman

"YES SIR, OUR new spy planes are hightech wonders."

General Roger P. Clayton said "high-tech" like it was one word, the way he might say shithead or draftdodger.

"Those planes," he continued with his hand imitating an airplane on a strafing run, "can tell if a penny is heads or tails from an altitude of fifteen miles."

He looked at me with a crinkle of humor around his eyes. "You ever heard the old rhetorical question 'Does a bear shit in the woods?'. I've got reconnaissance photographs that prove once and for all that they do." He laughed like a jackal at his own humor and slapped his leg just like Grampa Jones used to do on Hee Haw.

I looked around General Clayton's office. It was ninety degrees outside but here the air was cool. I looked for a moment for the air conditioner vents; they were subtly hidden in the grain of the mahogany paneled walls. Some pictures hung in studied symmetry around the room, General Clayton in front of a golf cart with Ronald Reagan, General Clayton in front of a B-2 bomber with a big possessive grin, General Clayton shaking hands with a corpulent Arab.

"Excuse me, Mr. Foldberg," he said, wiping tears from his eyes with a monogrammed handkerchief. He pointed at the telephone which had a red light blinking on it.

167

"Clayton here," he said crisply into the phone. I could hear a little voice in his ear piece; it sounded like a far away ant speaking Spanish. "Can't you assholes do anything right down there?" He put his hand over the mouthpiece. "They're having a little trouble finding your file, Mr. Feinberg. Could you spell your name for me?"

I took a deep breath and tried to think calming thoughts. "F-E-I-N-S-T-E-I-N," I said.

He repeated my name into the phone. "Okay, just get on it, dammit." He dropped the phone into its cradle. "Just routine, I'm sure you understand."

As he leaned back in his leather chair, he seemed to really notice me for the first time. He absorbed my worn out running shoes, the Levis faded to a threadbare pale blue, my rumpled shirt with the pens and pencils in the pocket and my eye glasses that kept slipping down my nose.

"So, you think you might like to work in our research department," he said with a distant look in his eyes. "Not easy jobs to get sometimes, but I always say, if you want to make a high tech omelet, you gotta have a few eggheads. Do you do chemical weapons?"

I shook my head.

"Too bad. They had a little slip up down there last week. Quite a few job openings if you know what I mean." He grinned and winked. "A few less pensions for the taxpayers to bitch about if you get my drift." He glanced up at the wall clock. "What have you got for me, Einstein?"

"That's Feinstein, General Clayton. Feinstein."

"Yeah, yeah, whatever. I'm a busy man. Let's get to the point."

"Okay, I think you'll find this interesting. The best way for you to understand is if I could do a little demonstration. This will sound a little strange but please bear with me. Please give me one of your nail clippings."

"A nail clipping?" he said as he took the nail clippers I offered. He looked confused but dutifully snipped a little from his index finger. "What the hell do you want a nail clipping for?"

I carefully pushed the sliver of fingernail to the front edge of his oak desk. I pulled the Thrifty Market shopping bag (A THRIFTY GAL IS A THRIFTY MARKET PAL) from under my chair. The bag rustled loudly as I opened it. I admired my creation for a moment before pulling it out. It looked just like what it was, a high school surplus microscope carefully modified with radio frequency Gallium Arsenide transistors, a traveling ray tube I got from Boeing Surplus and a ratty and colorful mess of interconnect wires. The General looked confused. I think he expected a three-thousand-page funding proposal with pie charts and a ream of spreadsheet pages.

"What's this? It looks like one of those Rube Goldstein contraptions." He seemed to think for a moment. "Hey, you're not related to Goldstein, are you?" he asked with a voice full of hope.

I didn't bother to correct him. I was just about to panic. The power switch had been turned on—probably while I was riding the bus to get here. The battery was run down and I didn't have a replacement. When I looked around the room, I noticed the General's desk clock was battery operated. I unscrewed the battery panel with the screwdriver from my pocket; the battery was quickly installed in my machine.

"I know," the General exclaimed. "Admiral Schenker sent you over here didn't he? He's still trying to get even with me for bribing his barber to give him a Mohawk. You should have seen him, a punk-ass Admiral." He laughed so hard that tears filled his eyes again. He dabbed at them with a silk handkerchief.

"General, if you'll just pay attention for a moment." I slid the nail clipping under the microscope focusing mechanism. "I want to explain about leverage. Find the pivot point where it takes minimum energy to disturb the balance. One day at work I was considering the implications of Heisenberg's uncertainty theorem. At the subatomic level, events occur in a probability cloud. For example, it is not possible to simultaneously measure the speed and direction of an electron. You can only predict an envelope of probability that describes events at that level. This factor of uncertainty can be called luck at the human conceptual level. When you think about it, our lives are guided by the field of subatomic events. Albert Einstein was proved to be wrong when he said that God does not throw dice. Have you been following the recent advances in chaos and turbulence theory?"

The General looked confused.

"I guess not," I continued. "To get to the point, the amplification and phase coherence of certain wavelengths of energy can influence the probability cloud that define events. I've shown that these events can be observed at our macro level. My machine demultiplexes, amplifies and adjusts the phase of radiation patterns that exist at the cellular level. I have some of your cells in this sliver of fingernail. They are still alive. My machine will influence the indeterminate factors of your life."

I looked at the General. His eyes were glazed; his jaw hung as if unhinged. He spoke as if the words needed to be dragged from his throat.

"I'm used to wild-eyed scientists giving me particle beam weapons and neutron bombs. What's with this Heidelberg stuff?"

"I guess I could be a little more clear." I pointed at my machine. "It boils down to this—when I press this little red button, a resonance in your subatomic structure is amplified, phase modulated and remixed. When I press this button," which I did as I spoke, "you will have mostly bad luck for a while."

General Clayton gasped like a beached fish.

"You-are-a-goddamn-nut-case-fucking-space-cadet..." He was interrupted by the telephone.

"Clayton here," he said in a small voice. "Bring it in. This should be interesting." He set the phone back down. The door opened and a sergeant handed the General a slim folder. The sergeant looked at me like a woman taking a last look at a spider before flushing it down the toilet. Clayton read the cover page and burst out laughing.

"You're a goddamned dishwasher at the commissary."

"It's not really that bad of a job. It does not interfere with my concentration. I do some of my best thinking while at work."

"You did not even graduate from high school. Admiral Schenker really got me this time. I spent twenty minutes listening to a damned dishwasher talk about comic rays and bad luck. Where's the 'America's Stupidest Home Videos' camera?"

He was grinning as he picked up the phone.

"Sergeant, call the fish farm and have two-hundred-thousand salmon fingerlings delivered to Admiral Schenker's limousine. And get this nutball out of my office."

Yes, I'm a dishwasher. As I said, it's not such a bad job. It pays the rent. It pays my bus fare. I get most of my meals at the restaurant (usually cheeseburgers, but if the manager is not around the cook will grill me a steak). I don't eat at home except for animal crackers and milk. A case of animal crackers costs about ten bucks at Costco and lasts about a month. What

171

more could a person ask for? In my own way I feel rich.

My place is not much, but I call it home. One corner of the dusty living area is dedicated to magazines, *Scientific American* and a few obscure academic publications. They are stacked in towering heaps. If you are curious about how a high school dropout and dishwasher can learn particle physics and chaos/fractal theory, just go to the library and look around. They know me by name in the Applied Physics library at the University. And, it's free, right?

I converted my dining room into a lab filled with wiring, surplus oscilloscopes, radio frequency signal generators and assorted junk. The kitchen is filled with dirty glasses lined up by the sink; I take them to work in a cardboard box and wash them when I can't find a clean glass. I might be untidy, but I'm no savage. The windows are greasy and allow only dim, unfocused light in. It doesn't bother me because I don't spend a lot of time looking out the window, do you? The bedroom is filled with empty animal cracker boxes. I keep thinking there must be some use for them. They are cute with their pictures of boxcars full of circus animals and the little wheels that pop out of the bottom.

Looking around my house, I have to admit that there is a lot of junk that could be hauled away. Sometimes at the military surplus store, I buy old equipment just because it looks cool; stuff that could be used for sets in 1950s B movies, *The Attack of the Big Bugs* or something. However, some of the stuff is valuable. I've got just about everything I need except a particle accelerator. I'll get that the next time I have two-hundred-million dollars laying around doing nothing.

Are you wondering if my bad luck machine works? I was able to follow General Clayton's life through the gossip mill at the base. The people who really know what is going on are the secretaries who type all the memos and the janitors who read all the papers in the trash as they feed it into the shredders. The rumor mill began filling with General Clayton's problems.

A few days after I visited the General, he was driving his big black Cadillac down the beltway. This was a huge car with armored windows, puncture-proof tires and tax-exempt license plates. He sped along smoking a cigar and listening to country music on the hundred-thousand dollar long-wave short-wave single sideband AM-FM Stereo system.

Near exit twelve he noticed the blue lights of a police car in the rear view mirror. The General pulled into the slower lane to let the cop go by. It did not occur to him that the cop would pull him over. The cop stayed on his tailgate. The General pulled to the side of the road, got his military identification ready and prepared for the pleasure of ripping this Smoky a new asshole. The cop cautiously walked to the window with his nine millimeter Taurus at the ready.

"Good afternoon, Officer," Clayton said, holding his identification out the window.

"Get out of the car. Keep your hands in sight," the officer ordered with the gun in the General's face.

"Put that goddamned cannon away, boy. Did Admiral Schenker put you up to this?"

"Shut up unless you want a kiss from my friend Billy," the cop said pointing to his riot stick. General Clayton was familiar with the club; it had about a pound of lead in the tip. He shut up. Within minutes, he was handcuffed and on his way downtown.

At the jail, the General was strip-searched, fingerprinted and dressed in ill-fitting jail overalls. He shared a cell with a couple of snoring drunks and a tattooed skin head who looked like he was on speed.

The General was stuck. If he called his lawyer, the news of

his dilemma would quickly spread around town. His wife was at bridge party with the Governor's wife, Admiral Schenker's wife and others. His wife would divorce him in an instant if he called her for bail money. He sat on the edge of a metal bunk with his face buried in his hands.

"All right, Clayton." The jailer clanged keys on the bars. "You can go home now."

"What happened?"

"Some asshole dressed as a General stole a Cadillac from the motor pool; we've got him in the holding tank. Next time you want to take a drive, use a driver. It looks suspicious for a General to drive his own car. You were looking for trouble."

When the General got home about four A.M., his wife bitched at him for being drunk and made him sleep on the couch. The General did not even try to explain.

There were a lot more General Clayton stories. Some were innocent enough—a flat tire in the pouring rain on the freeway, deodorant giving him a horrible case of hives and a gay son coming out of the closet. There was a grisly stomach pumping incident when the General ate bad macaroni salad. His dog bit a mailman whose brother happened to be a blood-thirsty personal injury lawyer. His wife came down with genital herpes. A seagull shit on his head while he was escorting the leader of the White House Arms Appropriation committee to lunch. His ball point pens leaked in his pocket. He couldn't eat without nasty green stuff getting stuck in his teeth. There was a near fatal attack of hemorrhoids and a situation involving a rabid IRS investigator who was jilted by the gay son. His daughter joined the Lords of Satan Motorcycle club and appeared nude in a sleazy biker magazine. A reporter got mixed up and ran his picture next to a story about UFO murders. Not really a good year for the General.

Animal crackers are quite underrated. Occasionally I enjoy Viennese shortbreads or Mari Lu biscuits dipped in Swiss chocolate, but on a daily basis, nothing is as satisfying as good old American animal crackers. I was trying to decide whether to eat a gorilla or a water buffalo when the doorbell rang. It scared the hell out of me; I didn't even know my house had a doorbell. I'd gotten used to the quiet—no phone, no newspaper. My magazines get delivered to a private mailbox. Just me, my animal crackers, and the dusty light that filters through the windows. I opened the front door and was blinded by the afternoon light. A disheveled (and recently demoted) Colonel Clayton brushed by me into the room.

"Come on in, Clayton. How have you been?"

"You know how I've been, you shithead," he said bitterly. "The IRS wants my financial records for the last seventeen years. I've been impotent for a year and my forty-five-year-old wife is pregnant. Tomorrow, I'm leaving on assignment in Libya."

He tipped magazines out of a chair, then sat down and buried his face in his hands. I could smell whiskey and decay on his breath. He was probably having trouble with abscessed teeth.

"Make this stop," he pleaded.

"I can't," I said while trying not to breathe in his rank odor.

"Feinstein, I'll have you drafted. Your house will be put on the toxic landfill list. Every nail and splinter of wood left after the place is torn down will be put in plastic bags and buried in Georgia. I'll tie your dick in a knot until your eyes turn yellow." He seemed to run out of steam. Tears hovered in the corners of his eyes and threatened to spill.

"Listen to me carefully, Colonel Claybird," I said reasonably. "If you are patient, I think the field will eventually

175

randomize again. You may even have a string of good luck for a while. I don't know if you've ever heard of the Second Law of Thermodynamics, but it goes something like 'Natural processes tend toward a state of greater disorder'. This is probably a concept too esoteric for you, but that it is the root reason why it is easier to destroy than create. In the case of my machine, it can disorder your fortune but it can't assemble it. It can give you bad luck but not good. It's that simple."

His eyes were unfocused—he nodded absently. He seemed convinced and shuffled out the door. The last time I saw him he was hopping away from my door, trying to remove gum from the sole of his shoe.

I was glad to see him go because I didn't want him to meet my new girlfriend. Her name was Heidi, and she was a stunning blonde college student from Denmark. I'd met her at the market where we were both trying to buy the last case of animal crackers. We decided it would make sense to share it instead of fighting over it.

By the way, I may have lied about not being able to create good luck; the experimental results are inconclusive at the moment. Unfortunately, I have to put my research on hold while Heidi and I spend my lottery winnings on a six-month honeymoon trip to Australia and New Zealand.

We'll send you a postcard.

Notes on *Feinstein's Weapon*

AP: Ken, I read this and it made me breathless. It's not every day we get personal insight into the illusive Ken Coffman, the man behind the scenes, the berry picker, cat food factory worker, dish washer, Air Force Sergeant, etc. But before I get really excited, this is partly autobiographical, right?

KLC: All stories are partly autobiographical—infused with bits and pieces of the author's life experiences, but I'm afraid you'll have to work a little harder to peer into my soul. Beyond a few accidental linkages, I don't feel that the loony Feinstein is me. My life is more structured, controlled, planned, deterministic and frankly, more boring than Feinstein's. My lovely wife is not a Danish blonde. Heh.

AP: I like the tone of the whole story; it reads as if Feinstein sat in front of a fire and remembered times and people who shaped his destiny. Also, Clayton's fate seems to have followed Feinstein when he refers to the Colonel's state in the current day. Is Clayton real?

KLC: My Lord, I hope not. He's a jerk.

AP: Is there a reason for Feinstein's interest in the Colonel's destiny?

KLC: Yes, it's karma in action for being such a clueless asshole.

AP: The descriptions are vivid. I would go as far as declaring this story holds the most vivid imagery I have seen so far in your work. All the words fall into place creating the exact surroundings and conditions of "ninety degrees outside but here the air was cool". Clayton is so well-captured that I could pick him out of a police lineup in two seconds. You must have felt really strong about this, right?

KLC: After rejecting the idea that I am Feinstein, I suppose these next comments will seem disingenuous, but you mentioned I was a sergeant in the USAF, so I have some

177

experience with military officers. Some of them were perfectly respectable people, but some were empty uniforms—perfectly-pressed uniforms with shiny baubles on the collar, but empty-headed, meritless creeps. I imagine that's where General Clayton came from. He's a bit of an unfair stereotype—Tom Clancy would not approve, but it's my story. I can do what I like.

My military years were spent in hot places (Texas and Mississippi), so details like that are mined from my personal experiences.

AP: You have a military background. What do you remember the most?

KLC: Are you sure you want to know? It is fashionable to glorify the military and I appreciate their service. Those that risk their lives to protect us at the proverbial point of the spear deserve our support and respect.

However, I have a strong sense of independence and a stubborn disrespect for authority. You can imagine what I thought of ideas like respecting the rank and not the man and following orders about haircuts and uniforms and saluting. I chafed at the idiocy and structure of the military. I hated it.

However, I had a technical job repairing and maintaining ground-based navigation equipment and I worked for a black Master Sergeant named Steve Stevens. He was an influential person in my life and I respected him immensely. Steve Stevens, a key character in my Glen Wilson series of books (he also appears in *The Sandcastles of Irakkistan*) is based on him.

So, I hated the military life. However, they recognized my aptitude and trained me in electronics (I knew nothing about electronics before my military training) and they paid for my schooling via the GI Bill. Since then I extracted literally millions of dollars of cash from this career. So, in some ways I owe everything I became and everything I accomplished to those few short years I spent in the Air Force. You'd think I'd be more grateful, but I just didn't give fuck-all for how shiny my boots were. An idiot with bars on his shoulders is still an idiot. Saluting a moron left a filthy taste in my mouth.

I realize this makes me an ungrateful jerk. In many ways, that's exactly what I am.

AP: What do you think about military nowadays? Over the years, has your opinion changed?

KLC: I am not an anti-military person. I understand the need. There are many tyrants in the world who'd love to reach out and steal wealth instead of building it the old-fashioned way by earning it. There will always be people who prefer plunder to work. You can't reason with these people; you have to deal with them with force and strength. Peace through superior firepower—that's what works in the real world.

I know there are smart and dedicated people in the military, but they were extraordinarily rare in my experience.

AP: There's a bittersweet feeling you create around Clayton…

> "You know how I've been, you shithead," he said bitterly. "The IRS wants my financial records for the last seventeen years. I've been impotent for a year and my forty-five-year-old wife is pregnant. Tomorrow, I'm leaving on assignment tomorrow in Libya."

How would you like the readers to perceive him?

KLC: As a hopeless man enjoying the fruits of his arrogance and stupidity.

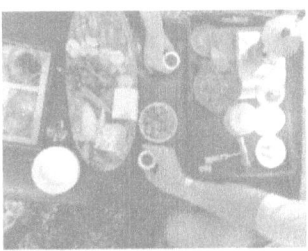

The Mail-Order Bride
Adina Pelle

EARLY IN THE morning, Ana took the first bus leaving town. Trains were too slow—taking long stops at unknown stations. A dense morning fog sat over the town. People emerged from the mist like birds emerging from eggshells—one head, one leg, and then hands full of luggage.

Everyone had luggage. Whether the traveler had many bags or a few was a clear sign of their stage in life. For Ana, her life was beginning, so she had nothing. Nothing. The beginning and the end are the same.

You come in with nothing and leave the same way.

Empty handed.

But, that morning, while stepping up on the bus, she held something dear to her heart.

Hope.

Precious hope.

The trip lasted several hours. She used this time to dream. Her favorite dream was about a little house wrapped in green ivy. Green, green fields and eternal spring everywhere. Green and sunlight were her secret love affairs. How she wanted a house full of light, with clear water from a well—sparkling water glistening in the sun. How much she liked the light. The dark, unsanitary houses she'd lived in until now were pushed aside in her memory. Darkness and mold. The damp smell of

181

poverty.

Next to the little house covered in ivy and light, she dreamed of a garden full of flowers; flowers of all colors and kinds. And more trees. A hundred trees with flowers, leaves and fruit and a pine tree to decorate in the winter. Evergreen. Immortal.

She would have a winding path through her garden where she would walk every night hand in hand with her husband. In life, no one held her hand. Never. Not even when she was a child.

She remembered their brief, banal telephone conversation repeated in her mind so many times—it became an obsession. She did not care what her husband looked like. Tall, short, thin, or fat, if his soul could love, it was enough. Emotion flooded her heart as she tried to imagine their first words. What would they say to each other when face-to-face? Between birth and death there is time for a grain of happiness and their first words had to be the seeds which would sprout that grain.

What would be the first word they shared?

With delight, she smiled.

The bus stopped in a town in the middle of nowhere. Ana was the only person who came off. The place seemed small and the immensity of the surrounding fields made it seem even smaller. Scorching sun. Burnt earth. Whitewashed houses covered with the road's stifling dust. No flowers, no tall trees—only a few stunted trees with poor foliage. There was no one to be seen.

Perhaps no one lived here. Perhaps the village was abandoned.

Or, maybe the people were vanquished by the heat and hid in their white-painted little houses. Looking around, she had a strange feeling that the entire area, village and all, was a huge scene suspended in nothingness. She felt the sensation of the finite contrasted against the infinite and was overwhelmed by a sense of cosmic loneliness.

Where am I? At the end of the world? Beyond the end, in another world which is a mirror image of the real world? What mirror?

The sky with its stunning light seemed apocalyptic.

What was she doing here?

Why did she come?

For a man she did not know.

What does he look like?

What kind of man is he?

She was driven by a desperate desire for a family and a home—because she never had one of her own? What was to be done would be done, because it was too late to turn back.

Walking down the main street, she cast a glance at a house. In the gray melting glass of its front window she saw a stout woman, neither young nor beautiful. Ana did not like what she saw, but this was a true picture, not one made up in her mind. The woman had a bleak, impassive expression; it was as if her features were eroded by torrential rainfall.

That's me, she whispered.

A door opened and a tall, heavily tanned man with a straw-hat on his head walked out.

He hollered in her direction.

"Want something? Looking for someone?"

"No—," she stuttered. "I'm just passing through. I fell asleep on the bus and I went too far. What time is the next bus?"

"Well, you'll have to wait some time until the next one. There is nothing to see in this town, and the heat is unpleasant. You can stay here and wait."

She entered the house and found herself in a dining room—maybe part of an inn with a bar at the back attended by a mustached bartender talking to a few customers.

Ana sat at a table behind a pillar. She did not want to order anything. The voices coming from the bar were loud; she heard them clearly.

"John found a new candidate for marriage."

"Another one? This one would be the third. His advertisement reads like a contest."

"A contest, right. With John as the prize."

They burst into laughter.

"Each one uglier than the other. The last one, he rode often and hard only to make the cost of the bus ticket worthwhile."

"And the first—a drunkard. Why didn't he chase her away the instant he saw her bleary face?"

The laughter continued.

"The one coming today, I think, is the youngest one yet. She had a thin voice on the phone and was very emotional. And the things he said he'll do to her...if she's a good one, maybe he'll keep her in his bed for a while."

And the laughter again.

"What *will* he do to her?"

The laughter continued. The men described the pornographic thoughts that crossed their minds.

Disgusted by what she heard, Ana felt sick. She tasted vomit and rose like a meek mouse to quietly leave the room. She walked toward the train station, which could be seen in the distance. She wanted to escape as quickly as possible, maybe take a one-way train going nowhere in particular, but far away from this dusty town.

It was a small station with one platform with three benches and a lonely lantern in a corner near a hydrant. Dry, wilted flowers struggled to survive in the scorching sun. On a bench, a homeless woman in a thin dress slept. By the woman's head was a nearly empty bottle of vodka. The woman was deep in sleep. She snored.

Ana approached the bench and looked at the woman. They were about the same age but the drunk had a puffier face. Then she looked at the train schedule posted on the board and saw she'd have to wait a long time until the next train.

The bus would be better.

I will take the next bus to nowhere.

She had no reason to go back to the city. There was nothing to go back to, especially since everyone would laugh at her. She could not go back.

She started walking toward the bus stop. There, she saw the man she'd met outside the sleazy pub.

He waited. This must be John, the man for whom she left everything behind.

They had nothing in common—no shared memories and no dreams for the future. No! I cannot stay here with him. I shall put away the thought that I could have slept with him. A stranger.

The man looked in vain among the passengers stepping off the bus—studying the faces to find the beautiful young bride he expected.

The darkness was dense now.

Where did the afternoon go?

As she walked back to the drunk, she reached out to pluck two flowers. Like Ana, they had brown eyes. Under dust, they emitted weak perfume. She closed her eyes and buried her nose in them. The flowers gave what they had. She arranged them on the bench near the bottle and stood for a moment soaking in the scene, then walked along the platform to step onto the bus. John looked for someone coming off and paid no attention to the woman getting on.

With a soulless grind, the bus slipped into gear. Through the dirty window, she watched John turn away and stand over the drunk woman. He shook his head in disgust and walked away.

Her mind was filled with green ivy when she felt a hand on her arm. The young man across the aisle held out a basket of strawberries. Being small and as brown as they were red, they were not beautiful. The young man's face held a shy expression. She had the sense that if she shouted, he would disappear into nothing leaving only his greasy-wool hat. A spray of angry pimples spread across his neck.

"You're pretty," he said, "and I'm older than I look."

She took a strawberry. It tasted better than it should have.

"Thank you," she said.

The bus gradually picked up speed and left the town behind. It was late and the road was long.

Notes on *The Mail-Order Bride*

KLC: This might surprise you, but I know very well the brutal reality of desperation and poverty. When I was teenager I lived in an unplumbed house on blocks with five brothers and sisters. This in a rich country where poor people around the world think the streets of America are paved in gold. I was able to save myself, but I don't know how to save anyone else. This strikes me as a contrast to the way you grew up—which is odd since you're from Romania and I'm from rural Oregon.

AP: America is one of the finest countries anyone ever stole, so they say. Over time, I developed an understanding of its controversial and contradictory nature.

Yes, paradoxically I grew up sheltered, happy and quite bourgeois in a country following an expired Marxist blueprint. I didn't miss a thing and all that time I fantasized about a country modeled after Beverly Hills 90210.

You are not the only one to be surprised at my upbringing.

My husband can't get it out of his head that while he, as a kid, was hiding under the desk from a potential nuclear attack by the communist bloc, I was taking skiing vacations and getting a top-notch education. That alone makes me a fierce socialist, but that's a discussion for another time. What's important to remember about America is its greatest strength, and its greatest weakness—a belief in second chances and that things can be made better.

KLC: I am addicted to Orwell and though I am not a socialist like he was, I understand the burning desire for justice and rescuing our fellow men from want.

> *At the back of one of the houses a young woman was kneeling on the stones, poking a stick up the leaden waste-pipe which ran from the sink inside and which I suppose was blocked. I had time to see everything about her—her sacking apron, her clumsy clogs, her arms reddened by the cold. She looked up as the train passed, and I was almost near enough to catch her eye. She had a round pale face, the usual exhausted face of the slum girl who is twenty-five and looks forty, thanks to miscarriages and drudgery; and it wore, for the second in which I saw it, the most desolate, hopeless expression I have ever seen.*
> —George Orwell, *The Road to Wigan Pier*

AP: Yes, Communism was done the wrong way.

> *Communism doesn't work because people like to own stuff.*
> —Frank Zappa

Nobody expected the Bolsheviks to take the lead. Everyone had their eyes on England as the most sophisticated society at the turn of the century—the one ready to make an evolutionary political change.

But, the fact that Communism was done wrong in the Eastern bloc doesn't make today's European socialism a failed project. Lessons were learned from the past and can be applied today. In the end, it boils down to this:

> Under capitalism, man exploits man. Under communism, it's just the opposite.
> —John Kenneth Galbraith

KLC: I remember my father once saying—this would have been in the early 1960s—that he wanted to run off to Russia and get work where everyone was equal and everyone had a job.

You have a lot more direct experience with Communism than me. If you had an endless supply of courage and heard my father say this, what would you say to him?

AP: Everyone had a place to work. Making no money but nevertheless, a job. Healthcare and education were available to all. Your father would have been employed, healthy and his kids would have a chance for higher education, but hold on, it's not that simple.

Everyone played a part in a masquerade. Your thoughts could not be voiced if they did not align with the CP[12] and Marxist doctrine. This led to controversy on human rights issues. People ended up in jail or worse simply because they spoke their mind.

---

[12] Communist Party

What does that make me? I don't know, I guess I was too young to qualify as a coward. I harvested a good, happy and safe childhood without a worry in the world. Depending on the age of the storyteller and their individual experiences, you'll hear a different tale.

KLC: Being a guy with active fingers on my computer mouse and keyboard, I stumbled across some of the websites where Eastern European women put up pictures and profiles—women like Ana looking for husbands. Here's an example from a pretty 47-year-old blonde—Irina in Mariupol (Ukraine). This is what she is looking for:

> *Partner of 45-65 years old. I am looking for a friend...partner...companion and lover for life...I believe the key to a long lasting relationship is communication. I want my man to be kind, reliable, caring, and generous for his family. I don't like men who drink a lot and don't respect their women.*

This must be a woman in a similar situation to Ana. Do you know any mail-order brides?

AP: No, I don't personally know any, but at some point I remember hearing about lonely farmers looking for strong women—and some happy endings coming from the arrangement. But, that was before the Internet when women were strong, men were good-looking and all the children were above average—to paraphrase Garrison Keeler.

KLC: I hope all the mail-order brides find happy lives. Am I wrong to have optimism for poor, sad dumpy Ana?

AP: There is always hope. Remember, that's the cruelest gift pulled from Pandora's box. Hope.

KLC: I don't think there are Internet websites for mail-order husbands. Please pretend this is not a stupid question. Wouldn't you enjoy seeing a catalog filled with freshly shaven, dolled-up men with nice haircuts who are desperately looking for an American wife to rescue them from the despair of their hopeless homeland? What am I missing?

AP: I think the balance between sexes has always leaned this way. It is a matter of inherent evolutionary behavior. The spheres in which we move separate the masculine parts of humanity from the feminine.

KLC: When thinking of poverty and despair, I naturally think of Dickens, but that's a cliché, isn't it? Instead of something obvious like Oliver and his porridge, what do you think of the names of Miss Flite's larks, linnets, and goldfinches?

> The old man, looking up at the cages after another look at us, went through the list.
> "Hope, Joy, Youth, Peace, Rest, Life, Dust, Ashes, Waste, Want, Ruin, Despair, Madness, Death, Cunning, Folly, Words, Wigs, Rags, Sheepskin, Plunder, Precedent, Jargon, Gammon, and Spinach. That's the whole collection," said the old man, "all cooped up together, by my noble and learned brother."
> —Charles Dickens, *Bleak House*

AP: There can be a romantic, quiet dignity associated with poverty. From Dickens to say, Frank McCourt in *Angela's Ashes*, poverty made a riveting backdrop for all sorts of heroes.

I remember being a kid and happy. I had food on the table and a loving family, but I envied the heroes who survived extraordinary conditions.

Googled
Ken Coffman

IN HER BEDROOM, Abigale giggled. Her BFF, Sharina, was sending close-up photographs of her cat's butt Photoshopped into videos of political speeches. Former President Barack Obama nattering about an oil well leak with a giant floating cat rectum hovering over his shoulder. Ex-Vice President Joe Biden blessing a foreign leader's mother's soul with a cat's bung in place of his mouth. Nancy Pelosi blathering on about the fairness doctrine with eyes replaced with cat's anuses.

Abigale could hardly hold onto her iPhone, she was laughing so hard. Her mother pushed open her door.

"Abby, didn't you hear us calling? I sent you a text message. You have visitors. From Google. Come down right away."

Google? What do they want with me? I'm a Bingurl.

"Okay, mom, I'll be right down," she said.

CUL8R, she I-M'd Sharina.

She ran a brush through her hair and touched up her lipstick before prancing down the stairs to the living room. There were three men sitting on the sofa. They stood when she entered the room. All three were dressed in suits, vests and neckties. Two were ancient, in their 40's at least, but one was younger—cute with curly brown hair and a Tweety bird necktie. They were all husky. Big men. They looked at her with unbridled curiosity.

She flopped down on an overstuffed, leather-clad chair.

"Hi guys. Whazzup?" she said.

The men, as if one, sat back down.

The man on her right nodded.

"Good evening, young lady," he said. "Please allow me to introduce myself and my colleagues. My name is Perry Winslow. I am the vice president of consumer research with Google and I work in our Waltham, Massachusetts facility. On my near right we have Caspar Gould. He runs the social media research group and he has offices in Munich and Bangalore. Finally, we have Donald Kay. He's a programmer out of our Mountain View, California facility. I want to reassure you, you're not in any trouble—that's not the reason for our visit."

Her dad leaned forward.

"Trouble?" he said. "Why would she be in any trouble?"

Abigale waved her hands dismissively. "Dad, please," she said.

"First of all," Mr. Winslow said. "Could I get the reason for the unusual spelling of your name? When we searched the web, the only statistically valid number of instances of your name spelled that way were typographical errors."

Abby's mother flushed very red.

"On the day she was born—it was very windy."

"Ah," Mr. Winslow said. "I understand. That would be a kind of play on words. I get it."

"What's this about trouble?" Abby's dad said. "It's not like you guys are with the IRS or something. You're just Googlers, right?"

Mr. Winslow shifted on the sofa as if experiencing rectal discomfort.

"Well, we were essentially deputized by the Obama

administration."

"Dad," Abby said sharply. "These guys are here on official business. That's why they're armed."

"Men from Google? Armed? That's absurd."

"I read about it in a forum," Abby said as if it settled the matter.

Donald grinned; a wide, happy grin that made dimples in his cheeks.

"Tell her that's nonsense," Abby's dad said.

"Uh," Mr. Winslow said. "Technically, she's right. We are armed and fully authorized by Homeland Security to carry sidearms when performing our official duties."

"They gave me a Glock Twenty-Three," Donald said. He leaned forward and reached around his back. He pulled out his black weapon…and carefully pointed it in a neutral direction. "These things are awesome. We shot watermelons with hollow points in training and it makes a huge mess."

"Donald! Put your weapon away."

"I don't want armed men from Google sitting on my living room couch," Abby's mom said.

"Please calm yourself," Mr. Winslow said. "We're not here to cause any problems."

"Then why *are* you here?" Abby's dad said.

"Can I?" Donald said to Mr. Winslow. Winslow nodded. "We're here as a matter of curiosity. Abby? You ordered a clarinet from the Musician's Friend website."

"Yes, she did," Abby's dad said. "She saved up half and I covered the other half. I put it on my credit card."

"It took me six months of babysitting to save up that money," Abby said.

"Musician's Friend has a contract with us," Mr. Winslow said. "They, along with many others in online sales businesses, pay us a lot of money for our services."

Donald interrupted.

"We collect a lot of data. That's no secret." He pulled an iPod Xtreemee from his Swiss Gear satchel. "I can show you your complete online history. You made your first blog post when you were three. It was cute. I can show you."

"Put that away, Donald," Mr. Winslow said, "we're wasting time." To Abby, he said, "When you were shopping for the clarinet, you did a lot of online research."

"Yeah, Abby," Donald said enthusiastically. "You were all over the place."

Mr. Winslow frowned at the interruption. "And, during that research—how many times was it, Donald?"

"Oh, I can talk now?" He turned to Abby. "While you were clicking around on the Internet, you were informed one-hundred-and-twenty-seven times that what you really want is an oboe. The market research is unambiguous. To achieve the maximum satisfaction rating—girls your age, with your demographic background, aptitude and interests, are ninety-seven-point-eight percent happier with oboes."

"The statistics are very clear about this," Mr. Winslow said.

"According to FedEx," Abby's dad said, "her clarinet should be here on Friday. We're very excited about it."

"Well, that's part of the reason we're here," Mr. Winslow said. "About that delivery…"

"I'm not exactly sure what an oboe is," Abby interjected.

"Gabriel Flotsam from America is Evil plays an oboe," Donald said. "The name means loud woodwind in French."

"Oh, the tubular thing with the long, curved hose. Now I know what you mean."

"So, we're here to explore. When the statistics are so clear with regard to consumer satisfaction, why did you ignore our advice? We take our recommendations very seriously and rarely are the numbers so obvious."

Mr. Gould finally spoke. "Simply put, young lady—you are not a clarinet person. You are the textbook example of an oboe person."

"Yeah," Donald said. "We invested about ten-thousand man-years of code. Heuristic programming running on a dedicated server farm. We pride ourselves on our accuracy and we can't figure this out."

"What did you mean about the shipment?" Abby's dad said. "I have an order confirmation and a tracking number."

"Wait a minute," Donald said. "I think I figured this out. Abby, did you say an oboe has a curved crook?"

"The tube thing?"

"Yes, that's called the crook, though the formal name is the bocal."

"Yeah."

"The thing with the curved bocal is the bassoon. The oboe has a straight reed sticking out of the end of it."

"Oh, those things are cool."

"Right," Mr. Winslow said. "That's what our gentle guidance was trying to tell you."

"I can show you what they sound like." Donald poked at his touchscreen and brushed his fingers on the display. A low-pitched melody began.

"Hey, I like that," Abby said.

Mr. Winslow exchanged a glance with Mr. Gould.

"The big one is called a heckelphone," Donald said. "They make a very pure tone with very limited harmonic content."

"Dad, I don't want a clarinet. I want an oboe. Is it too late to change my mind?"

Mr. Winslow cleared his throat. "As it happens," he said, "we brought an oboe with us. It's out in the Escalade."

"Cool," Abby said.

"I'll go get it," Donald said.

"I'm glad we resolved this," Mr. Gould said. "It was driving us crazy."

Mr. Winslow waved his finger at Abby. "In the future, miss, would you please pay more attention to our recommendations so we can avoid all of this turmoil?"

"Yeah, sure, whatever," Abby said.

Notes on *Googled*

AP: The architecture of the new world creates vexing questions of spying and control. When they are answered, we get a story like *Googled*. What were you thinking?

KLC: With so much of our life online, there are many opportunities to capture and exploit our behavior patterns. Every link you click, every purchase you make, every friend you link with, every photograph you share and every unencrypted e-mail you send or receive on a public network is available for analysis and exploitation.

It bothers me that computers watch, record and peer into our souls purely for the sake of commerce. I hate the idea that my essence can be boiled down into a few categories and niches and we're only at the very beginning of what can and will be done.

AP: I could not stop smirking at your usage of online lingo...

KLC: Our language is being reinvented at a startling pace. Slang is nothing new, but I think the terseness, randomness and the lack of a controlling authority is interesting. I'd say most of our kids have never heard of the Oxford English Dictionary and would LOL at the idea of authoritative guidance from a bunch of old fogies. If they want a word, they'll invent it themselves—they don't need help from ancient, obsolete generations.

AP: Email and online news sites are increasingly popular. Today, 92% of adults write and read email on a daily basis. The lack of privacy is the price—which leads to the question: is it all worth it? Does the technological end justify the intrusive means?

KLC: I work for a Fortune 500 company in a remote location and live in a small town in very pleasant surroundings. This lifestyle is enabled by the Internet and electronic communication. I am in constant contact with my customers. My boss, from thousands of miles away, can reach out and touch me with a text, email or a cell phone call at any time. For all of the hazards, I love my lifestyle so much, I would never voluntarily give it up. I could turn off my computers and break up my cell phone with a hammer, and some days that urge is overpowering, but I am wired in. I would never give it up.

AP: There's humor, or rather satire, embedded throughout this piece. I look at it as a caricature of our new way of life. Do you find it funny, creepy, worrisome or have you simply made peace with the situation?

KLC: I share the feelings of paranoia and fear of others, but everywhere I have a choice, I focus on the humor of it all. At our core, we're silly creatures running around with an inflated sense of self-importance. For me, the things we take most seriously can be the source of great amusement when you examine them in context—particularly in the largest schemes of things.

AP: I wonder what would have happened if Abigale hadn't changed her mind?

KLC: There's a reason the Google agents are armed—in case deadly force becomes necessary. Silly, right? Absurd?

Nonetheless, the Google algorithms are very clever and wise. Why would they make a mistake?

AP: Now I know the difference between an oboe and a bassoon...

KLC: Thus we prove this goofy tale was not a complete waste of time.

AP: I agree with your observation that we are a society of consumers. We are subliminally told what to buy and are viewed as faceless agents of the economy.

KLC: The concept is no different than the grocer noticing lettuce in your shopping cart and suggesting leeks for your salad. The part that bothers me is how accurate the algorithms are and whether the computers will eventually figure us out completely. I don't mind a helpful, friendly suggestion from a knowledgeable source, but I hate the idea that my choices are damned predictable. Am I an individual or just another drone?

To the extent that the computer makes reasonable suggestions and does not waste my time with products I will never buy, I am appreciative. But, when the computer knows me better than I know myself? That's scary.

Two Memories
Adina Pelle

1950

IT IS SAID there are three dimensions to human consciousness. We are born and grow old with them. I am old as my mind weaves the threads of the past, but young as it all comes back to life.

I do not know about others, but when I think of my childhood, I feel like holding my head in my hands—maybe to support the heavy weight of old memories. It's not just elderly people who think the past is everything; and it's not only the young who believe only in the future. No one can live only in the present like a wild, stubborn horse.

When my parents first moved into the rooms where we lived for ten years, they knew no one. They had just come from a Russian-Jewish refugee camp and were happy to be alive—ready to make friends and enjoy a new life after the war.

It did not take long for my mother to become friendly with the other renters. Vasea and Little Marie were the most colorful—they lived directly behind our two rooms in a one-bedroom space. Their existence fueled curiosity throughout my childhood, mainly because of the things that happened in their room. Liquor shared on payday nights had fabulous powers—not only on their skewed reality but also over my everyday life by distracting others from my strangeness as a child and delivering me many nights of entertainment.

Despite her name, Little Marie was not; she was a tough woman who could hold her liquor. Though large, she was powerless against Vasea's quick fist. After an argument came to blows, she would show up in the yard telling the same story the following day with a black and purple eye.

"The door hit me."

One Christmas Eve, Little Marie surprised my mom by pulling a little white and blue dress from a box…and handing it to me. It was the most beautiful dress I had seen—with white and blue bows attached to its hem and a marine motif on the upper part. The minute it took me to dress up extended into eternities of blissful happiness twirling in front of the mirror and running up and down our stone-paved yard. My mother was touched by Little Marie's gift and invited her and Vasea the day after Christmas to a neighborhood bodega— hoping to return her friendly gesture.

What my mother did not know was the effect of liquor on Little Marie. After a couple of beers, to my mother's shock and my tearful disappointment, Little Marie asked for the dress back with no explanation. I was devastated—especially because I did not understand the mechanics of the very cruel game grownups played.

Since I was a well-behaved child, when I did foolish deeds, I could remain silent, saying nothing, and get away with my crimes. After my first disappearance that Christmas Eve following the blue dress fiasco, my father found me hours later, freezing cold and talking with two wet, skeletal dogs huddled at my feet. He took me home without a word and fixed two hot chocolates—expecting, certainly, an explanation, an answer, for me to say anything.

"Why, why did you want to run away? How could you think that that was the way?"

"I do not know," I sadly answered without my usual smile. After half an hour, with no explanation for my wandering, he told me of a friend from work who had a cat and was looking for a little girl to take care of its kittens. Taking care of two little black-and-white kittens kept me entertained and alleviated the monotony of my life as a small and peculiar little girl.

We lived in two rooms—my room and the kitchen-living room, which was also my parent's bedroom. In an olfactory trance, many memories come to mind as the warmth of our simple, frugal life finds its way back into my thoughts. The kitchen-bedroom smelled of plum pudding and other simple delights my mother put together with the food ration all the war refugees shared. Our little house with its flower garden in front seemed like a corner of paradise. I always found my mother bent over something, washing or ironing or baking some little delight. I was convinced she could breathe life into inanimate things. All my childhood I drank milk from a nice porcelain cup with red and blue flowers. Mother's hands pushed the cup forward so slowly and graciously—suggesting that this cup was not a simple object, but an enchanted one.

The next Christmas Eve after Little Marie's cruel game was played on my feeble mind, I went to bed early with one hand under my head, uncovering an ear so I could hear dishes clinking in the kitchen as my mother washed them, mumbling a little song as light as a sleigh pushed by the wind. All I wanted was to see snow falling—the year before I'd missed it.

In the morning, oranges were lined up on my dresser. Later, mother cut and simmered their flesh until the house smelled like a magical fairy tale.

1954

FOR SEVERAL YEARS, nearly every evening we met behind the school building and chatted or walked around our neighborhood looking at the pretty houses—imagining a charming, impossible life. After the big war, only movie heroines enjoyed perfect lives.

Her name was Mira. She was my best friend when we lived in two rooms alongside many other renters in the tenement sternly managed by Miss Iris.

I liked Mira's spirit—her combativeness with anything crosswise in her complicated life. She ate sunflower seeds like a gypsy, spitting shells with an ironic smile teasing the corners of her mouth. There were always remnants of leftover shell— black and thread-thin—on her upper lip. She had pockets full of sunflower seeds at all times, getting her supplies from old Manda, her Gypsy grandmother who lived on the other side of the tracks over the ditch carrying dirty sewer water out of town.

My world was familiar up to the railway, the *good world* as Manda referred to it with nice houses and apartment buildings and long, narrow alleys and streets named after famous composers. Mozart, Chopin, Bach, Puccini....

The area on the other side of the tracks was known as 'The Pit'—with long, muddy streets lined with rotten old fences surrounding nearly identical dilapidated houses.

In Manda's yard, other than broken clay pots and rusty old copper vessels with peeling enamel, there was nothing else but mud. The threshold to her hut was dull and dirty with the yard's sticky sludge.

When I followed Mira to her grandmother's hut, I tripped over old shoes and galoshes lined up like little soldiers by the front stoop. Seeing that I was embarrassed by my clumsiness, old Manda asked a question.

"What, you do not leave your shoes at the door?" With a small shrug, she answered more quickly than I could. "You live in another world—in a real house with a porch. Not like me stepping into my house directly from the mud."

In a corner of the room was a stove with a hot plate and a big black pot where Manda roasted her sunflower seeds. Alongside was a bed of rags thrown one on top of the other. The dirty hut had one bedroom and a kitchen, just like our house. On the dirt, rugs were thrown in disarray. The room smelled of roasted seeds and salt. Their smell was so pungent that it masked the smells of mold, wet earth and dirty laundry.

While in the hut, we laughed at the way the old woman spoke and tried not to trip over pots filled with rotten food scraps strewn around the room.

When we returned from Manda's with pockets full of sunflower seeds, it was cold outside, like all November evenings. When crossing the tracks, the place looked deserted and dark. I was afraid, but did not dare admit it, knowing how gutsy Mira was.

Suddenly, looming from the darkness, a shadowy man made an ominous appearance. While passing, he lit a cigarette—in the matchlight, I could distinguish some of the man's features. On his forehead, he had a gash that appeared be cut with a knife. He stopped next to Mira and pulled the cigarette out of his mouth.

"What, Mira, you walk around with the better world and ignore us. For an intruder? A white girl? You know talking to anyone about us or what you see will get you in trouble, right?"

Mira remained silent. It was too dark to make out her expression. I never knew if she was afraid or not. I spoke to her when we drew close to my home.

"He threatened you. What will you do?"

"Don't worry," said Mira. "He meant nothing," she added, before disappearing into the darkness behind my house.

The next day, toward evening, I went to our meeting place. Mira was already there—sitting on the bench behind the school building, eating sunflower seeds and spitting the black shells into a bush.

"Sorry," she said, "we cannot see each other anymore. Tonight is the last time we will meet. He made me choose between you and them. He threatened me. If I don't choose them, I'll pay."

I sensed that Mira was filled with unshakable determination, but I could not hold the question back.

"Can't we see each other just for a half an hour in the evening?"

"No, because we cannot be seen together. In my group you are considered an intruder. They see you as a threat. We cannot change that—we come from different worlds and however I feel about you, I cannot give up my world."

With that, she disappeared from my life.

A few days later, in that desolate place we visited so often, she was found near the railway laying in snow reddened by her blood—with a knife stuck in her heart. She was not yet fifteen years old.

The Mira-less days that followed were hard.

Her ironic, irreplaceable smile remains frozen in my memory. I planted a sunflower, but it did not bring her back.

Notes on *Two Memories*

KLC: When you talk of gypsies, are you thinking of ethnic gypsies like the Roma or are you thinking more metaphorically?

AP: No, the reference is very earthy. Roma gypsies are all over Europe, particularly Eastern Europe.

KLC: I want to return to Orwell...

> But the word 'caravan' is very misleading. It calls up a picture of a cozy gypsy-encampment (in fine weather, of course) with wood fires crackling and children picking blackberries and many-colored washing fluttering on the lines. The caravan-colonies in Wigan and Sheffield are not like that. I had a look at several of them, I inspected those in Wigan with considerable care, and I have never seen comparable squalor except in the Far East. Indeed when I saw them I was immediately reminded of the filthy kennels in which I have seen Indian coolies living in Burma. But, as a matter of fact, nothing in the East could ever be quite as bad, for in the East you haven't our clammy, penetrating cold to contend with, and the sun is a disinfectant.
> —George Orwell, *The Road to Wigan Pier*

From your writing, it's clear that gypsies are an important influence on your thinking. I don't know how unrealistic my thoughts are on their tribal, nomadic heritage and culture. I tend to think of them as free spirits, but there is more to it than that. There was horrible discrimination against them in Europe and they have a nasty reputation as liars, swindlers and cheats. In the U.S., gypsy is not considered a race, but more of a lifestyle like that represented by the Irish Travelers from

South Carolina. From your point of view, how much of the negative stereotype is based in fact and how much is unfair?

AP: Gypsies could easily be viewed both ways. I choose to look at their traditions and way of life through the magic lenses of my youth. They pack as much mystery and wonder as the 1001 Arabian Nights stories. Their reality could be viscerally dissected and explained in politically correct terms. My question is, where is the fun in political correctness?

KLC: I always wonder how much of a story like this is literally autobiographical. If I forced you to answer—what percentage of this tale is a true recollection? I will make a guess. 80%. How did I do?

AP: Pretty good. The 100% true stories are the ones that spring from my mother's memories.

KLC: I've always been interested in the stereotypes. If there weren't grains of truth to them, they wouldn't be so ubiquitous. I once hired a Hungarian—I'll embarrass him by giving his real name, George Zatloka. When I interviewed him, he told me he'd work twenty-six hours a day if I hired him. Of course, when he'd leave at five or six o'clock in the evening, I would remind him he had not put in his twenty-six hours yet.

One day I asked George about stereotypes from his home country. Here's what he said (and I hope you'll imagine this said in a Hungarian accent).

> *Ken, I will tell you. We have a story about a Scotchman. One day, his son comes home all excited and happy.*

> *"Father," the boy said, "I saved twenty-five cents by running behind the schoolbus instead of paying the fare."*
>
> *His father thinks for a moment, then scolds the boy.*
>
> *"You fool," he said, "you could have run behind a taxi and saved two dollars."*

If a stereotype for being thrifty is common in far-distant countries, then surely we must acknowledge they contain some truth, don't we? Have you ever welshed on a bet, been jewed down on a price or been gyped on a deal?

AP: No. You earn yourself a puzzled look because I have no idea what you are talking about.

KLC: I want to ask you about the following passage.

> *No one can live only in the present like a wild, stubborn horse.*

I don't want to forget the past, but I understand it can represent a lot of old baggage we'd be better off without. Do you have any respect for philosophy-of-the-now?

> *Realize deeply that the present moment is all you have. Make the NOW the primary focus of your life.*
> —Eckhart Tolle, *The Power of Now: A Guide to Spiritual Enlightenment*

AP: I believe our past makes us who we are. I refuse to live in the past (except for short literary immersions) but I acknowledge it as my maker. In other words, I exist as I am due to everything that happened in my past.

KLC: The four-year span of this story shows a quite a difference in the life of the young woman. She moves from worrying about pretty dresses to literal life-and-death issues. I know that's an important theme of this story—childhood to adulthood in four short years. I want to hear more about Adina at eleven and Adina at fifteen.

AP: This story of two memories is based on my mother's experiences. Speaking of myself, I grew up overnight. One day I was a dreamy girl reading *War and Peace* and laughing/crying with Natasha. The next day I had my own drama and life story in the making...

KLC: Why was Mira murdered?

AP: Mira was part of a very ruthless gang who would not accept her desire to live a different life on the other side of the tracks.

Glen Wilson's Guitar Lesson[13]
Ken Coffman

AFTER A LONG minute, David 'Razor Blade' Smith emerged from his trance. He looked over the mob. There were a hundred screaming people crammed into the tiny bar.

"And now, we have one more special treat." He made eye contact with Glen. "My friend Glen will come up and show us how things are done."

He picked up the Epiphone and wove through the crowd.

"Here you go, Glen," he said.

Glen was drunk and in a bad mood. Jesus was right; he was pissed off after being barred from the band's van. Then tequila; he was always angry when drinking tequila. He'd had a massive amount, so was awash in a massive fury. In his distorted vision, the room appeared splattered with red paint while speckles of wrath dripped from the walls.

Raz, one of the world's finest rock guitarists, threw down a cruel challenge to an amateur with a crippled hand. Glen should have congratulated him on pulling a good practical joke. That would have been the mature thing to do.

Unfortunately, the Glen Wilson way is often not the mature way.

He had a card up his sleeve. In the years he'd spent in a prison-like North Dakota facility, he played endless hours on a

---

[13] —from the novel *Toxic Shock Syndrome*

battered nylon-string acoustic with five strings. An intern helped him tune it and showed him a few simple chords.

In deference to Glen's mutilated hand, the intern urged him to play left-handed, but that was hopeless. He *could* play a few simple chords and work his way around a 12-bar blues sequence. With malformed finger stubs on his left hand, he could only reach a few notes and the damaged, hyper-sensitive skin hurt like hell, but he learned to tap out right-hand patterns on the fretboard, playing it like a hammer dulcimer.

He took the guitar. Raz, with a mocking smile, offered his pick, but Glen waved it away.

He told the band what he wanted. *Devil Got my Woman*, the 1931 Skip James[14] version, played in A-minor. They started by playing it too fast, but he cursed, threatened and waved his hands in tempo until they settled into a glacial pace; a dirge to suit his mood. He held the guitar to his chest like a lifesaver before starting to sing.

> *Must have been the devil,*
> *Believe that woman has gone mad…*
> *Must have been the devil,*
> *Believe that woman has gone mad…*
>
> *Nothin' but the devil change my baby's mind*
> *Nothin' but the devil change my baby's mind*
>
> *Laid there last night, laid there last night,*
> *Tried to take my rest*
> *My mind got to ramblin' like wild geese from the west*

---

[14] Skip James, Nehemiah Curtis "Skip" James, 1902-1969, early-era Mississippi River Delta blues musician.

Must have been the devil,
Believe that woman has gone mad...
Must have been the devil,
Believe that woman has gone mad...

Woman I love, woman I love
Took off with my best friend
Woman I love took off with my best friend...

He held out his deformed hand so everyone could see it and then picked out notes and multistop chord fragments, pinching and plucking with his right hand. Like foreplay with a woman he cared about, he started slow and teased the audience. He was in a zone. When he hit a bad note, he bent it up, up-up-up until it screamed in pitch. The main thing was to show no fear—to let the night and alcohol feed his arrogant confidence. This confidence was based on an unfiltered hatred of the audience. They were not remotely worthy. If they were too dumb to appreciate what he offered, they should fuck off and die.

It didn't matter that he could not play well—he could make the audience *feel*. Channeling the Reverend Nehemiah Curtis James, the spirit was drawn from the cold grave. Seeking comfort, dancers pressed together. Drinkers stared into their lonely glasses. In tribute, Arthur Brown raised a sloshing bottle of Jack Daniels and grinned like a ghoul. Josh raised a bottle of Budweiser and howled.

Glen twiddled knobs and turned the guitar down low, and then walked to the amp and cranked every knob to the right as far as they would go.

Must have been the devil,
Believe that woman has gone mad...

Must have been the devil,
Believe that woman has gone mad...

With his right hand on the frets, he played wild vibratos. Tortured notes screamed from the overheated amplifier. Then he played the few patterns he knew as fast as he could—arpeggios filled the room like a flurry of black leaves. The band caught the spirit and pounded their instruments with hot fury. He rubbed the guitar neck on the microphone stand and feedback howled like a hungry wolf.

I believe that woman has gone mad...

He whipped the guitar off his neck and smashed it against the amp. It died with screaming white-hot feedback echoing endlessly in his ringing ears. He was left holding the pickguard with ragged pickup wiring. He weaved through the dancers and tossed the pickguard at Raz. Murphy made ready to jump in the fray.

"That's the last free lesson you'll get from me, kid," Glen said.

"Impressive," Raz said. He held up the mangled guitar pieces. "I might have been in the mood for a few more songs."

"You didn't want to follow that performance," Glen said.

The bar band's guitar player, looking ashen and angry, grabbed Glen's arm.

"I liked that axe, man," he said.

"Shut the hell up. It was a Korean knock-off, not a real Gibson. Besides, Raz will cover your cost."

Competing emotions washed across Raz's face, but his face settled on a wan, thin smile.

"Okay," Raz said while gesturing to Murphy to hand over money.

When the pile got high enough, the guitarman grabbed it and stomped off. Raz signed a few autographs as the place cleared out. Real people needed a few hours of sleep before going to work.

Raz, drinking a Snapple, stared with piercing eyes while Glen and Jesus puffed rekindled cigars and passed the nearly-empty Cabo Wabo bottle back and forth. The night ended for Glen when he passed out.

Notes on *Glen Wilson's Guitar Lesson*

AP: Ken, you made my day with this snippet. I am a big fan of Glen Wilson. He's the dysfunctional alcoholic you love to hate or hate to love, depending on the axis you are leaning on.

I have to ask, where is he coming from?

KLC: It's hard to believe the first Glen Wilson book was written so many years ago. *Alligator Alley* was written in 1994 and 1995. From my teenage years, I loved books and knew one day I would be a novelist, but beyond software and technical documents, I never wrote much other than a few failed starts at novels and some lame short stories.

As I got older it became clear that if I ever would be a novelist, I'd better get busy. At that time, at random, I stumbled across some wild tales written by Mark Bothum. I loved his stuff and felt like I'd stumbled across a unique talent (ha, see *The Talent Scout*). I still think that now—he's a far better natural writer than me. Compared to Mark, I'm more of a turn-the-crank technician.

I tracked him down and suggested we write a novel together. To my surprise, he agreed. So, what to write about? I knew a rather wild fellow who always seemed to come out on top of every crazy situation he found himself in. And so,

Glen Wilson was born.

Many people accuse me of being the prototype for Glen Wilson. This is not true, but I will mention something. The more I act like Glen, the better my life seems to get. So, Glen Wilson is not me, but I'm becoming more like Glen Wilson.

AP: Among an array of social handicaps you pile on Glen is the fact that he is a misanthrope and very happy with being so. Is this something personal? The reason I ask is because I sense so much personal, writerly satisfaction coming through. You use sharp words like:

> *They were not remotely worthy. If they were too dumb to appreciate what he offered, they should fuck off and die.*

However, ultimately you use Glen to point a way out of a handicapped society. Do I have a right sense of this?

KLC: I don't think Glen hates humanity. In fact, I think he has a kind heart and an innocent optimism about people—it's easy to take advantage of him. However, he seems to have a knack for getting into trouble and fighting against the worst examples of our fellow men and women. He has no patience or misplaced sentiment about the bad parts of human nature, but I wouldn't say he hates humanity in general. Is there any doubt he'd die for his motley team? However, he does seem to be a big advocate of tough love.

With regard to the quote, I have a horrible stage fright. When I was younger, it was difficult for me to stand in front of a crowd. I refused to give in to this fear, but this was a tough thing to overcome. It helps to despise your audience. I think a lot of successful public speakers are creeps who embrace this sentiment.

You mentioned handicaps. That's something I hope comes through the continuing adventures. Everyone has limitations and faults. So what? What are you going to do about it? Everyone should try to transcend their limits to achieve their productive destiny, whatever it might be.

AP: Of course, the music. I have to bring up the music. Is he playing your kind of music?

KLC: No. I know very little about the blues. As a bass player, this kind of music (along with country music) is the most boring kind of stuff to play. I'm much more sympathetic to the obscure Swedish progressive rock mentioned in my novel *Endangered Species*.

AP: What is the first thing would you ask Glen if you had him across from you?

KLC: Interesting question. I don't think I have any questions for him. He and I share an odd telepathic connection. I know him better than he knows himself.

AP: Do you want people to love him or hate him? For myself, I look at him as an addiction. You know it's bad for you but you can't shake it off.

KLC: I hope Glen is the man you love to hate, but I can go with the converse too. You can never measure a man until the end of his life because it can go irredeemably wrong in a flash. And, every evil man might be saved by some terminal act of glory. Glen has a final destiny and I know its nature, but I hope the reader is unsure (and worried) until they read the last word on the last page of the last novel.

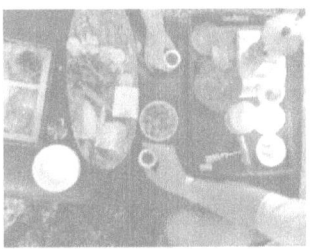

The Illusion of Sex
Adina Pelle

SHE CAME TO his room with no fear, knowing everything that was meant to happen—would happen. It was always that way.

He sat on the bed, lit a cigarette and inhaled a leisurely drag—erotically taking the smoke deeply into his lungs as if to remove all the air between them.

She watched. She was a very strange girl, disconnected and generally cool and composed, but not today.

They laughed a little about something or the other but who remembers?

She lay on the bed next to him. Her dress was molded to her body—emphasizing each curve and soft feature.

He touched her gently. From neck to knees, he explored her body like a blind man—a man possessed by a harmonic, hormonal addiction. His throbbing pulse was visible in his temples.

She arched her back, and then, through a whisper and a soft sigh, let her desire to be possessed be known.

He no longer looked in her eyes. There were other attractions. Her dress was a crumpled pile the floor.

Shoulders. Belly. Thighs. Peach-colored skin.

His eyes traveled across her body, flicking like a lion pacing in a cage too small to hold his desires.

Clavicle. Lips. Cheeks. Knee caps.

Their dance slowly moved toward its end. He touched her bellybutton with an adventurous forefinger which moved slowly in ever-larger circles.

A kiss. A long soul kiss.

She thought about antelopes—how they scatter when a hungry lion approaches.

 And the look in their terrified eyes.

His overheated palm moved on her belly confidently, as if he knew the pleasure his ovary-warming hand delivered. Naked with no uncertainty that would come with later years and time's cruel side-effects. Her eyes were filled with solid knowledge borne of youth, optimism, ignorance and inexperience.

He was slow and cautious in approaching the consummate act—perhaps for fear of too much sensation drawing closed the curtains of their passion play. He filled his eyes with her.

"Enter me," she said.

He did—and broke the magical spell.

They enjoyed the illusion of sex; visceral, real—and sad, decorated with moans and theatrical whispers. Words cut in quarters and delivered in pieces.

The jigsaw puzzle of life.

Hers. His. Mine. Yours. Ours.

The more I know the more I realize I know nothing.

Is that the famous saying?

Notes on *The Illusion of Sex*

KLC: At fifteen, you started a relationship with your nearly forty-year-old art teacher. You married him and he died of a heart attack when you were twenty-two. You must expect us to think of *The Illusion of Sex* as autobiographical. Right?

Ken Coffman and Adina Pelle

AP: Among many others, sex is a subject I cannot write about without touching the personal resonance of my life history.

KLC: It is a cliché and a stereotype that older men exploit young, innocent girls. Of course, there is a solid grain of truth in every cliché and stereotype. Speaking of this story and nothing else, is the young girl a victim—someone exploited by the older man?

AP: I don't write about victims for a variety of reasons. For one, you can't reverse or rectify a situation by writing about it. I believe in everyone's right to make choices, even if those choices lead to bad consequences.

In this story, I focused on an intense and honest look at desire which climaxes in the sex act.

KLC: I want to argue about the title a little bit. They did not enjoy the illusion of sex—you make it vividly clear they had real, actual sex. You allude to an alternate meaning of 'illusion', i.e., they enjoyed the false paradise or ecstatic-delusion of sex. To what extent are you toying with us with the title you selected?

AP: Through the thick and foggy lens of time, I thought back to the days of my youth—about my sexual ideas and illusions.

My urges and desires were unmistakable and undeniable, but the consequences bore an impenetrable shroud of mystery.

KLC: Based on the twists and turns of your life and what I know of your personality, I think you'd be a tough, drill sergeant type of sex therapist. Imagine sitting in your fancy office with diplomas on the wall and thick books on the shelf. If a woman comes in and wants help dealing with anger and frustration caused by a philandering husband, what would be the nature of your advice?

AP: You are right about me being a drill sergeant hidden in a civilian's body. I don't believe in talk therapy. That comes from my upbringing. My family would never tolerate the nonsense of self-examination or agonizing over useless things like feelings.

Everyone has the capacity on their own to solve their life dilemmas and facilitate their necessary healing—forgetting, forgiving or simply moving on.

KLC: This story is sexy, but not graphic. Your expressive language fills our heads with images in clear, vivid focus.

> *...emphasizing each curve and soft feature...*
> *...harmonic, hormonal addiction.*
> *...her desire to be possessed...*
> *...peach-colored skin.*
> *... time's cruel side-effects.*
> *...words cut in quarters and delivered in pieces.*

I don't have a question; I just wanted to repeat those lovely phrases. You might have made a tough sex therapist, but you have a delicate way with words.

AP: I love poetry—it is a joy of my life.

KLC: In your last two sentences, clearly you refer to Plato's quote of Socrates:

> *As for me, all I know is that I know nothing...*
Let me quote a friend in a similar vein:

I hope I have been able to clarify things a little bit, or at least caused some creative confusion. When I teach thermography I find that the more you learn the more confused you get, but on a higher level. Every question answered raises a few more, which grows the confusion exponentially. It makes the subject interesting, though.
—Mikael Cronholm

Often, I feel like a blind man in a forest. Is there anything you would point to as absolute, immutable fact? Something we can anchor ourselves to?

AP: No. Life is a journey of personal discoveries—it is the string Ariadne gave to Theseus to lead him from the Minotaur's maze. It is the thread measuring the length of life cut to length by the Fates. Life gives us many more questions than answers.

Brutal Honesty Day
Ken Coffman

CLIVE STOPPED ON the concrete steps and turned to look back over the stairway, the sidewalks and the street. Kids, most of them black, milled around the common area, emerging from mostly-older, battered cars. They wore backpacks, sneakers and colorful jackets. This urban neighborhood was not a rich one, but the kids looked well-fed and spiffed up for school, with the girls' hair braided with beads and the boys wearing clean jeans, though huge and drooping off their asses in the current style. A set of flags rippled over the brick school entry—U.S. and state. A patch of struggling ivy climbed the brick wall that towered five stories overhead.

The concrete walkway was dotted with trampled blobs of gum.

Blah.

It was Brutal Honesty Day. Clive sighed.

Always a tough day.

But there was no relief; the job had to be done.

He turned and continued up the stairs and entered the school. The assigned classroom was on the second floor and was filled with chattering third-graders. As he walked in, he made eye-contact with the exiting teacher. He could not read her blank expression, but she seemed unhappy. She pulled the door closed firmly behind her.

Clive stood in front of the class and tapped on the teacher's desk. The clamor quieted only slightly.

"Could I have your attention, please?" Clive said with a firm voice.

He turned and picked up a dry erase pen…and scrawled his name on the white board.

"My name is Mister Colgate," he said while writing.

A girl in the front row raised her hand.

And so it starts. Brutal Honesty Day. I have sworn to tell the whole, unvarnished truth.

He took a deep breath and pointed at her.

"Do you have a question, young lady?"

"Who are you?"

"As I wrote," he gestured over his shoulder, "my name is Mr. Colgate and I work with an international non-governmental organization which funds programs for selected children."

Several kids in the back of the room still had not taken their seats and were talking. One of the kids strutted in a circle.

"My name is Mister Cockgate," the kid said as stuffily as he could manage in imitating Clive's English accent. "And I like cocks."

The boys laughed heartily. Ignoring the insult, Clive continued speaking.

"The name of the organization is a little difficult—I'll write it down."

He turned and was about half-through with writing the name when a wad of soggy paper hit the board with a thunk. A nasty mass of sodden paper slowly slid down the white board's surface—leaving a trail like a slug.

"Okay, I guess the name is unimportant," he said. "Please

take your seats." He lifted his heavy backpack and dropped it on the teacher's desk. "I have some things you might be interested in. How many of you like television?"

Most of the kids raised their hands eagerly.

"I have Zune video players and headsets."

A boy in the middle of the desk area raised his hand.

"Do we get to keep them?"

"Yes, you can keep them."

The video players were small, with three-inch screens. They came with earbuds in little plastic bags. Clive passed them out.

"Can we watch them now?"

"I have some things I want to talk to you about, but if you prefer to watch a movie, that's your choice. The memory has Shrek and a few other shows recorded for you. If you prefer video games, there are some. Can I get the people who want to watch a video or play games to move to the back of the room, please?"

The room was filled with milling children. Of the thirty kids, seven sat in the front rows clutching their Zunes and looking at Clive expectantly. Two girls and five boys.

Seven out of thirty. Twenty-three point three percent.

For an instant, he couldn't prevent a scowl from decorating his face.

It is what it is.

One of the seven changed his mind and eagerly tore at the plastic as he wandered to the back of the room.

Bloody hell.

Six.

The room was eerily silent. The only sounds were creaking chairs and tinny music escaping from the earbuds.

"I am going to give you a little puzzle to solve."

A boy wearing close-cropped hair and a Lakers basketball

jersey raised his hand.

"Is this a game?"

"What's your name, young man?"

"Richard."

"Richard. Okay. No, this is not a game. I am going to draw some symbols. This one that is straight on the left side and curved on the right side represents an *AND* function. When the two inputs on the left are *ones*—then and only then—the output on the right is a *one*. This symbol with a curved side on the left represents an *OR* function and the output is *one* when either of the inputs on the left are *ones*."

He drew the symbols on the board with little charts to describe their function.

"The charts are truth tables—they describe what these symbols do. Now, I'm going to draw a group of these symbols with inputs and I want you to tell me what I will get at the output point." He pointed. "Here."

"This is stupid," one of the boys said.

He got up and moved to the back of the room.

Five.

Clive passed out a photocopied sheet so the kids could work through the logic circuit.

After a few minutes, a boy raised his hand.

"I got it," he said.

"What's your name?"

"Ray."

"Very well, Ray. What will the output be?"

"It's a *one*," he said proudly.

"Okay," Clive said. "That's good."

Richard raised his hand.

"I don't think there *is* an answer."

"That's interesting, young man," Clive said. "We're talking about ones and zeroes, how can the output be

225

undefined?"

"It's because of this line here that goes from the output back to one of these or-gate things. We have to know what that was before we can figure out what the output is."

"That's stupid, Richard," Ray said. "The output should be zero when we start, that's the only thing that makes sense— that means the output is a one."

"If we don't know what the output starts as, then we don't know how it ends up. Mr. Colgate did not say anything about how we started."

"You're always arguing about stupid stuff that doesn't matter, Ricky."

"I'm trying to think about what Mister Colgate said and he didn't say anything about how this puzzle starts out, so we can't know."

"Mister Colgate, who is right?" Ray said.

"What do the rest of you think?"

The other three kids looked uncomfortable—fidgeting in their seats and shooting glances out the window.

"I don't know," one of the little girls said. "I tried but I couldn't figure it out."

"Tell Ricky he's full of garbage," Ray said. "The answer is *one* isn't it?"

"Yes, Ray," Clive said, "the correct answer is one."

Richard stood up and leaned over his desk.

"But," he complained, "if the output was originally a one, then the answer would be different. You didn't tell us nothing about how this thing starts, so you can't prove I'm wrong, can you?"

"Tell Ricky to shut up. He's stupid."

Clive scratched his head and pondered the situation, then laughed.

"I see Richard's point, Ray," he said. "In the strictest sense, he's correct too. If you don't know the initial condition, you can't know the output state. It's undetermined. To be rigorous, I should tell you the initial condition. The problem assumes the initial states are zeroes, but that's not explicit in the question, is it?"

Richard did a little dance and waggled his index fingers at Ray.

"I'm nine times smarter than you, Ray. Maybe ten."

I can only choose one, but screw the rules, I like this kid.

"Okay, I have a card for both of you." From his backpack, he pulled two laminated cards and handed them to the boys. "Go to the website address on the back or ask your mum and dad to call the toll-free number—we'll explain to your parents what we have in mind for you."

He zipped up his backpack and pulled it over his shoulders.

A little girl raised her hand.

"What about us, Mister Colgate?"

Brutal Honesty Day.

Damn it.

"What's the difference between *being* smart and *acting* smart? If you accept wise guidance, live by a solid moral code and avoid the worst of life's pitfalls, then you can enjoy a great life. But, there are many hazards and dangers in our world and we need our very best minds working on solutions."

"Did you hear that?" Richard said. "I have a superior brain." He did a little dance and spun on his heels—stopping with a finger pointed at Ray's head like a pistol. "Bang, you're dead. I'm the sharpshooter, baby."

Ray leaned his elbows on his desk and covered his face.

"I hate you, Ricky," he said.

Clive opened the doorway and stepped into the hallway. Leaning against the far wall, the teacher waited.

"I hate how you separate the kids," she said. "People

227

shouldn't be inspected and graded like cuts of beef."

Clive shrugged. "I don't like it either, but it's my job. Good luck with getting the video players out of their hands."

"Yeah, thanks for nothing," she said. "They'll be hopeless for the rest of the day."

"See you next year," Clive said.

With her hand on the doorknob, the teacher took a deep breath before opening the door and going in.

Notes on *Brutal Honesty Day*

AP: Honesty pays, but it doesn't seem to pay enough to suit everyone.

Aside from everything else, I love the idea of a day in which everyone is honest. It would serve well the individual and the society. Or maybe not. Why do you think people are not honest on a regular basis?

KLC: Are you kidding, Adina? The maxim is that *crime* pays, not honesty. Why are we dishonest? Because it profits us in some way. We all want something for nothing.

The parts that interest me most are the facts we're unwilling to face straight up. I put this quote in *Alligator Alley*:

> *A few of us now know from the closed-system experts that the golden rule doesn't work. Those few of us who are rich and who really have the figures know that it is worse than one chance in one hundred that you can survive your allotted days in any comfort. It is not you or the other fellow; it is you or one hundred others. And if you are going to survive...you're going to have to do it at the expense of others. So, do it as neatly and cleanly and politely as you know how and your*

conscience will allow.
—Advice from an "uncle" to R. Buckminster
Fuller in 1913 as related in *Utopia or Oblivion*

Unfortunately, many are in a hopeless position and it's often not anyone's fault, it's just the way it is. Were you born ugly, stupid or poor? Well, I'm sorry, but you're not going to be Johnny Depp or Jennifer Aniston. Watch football on TV and be happy.

AP: You brilliantly capture a fault with today's society. Consumerism—everyone is a cog in this complex system and it's a tragedy that children are nothing but a blank canvas to be exploited by marketers.

KLC: I was trying to make a point that opportunity might present itself, but you have to pay attention and be ready to answer the door. Some of the kids in the back of the room might have been smart enough to earn a ticket out of poverty and obscurity, but they're too busy watching TV or playing games and don't have the context to understand what might be good for them in the longer run.

AP: Having grown up in a communist country as I did, I experienced the political assault on our subconscious. We were supposed to be brainwashed into being brave little Marxists. Marketing as we know it, targeted at the buyer, was nonexistent. And yet, the buzz about the Snickers candy bars or electronics or you name it seeped into our brains—we wanted the best product and to have better things when compared to the Joneses.

None of the Marxist propaganda worked but remote marketing from the west did. Interesting, no?

KLC: Yes, it is interesting how commercial styles and fashions and trends seep through borders and cultural barriers. Why are Marlboro cigarettes popular in Japan? Why are pop songs from around the world almost always sung in English? When my visitors come over from China, why are they wearing wingtip shoes, business suits and neckties?

AP: Can I quote Santayana?

> *Advertising is the modern substitute for argument; its function is to make the worse appear the better.*
> —George Santayana

Do you agree?

KLC: I didn't get to where I am today by arguing with George Santayana. Can I volley back with another of his quotes?

> *Intelligence is quickness in seeing things as they are.*
> —George Santayana

AP: It's interesting how you focused on kids in your story.
"I have some things I want to talk to you about, but if you prefer to watch a movie, that's your choice. The memory has Shrek and a few other shows recorded for you. If you prefer video games, there are some. Can I get the people who want to watch a video or play games to move to the back of the room, please?"

The room was filled with milling children. Of the thirty kids, seven sat in the front rows clutching their Zunes and looking at Clive expectantly. Two girls and five boys.

> Seven out of thirty. Twenty-three point three percent."

With the risk of sounding like an old cliché with 'back in my day', but it's only in the past 15-20 years that I heard about ADD or ADHD when referring to children. I think the paragraph I just quoted speaks tons about what the real problem is: the assault of the entertainment industry gives our kids the attention span of a moth. Would you agree?

KLC: We live in a very wealthy society. In general, our kids are not breaking their backs in a field; they are sitting around watching TV, playing video games or sexting each other. Normally, we are rich enough to freely do what we want—and it turns out we want to laze around.

We are closer than ever to having the ultimate in free time to achieve a final human destiny, but it looks like that destiny consists of sitting on a couch with our eyes on a video screen and our minds in idle mode—while stuffing our faces with junk food.

Sounds good, doesn't it? Let's go get some ice cream.

Whatever Happened to Faust?
Adina Pelle

WHATEVER HAPPENED TO Faust?

The creepy, hollow look in his eyes made me nervous. While sitting in one of the room's chairs, he cast his eyes around the room—surveying the area and sucking in deep draughts of breath like someone recently freed from a confined space. He settled his gaze on me—as if trying hypnosis. His voice was nearly a whisper.

"I am Satan," he said.

I maintained my serious expression and studied him carefully. He was a man with a solid build—tall, about thirty years old with pale skin and short, black hair, a very wide forehead, snubby nose, thin, almost feminine eyebrows and eyes with glassy, opaque-blue irises.

He crossed his legs, slowly drawing his left leg over the right. The thin fingers of his hands were bound together over his knees. The defiant smile on his lips mocked me.

He spoke in a reproachful tone.

"Find it funny?"

The question surprised me. My aplomb was well-practiced. I was sure no feature of my face betrayed amusement.

"Not funny," I said. "Just incredible. Hard to believe."

"I often earn that reaction."

232

Something in his body language—maybe a sneaky hint of smile—suggested a state of existential glee.

"How often does this happen?" I said.

"Normal people should not expect an easy confession. Me. Satan. It's inconceivable, right?"

"Yes, it is. There are many who claim to be Jesus or Moses. Until recently, I never talked to a real demon."

He erupted with a gale of laughter which stopped just as abruptly. He spoke with a serious look on his face.

"How can I convince you?"

"It is well-known that demons have supernatural powers. You could, for example, burst into flames or make yourself invisible for a few seconds, then reappear. That would do it."

His ironic smile and defiant look melted the amusement from my face.

"Unfortunately," he said regretfully, "I can't prove my identity. When we take human shape, we are deprived of our powers and are not allowed to show our true appearance."

"Why did you take human form?"

He leaned toward me and spoke with a confidential whisper.

"It's punishment. When a devil neglects his duties he is exiled to live with men and forced to live a mortal life. Deprived of his powers, he must convert three people—that's the price of redemption. If successful, he regains all his privileges."

"Shouldn't this be a secret? Do you risk anything by telling me this?"

"No, because you are my first soul—a soul I'm determined to claim."

His calm silence grew uncomfortable.

"Why were you exiled?"

He face twisted with the memory.

233

"It happened many years ago. It was an easy task—I had to claim the soul of a young woman. Her name is unimportant. I spent hours and hours studying her—day and night observing. I walked with her, watched her sleep, listened to her voice and smelled her scent. She was an innocent virgin. Ah, misleading senses. When the time came, it was discovered that I spared her soul, so I earned this punishment. Because of a woman, a mortal." Spasmodic laughter died in a sigh. "The love of a woman!" he exclaimed, shaking his fists in despair.

I thought I saw tears in his eyes. He rose from his chair and stomped across the room like a lunatic. The door opened and the attendant entered.

"Is everything all right, doctor?" he asked.

"Yes," I answered, regaining my calm. "We're done. Can you take him into the sitting room with the others?"

My assistant motioned to the patient to follow and shut the door behind them.

I drank a glass of water and wiped sweat from my forehead with the back of my hand.

Twenty-seven patients who claimed to be the devil.

Why did I always get them?

Notes on *Whatever Happened to Faust?*

KLC: Many years ago, I wrote a song called *Faust Food*.

> *I watched you from old darkened halls*
> *As you played out in the light*
> *I followed in your footsteps*
> *As you wandered in the night*
>
> *Same old story, same old game*
> *The faces never change*

When you're feeling lonely in the night
I have a contract we can arrange…

What say you? I have a sense that, despite a wide gulf of differences, in many ways we think alike.

AP: Yes, we come at things from the same angle. I've had a lifelong fascination with Mephistophelian transcendence. What kind of deal would we cut in exchange for a serving of the forbidden fruit? What would we trade for love, youth and immortality?

KLC: The Faustian legends go back many hundreds of years—who knows how old the original stories are?

> *Again Doctor Faustus departed from the spirit all melancholy, confused and full of doubt, thinking now this way now that, and pondering on these things day and night. But there was no constancy in him, for the Devil had hardened his heart and blinded him. And indeed when he did succeed in being alone to contemplate the Word of God, the Devil would disguise himself in the form of a beautiful woman, embrace him, debauching with him, so that he soon forgot the Divine Word and threw it to the wind.*
> —Historia vnd Geschicht Doctor Johannis Faustj des Zauberers, 1587

When writing this story, which version of Faust were you thinking of? The Marlowe translation (*Tragicall History of D. Faustus*, 1601) or some later version?

AP: Goethe, without a shadow of a doubt. When I think of Faust, I think of the version that sprang from Goethe's pen.

KLC: Our struggles are truly timeless, aren't they?

> *This life of earth, whatever my attire,*
> *Would pain me in its wonted fashion.*
> *Too old am I to play with passion;*
> *Too young, to be without desire.*
> *What from the world have I to gain?*
> *Thou shalt abstain—renounce—refrain!*
> *Such is the everlasting song*
> *That in the ears of all men rings,—*
> *That unrelieved, our whole life long,*
> *Each hour, in passing, hoarsely sings.*
> —*Faust,* Johann Wolfgang von Goethe, 1806
> (as translated by Bayard Taylor)

AP: Yes, you capture the exact frame of mind I was in.

KLC: This story is very simple, but it has a wry, subtle humor to it. Am I kidding myself? Did you intend this to be a sort of divine comedy?

AP: Yes, more or less. I meant to take a casual tone for a very metaphysical subject. Mankind is corrupt and sometimes we revel in the evil and disaster we leave in our wake.

Energy Independence
Ken Coffman

PETER BEKMANN, READING a book while sunk deep in the tattered cushions of his threadbare La-Z-Boy recliner, was comfortable and had a policy of never answering the door or the telephone if he was busy. And, he *was* busy. Very busy—reading *Farnham's Freehold* on his Kindle. It didn't seem like the knocking would add anything significant to the cacophony. Peter was used to the cats mewling and the kids fighting—but the pounding on the door was abnormal and annoying.

The person banging on the door would not take the hint and go away.

Peter's kids argued over their books at school. School was a card table in the corner of the room. Sherrie pulled pages from a Doctor Seuss book and ate them. Barry, with his head and thoughts deep in a Networks Analysis book, chewed on the end of a pencil and nibbled Bing cherries from a giant bowl. Cassie splashed color on a paint-by-numbers Mona Lisa with her own selected tints—with a strong emphasis on a froggy, putrid green—a paint she had a lot of because the Goodwill store had a case she bought for three dollars.

"Tanya?" Peter called out. "Would you get the door, please?"

Tanya came out and stood in the kitchen doorway with a mixing bowl and spoon. Her dark-blue cotton dress was covered with brown flour and the hair over her left ear was stiff with a dried glob of batter from their breakfast pancakes.

"Sure, honey, I don't have anything else to do. I'm just making dinner for you and your children while you sit on your ass in that dad-blasted chair. I'd be honored to get the door for you."

Peter grinned. "Thank you, baby."

Tanya was a huge woman; not obese, but far from thin— she was tall and husky. When she stood up straight, she was six-feet-six-inches tall. She looked scary and mean, but was actually a sweet-tempered, gentle woman. With the mixing bowl under her arm, she pulled the door open. A man dressed in a three-piece suit stood smiling in the doorway.

Instantly, Missy, a giant white and orange cat, weaved through his legs and purred like a piece of earth-moving equipment. The man looked down—already his wool slacks were decorated with fur. His smile grew strained. Peering at Tanya, he looked up with his neck at an uncomfortable angle.

"Oh, my, you're a tall woman. I suppose you hear that a lot. I'm sorry. I apologize for being so persistent, but I could hear the kids, so I knew you were home. My name is Gordon Bell and I'm from Puget Sound Energy. I wonder if I might come in and talk with you and your husband for a few minutes?"

Tanya turned to Peter.

"It's for you."

Peter sighed and dropped his ebook on the little table beside his chair.

"Tell him he can come in if he takes off his necktie."

"Sorry," Tanya said to Gordon, "he doesn't allow senseless apparel in his house. At the same time, he's always after me to wear nylon pantyhose and ribbons in my hair. I know it's stupid, but what can I do? The man is impossible to reason with."

"Necktie?" Gordon looked down. He wore a silk Hathaway tie covered with baseballs—a Father's Day gift from his daughter. "Uh, yeah, sure."

While gently moving the cat away from his slacks with a shiny leather shoe, he fumbled with the tie. He worked it off and slipped it in his jacket pocket. As if offended by rejection, Missy wandered off, but was replaced by Rascal, Tom and Alice who took over the attack on Gordon's trousers.

Stirring vigorously, Tanya strolled back to the kitchen— leaving Gordon standing in the front doorway.

"I can come in?"

Peter gestured.

"Sure. Make yourself at home. Take a load off. My house is your house. Pull up a seat and we'll chat."

Gordon looked around, but there were no chairs nearby. Along the wall, under a massive, out-of-control dieffenbachia, he spotted an old oak kitchen chair. There, a cat sat on a stack of old Wall Street Journals. He looked over his shoulder at Peter.

"Go ahead. That's old Clem. He'll move."

Gordon tilted the chair—the newspapers and Clem slipped off. Clem looked up at Gordon with insult in his eyes, and then moseyed off. Gordon brushed off the worst of the cat hair from the chair and moved it near Peter. Immediately after Gordon sat, Sherrie jumped from her chair, toddled over, and wrapped her arms around his leg.

"I love you very much," she said.

Gordon looked up a Peter, then back at Sherrie. She had strawberry jam on her cheek. She rubbed the gleaming mess on his pant leg.

"Uh," he said while calculating the dry cleaning bill in his head. "I love you too."

She picked up the orange and white fur ball—and hugged her to her chest.

"And I love Missy," she said, before wandering off to the kitchen.

"You look familiar," Peter said.

"Yeah. I was a year behind you at CalTech. In the physics department. I remember you arguing with Professor Rossman about radiation effects on minerals in the analytical techniques lab."

"Yeah, those days were a lot of fun. I was thrown out shortly after that."

"I always wondered. What happened?"

"Oh, my grades were terrible. I wanted to learn—but I didn't care a whit about keeping score. I lost my scholarship, but it was okay. I met Tanya and we were more interested in making babies than college classes."

"She's very tall."

Peter beamed with pride.

"Yeah, man, ain't she something?"

"And you're..."

"Yeah. Five-foot-three-and-a-half. A man like me has to hang on tight when she gets her passion up, if you catch my drift. A horse is bigger than a man, and you don't see the man complaining when he's galloping around, see what I'm saying? Same thing in the sack. Don't knock it 'til you try it, but get your own woman. Mine's taken."

"Right. Of course," Gordon said.

Tanya came in with two massive, mismatched ceramic mugs filled with steaming brown tea.

"He's not comparing me to farm animals again, is he?" she said.

Gordon caught a whiff of the tea and waved it away.

"Oh, no thank you," Gordon said.

"Everyone drinks my Masala Chai and barley tea and likes it if they know what's good for them. It goes real good with the farina-sesame bread."

"Okay," Gordon said.

He took a sip and looked for a spot to place the cup where the cats would not get it.

"Better hold on to it," Peter said. "The cats are big believers in sharing. Socialists, every one of them. To each according to their need, know what I'm saying?" He took a big swig of his tea and sighed with pleasure. "Damn, that's better than a wet teenage kiss under a blanket in the back of a station wagon. But never mind that. What brings you out this way, Gordon? I don't think I have any business with Puget Sound Energy."

"Ah, that's the thing," Gordon said. "I'm here to talk about the green energy rebate program."

"I read about this in Mother Earth News. You guys essentially buy power from home generation—people who put solar panels on their roof."

"Right," Gordon said. "Exactly. Smart power meters run backwards when you feed power back into the grid. To encourage that, we have an incentive program—the government is involved too. Anything that contributes to green energy and reducing our dependence on foreign oil, uh, we want to promote that."

A stern look crossed Peter's face. He leaned forward.

"Green energy, eh?" he said.

From across the room, Peter's son—Barry—spoke.

"Be careful, Mr. Bell. Daddy gets mad when people talk about green energy."

"Uh, green energy carried by green electrons, brown

electrons, black electrons," Gordon said. "We know an electron is an electron, but we craft a simple message for the public."

"I don't like it and I will not tolerate that kind of talk in my house," Peter said. "Energy is energy. Are we through?"

"No offense intended. Please forgive me. I won't say anything more about colors and energy, okay?"

"Very well," Peter said, "but watch your filthy mouth around my children. I don't want their brains filled with nonsense. If we could get to the point of your visit, I would appreciate it."

"Okay." Gordon took a deep breath. He almost took a sip of his tea, but the odor changed his mind. He placed the mug on the floor. In less than two seconds, Rascal had his nose in the cup. "To my point. Yes. It's obvious you do not have solar panels on your roof."

"I hate the damned ugly things. I don't want mounting holes on my roof and I don't want to climb up there to clean off the bird shit every year. Besides, with an average generating capacity of something like three-hundred watts-per-square-meter, there's no way they're worth the bother. Not even close."

"Right. You don't answer our phone calls or letters, so maybe you don't know this, but you've run up a large credit on your power bill. Over eight-thousand dollars. So that's the question, right? How are you doing that? We checked your meter; its working fine. Twenty kilowatt-hours fed back into the grid twenty-four hours a day. Where is this energy coming from?"

With a smug look on his face, Peter leaned back in his chair and took a sip of his tea.

From across the room, Barry spoke again. "That's easy—Daddy is a genius."

Ken Coffman and Adina Pelle

"So," Peter said, with a smirk spread across his wide face, "I see why they sent you. You're here to steal my design. You guys are funny."

"It's a simple matter of idle curiosity now, but, of course, something like this will attract attention. If we have to, we'll get the Feds involved. How do we know you're not doing something very dangerous?"

Peter laughed.

"You wouldn't be here if you detected anything hazardous. Radiation? No, we're not emitting any, are we, Barry?"

Barry looked up from his book.

"Our yearly emission is less than forty microsieverts. We absorb more background radiation than we emit."

"Okay," Peter said, "suppose we remove the power meter and I disconnect us from your grid? Then will you leave us alone?"

"Don't you think the public has the right to know how you're generating power?"

"No, I don't. The public should mind its own damned business. Besides, I figured it out and it's not that complex. Someone at GE or Westinghouse will figure it out. Someone will dig deeper into Nicola Tesla's obscure papers. Or, like me, some knucklehead rethinking what he or she learned in college—unlearning bad paradigms about electron orbits and the like..."

A young woman, about sixteen, with her hair wrapped up in a bath towel, came out of the kitchen with the teapot. She was not as tall as her mother, but she was headed in that direction. She wore a short terrycloth bathrobe. It had holes showing bits of random, intimate skin. Her breasts were large—scattered freckles decorated the ivory flesh of her cleavage. Gordon's eyes ate her up.

"Bonnie," Peter said sternly, "I told you not to wear that

nasty old bathrobe when we have company. Take it off."

Gordon froze in his chair as if paralyzed.

"Daddy, knock it off," Bonnie said. To Gordon, she said, "He does that to freak you out. What was that guy's name from the Department of Energy?"

"Garte," Barry said.

"Yes, thank you," Bonnie said. "Doctor Garte. I thought he'd have a heart attack when Daddy said that. What's the big deal about a little skin? I don't understand it. Would you care for more tea?"

Gordon took a deep breath. He nudged Rascal to get his nose out of the mug.

"Yes, please. I'd love some."

She leaned over to fill Gordon's cup. He didn't know where to point his eyes, so he closed them.

"Thanks, Bonnie," he said.

She winked and turned away. Her panties were pink— visible in swaths under the shorty bathrobe as she walked away.

Good Lord, Gordon thought.

"Where were we?" Peter said.

Gordon took a moment to allow his heart rate settle.

"Your power. I need to know where it comes from."

"Ah, well, it comes from the same place all energy comes from, silly. It's all around. In every cell, every atom, every photon, every electron—green or brown or black or purple. You're a clever guy, you figure it out. Think about this: Al Einstein figured gravity is not a force; it's a warp of the fabric of the space-time continuum. See?"

"No," Gordon said.

Peter sighed.

"Okay, do what I did. Imagine the universe will provide what you need. In other words, if you need clean, cheap energy, then it exists and all you have to do is find it and put it to work for you. Why? Because God is your friend, okay? If it helps, think of it that way. Can you imagine the universe working that way?"

"No."

"Fine," Peter said. "Then it won't matter how much I try to explain—you're not going to get it."

"If it was up to me, I would accept your, uh, position. But, the public interest trumps your privacy. I'm sorry, but that's the way it is. You'll disclose your energy system in detail."

"No, I won't."

"We'll come in and tear your house apart and haul everything to a lab in New Mexico. We'll split up your family. We'll throw you in prison and toss away the key—until you cooperate. I'm very sorry, but that's the way it is."

"No you won't."

Gordon rubbed his forehead.

"Okay, I'm curious. Why not?"

"If I press the red button—what did we figure would dissolve, Barry?"

"A sphere about forty miles in diameter."

"Yes," Peter said. "A big chunk of the earth would be disassembled into leptons. Instantly. You know how much easier it is to make a bomb compared to a controllable power generator, so I think the fruitful part of our conversation is over. Can I get back to my book now?"

Gordon put the mug of tea on the floor, and then stood.

"Our guest is leaving," Peter called out toward the kitchen.

Tanya came out with a small bundle wrapped in a paper towel.

"Please take a groat cake for the road, Mr. Bell," she said. "I make them with lots of squil."

"Uh, thanks, I think," Gordon said.

He walked to the door and hesitated for a moment with his hand on the knob.

"Goodbye, Mr. Bell," Barry said.

Without speaking, Gordon opened the door and left.

"Dad," Barry said.

Peter picked up his ebook and pressed the buttons to find his bookmark. His place was lost when the cats stepped on the navigation buttons. He shifted a little to make room for Alice—a giant, furry, black-and-white cat—in her usual spot beside him.

"Yes, son," he said.

"We should actually get a big, red button. I've seen them in the Grainger catalog—ergonomic mushroom switches. Make a box with an antenna. Put the switch on the box? Wouldn't that vex the knuckleheads?"

"Whatever you say, Barry. If that's what you want. I suppose you want me to pay for it too."

"Yes, dad, that's what I was thinking. I'm saving my money to buy a spectroscope on eBay."

"I think it's interesting how all of the great ideas around here end up costing me money."

"If you agree to pay the Grainger bill, I'll leave you alone for an hour."

"Great, now it's extortion. Fine, okay, son. It's a deal."

Alice worked her head under his hand until he stroked her.

To Alice, he said, "I sure am glad someone around here loves me for me."

Notes on *Energy Independence*

AP: I think I read this story at least five times so far and most likely I'll read it a couple more times only to come up with a different interpretation every time. The story is like looking at the world through a kaleidoscope lens. Are you satisfied with the view?

KLC: Yes, of course. There is a lot going on—I try to create stories and books that are crammed full of ideas and concepts and teasers. It takes me a long time to craft things the way I want, so I'm happy if the words earn extra readings. There should be things you wonder about late at night—or little discoveries that pop in your head when you're in the shower.

The story revolves around such an absurd idea—the idea that a man can create enough power for his house and also feed quite a lot back to the grid. Energy independence is a political concept with a lot of standing these days, so I extend this idea to its logical conclusion—the independence of the household.

AP: My first thought, of course, given my arts background, goes to the cinematic quality of the scene. Your composition strikes me as a combination of a modern Vermeer with his masterful eye for light and detail and Hieronymus Bosch whose work used fantastic imagery to illustrate moral concepts and narratives. The six foot tall woman certainly stands for more than just gentle giant character. What did you have in mind when you created the scene prior to her opening the door?

KLC: I wanted a very recognizable and normal domestic situation with chaos and cats and kids all interacting. There's a lot I'm playing with. If I can get you to *buy* the normalcy of the household, then I think that draws a more interesting contrast to the weird science going on in the background.

AP: The sassy comment about the giant woman in the sack is hysterical. It adds so much more to the domestic setting where everything is either burlesque or mainstream and of course links Peter's coital identity (for lack of better words) next to his socio-political persona. The reader is pushed and pulled back and forth in trying to internalize and factor the scene and personalities.

KLC: Peter is this tiny little guy married to a huge woman. Perhaps society would judge this couple as freaks, but they make their own way in life. A lot of things in our lives are created by our viewpoint and attitude. It amused me to have this little-bitty guy as the master of the house. The king. Is he ashamed to be so small when his wife is so large? No, he revels in it. I've noticed this in my life—why be defensive about things? Don't accept what others might see as problems. Be aggressive about forcing others to accept you as you are and as you want to be; they can always bugger off and associate with others if they prefer.

AP: And then comes the real color Peter adheres to—which is not green, that's for sure. This is where your message is carefully tucked away. Is this something you tried explaining to many people in numerous and diverse ways? I get the feeling that you tried passing on the message related to green energy many times before with mixed results. Is this true? Is the new approach to your polemic working better?

KLC: No, not at all. You wound me, Adina. How could Peter be more 'green'? He's the epitome of 'green'.

You're married to a technical person, so you know the worldview. Facts are facts and truths are truths. I am analytical about the world...science, sociology and technology. That doesn't mean I don't make mistakes, because I do all the time. But most people are uncomfortable with an objective reality, whereas I force myself to look the world directly in the eye and let it be what it is.

For fun, I argue with progressive activists all the time. They are so sincere about trying to save the world and get so upset when others won't get out of the way and let them do their good works. We're not so far apart—I agree with a lot of their positions. We should increase energy efficiency. We should reduce particulates in the air. However, we have so many serious problems; it doesn't make sense to dream up fake ones, particularly when the objective science is so clear.

Today, the progressive activists want expensive government programs to support this or that great idea. Lovely. Do you think it was a government program that moved us from horses and buggies to internal combustion automobiles? Was it a government program that created the iPad or the smart phone?

Of course it wasn't.

One thing we all agree on is we need new sources of safe, clean and cheap energy. If you're looking for energy, why not look where there are huge amounts of it? In the atom. There's a lot about physics we don't understand and here's something I'm quite serious about—the breakthroughs of energy generation will not be made by governments or big-company programs. These are poor incubators of breakthrough ideas. I believe some very clever person will re-examine the information we have and figure out another way of viewing the atom and answers, like magic, will fall onto his or her lap. This is essentially what my novel *Hartz String Theory* is about.

In some ways, I'm 'greener' than the progressives. I don't think we should waste time and resources on dead-end technologies.

Flowers from Luther
Adina Pelle

SHE KNEW IT, it was obvious; something would happen to her sooner or later. If you play God, your destiny becomes complicated. She doodled and played with God's grand scheme, and, of course, was rewarded with a cosmic slap to the face.

Noisy families lived in her building—a tower deep in a low-income ghetto. The too-familiar acoustic landscape included screams, arguments, fuss, howling children and swearing men and women moaning under the weight of men's smelly bodies.

Once in a while, an unwilling visitor like a policeman, plumber or hell only knows—perhaps a disgruntled neighbor—briefly disturbed the cacophony of noise pollution. And, once a year, a new neighbor moved in the building— when someone died.

When she came home and found flowers from Luther and two large pizzas in cardboard boxes, she knew someone had died.

It's been a year already?

Last year a man killed his wife because he was tired of finding the bathtub drain clogged with clumpy strands of her long, blond, hair. He loved her pretty hair, but not when it plugged the drain.

"How much do you expect a man to take?" the man had said. "Get the fuck more careful. Clean up after yourself."

Now, she's dead and clogs the drains no more.

Scary, but that's life—in the projects or in the suburbs.

When she entered her building, Lesta, the woman who lived directly below, stood in the hallway with her baby—Lamar—on her hip.

Lamar is a minor character; he should not even have a name. And he is too young and innocent to be a prisoner of the projects.

He cried incessantly.

She spoke to Lesta. "Who died?"

"Your next-door neighbor," Lesta said. "She was a busy girl with a visitor every night; a different man parking his fancy car in the parking lot."

"How do you know all this?"

"From the old lady who watches," Lesta said. "Agnes, on the second floor, you know her? She has white hair? Always sitting on the front stoop? Watching?"

"Aha—and how did Agnes die? Of old age?"

"Agnes is not the one who died," Lesta said with an astonished tone. "The police say the dead woman slipped in the bathroom and hit her head on the bathtub. No one saw anything. But, what kind of woman receives a different man each night, huh? I mean—she had a brothel going on right here in our building, right?"

"Maybe, but..."

"No 'buts'. She got what she deserved," Lesta interjected. "What she did was not right."

"Was one of her visitors to blame?"

"What? She's dead. It was an accident. Forget about it."

She shook her head at Lesta's badmouthing the poor, dead

whore and realized how death had no real impact on anyone. Mortality was simply a minor disturbance of the building's monotony.

As Lesta finished talking, Agnes slowly approached.

She had news—the record needed to be corrected.

Agnes-with-the-white-hair said men showed up every night to visit the woman next door, not the one who died. The dead woman quietly lived in the building for many years and she had a boyfriend nobody saw. Fresh flowers and two large pizza boxes were found on her kitchen table with a scented note.

The note was written with a man's heavy hand.

To my angel…

—from Luther

"It was God's will. He took her because she was in everyone's way," Agnes said.

"Let's forget about it," Lesta replied.

Notes on *Flowers from Luther*

KLC: It would be natural for a reader to look over a story like this and judge it to be a simple little throw-away thing—it's very short at just over 500 words. However, words have bulk. Density. How do you approach a thought like this? What leads you to the right length?

AP: I started this story at around 1,500 words but kept going back and gnawing at it because I felt like the story was too complex when told in that many words. I used the majority of them, the density you refer to in setting up the visual aspect—

the projects, crying children, domestic abuse and gossip. I wanted the gist of the story to hide behind this curtain.

KLC: By now, the reader is used to you being slippery. You set up a vividly-described scene and anchor us in it, but then twist what we think we know. Your technique is very smooth. My question is: where does this come from? Did you read the Russian absurdist masters as a child or young adult? Gogol? Kafka? Bulgakov? Who?

AP: I was, and still am, on a quest to find the true 'messiah' of Russian literature. I may never settle for only one favored author. While in school, I fed on Alexander Pushkin, Nikolai Gogol, Fyodor Dostoyevsky, Ivan Turgenev, Nikolai Nekrasov, and many others. They are all in the first rank of human treasures—they focused on the misery of 'the people' and the travesties of the social institutions which prolonged their misery—this theme has never left my subconscious.

KLC: The story of the man who killed his wife for leaving hair in the drain—it strikes me this is a snapshot of lost love. It's sad. He once loved her blond hair, but that love died. It reminds me of a master painter who applies a few brush strokes and leads you to see something that is not literally there. We instinctively *know* the arc of their love story as it starts in joy and descends into tragedy. I've already used more words discussing this snippet than you used. This is not an easy trick. How do you tell a long story so obliquely and with so few words?

AP: It's funny. Love comes and goes as it pleases—regardless of our will. I once read a newspaper story about a man who shot his wife because she put the milk in the back of the

253

refrigerator. For twenty years he calmly asked her time and time again to leave the milk upfront, but she wouldn't do it. Obviously, this is a psychotic example of madness and love expiring over time. In addition, I was thinking of Dr. Spark's book, *The Man Who Mistook his Wife for a Hat*. It fascinated me and I used it as a backdrop for several stories. You are right, there is much one can unfold from a line like 'the man who killed his wife for leaving hair in the drain', but a writer needs say no more beyond this sentence—everything else unfolds in the reader's mind.

KLC: Once again, I think you toy with us by casually using a name with deep resonance: Luther. I can imagine this story nailed to the door of some busybody neighbor. You might claim the name was picked at random, but I will not believe you. Can you defend yourself?

AP : No, of course it's not a random name. I had Lucifer in mind and I played around this Mephistophelic approach until I came up with Luther.

KLC: The most interesting thing about this story is: it's a bit like a suicide note. In other words, the unnamed *she* of the story, in playing with God's controlling role, finds herself the victim—a Greek Icarus type of character—which makes this tale a sort of modern myth. You're a skilled storyteller, but I sense divine intervention at work with this one. Tell me about the spirit that visited your house and guided your fingers on the keyboard when you wrote this.

AP: Can I answer with a quote?

There are things which a man is afraid to tell even to

himself, and every decent man has a number of such
things stored away in his mind.
—Fyodor Dostoyevsky

Dark spirits peep over my shoulder when I write. These spirits demand complete honesty and courage when facing down personal demons in shadowy places. They press me to do things in a certain way. Thus, I write about betrayal, love and the general human condition—at its best or at its worst.

King for a Day
Ken Coffman

AS I PEERED into the dusty distance, I pondered the goddamned dumb idea of riding a bicycle from Cabo San Lucas to San Diego; it was one of those ideas gestated in a beer glass and born in a bar.

It seemed like a grand, once in a lifetime adventure—a pleasant, joyous ride through the desert—roughly following the famous Baja race course. A communing with nature and replacing the stress of city life with peace and solitude. That's what led me, Warren Smythe, computer jockey and full breed city boy, to be stuck here in hell.

I should have discarded the idea when my ex-wife and riding partner, canceled. Now I'm down to a pint of water one-hundred miles from the nearest phone, carrying my bicycle through the sun-blasted Mexican desert. Late September was supposed to be cooler than summer. If so, I would sure hate to see what July was like.

There would have been a good chance of catching a ride with an empty produce truck returning to San Diego if I'd stayed on the main road, Route 1, but I had to get away from the traffic. I felt like there was a target on my back with so many crazy drivers spitting and pegging Carta Blanca beer bottles at me. Too much dust and blue smoke.

I brought plenty of tire patches and a spare inner tube, but a half-dozen tacks ate one tube and a split seam took care of the spare. I considered abandoning the bike, but I paid $850 for just the frame—damned if I would leave it behind while I could still walk.

I got up early in the morning to get in mileage while it was still somewhat cool. I was ready to find shade to rest in during the toaster-oven part of the day if I could find a place that wasn't already claimed by a sidewinder. I was startled to see a child of about eight peeking from behind a thorny bush—he was giggling and sucking a dirty thumb. The kid was funny-looking, with blue eyes and frizzy blond hair, dirty trousers and those ubiquitous sandals with soles made from old tires.

Huaraches.

I knew twenty-six Mexican words and *huaraches* was one of them. I thought—if I could find where the kid lived, I could at least get some water, perhaps even a ride in the back of an old pickup to any place a phone could be found. For the hundredth time, I cursed myself for sleeping through my high school Spanish class. I could ask for a beer or call someone an asshole, but neither of these skills were useful at this time. I searched the rolling hills for some other sign of life but I saw nothing but dust and blinding sunshine. The kid motioned for me to follow and I obliged. We set off down a dusty track toward the west.

After a half hour of walking we were joined by a dark-skinned young girl of about seventeen. She had a goatskin filled with cool water which she handed to me. I tried not to be gluttonous but the water was so good—soon my stomach sloshed as we walked. I couldn't take my eyes off her; she was on the cusp of womanhood. As she got older, her hips would widen and she would have the common stocky frame of the local *Cochimi* natives. Regardless of what she would look like later, for now, her breasts were shyly and subtly tenting the front of her rough-cotton blouse and I couldn't stop watching the sway of her slender rump as we proceeded further from the road and deeper into the endless Mexican nowhere.

Later I would wonder why I felt comfortable following these strangers. It didn't occur to me that I might be in danger; from what happened later, there must have been clues that would have saved me had I been more alert.

However, I'm getting a little ahead of my story. Let me continue.

We walked for several hours without seeing any other signs of life except buzzards drifting in heat waves and an occasional scrawny jack rabbit. I wondered what these two kids were doing wandering so far from home. This was the first time it crossed my mind that they might have been waiting for me or some other hapless traveler.

Every half hour we would stop for more water. I remember being entranced by the wispy hair under her arms—glimpsed when she drank from the goat skin. I couldn't keep my eyes from traveling over her dusty legs and into the folds of her blouse which allowed pale patches of skin to peek through. This did not appear to bother her—she rewarded my attention with a Mona Lisa smile. She had a direct way of looking at me which was disorienting. The women I knew back home were trained to understand the danger of direct eye-contact with a strange man. This girl, whose name I finally understood to be Magdalena, showed no fear what-so-ever.

As we continued walking, I was so blinded by the late afternoon sun that I could barely follow the trail. Even my aviator sun glasses didn't help with the sun directly in my face.

There wasn't much to look at anyway. Rock outcroppings, lizards darting across the trail and mesquite bushes tugging at my clothes. I finally gave up on the bike and left it with the thought I would pick it up on my way back. Magdalena dragged the bike off the trail to rest by a patch of prickly pear; it's probably baking there still.

We walked for hours, later catching an occasional breeze off the Pacific that would cool the sweat on my shirt. As we walked I thought about how it would feel to press the girl against my chest and tear off her blouse. I would follow her to the Patagonian tip of South America to make that happen.

We came to the top of a rolling hill and stopped for a moment, looking over a village. It was untypical because I could not see roads in or out; the shacks were made of adobe, not of scrap wood and old signs. The place was still. I could see burros staring at us from meager shade. A few people pointed and whispered among themselves. There were no power lines, no telephone poles, not even any of the ever-present satellite dishes found even in the poorest parts of the Southwest. Chickens pecked at the dusty ground and there was an acre or so of limp corn stalks. I asked the village's name. Magdalena smiled and shook her head.

As we walked downhill I could hear the people laughing. There was an air of festivity. The village *had* looked quiet and sleepy. Now there was laughter, kids running around stirring up the goats and women hanging kerosene lanterns. Where a board was missing in a hut, I caught a glimpse of a man's white face. There was an unfathomable look in his eyes, perhaps relief mixed with dread? I'm probably coloring this with the way I felt later. How could I read dread-relief from a few seconds of eye contact with a man who probably just looked damned?

The women looked at me in an odd way, as if eating me with their eyes like parasites. Creepy. I can't explain why I felt uncomfortable—like a pretty girl walking by a group of lecherous construction workers.

Most of the women were dowdy and matronly, but some

were young and thin. Like most men, I had the habit of searching loose clothes for flashes of secret skin. The girls knew what I was thinking and teased me with their eyes. I felt like a marlin that knows there is a hook in a smelly hunk of fish, but can't resist striking anyway.

We arrived at the center of the village and I was led to a small hut. A fire ring dominated the center of an open area. A twelve-foot stack of dry wood looked ready for the torch. I wondered how long it took to gather so much wood. This area isn't exactly a forest.

As I looked around, I noticed that the few men left were packing their bedrolls and food for at least an overnight trip. It looked like I was going to be alone with the women and children. The prospect was idyllic.

Magdalena gestured for me to sit and another of the dark-haired girls brought me a drink. The drink, obviously alcoholic, burned my throat as I choked it down. Thick like syrup, it had a bitter aftertaste. Sickening, but after it was gone I immediately wanted more. The bustling girls took care of me—one took my shoes, one washed my feet with cool water and another brought a basket of fruit. The older women strung flowers at the edges of the clear area around the fire ring. As far as I could tell, one hell of a party was imminent and I would be the only man around. My imagination ran wild with visions of being chased around the fire by naked women.

Thinking back, there must have been more than alcohol in the stuff I was drinking. Perhaps extracts of agave, peyote and mescaline and who knows what else? Why wasn't I suspicious enough to notice that I was the only one drinking? All was probably lost after the first drink; I won't worry over what's over and done.

I was immediately woozy, but I noticed I was mistaken to think I was the only man around. There was a guy helping with the decorations. He looked directly at me and something would pass between us that was beyond words. He was Caucasian. Even with very tanned skin, he stood out against the darker women. Though I now understand what he was thinking—at the time he appeared mysterious and doomed.

At some point I fell asleep or passed out. When I woke, I could tell by the position of the sun—barely hanging over the western hills—several hours had passed.

The circle had been transformed with torches waiting to be lit. A pig roasted over a cooking fire across the clearing. The women had painted their faces and put on bright clothes. They lined up around the fire ring. I was pulled to my feet and ushered around the circle. The women plucked at my clothes and chattered as I staggered around the loop. I noticed an odd contraption—with a large weight suspended above the ground and a leather harness—arranged around a flat rock. As the sun faded behind the hills, a torch was applied to the bonfire and the ceremony began.

The fiesta started with the women feeding me; each put a bit of fruit or steaming pork into my mouth. I had never been so hungry—as fast as they could stuff me, I chewed and swallowed. Some poured thimbles full of their bitter brew down my throat—it tasted better with each serving. Like a dream, I was the king surrounded by female subjects. I knew these women lived to serve me because they were so happy when I devoured their offerings. Inevitably, my thoughts, such as I was capable of, were of making love with any of them, or better yet, all of them, giggling and blushing. I'd like to screw this one or that one. Which would like to be my happy queen? When the sun wore away into faint stains on the horizon, the dancing began.

The women glowed in the firelight. Even the older ones took on breathtaking beauty. They whirled me and I stumbled between soft arms that warmed and supported. Each face and body appeared as if from a fog; each more lovely and desirable than the previous.

I don't know how to put this delicately—I got hard. I thought of the story about the disco dancer who broke his leg. When the paramedics cut off his pants, they found a sausage taped to his leg.

Well, ladies, that's no giant sausage throbbing in my pants. Just me. If I could, I would share it with all of you.

Who was it that said you should be careful what you wish for?

From a more advanced perspective, sex seems like such a waste of time. We spend so much time thinking about it and so little time doing it. If we ever do have a female president with the fate of most of the world resting in her hands, half of America would be wondering if she was any good in bed. I wonder if the politicians thought of this; it would be a very effective distraction while they loot our economy.

I was proud of my erection. My ego was equally inflated; I remember thinking that I had an amazing gift to share with these lucky ladies. Of course, they knew exactly what I was thinking. They rubbed against me and leaned so I could glimpse their breasts twitching under their blouses. I imagined my penis would rip through my jeans with a flash of lightning and a roar of thunder; all present would fall to their knees in worship. Magdalena appeared and my hands tore away her shirt—leaving her supple chest glowing before me. She walked backwards with her arms out-stretched.

In the same way iron has no choice but to trace the flux lines of a magnet, I followed. At this point, I knew what was coming (no pun intended).

I was led to the flat rock, pressed onto my back by a hundred hands and strapped tightly down. A leather rope was tied around my penis which stabbed the sky like a granite monolith.

I should have screamed and kept on screaming. Instead, I watched with a desire that filled the universe as Magdalena lifted her skirt and slowly lowered herself on me. My entire being entered her hot envelope. I rose to the highest heights of heaven as she took me in. I crashed to the deepest depths of hell when she raised herself off and I was exposed to the cold.

If I could speak, I would beg her to stay. Magdalena backed away and an old woman took her place. Her toothless grin mocked me as she took her turn. She was replaced by a girl no more than fourteen—she was helped by the older women and took her turn with a look of pain and fascination on her face.

I was just an observer—my dick and the women were the active participants. I'm not sure how long this went on. With no doubt, it was my greatest sexual performance. I know guys back home who would pay a lot to get some of the magic recipe that would permit them to extend their love making like that.

To tell the truth, it got kind of boring after a while. Each woman would swim into my focus, impale herself on me and then get back in line. I looked around as my penis continued its performance. I realized what sort of apparatus I was strapped into; in an instant I knew would happen when the women were through with me. This knowledge should have terrorized and left me limp and screaming for help. Instead, it added a new dimension to my fever. I recall thinking I'd better keep serving these women until they all got tired.

Perhaps if I lasted until sunrise they would let me go?

Hope springs eternal.

Heat built in my groin. The flushed faces and parade of nearly nude bodies were too much. When the girls were on me I would twist and thrust as much as I could—not much since I was tied down well. Finally, Magdalena came around again with her little smile and a mist of perspiration on her upper lip. There came that moment known to all men (and perhaps to women, I don't know) where the world recedes and the thundering conclusion of the sex act becomes yearningly and sweetly inevitable—the point of no return.

I've read of the sexual climax being described as little deaths. As the French put it: *Le Petit Mort*. Well, this was the big death, a shuddering, intense blast into deep space. My fluid came from the depths of my soul to launch into Magdalena's welcoming void. I was beyond reason or pain at that instant, but I felt—or imagined I felt—the leather rope tighten and the sound of someone screaming.

The world dissolved.

Time has passed. As I write these words I cannot describe exactly how I feel. After a month of nursing the bandages came off and I was healed. You might imagine I feel immense regret or loss, but I'm happy in my own way. I help the women with their work—they showed me how to grind corn and prepare wool for weaving. I watched Magdalena's belly swell with our child. I think about leaving. The fact that I have not seen the other white man around (though I noticed several children of mixed ancestry) makes me imagine I won't survive next year's celebration. I don't care. I'm content and have little else to lose. I was king for a day and that is more than most men ever achieve.

I admit there is one thing that really bothers me—though as time goes by perhaps I'll get used to that too.

I still consider myself somewhat of a man and really don't like squatting with the women to pee.

Ken Coffman and Adina Pelle

Notes on *King for a Day*

AP: Oh, man, I'm tripping out with Ken Coffman. What a kaleidoscope of psychedelic images—and exploration of the subconscious. Have you ever tried any of the hallucinogenic drugs? I haven't taken them, but the trip is vividly described. It leaves little doubt about the origins...

KLC: I had exactly one experience with psychedelic mushrooms. A friend gave me a baggy with the shriveled fruit-of-the-earth—I brewed up a tea and drank it. The promised "trip" did not materialize. I spent a few hours feeling paranoid and frankly—terrified. For a guy like me, the only thing I have to offer the world is my mind and it's not something I should mess around with.

The world between my ears is odd enough on its own; it needs no outside help.

AP: Obviously, next to the psychedelic experience, this story illustrates a reverse Freudian fantasy. I say reverse because Freud, to my chagrin, never imagined men as the subject of their own fantasies or hysterias. It took confidence as a man to write a first-person story where testosterone is used and abused.

What were you thinking?

KLC: Beyond an obvious commentary on culture, I was thinking about the nature of our experience. How is satisfaction or success to be measured? Is a long-term general satisfaction equal to a life with a lot of horror, but moments of sublime ecstasy? Should we trade a lifetime of pain for a few moments of transcendent pleasure or joy?

AP: In some Amazonian tribes, young men's fantasies are fulfilled through physical abuse. And, he likes it. Would a woman in the same position consider herself queen for a day? I smirk as I write this...

KLC: Surely you're well-aware of the tortures women voluntarily tolerate. High-heeled shoes come to mind.

AP: Moving away from the sexual catharsis, I thought the descriptions were stunning. Not only providing clear visuals for the reader but the collection of vivid sensory experiences...

> The circle had been transformed with torches waiting to be lit. A pig roasted over a cooking fire across the clearing. The women had painted their faces and put on bright clothes. They lined up around the fire ring. I was pulled to my feet and ushered around the circle.

Or...

> The women glowed in the firelight. Even the older ones took on breathtaking beauty. They whirled me and I stumbled between soft arms that warmed and supported. Each face and body appeared as if from a fog; each more lovely and desirable than the previous.

Simply awesome writing, my friend.

KLC: Thank you.

AP: Do men fantasize about being sex objects?

KLC: Young men do, but old guys like me? No, not so much.

AP: There has to be reproductive pride even if only fantasized. Men have a role to play in propagating the species. Without masculine self-confidence, the human race would perish. Am I right?

KLC: You're right. If women universally pointed at a man's *equipment* and laughed, mankind would be extinct in a couple of generations.

Farewell, Fair Cruelty
Adina Pelle

MANY THINGS REVERBERATE though a lifetime, framed by the fleeting zodiac of ephemeral time. Among these things are the intimate encounters between man and woman.

Nothing is more exciting than the clash of two mentalities. The battle of the ages, as always, is accompanied by advance, retreat and surrender. Love—and its heavenly glory—are not always the pinnacle of a relationship. The sexual bazaar—with its surrounding tents, muddy streets, garish awnings and dark alleys—is what stands out through time.

There is nothing more elemental and real than raw sensuality. As the mad doctor claimed while peering over his grubby notebook, sex is a sure cure for madness and cruelty. It fulfills our temporary craving. It confirms our being. On the other hand, true love is an illusion. Love extends no further than the reach of a woman's arms. Everything beyond her reach is wishful thinking. Fantasy.

Late at night in the lonely light of a flickering candle stub—with a dull pencil and recycled paper, he believed all this. In his forgetful heart, he had a man's hopeful courage, the courage that made him ready to try again after losing everything. The manly valor to start it all over again.

Once he spent a night with a woman he barely knew.

268

Why?

In the morning, he was awakened by her fiancé. They sat—the three of them—around a kitchen table with coffee. Yesterday's bagels. Dust and dead bugs. The sun seeping through a torn blind tried to pierce the gloom, but failed. With bold bravado, he proposed that she choose. The pain-filled morning wavered back-and-forth. Then, in the afternoon, the fiancé left. And months later, he left too when she found someone else.

Then he met Zelda and she seemed perfect. Sexual ignorance fueled her awkward beauty. She injected excitement into his life.

"I would have liked being the first man in your life," he whispered in her ear.

"A woman does not always become her real self the night she loses her virginity," was Zelda's answer.

She had a tiny frame and was uninhibited and agreeable. Easy and silent, she never worried about what was to come. Her grandmother said there's someone for everyone. They considered themselves living proof of the adage.

He was a writer. She wrote nonsense poetry that got published and—amazingly—attracted tiny checks and fan letters. At night, they danced tribal, primitive dances—not invoking any particular god but satisfying the hunger of their bones and flesh.

They drank cheap wine, talked about symbolism and James Joyce and listened to rhymeless and rhythmless musical experiments while friends talked about her poems capturing the essence of the human message.

They made love and slept on a bare mattress on the floor next to a rattling, feeble radiator. They ate at snack bars or, sometimes, from tin cans at home. They shared a cup of coffee at the corner pastry shop where they talked of many things, but not of plans for their future.

As escapees from the city—lonely urban refugees—they withdrew to the mountains and arrived at the epicenter of nowhere and stayed, giving themselves to each other with unconscious abandon. They were intoxicated by passion with no thought of consequence or retribution.

Often Zelda asked empty questions. For example, if the stones, the stars, the moon and the sun were in love with each other. She was the absolute antimatter—the catastrophic element every sane man feared. However, while she knelt before him in submission and seminal supplication, he forgot about the future. It was not directly in front of him, so it did not exist.

In the morning he would be a guilty spy as she bathed in the lake. He drank the sight of her beautiful nakedness. Tired from swimming she would lasciviously lay on the rocks, disturbing the jealous light of Venus.

Zelda.

For a month, it was the only meaningful word he spoke.

She usually slept sprawled on the bed as if crucified—with her right arm and right leg hanging over and her hair a black mist spread across her pillow.

Bedside, he knelt in the light of her reading lamp and touched her, beginning with immaterial hints and then working at her breasts until her pink nipples fought for freedom by pushing upward through the sheets. He stoked the chemical fire in her belly—pressing on her ovaries with warm, soft palms.

She woke when he climbed into bed. Her lips curled with vague, unfocused fright, trying defense at first, then reversing and thrumming under his heaviness. Panting until something broke in her; she screamed and pressed her body into his.

Afterwards, absorbed in drowsy reverie on the lumpy

mattress, they looked at the walls.

"Sometimes I don't know how to talk to you," he said.

"You could write to me. You are a writer."

So it was. Every night he wrote a page and she read it during their morning coffee.

At night, after they finished their coupling, calm replaced her limitless, unrestrained energy. They listened to music, drank wine and smoked cigarettes. With incapable, sated bodies, they tried to re-penetrate each other's souls, but retreated into unshared memories. For a long time, Zelda, fresh and beautiful, slept in peace like a baby, but it was the calm before the storm. He sat beside her while she slept—writing with mad fury and abandon. He knew, in the morning, she would read his work and they would talk about the end of the world.

"Having the courage to let go is the essence of true living," she said. "If you surrender to your heart, time's conquest is meaningless. That's when you lose—not just this or that, but everything. You slip into indifference and that is death's first victory."

As she spoke, he remembered one particular fall—with endless cold, windy and wet days. The pear tree in his yard fought against the season. Full of ripe pears, it refused to let go. Winter was denied. The tree taught him a lesson.

Anything in the world can hold on and win.

Unfortunately, love was different. Their last days, before Zelda disappeared, were stale and obscene. The golden living was gone—replaced by a poverty of gesture and affection. Even the last episodes of animal lust were a bad dream, a mistake. An annoying act of obligation.

Without her, he spent sleepless nights with boulders pressing on his skull. His fractured, scattered thoughts refused capture on paper. He realized Zelda took his best thoughts

271

when she left.

He was left with scraps.

Rootless, heartless woman. Woman I loved. You feared something bad would happen and it did. You will never know how and why I loved you with such bittersweet abandon.

Years passed.

Then he received a letter—without a return address.

He instantly recognized her handwriting.

> *Every time I think of you, my body responds. Heat invades me. My empty womb shivers and cries. All because of you.*

And he knew it.

You could bid farewell to cruelty, but it would never leave.

Notes on *Farewell, Fair Cruelty*

KLC: This might surprise you, but some people think you write pornography, partly because of Warren Adler's comment about *Ghost Words and other Echoes…*

Here's what he said about your work:

> *A true exploration of a woman's emotional and erotic life.*

Farewell is an example of one of your sexy stories, but there is nothing graphic about it. There is no explicit gynecology. However, there's no mistaking the nature of the interaction between the couple. How do you stay on the proper side of the line in communicating clearly about human sexuality without being crude or obscene?

AP: I never intended to dabble in erotica or anything like it. Besides, what exactly is pornographic literature? To me, that phrase is an oxymoron. The answer is complex and differs depending on the reader's interpretation.

I write as honestly as I can and I avoid gynecological details—not because they make me uncomfortable—but because I respect the power of words. I am mesmerized by the cathartic energy a turn of a phrase can release. Graphic description has its place, but in my work I treat sex as a character in the story. I approach it carefully—with the same candor and intimacy I do with everyone who lives in my invented worlds.

KLC: I describe some of your stories as parables. Often I think there are moral messages in your work, particularly for young girls. Are you mining your experiences to provide cautionary tales for young women?

AP: I could not think of my writing or my experiences as inspiration or accidental role models for anyone. The stories I wrote for my first book (*Ghost Words and other Echoes...*) packed a certain amount of naïve—albeit liberating—semantic. I escaped into modern fairy tales and sweet childhood remembrances; a world I can always return to—since it's now printed and captured in black on white. That gave me the courage—or rather the need—to be more courageous in my second round of stories and parables—to look at dysfunction, untamed love and loneliness straight in the face and let the reader take away what's suitable.

KLC: It's a cultural and historical fact that men exploit women. However, conversely, sometimes young women take advantage of men. In this story, it's unclear who is the victim and who is the aggressor. What can you say about this from your experience?

AP: I don't believe in stereotypical male aggression or stereotypical responses when women encounter male aggression. Whether for good or naught, and whether they use it or not, women have power over men. It's true that in any love story, one loses and the other wins, but it's never fully clear who the victim is. Like every war—the winner finds peace and avoids emotional abstinence.

KLC: Some of your phrases are infused with huge amounts of poetic resonance and imagery. The *sexual bazaar*, *zodiac of ephemeral time*, *love's heavenly glory* and *forgetful heart* are examples. It surprises me how your choice of a very few words can trigger deep and complex thoughts in the reader's mind. How intentional is this? In other words, is there a sort of mental calculus happening when you're writing or is it more a matter of words and phrases floating to the top of your mind during the creative process?

AP: I craft every phrase and word with a specific purpose. Like a small, insignificant creek becomes the mighty Mississippi River, I like my writing to start as a gentle trickle to the stream of consciousness and become splendorous in the immensity of an ocean of thoughts, ideas and memories. It's like Proust and his olfactory reverie around a freshly-baked madeleine; the words and overlapping references link to a literary world that helped me survive to my middle-aged years and carry my message into my stories.

KLC: You don't cater or talk down to the reader. For example, you could make your story more clear when you obliquely mention Dr. Freud or James Joyce or when you pick a name like Zelda (which, of course, draws us to think of Zelda Fitzgerald) or when you refuse to name the main male character in this story—allowing us to imagine Scott if we wish. We know you're talking about your own life—at the same time you reference autobiographical aspects of Scott and Zelda's lives. The reader doesn't have to figure all this out to get the heart of your message, but it's there if they care to pick up on it. How do you balance the flow of the story, the communication of your message and the deep background details which thrill the educated reader?

AP: I carry a secret fear that my constant references and quotes will pester or bore a reader to death. I hide my Machiavellian goal by luring and enticing the reader deeply into my story by planting extravagant detours through well-known gardens.

KLC: I think you tease the reader without mercy. For example, this story is an emotional roller coaster taking us from blissful high to low despair. The title gives away the punch line, but it's not clear until the end *who* is cruel and *who* is the victim, and then it's a reversal from the easy stereotype. I think it relates to your background as a visual artist; you adjust the angular perspective and splash this or that color to create the composition. In addition, some of the details are very real and vivid, but other parts are in soft focus and only hinted at. Am I right about the way you compose a project like this? Does it come from a painter's perspective?

AP: I never thought about it this way, but I suppose you are right. I start with a blank canvas and play with the hues until I have the picture I want.

275

Mesh

I'm always looking another direction while everyone else stumbles over the obvious. Nothing is clear until the end. Love, out of all things in life, likes to surprise, exalt, liberate and disappoint—all within a blink of an eye. As Bizet's Carmen sang from her heart:

L'amour est enfant de bohème
Il n'a jamais jamais connu de lois

[Love is a Bohemian child
It has never, ever known laws]

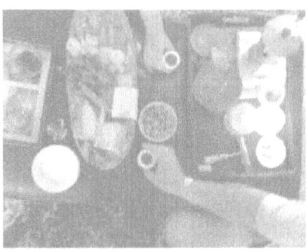

The Malevolent Dictators
Ken Coffman

KURT, WHILE WAITING for Josef to appear, fiddled with the sound level on his recorder. The twenty-seventh floor hotel room was lavish with fresh flowers in vases in every corner. Far below, city lights glittered. Josef's assistant, a large man nearly as broad as he was tall, came in and scanned the room with a handheld meter. He spoke into his headset.

"All clear, boss," he said.

Josef, also a very burly man, swept into the room. His hair was black—artificially black. Kurt had never been close before, so he didn't know if Josef wore a wig or dyed his hair. Kurt looked closely. Hair implants, dyed—excellent, expensive work by the surgeon.

No expense had been spared.

Kurt stood and extended his hand which Josef shook with firmness and vigor.

"Sit, sit," Josef said with a wide grin that showed off a mouthful of large, brilliant white teeth.

"How shall I address you, sir? May I call you Josef?"

"Calling me 'Father of the Peoples' or 'Glorious Leader of Progressive Mankind' would be very awkward, wouldn't it? Please call me Comrade Stalin. And I will call you Kurt. Our time is short—shall we begin?"

"Of course, Comrade Stalin," Kurt said. "I'd like to go back to the beginning. It was a stroke of genius on Trotsky's part to suggest putting aside your differences to start a death metal band. At the time, such a thing was inconceivable."

Josef laughed. "Yes. It's no secret I'd already sent instructions to an assassin in Mexico City when I received Leon's cable. It took a while for his suggestion to sink in. He had a vision of the decadence of the post-war West and how we could achieve *all* of our goals—and more—by combining heavy metal and punk. He was right. Completely right. And, he's a hell of a keyboard player too. No one nails industrial grind on a spinning Leslie and Hammond B-3 organ like he does."

"So, you immediately thought of the other players?"

"Yes, that's what made the idea come to life in my mind. I'd been jamming on and off with Nikita Khrushchev on bass and Vladimir Lenin on drums, but the idea of assembling a serious band was the last thing on my mind. The endless possibilities did not sink in until I got Comrade Trotsky's cable." Stalin laughed. "Fortunately, I was able to call off the assassin in time."

"Yes, that is indeed fortunate—for rock-n-roll history. Tell me about your first gig?"

"You probably mean the outdoor concert in Red Square. We played a few warm-up shows in small clubs. The songs were coming together nicely, so we scheduled our grand unveiling. We didn't want to *build* an audience—we wanted to start with a big splash. We raided the museums and what was left of the coffers in the Kremlin to finance a real spectacle."

"How did you get the Beatles to agree to open for you?"

"That was easy; we just threatened to kill their families— and cut off their legs." Josef chuckled. "Can you imagine if they had to shoot their famous Abbey Road photograph crossing the street in wheelchairs? With stumps for legs? That would have been something."

"Were you serious or was that just a ploy to get them to cooperate?"

"Oh, no, we were serious. We dispatched a dozen loyalists. They were going to use meat cleavers. It would have been an ugly mess. It was better for everyone that they signed the contract. We paid them one ruble each."

"That's a good deal. Four rubles for the Beatles at the height of their fame..."

"Well, we also had to pay for their meals and lodging—which added up to a lot more than four rubles, but that's—how do you say it?—water under the bridge?"

"Let's move forward. How did you get Ernesto Guevara to join up as your lead guitar player?"

"Of course, he was one of the premier players of the time. You couldn't mention Clapton, Hendrix, Jimmy Page or Jeff Beck without mentioning Che in the same breath. Wearing the green uniform and the beret—and with his revolutionary street cred? There was no one cooler. We had to have him. There was no other choice. And, from the first jam session, everyone knew we were onto something special. It was magical—he kicked his guitar playing into another dimension. It was good for everyone."

"From the beginning, you were more than just a rock band. You guys were trying to change the world."

"That goes back to Trotsky's insight. He saw a future where governments would have limited influence on a wealthy, fad-obsessed pop culture and that music was a great vehicle for progressive change. We owe a lot to him. Before him, no one else thought that way. He was absolutely right. We didn't have to put our jackboots on the necks of the people. All we had to do was raise our feet and play our guitars

Mesh

loud—and people would voluntarily put their necks beneath our boots. There is a deep, instinctual human need to serve their superiors."

"There's no denying your success. You sold more records than any other musical act in history. Combined. Beyond predicting and riding cultural trends, how do you account for your incredible achievement?"

"Well, when a competing act gets traction, we discourage them."

"Comrade Stalin, what do you mean when you say 'discourage'?"

"Well, for example, when John Kennedy picked up the guitar and brought on Marilyn Monroe as lead singer? That turned a few heads. They would have been a hundred times bigger than Sonny and Cher. I don't think I need to say anything more."

"You're suggesting…"

"I'm suggesting we move on to another question."

"Okay." Kurt looked over his notes. "Let's talk about your fans."

"The best people in the world."

"Right, but some criticize their violence against critics. Do you accept any responsibility for their murders and vicious attacks?"

"We can't control everyone in the world. If a critic says something hostile about us and a fan takes it upon himself to see to his…re-education…what can I do?"

"You could take a stand against violence. Denounce it."

"You're an amusing man, Kurt. Next question."

"Let's talk about your female fans."

"Aren't they beautiful? I love our groupies to death."

"That's the thing, Comrade Stalin; it seems like many of them *do* die from the mutilation."

"Mutilation? What you call mutilation they call a release from the slavery of the fads of beauty. These women come to us of their own free will and we release them from the bondage of societal norms—we make an important statement about what is attractive or desirable. I see them when they come to our show the following year—after the scars heal—and they are beautiful."

"You cut them up."

"They line up and beg me to work my artistry on their flesh. Are you being critical? You agreed to a—treatment—in exchange for this interview. It doesn't have to be a broken hand or a few broken ribs. We could get more creative. I'll grant you one last question, then we're done."

With a satin napkin plucked from the coffee table, Kurt dabbed at sweat on his brow.

"Comrade Stalin, my sister got your *treatment* last year..."

"Is she happy?"

"Yes, she's thrilled, but you cut off her..."

Stalin held up a massive palm to stop him.

"Okay, we're done," he said. "This is for a Rolling Stone special edition, right?"

"Of course, Comrade Stalin. A whole edition dedicated to nothing but The Malevolent Dictators."

"Okay." Stalin raised his voice. "Adam?"

The large aide poked his head in the room.

"Yes, sir," he said.

"Bust this guy up good—he's impertinent."

Kurt stood up.

"Thank you for your time, Comrade Stalin," he said.

"You're welcome," Stalin replied. He held up his hand and formed the rock-n-roll devil-horn gesture. "Rock on, brother," he said before sweeping out of the room.

Notes on *The Malevolent Dictators*

AP: I really enjoyed this delightful intellectual and social fantasy—and the way you mixed politics and pop culture. The cruelty of Marxism is deeply embedded in my family's history and our collective consciousness. First of all, let me ask this—where did the idea for this story come from?

KLC: If you look what influences our culture, you see there are a wild mix of factors. There are traditional influences, like government and religion, of course, but also television, social networking, movies—and music. The root of this story probably came from listening to proselytizing activists like Danny Glover, Sean Penn, Sting, Sheryl Crow and others. Ubiquitous, noisy media stars—people with the odd notion that success in the entertainment field qualifies them to be vocal advocates of this or that serious cause.

In addition, I was thinking of The Ramones playing at the fashionable Olympic Ballroom the first time they came to Seattle. It was a big deal for our little corner of the world. They played very simple two-minute songs. There was little musical talent on display. But, it didn't matter, because they represented a cultural movement. The music and their musical talent were irrelevant to what they were doing. In fact, if they had more skill, it would have detracted from their low-tech charm.

I touched on the idea of rock music as the motivating engine far beyond entertainment in my novel *Toxic Shock Syndrome*. This kind of thing is often on my mind.

AP: It is refreshing to read a story about Stalin that is funny, absurd and extremely imaginative when everything else bearing his name is dark and macabre.

KLC: I'm glad to hear you say that. With your family's history, I was worried you'd take offense at my silly and frivolous trivialization of a very ugly period of human history. How many people died under Stalin's reign? A hundred million? And here I am using these people in a ridiculous comedy piece.

One of my goals was insult the despots of history—to tarnish their memories by making fun of them. This is a classic Alinsky tactic turned back against the exploiters.

AP: I know you played in rock bands in your youth. Did that provide a foundation for your characterizations?

KLC: Sure. Music remains a big part of my life. Though I don't have the talent or dedication to achieve much, I still mess around in my recording studio in my spare time. I have a lot of musician friends and I get to enjoy their lives vicariously. I'm happy I don't have to deal with the vagaries of the marketplace—the brutal competition and the uncertain scramble to make a living.

AP: Kurt, who is he? Is that you?

KLC: No, I was thinking of Kurt Loder, the famous *Rolling Stone* interviewer, essayist and MTV personality.

AP: The names peppered throughout denote you did your reading about the characters who made history. What made you approach this story from this angle: Stalin meets the Addams family while waiting for Godot?

KLC: I was just playing with the personalities. For example, you see Che Guevara's image all over t-shirts and handbags.

He is a cultural icon far beyond anything he deserves. He was murderer and a thug, but that doesn't matter to the trendistas because he looks so stylish and cool in his beret. So, he's a natural candidate for my mythical rock band.

AP: Lastly, what would the music they played sound like? Did you have a sound in mind?

KLC: Yes, sure. Loud, thrashy punk-death-metal; a loud, rhythmic assault—like sticking your head in a jet engine.

Comedy
Adina Pelle

All I need to make a comedy is a park, a policeman and a pretty girl.
—Charles Chaplin

MANY MOONS AGO, I was a curious child walking around my hometown pursuing diversion and amusement. Endlessly, it seemed. Day-after-day.

One day in the town center, I noticed a vagabond sitting crossed-legged on the grass of the village green. He was lost in thought with his head supported by his dirty hands—staring at a point in space only of interest to him.

Contemplation, I noticed, manifested on his forehead and neck in the form of small beads of sweat. From time to time, he wiped these discharged thoughts with a dirty handkerchief—followed by a motionless posture for the next second or two.

Until a policeman came into the scene.

The officer spoke in a croaky voice. "What are you up to, bum?"

"Nothing, sir," the drifter replied respectfully. "I am sitting in the shade resting after a long day on the road. God bless you and your handsome hat."

"Cut the crap. Move on, you're ruining the grass."

The bum didn't move from the grass. Instead, he stared at the cop with a puzzled expression—as if the cop spoke with a foreign tongue.

"Did you hear what I said? Move. You're defacing the town's greenery."

Slowly, the bum stood and shuffled toward the sidewalk.

The cop rolled his eyes in exasperation.

"Not there, you'll get in everyone's way."

"Well, officer, nobody is on the sidewalk except this kid," replied the hobo.

He pointed at me with a filthy index finger.

"There are lots of people walking. Everywhere. If you continue talking back, I'll take you to the police station."

"What did I do wrong, officer?"

"Something. You did something and we'll find out what at the station, unless you walk away as I said."

The drifter responded, unafraid, but unwilling to tolerate the headache.

"Very well, officer. I'm out of here."

After the bum walked away, the cop winked at me and laughed. The laugh was a deep one emanating from the depths of his huge belly.

"Did you see how I scared him off?"

Impulsively, I spoke. "If you told him there was a snake in the grass, he would have fled immediately cuz' everyone is afraid of snakes, and you could have avoided aimless talk and wasted time. Blabbing goes hand in hand with stupidity and stupidity travels in the luggage of ignorant people, my dad says."

"Are you calling me stupid?" The cop said.

"Not exactly," I said.

The cop didn't buy it. He started toward me with his

hands raised.

I took off as fast as my little legs would carry me.

I reached the edge of the town square. There, the vagabond—now seeing the policeman running behind me—began running too. A car thief, working at the window of a shiny Jaguar sedan, saw our scamper and thought the cop was coming after him too.

The officer, with his hat clasped in his fat fist, ran after us—waving his baton furiously in the air. Soon, a stray dog scurried along with us. After fifty yards of huffing and puffing like a locomotive, the policeman stopped. He propped himself against the wall of a house with his face as white as a sheet of typing paper.

Eventually, an ambulance came and took him away. At the hospital, they performed tests and discovered a ragged hole in his heart.

Immediately, he was hauled to the operating room and attended by surgeons and nurses. After a few days of recovery—with rediscovered youthful vigor—he went home to his wife. As they had in her youth, her cheeks had reason to blush. She was happy.

These events started with a lost-in-thought bum bothering no one in the town's green center.

It was a valuable lesson I never forgot.

Notes on *Comedy*

KLC: Adina, you must admit this silly story is quite absurd...

AP: Of course it is. Have you forgotten who you're talking to?

I was asked once about what feeds my funny bone—early in my life I realized my life spins on a different axis than the majority. Frankly, I wouldn't have it any other way.

KLC: I don't really want to return to a painting analogy, but you start this story with very broad strokes, as if you're not even using an artist's brush—but a crude, sloppy, house-painting brush. The village green, a sweaty bum staring into space, a cop. As a writer, I realize you could add a lot more depth. It would be easy to describe the day and the town in much greater detail, but it would slow the story's pace and add unnecessary gravitas. This requires a lot of discipline. This is a lazy cliché, but it's true: sometimes less is more. How do you balance the trade-offs of intricacy and pace to strike an artistic balance for a story like this?

AP: I wanted only the kid and the other characters in focus. Imagine a soundtrack performed by an old, out of tune piano accompanied by the sound of a film reel spinning in the background.

KLC: The opening quotation brings us into the proper mindset very quickly. Was the quote something added later—or was it the inspiration for the story from the beginning?

AP: The Chaplin quote is where I started. A friend challenged me to a writing exercise—where the result was a new, spontaneous bit of flash fiction.

KLC: I'm curious about the allusion to old comedy movies. The chase scene brings to mind the Keystone Kops and comedy films from that era. As an adult or young adult in Europe, were you aware of these films? The reason I ask is because I find it hard to imagine you as an adult sitting down to watch old Chaplin or Buster Keaton films. I don't know how much exposure these films got in Europe—particularly the Eastern Europe of your childhood.

AP: I grew up watching endless old silent movies. Chaplin, Keaton, Errol Flynn (who made the best Barrymore in my opinion [in the 1958 film *Too Much, Too Soon*]). Even now, I still have a video library of old Chaplin classics: *The Kid*, *The Gold Rush*, etc.

KLC: The image of your mouthy, overly analytical kid amuses me. Except for the line about the happy wife which I'll mention later, this might be the funniest aspect of this silly comedy. The kid is a troublemaker. I know you were a rambunctious and troublesome teenager, but what were you like at the age of this kid, who I imagine to be about ten-years-old?

AP: I was shy and withdrawn at that age. There was no way I would have even raised my eyes from looking at the ground, but I spent a couple of summers with my cousin Dan who questioned and challenged all boundaries.

KLC: These two lines take about two seconds to read.

> *As they had in her youth, her cheeks had reason to blush. She was happy.*

I can't quite pinpoint why this is so amusing. I imagine the reader sliding by, then stopping and going back with the thought:

> *Wait, what did she just say?*

Is it safe to assume you're not talking about youthful vigor in weeding the garden or washing the dishes?

AP: Oh, I definitely composed that sentence to include sexual facetiousness. The author hides in the background as an observer throughout the entire brouhaha.

This little comment is the only time in the story where my unfiltered voice is heard. It's there to indulge myself with a slightly scornful, but jovial reason to smile.

KLC: You don't have to answer if you prefer to leave the undefined tutorial to the mind of the reader, but I think there are a few lessons you might be talking about. It can't be to leave an innocent bum in a park alone, because this tale has a happy ending—which came about from the cop's cruel harassment. What kind of lesson is that?

A lingering thought one might retain from this story is to always mess with authority when you can. What do you have to say about that, Adina?

AP: That's exactly it. When I was writing this story, beyond its historic, silent movie dynamic, I was thinking about how I always despised the police abusing their power and exaggerating their role in society's social chain. Adults deal with bigger and more complex issues when face-to-face with authority figures, so I saw the mouthy kid as the best focal point for the cartoon-like absurdity of the scene.

The Voodoo Lady
Ken Coffman

"SOMEONE NEEDS TO fire the voodoo lady," he said.

I was using nitric acid to etch plastic epoxy from the body of a failed integrated circuit. The chip was in a vented enclosure and I handled the tiny spray nozzle with heavy gloves that protruded into a glass-sided, hermetically sealed box. Scrubbing air filters hissed disapproval at the interruption.

"I promised to get a failure report done tomorrow. Don't come around here with your bullshit while I'm working. Besides, I can't fire Zonara. I have a PhD."

"She works for you. Besides, everyone in this lab has a PhD."

Avery was right—good, high-paying jobs in Maine are rare, so the company hired PhDs by the peck and bushel. Even the nighttime building maintenance guy (janitor) had a PhD, but his was in 17th century French Literature. You had to be careful not to make eye contact with him or suffer an hour-long lecture on Louis the Fourteenth, The Sun King.

Yes, I know Louisiana is named after the Sun King, thank you very much.

I shuddered at the thought of hearing about it again.

The chip I worked on was the size of a fleck of coarse-ground pepper, but it had caused the failure of a twenty-thousand-dollar multimedia server board. I focused on the microscope's high-resolution display and activated the joystick control that manipulated the probes on the tiny chip. I could sense Avery still behind me. He did not go away.

I pushed my lab chair back on its squeaky wheels.

"Yes, she reports to me, but that's a technicality. You slipped her across the bottom of the org chart when we reorganized."

"Marcus signed it."

He was right. Marcus, the company president, had signed it. This made the technicality a practical reality.

"She does good work."

"She does great work. The cumulative yield from her machine is fifty parts-per-million above the norm. That's not the issue."

"Then what is it?"

"She put a hex on the boron ion implanter."

"So what? You don't believe in that juju horseshit."

"The other ladies on the assembly and test line do. They are calling in sick and refusing to work in that part of the factory."

"Damn it." I removed my hands from the manipulator and rubbed my clammy palms together to restore circulation. "This does not have to be complicated. I'll transfer her to Crowder's department; he fires everybody."

"No." Avery shook his head. "She worked for him for about five minutes. He's the one who slipped her into *my* group. *You* have to do it."

"I'm a scientist, remember? I won an award for my paper on microstructural changes in ceramic substrates with ion and electron beam superprocessing."

"Try to get her out this week: we're behind schedule and need to step up production. Get it done and I'll buy you lunch, okay? Sarku Japan? Sushi, on me. Talk to you later."

The door seal hissed as he left.

Zonara waited for me in the Moose Crossing conference room. The official name of the room was Building One Conference Room 1C3, but some scoundrel mounted a yellow Moose Crossing sign near the intersecting corridors. The sign was long gone—purged prior to a visit from a wolf pack of investment bankers—but the nickname stuck.

Before entering, I watched her through a strip of glass set in the door. She fluffed her tangled hair with glossy fingernails. Her dark eyes matched a navy blue turtleneck sweater that covered her from wrist to neck to waist and hugged her shapely figure like a shadow. My hands sweated as I grasped the sheaf of paperwork. With written reprimands going back many years, there was no legal problem with her dismissal and I'd negotiated a generous severance package with the stuffed suits in H-R. If she waived her right to sue, then she'd get eighteen more monthly paychecks.

Someone should wave that deal in front of my face; I'd be all over it in a nanosecond.

She stirred a bundle of bones on the walnut table top and stared into them intently. They were too small to be quail bones, perhaps they were frog? I was idly curious, but I was not going to ask. When I entered the room, she swept her bones into a leather bag and slipped the cord around her neck.

"You're going to fire me," she said.

I settled in my chair and arranged the paperwork.

"We prefer to call it a reduction-in-force. I got you a year and a half with pay. Just sign the spots marked with an X and you can take a long, paid-in-full vacation."

Her eyes flicked at me as she scribbled on all the pages.

"I curse you."

I sighed. "Zonara, you aren't Haitian or Slovakian. You're a lapsed Mormon from Pocatello. Your real name is Susan Kelly."

She stood up and spat on the table. "Pah." With a thin finger, she peeled back her eyelid. "I put the evil eye on you."

She tried to slam the door but the pneumatic mechanism resisted. Through the narrow window, she redundantly pointed a finger toward her eye then at me.

Yes, the evil eye, I get it.

When I got home, my cat, Gallium Nitride, slept on the sprawled-open pages of a technical journal. The journal title was sexy: *The Materials Research Journal of Group III Nitride Semiconductor Technology.* Over breakfast, I'd been reading an interesting article titled *Topochemical Control of Solid State Conversion of Cyclotrigallazane into Nanocrystalline Gallium Nitride.*

Gall was critical of the discussion of polymeric solids; she'd left a yellow stain on the string of formulas. I aimed a kick at her but only succeeded in toppling a stack of magazines. *Applied Physics Letters* and *Electrochemical Proceedings* scattered everywhere. It would take half an hour to arrange them back in chronological order.

Damn it.

Unconcerned, Gall sat on a barren patch of carpet and licked her tail while I dabbed at the journal's yellow-stained pages with a paper towel.

There were too few hours in the day, yet I wasted precious time with cat pee and administrative overhead. There was no justice. Before I could get back to my research there was something I had to take care of. It took a moment—leaning back in my chair and thinking—before I remembered.

It's always something.

I moved a stepladder to access books high on a dusty shelf.

I ran my thumb over the spines until I found the one I was looking for. It was hidden between *Applied Crystallography* and *The Intuitive Guide to SubQuantum Entanglement*. The pages smelled musty; I stifled a sneeze. I'd inherited this particular book from my Uncle Gabor. It was more than a hundred years old. Fortunately, metaphysics does not evolve as fast as semiconductor physics, so old books are just as good (or better) than new ones.

I took the book to my desk and settled in my chair. It creaked on its springs as I leaned back and put my feet on the desk. Unconsciously, I lifted my coffee cup for a drink, but it was filled with fuzzy dried crud. No telling how long it had been sitting there. I flipped through the pages until I found what I was looking for.

Warding off the evil eye.

As I read the passages, my heart sank. This needed to get done right away, but where in the hell was I going to find the right eye of a hyena at this hour of the evening? Fortunately, a nice Azerbaijani family ran the Stop'n'Shop on Running Hill Road. They probably had a private supply of hyena eyes, both left and right. I read through to the end of the section. As an additional benefit, this potion would remove black energy from my blood. In my experience, one could never get rid of enough of the blood-borne dark energy.

Though I was tired after a long day at work, I couldn't put off this chore.

Gall, wary of my intentions, eyed me as I stepped over the talus of strewn journals and found my jacket and car keys.

"Stay off my desk while I'm running this errand," I said, waving a warning finger at her.

Do other cats know how to be insolent?

Mine does.

I flipped on the porch light and hurried out into the night.

295

The Stop'n'Shop parking lot was empty except for a sleek Corvette. There was no mistaking it; the license plate said PLANAR. It was Marcus, the company president.

What was he doing out this late at night?

I toyed with the idea of coming back later, but I saw him walk from the back of the store with a grease-soaked paper bag. The contents were soggy and heavy.

I heaved myself from the car and passed Marcus at the cash register.

"Hey, boss," I said. "What brings you out this late?"

He scanned the counter and grabbed a couple of snacks from a rack.

"MoonPies," he said.

"Can I take a peek in the bag?"

His face scrunched.

"Okay, you got me. Fresh aardvark entrails. Satisfied?"

I already knew, I could smell them.

He continued. "That Haitian we hired in government compliance last year? Turns out he's a Papa Ghede priest and was disappointed with his salary increase. He's turning *Les Invisibles* against me. You?"

"The Voodoo Lady gave me the evil eye."

"That's a tough one. Hey, we need to talk tomorrow. I think the ion implanter can go to a semi-annual calibration."

"Maybe," I said, "it all depends on the parametrics of the nickel silicide mesotaxy. I can review the data and see what can be done."

"Wait, the Voodoo Lady? I heard she put a hex on the boron ion implanter..."

"I heard that one too."

"It's nonsense, of course, but what do you think we could get for that machine if we sold it on eBay?"

"I can look into it."

"Yeah, why don't you do that. Well, I gotta…" he said, gesturing with the bag.

"I know, same here," I said. "I'll see you tomorrow."

"Yes, until then," he said. He lifted his bag of entrails. "Look, I'd appreciate it if you didn't say anything about this back at the factory."

"About what? We're just a couple of snack hounds buying late-night MoonPies."

"Precisely so," he said, nodding. "Precisely so."

I watched him get into his Corvette and drive away. I turned to the counter. Mr. Aysel smiled.

"How can I help you, sir?" he said.

"I need a fresh hyena eyeball. Right, not left."

His smile got deeper and broader.

"Then you've come to the right place, my friend," he said. Then he shook his head sadly. "Though the price this time of year…"

I was able to negotiate him down from grotesquely expensive to alarmingly outrageous before we shook hands on the transaction.

He was a nice guy and threw in two MoonPies to sweeten the deal.

With the little sack in my hand, I stood by the door.

"Goodnight, Mr. Aysel," I said.

"Goodnight, sir," he replied.

Notes on *The Voodoo Lady*

AP: Ken, this is another story I had to go back and read again a few times. My first thought, and you can snort if you like, is that this is one of the best satires written only for a select audience: engineers. Is that what you had in mind?

KLC: No. I wanted the technical and engineering details to be reasonably plausible, but I tried to write it so anyone could follow the storyline. I hope you don't have to be a scientist or technologist to understand the personalities and the story arc.

The story was embedded in my mind after a casual comment over dinner by my friend Karen Wespi. In the course of a conversation about odd historic events at the Fairchild Semiconductor factory in South Portland, Maine she idly mentioned they once had to fire a voodoo lady. That was enough to get my mind working over the possibilities.

AP: The story grabbed me. Looking back, I'm not sure what scared me more—the fact that I actually understood what you were talking about or the voodoo lady herself. That realization brings me to the most important fact: the story only *seems* highly technical, when in fact your craft as a writer smoothed the edges and made it entertaining. How do you pull that off?

KLC: By working at it and playing with the pace and the amount of arcane detail. I mix human character we can all relate to with complex ideas and terminology. I hope there are no big, dense chunks the reader will choke on and give up. I tried to make it light and fun and humorous but give the reader something to think about. Sometimes I succeed.

AP: Memorable lines like, "metaphysics does not evolve as fast as semiconductor physics" make this story one of my favorite ones. Your talent as a writer seems to battle against the engineer in you. Which is going to win?

KLC: First of all, there is no hard line between art and science. Artists and philosophers contribute a lot to defining what is humanly possible and the best technologists are artists in how they architect and implement their designs. There's no conflict between literary grace and style and inspired engineering.

But I understand what you're saying. For the final battle for my soul, the artistic side will win. Because, as I get older and my brain fails more and more, I hope to still be able to synthesize and capture interesting ideas in an entertaining and culturally valid way. It takes a certain amount of raw intellect to do engineering and I can see a day when my memory and acuity make me a poor engineer. At that point, I should be semi-retired and writing crazy stories and publishing, not designing sophisticated electronic products.

AP: Are there such publications as *The Materials Research Journal of Group III Nitride Semiconductor Technology* or *Topochemical Control of Solid State Conversion of Cyclotrigallazane into Nanocrystalline Gallium Nitride?* I love this strange specificity.

KLC: There may not be literal versions of these journals, but I assure you—there are much more exotic and esoteric ones out there. My imagination is vivid, but it can't create anything odder than the real world. When examined carefully, the details of our life on earth is far stranger than anything I could dream up.

AP: In this story, I see the juxtaposition of superstition against practical thinking as the major hook. Scientists guided by the irrational. We're in Dr. Frankenstein territory.

KLC: That's exactly what I was trying to illustrate. There's a famous quote by Arthur Clarke that has become a cliché, so I won't repeat it. But, it's true, the far advances of technology *are* like magic. It amuses me to mix plausible high technology with traditional superstition. At the fringes, both are equally silly. I don't see any limit to what we can and will do with microelectronics, sensors, energy, medicine, genetics, artificial intelligence (that's an oxymoron, isn't it?) and all the other advances of science.

That stuff is a lot weirder than hexes and hyena eyes.

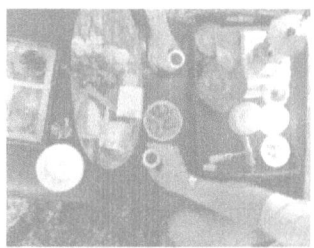

A Quick Fantasy about the Ingredients of the Soul
Adina Pelle

IMAGINE THIS: GABRIEL and Damien, each with a ladle in hand, lazily mixing souls in a cauldron.

"Do you think we have enough?"

"For the ones born today, I think it's enough," Damien said, "and there will be some leftover for tomorrow."

Their roles are simple—to mix up the ingredients for the souls born that day.

Gabriel favored compassion in his recipe; Damien laid in malice by the dollop. While Damien's back was turned, Gabriel added a spoonful of ambition. When Gabriel went down into the cellar, Damien tossed in a fistful of ego. And so on—measures of talent, tolerance, selflessness, laziness, spite, sloth, envy and greed.

Once mixed in the caldron, each ingredient has a distinct color, but as a rule, Gabriel's dishes are brighter and more eye-catching. Both a benefit and a fatal flaw, *intelligence* follows a different color rule, often making it indiscernible from the other ingredients. Combined with negative attributes, intelligence is often an unfortunate catalyst—frequently and unpredictably emphasizing the dark side of life.

As a result—in contrast to all other ingredients—

301

intelligence is mixed in small quantities and is rarely used in combination with intolerance or altruism. Hence the proverb:

Dumb, but good-hearted.

This is how things are done today, but there was a time long ago when things were done differently. Perhaps you've heard the story? Eternities ago, a crisis was born at the soul factory and nothing was ever the same again.

As the tale goes, the supreme power, let's call him or her or it "God", equipped the kitchen pantry with equal stores of ingredients: the affirmative and the unfavorable.

Then, when no one watched (except God, of course, but who knows God's intent in this drama?), Damien exercised his evil genius and overstocked negative ingredients—disturbing the human stew's proper, delicate balance. Then, he feigned interest in Atlantis, the continent housing most of the world's population at the time—hyper-inflating its value.

Convinced of its worth, Gabriel, in a fever of speculation, purchased the obsolete continent—falling for the oldest trick of financial shenanigans. At first, all was well. The people of Atlantis became the spitting image of perfection—though, deep inside, the caldron's ingredients were unbalanced.

For a time, the unconstructive and damaging elements were hidden away.

Arts and sciences peaked at unprecedented heights on the fortunate continent. To all, it appeared the Earth hosted a perfect utopia.

Then one day, according to the plan, while Gabriel napped, Damien sank the continent. The invested effort was lost in the deep, cold waters of the ocean.

The repercussions were endless. How rarely reason prevails over madness, for example, very few understand. This comes from the fateful day when Atlantis was eaten by the sea.

Now, Gabriel's eternal hope is that the fusion of

ingredients will make people chose kindness over malice. With new tactics and ladles of luck, the rebirth of perfection is Gabriel's ever-constant goal.

Damien remains amused by the optimism of his nemesis. Deep down he knows the fruit of genius is not just joy, but crime and war and evil too. He pretends not to notice when Gabriel tries and tries to fix the mix.

"Perhaps, my friend, we'll add just a little dash of piety along with the hope and change," Gabriel suggested.

"Yes," said Damien, "with a pinch of sour covetousness to balance the sweetness."

And so the afternoons go in God's steamy kitchen.

Notes on *A Quick Fantasy about the Ingredients of the Soul*

KLC: The names Damien and Gabriel are interesting selections. What were you thinking when you named these characters?

AP: Though I am not religious by any stretch of imagination, I always love a good story. The biblical accounts are action-packed and filled with intrigue—they have everything: lust, revenge, greed and gluttony. What more can you wish for in a story?

By legend, Gabriel is the gatekeeper. Damien is a word game, a mix of Damned and Omen. I watched the antichrist movies and it amuses me that the antichrist (I cannot believe I am using that word) is always some pretty boy with a smooth name.

Sometimes I imagine myself arriving at the Pearly Gates and causing a total ruckus—confusing everyone like I did throughout my life.

KLC: It seems like the personalities could easily have been reversed with Damien the more innocent and positive person and vice versa—why did you assign them the way you did?

AP: Personalities? In this story, I worked on the perpetual struggle I always face. To do well, excel and be special. The lines between the competing parts of our essence are often shady. Can you be special when mediocrity is the common denominator? Can you be unique when seeking integration—the acceptance of the crowd? If you succeed, you're simply average. Gabriel would like to *be* Damien one day, but he is too timid and naïve. Damien is a practical man who does not stop to analyze silly scenarios.

KLC: The idea of two rivals mixing up souls is playful and childlike—which is a tone you take for many of your stories. Does the initial thought about this story come from a childhood thought or experience?

AP: The idea of souls in a caldron being stirred by delusional characters is strongly based on what I have observed—what I think other people believe. I am not making a mockery of the common belief in a greater power that controls our destinies. But, on the other hand I enjoy tweaking Judeo-Christian mythology. Personally, I put my faith in a black and white reality. In my writing, I attempt to give purpose to that which looks wacky, unfair or random. I was brought up against the current. Think of Nietzsche's intimate candor; God is dead, so we should move on. I always like exploring this theme.

KLC: Atlantis is another interesting creative choice because of the resonance of the legend of the lost island. In addition, you sometimes use Atlantis as an Internet name, so, clearly, there is some special significance to the legend in your mind. Does this go back to your childhood in Eastern Europe or are your thoughts about Atlantis from later in your life with a more western correlation?

AP: Atlantis is a fictional space for most people, but for me it is a place where I can escape from reality. I like the myth of Atlantis—beautiful people and perfect lives sunk without a trace. Greek mythology is mirrored in Atlantis where the Gods lived among the mortals. Plato dangled the idea in front of the Athenians and they were intrigued. So am I—ever since I read Plato all those many years ago.

KLC: There are quirky ties to modern events in this story, which is a creative—and frankly brilliant—aspect to much of your work. In this case, I'm thinking of the mad real estate speculation which ties into the market meltdown we're still struggling to escape. You feel no need to solidly set your stories in one historical period. What inspires you to mix current events with your playful revisiting of ancient myth?

AP: After an astonishing amount of reading, especially history, I'm convinced age is not chronological or geographical. Age is a philosophical concept. History repeats itself over and over and will do so again.

When I was twelve or fourteen, my mother (who was a history teacher before retiring a couple of years ago) had to pass some accreditation with professional tests required by the school system in Romania. I offered to help. I held her history books and verified her answers to all the practice tests she studied. There was a full summer where I did only that...

So, why do my thoughts about history and current events mix? How could they not?

305

The Flower
Ken Coffman

KEN STOOD ON his deck sipping a cup of organic French roast coffee. The barista knew better, but his eight-ounce cup was filled with seven ounces. He always asked for six ounces and explained the situation over and over.

"Lactose is not exactly my friend. I get cramps and gas. Need I say more? And soymilk tastes like transmission fluid, so that's not an option. I can tolerate six ounces, no more."

Weren't the tips big enough? Would his suburban nightmare never end?

What?

Ken squinted. Did his eyes deceive him? In the corner of the yard, hidden by an ornamental patch of boxwood...

It appeared the gardener missed a dandelion. In a gentle breeze, the lurid yellow blossom nodded and mocked.

Intolerable.

He put his coffee down and stomped to the garage to locate utility gloves, garden clogs and a spade.

You have to dig deep into the root system or the dandelion comes back. Everyone knows this.

He stood over the offending weed with his foot on the spade.

"I wouldn't."

Ken turned. It was his neighbor Vasili—who spoke in a

306

thick Romanian accent.

"Excuse me?" Ken said.

"You should always leave one to please the desire of nature."

Ken turned with exasperation written on his face. He waved the spade around his yard.

"Look, you old fool. My yard is perfect except for this god-blasted frickin' weed. I don't tell you how to take care of your—yard." It was painful, but Ken looked over his neighbor's faux pas of landscape. "What are you growing? A briar patch? What's this stuff with the flowers and thorns and—what's this? Mushrooms?"

"The flowers are Syrian Rue Peganum harmala."

"What?"

"We call them steppenraute."

"I don't care what you call them as long as they stay on your side of the line."

Ken paid a surveyor thirty-three hundred dollars to mark the property line to an accuracy of one centimeter. White stakes and rebar were pounded in the ground every ten feet.

"If you leave a weed, the blemish accents perfection. Know? Like a beauty mark on an actress? See? Then, sometimes the earth mother will pass you by when she's angry."

"Know? See? Nonsense," Ken said.

He stabbed the spade deep into the earth and uprooted the dandelion. After shaking soil from the root, he tossed it on the sidewalk and tamped dirt into the hole. Soon, he was satisfied.

He walked over, picked up the wilting dandelion and waved it at Vasili.

"See? Dead. It's nothing."

Vasili shrugged. "You're right. It's nothing," he said.

Ken walked to his garbage can to dispose of the weed.

Across the yard, Vasili whispered.
"Or everything."

Notes on *The Flower*

AP: The idea that Mother Nature needs to be appeased is an old one in Romanian folklore. Peasants work their land as if it's not theirs but borrowed from the ever-so-benevolent Mother.

KLC: I'm making fun of western materialism.

AP: What do you think about nature? How do you relate to it?

KLC: I grew up in the outdoors and felt connected with woods, meadows, creeks and wildlife. However, as I get older, I value my personal comfort more and more. I can live rough if I want—it wasn't that long ago that we enjoyed outdoor plumbing and no running water—though enjoyed is not a precise or exact word to use. 1988-1994. Oh boy. I just want a fire to warm my bones and a comfortable chair to sit in while reading a good book.

Like everything in life—my relationship with nature is mixed. I appreciate snow-capped mountains, but Mother Nature has a nasty temper. Turn your back for an instant and she'll drown you in a flood or tear you to pieces in a tornado. Think of all the hazards of nature: earthquakes, pestilence, disease, volcanoes, tsunamis, meteorites. The list of things to worry about is endless.

I remember watching a speech by Sallie Baliunas[15] on YouTube where she mentions a storm front that dropped a

---

[15] http://www.youtube.com/watch?v=8C1CKKhN7ng

meter of hail on central Germany on May 24, 1626—this was followed by a severe cold snap that destroyed crops and caused terrible destruction. To forget how nasty Mother Nature can get seems like a terrible error to me.

AP: Earlier, you mentioned that you grew up in Oregon. Which part? Rural or urban?

KLC: Eagle Point in southern Oregon could hardly be more rural—and it was a six-mile walk (which I did many times) to get to Eagle Point from my house.

AP: I don't know him well, but I like Vasili.

> Vasili shrugged. "You're right. It's nothing," he said.
> Ken walked to his garbage can to dispose of the weed.
> Across the yard, Vasili whispered.
> "Or everything."

KLC: Thank you. Sometimes I accidentally stumble across an interesting thought.

AP: How about a Romanian proverb?

> Without weeds, there is no garden.

KLC: Well said.

AP: Here's an example of how assorted, for lack of better word, my upbringing was. This is a Jewish proverb:

> Ask about your neighbors, then buy the house.

And here is a Romanian one:

Fear keeps the garden better than the gardener.

KLC: You'll have to explain the second one—I'm not with you.

AP: They are poorly—word-for-word—translated. The gist is the Romanian peasant bears the fear of God in everything he does, including gardening—whereas the Jew is only interested in the sale, not the garden.

As I think about this, the proverb ties into our conversation about stereotypes, doesn't it?

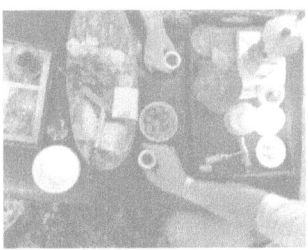

The Poet has Many Lovers
Adina Pelle

The long sobs of the violins of autumn
Lay waste to my heart with monotone boredom
—Paul Verlaine, *Chanson d'Automne*

"Father Fyodor," said the deacon, while tilting his head to one side and pressing his hand to his heart. "I am an uneducated, slow-witted man, while the Lord entrusted you with judgment and wisdom. You know and understand everything. You master anything, while I know not how to put my words together sensibly. Be kind, sir. Tell me how to write a letter. Teach me what to say and how to say it...."

"What is there to teach? There is nothing to teach. Sit down and write."
—Anton Chekhov, *The Letter*

One

ON THIS MORNING, Karl is displeased.

Ruthless light attacks his eyelids and scares him when he tries to open his eyes. He suspects reality to be like a boring novel—an obsolete, archaic novel filled with dull details no one cares about.

Sleep: a slumber fortress.

His sanctuary from life's cruel, day-to-day reality.

The night had not left him. He was in an unstable state of nonequilibrium. Though every affirmation finds its terminal denial, his path to balance was unknown.

Morning light blasts through cracked windows—the porous walls provide no barrier against the marauding music of a magical violin. On the street below his window, heavy-breathing, club-foot people march to and fro on the sidewalks. In cold morning air and trampled silence, the rattletrap world wakes and chases away the dream world.

His room smells like dead ashes, his fermenting body and vodka. The simple task of getting out of bed exhausts him. Stingy light, like fine threads of candlewax, slides across his dusty books.

He makes a solemn promise.

Today will be different.

His bladder makes urgent demands—he is forced to rise and face the day. In the bathroom, he splashes cold water on his face.

The day before, he'd written line after line of unconscious poetry while smoking ceaseless cigarettes. Then he found himself at a bar where women with soft bodies and hard hearts palmed his money and laughed at his quips. It was dawdled time in the preordained theater of wasted life and artificial love—like a Wagnerian opera with Isolda's legendary time expired.

Examined in the morning light, he was fascinated by the dream of a new life—a life where he was unchained—bearing a fresh name and a different mask. Naked, he sat at his writing table and wrote a letter to the mad, deceased poet Verlaine.

To think—Verlaine could accuse me of plagiarism?
He smiled.

All transformations—coming or going—that were easy and comfortable in his youth now scared him. The fear fed words, which found their home on the paper.

Yes...I want stillness. Motionlessness is what I prefer.

Tomorrow, tomorrow with no more eternal delay.

The spring aroma of sycamores crawl through the walls; everywhere but his room which remains the same—dank and saturated with the smell of moldy books.

He lives in a condemned, falling-down building but is untroubled by it. He is a natural part of this community's body of artists and their clearly-defined hierarchy. Collective intimacies and dependencies are like a morphine addiction.

Under all circumstances, Karl emits indifference.

Ulm is his neighbor—a painter in a stereotypical too-long black poncho and black hat—wearing round glasses over his swimming eyes. Karl needs not hear Ulm to feel his presence; he knows him without ever seeing, building an image with an artist's imagination, bearing the footprint of a world bathed in random shades.

One day Karl spoke to Ulm.

"I am impressed with your hands," he said.

He referred to Ulm's paintings, but the words fell like useless spring rain on red clay tiles. Once, they shared a lover, Lascia, and her portrait divided the dark corners of their minds.

"I know how to reach inside every woman and outline her form to give her volume, finesse, and an unmistakable, triumphant lasciviousness," Ulm proclaimed proudly.

Karl's thoughts ran rampant, but he remained silent.

To paint on a piece of canvas is easy. To paint on—in—the body of a woman with teeth—wild, hungry wolf's teeth—represents a conquest and triumph over life.

He had no reasonable motivation for hating Ulm for seducing Lascia. Unfortunately, the illusion of love for Lascia filled every thought. They met in parks. Then, sometimes he walked her home and other times they stopped at a restaurant where he gulped fortifying glasses of vodka. On these nights, he was overfilled with joy. Her eyes were alive—large, green and wild. He squeezed words from his heart and wrote daily letters, but never mailed them. Instead, he handed them over like Chekhovian secrets—with urgent whispers.

Here is the seagull—I killed my heart, it bleeds.
Take it with you, it belongs to me no more.

He hoped one day she would look into his eyes and say yes, I love you.

Instead he accepts a solitary life alone—a life of useless dreams and desolation. The ocean is a heavy blanket under the cruel sky—with clouds driven by malicious winds.

Spring dwells in me even if this is the end of the world.
If I had one wish?

That love was more kind.

Two

LATELY, KARL SLEPT with the lights on—with a finger stuck between the pages of his book. He had returned to his habit of spending his nights alone. This way, in the morning, there was no white leg draped over his—offending the morning by exposing flesh and blue veins from under the rough blanket.

He woke thinking he was a character in a Kafka story—created from the thin, stale air of the morning. He felt dumbfound, suffocated and convinced that one day he would experience a weird metamorphosis. This madness occupied every conscious moment and bothered him every day. He felt ragged and half-alive with blood as dry as chalk dust.

Occurrences, it seemed, had no logic. Instead, they happened by accident. Looking for a fulcrum in his fast-passing thoughts and recollections, Karl felt the thin memories of women passing through his life; how fleeting were the images that remained imprinted on his corneas.

Fifteen years prior, he was in Switzerland in self-imposed exile. In the central park of the castle, while lying stretched on a blanket white as a cloud, he dreamed of naked women coming from the gardens and sidewalk stones—with slender shadows lingering gracefully on the walls of the palace.

One in particular.

He noticed her ankles first—then long legs under a flapping dress—left naked with each breeze.

What could I say?

Should I start by asking for her name?

"Wie heißt du?"

She smiled faintly without engaging his eyes and did not answer. This arrogant Teutonic woman with unveiled legs. Green grass framed her fecund thighs. Karl imagined her vagina as a slot splitting the heavens—holding both the nativity and disintegration of the world.

Woman is an extended God men follow.

He thought back to an earlier time.

Usually the male is dominant, confident, proud, and gallant, but in Karl's life, everything was reversed. Every woman he had a relationship with became abusive and showed her malevolent inner shape. Every time, the game led to his broken ego and mewling indignity.

The beautiful Amazon on the grounds of the old castle caught him in her web—he crawled like a snake into her blood. All doubts of his troubled mind melted under her gaze.

One sticky night, he saw her on the street holding another man's arm. That night he locked himself in his room and worried at his imagination like a puppy tearing at an expensive shoe. In his dreams, he lost another battle and took back a flayed heart in return.

He got drunk and wallowed in sadness. She'd promised him nothing and not even rejected him.

He whispered to himself about the futile love of his heart.

Ich liebe dich ganz Leben fur.

The words were eaten by the wind and he got nothing in return.

Liandra

REGULAR DAYS PINCHED Karl—not pleasantly, but in an annoying, good-for-nothing way.

He lies in his bed every morning and wishes for a visit from his benevolent muse but winds up feeling like a fool moving a blunt pencil across a piece of paper and realizing he cannot connect two words.

I am not sleeping; I am dreaming.

Last night's dream had something to do with his hands and shoulders growing ostrich feathers—morphing in a homemade, primitive underachieving parody of the proverbial Icarus. There was no sun in his dream; instead, he felt sheets of cold rain on his skin like a frigid ocean wave. Borne on the winds of this sad dream, his inadequacies, memories, and insecurities suddenly became clear. He expected to wake up wet, but instead was dry—with eyes blinking at the white ceiling while a morning breeze riffled and teased a blank piece of paper on his desk.

Awake and tormented—or rather challenged—by the need to link words in sentences and rhymes, Karl thought

316

about Liandra instead. Long ago, she'd borrowed his thoughts and never returned them.

Passive Liandra, looking at him with impertinence in her eyes.

Liandra, is that you?

Usually she did not reply. On some days, she came forth naturally like the morning light. On other days she devised a reason, like picking up one of her belongings—an object she left deliberately behind. One day she left a hair clip on the bedside table. On another day she left a silk stocking and cutout gloves of her stepmother's mother. These odd habits—together with her love for Karl—were equal parts of her anxiety and comfort.

Naked, she walked into Karl's room wearing only a scent of apples, oblivious to anything resembling reality. She floated like a blaze through the rooms, bringing all the light around herself.

Karl asked for nothing, watching her for as long as he could until the door closed behind her young shadow. He watched her fire passing first through his space and later felt it burning his flesh.

"As of today I have no need for myself," she whispered. "I am all yours, living through you. Do not forget."

Liandra had three sisters. Matia, the oldest, committed suicide. It is said they came from a dysfunctional family with an alcoholic father and a mother who abandoned them when they were very young. The girls were helped by men who wanted a woman for the night, a week or a year, but never forever.

In her presence, Karl was overwhelmed and scared. He had a fervent fear that reality could be only a dream; a fantasy of women who teased him and wrecked his life. He made love to her as if she was a virgin and an angel, fragile and pure of soul.

She left him one hot summer day, but Karl remembered how the room walls felt frozen and the windows icy. Since Liandra left, he left open the door to his room. From the hallway, his table in the middle of the room, two chairs with three legs carved from linden wood and a huge chest where he keeps his clothes could be seen. In the other room, the bed and the mountain of moldy books. He was the king of despair.

He found an address for her and he wrote a letter. Her husband sent him back a message.

Liandra hung herself last spring.

God rest her soul.

End

KARL HATED THE uncertainty of his past, present and future, though he was used to its presence. Life, lately, felt like a finicky concubine starting to ignore him.

In the days to come, he sold or gave away most of his furniture. Every time he looked at his writing table, exhaustion dissolved his spirit. Like a gourmand after a big meal, he was drowsy—drained and bloated with despair.

I want to stop.

I do not want to take another false step.

I am afraid to stir the air in the room. The celestial poker game is over and God collects his winnings—carefully placing the cards in their box and throwing them in the drawer until the next game.

The sight of his books choked him. For the first time, the moldy paper smelled terrible.

Air, more air, absorbed the stale odor of his writing which was trapped in forgotten history. The past intruded on his words without his knowledge and resulted in a delayed disruption of his inner self making him feel caged, the same way every woman made him feel in his youth.

Shy and lonely and trapped in his memories, he was afraid of wide-open spaces. He searched each memory with a clear mind and closed it in his own defined space. There was nothing to write about anymore.

Write about what?

The many nights he loved? The memories were arranged in time on a path through his lifelong resignation and surrender to women.

When Ulm knocked at his door, they deflowered a few bottles and emptied them quickly.

Now sight of the empty bottles, lined up like naked courtesans in front of the Athenians filled Karl with a terrible anguish.

Ulm, good old Ulm, looks towards the windows and Karl is suddenly expecting the glass to shatter from the intensity of his stare. Instead, silence takes a seat between them with legs crossed like a cultured woman.

Finally, while wet morning light slithered under the door, Karl grabbed an old notebook and wrote feverishly.

Today, Karl, the great writer, holds onto the past because he is afraid he will collapse numbly into the future.

He was pleased with how graceful—soft as cotton candy—his words sat on the page. He carried on with his scribbling.

Unique poetry is drawn from the soul; prose from experience.

He looked at Ulm and asked his question as if the painter could hear his thoughts.

"Did you know this, my dear old friend? Liandra, ten-years-ago—before she hung herself—gave birth to a child." Karl continued, "but the child came out purple like an eggplant—a soft, indigo-colored blob of flesh. They quickly wrapped and buried the baby in a lonely wooden box. A white box."

The baby looked like Karl, they say, and every time Karl thought about him, he dreamed of how this child could have written poetry so beautiful that words written by other poets struggled unsuccessfully to escape the chambers of their minds like blind sparrows captured in a cage. Maybe God hears the child breathing in the labyrinth of the past. His father did not know when he came or where he went, and now feared the child eternally asked his mother two soul-wrenching questions.

"Where is my father? Why did he forsake me?"

Crazy women, eager to see him in his drunken, free-spending haze, appeared in Karl's mind smelling of their past. Misunderstood, peeling images of memory overlapped each another until they all appeared clear in his mind.

He looked for peace, but the years were a deep hole making a prison of his writing table where he spun tales and talked to the pagan ghosts of women embedded in the walls of his room. These spirits were accepting, deeply embracing creatures concerned only with their shadows. Only *they* knew how to proceed without disturbing the quivering harmony Karl created while locked in his vertical fortifications.

Even so, when the gray women hidden in his walls ran to the harbor to welcome the sailors, he was intoxicated by their aroma. Loving them desperately and seeing them so clearly, he looked past their lack of sophistication to restore and repair their virginal integrity upon their return. Their inner light was like the freshly undressed shape of a mythological water nymph.

They intruded and lived everywhere. From the tip of his tongue buried deep in the fragrant night between their thighs, to his feelings, thoughts and sensory trances, through the salty taste of blood hidden in his rough beard that grew in wild tangles on his weary face.

A ripped and ragged silk stocking replaced an entire philosophy. Painstaking, intricately developed pictures of wonderful faces became madness, restlessness and the ugliness of today, tomorrow and forever.

Liandra left before he knew her, so he must forget her. He dared not touch the face Lascia painted on the small canvas. Instead, he placed it between books on his memory's dusty sill.

Penelope, the Greek woman as he imagined her, never protested. Instead, she was amused by his fruitless antics. A delicate rosiness lived on her olive skin and prominent cheekbones. Almond-shaped eyes with irises like two huge black cherries focused on him. She smiled like a child receiving a desired toy.

She seemed a lot like a desperate woman ready to seize on anyone to prove the power of her enticement. The kind of mentally unbalanced woman that offers herself unconditionally, only to watch black energy invade men's bodies, completing a desire to dominate and trample men under their feet.

From the first night, they fit together well. So well that for the very first time in his life, he felt relaxed. He discovered and experienced all sorts of things in Penelope. For example, in one club they found a room called simply The Dark Room—a special place for those who wanted to fuck with no strings attached. Dark inside, no one talked or knew who their partner was. However, for he and Penelope, The Dark Room meant something else—it represented a method of recognition. In complete darkness, they found each other. It was very exciting. And the most amazing fact was: they always ended up together.

Maybe destiny is a wine that fills a glass. You drink one and then another, until you are drunk and fall sleep in a ditch—a ditch so vast that if you look down from afar you see

321

it is a line in the palm of someone larger than you are—
someone with a name you can never remember.

Memory is like a vortex sucking at his life while he seeks
meaning. He is awake to the foreign eye and enjoys a cigarette
with greed while remembering fondly his old neighborhood
with streets shaded by linden trees in the summer.

Poets of yesteryear are still here but what about him?

What of the new geniuses of our age?

Notes on *The Poet has Many Lovers*

KLC: At three-thousand words, this is one of your longer
pieces. We've talked about this before and you've told me
many times that long forms like novels and novellas are not
your forte. If you can pull together three-thousand words, why
don't you think you'd be successful with longer tales?

AP: This piece is—without a doubt—an homage to poetry,
specifically French poetry. I secretly fantasized about taking
this train of thought deeper into my mental frontier. I get lost
in poetry like a child in a candy store.

> *There exist only three beings worthy of respect: the
> priest, the soldier, the poet. To know, to kill, to
> create.*
> —Charles Baudelaire

KLC: This story strikes me as an example of a classic,
European style. Can we talk for a minute about other classics
and how they influenced your thinking and your work?

> *The candle-end had long been burning out in the bent
> candlestick, casting a dim light in this destitute room*

upon the murderer and the harlot strangely come together over the reading of the eternal book.
—Fyodor Dostoevsky, *Crime and Punishment*

In what language did you originally read the Russian classics?

AP: My parents and grandparents spoke Russian in our home, so I grew up with it from the cradle. It was a special treat to read the Russian bards in their native language and I must say, Tolstoy's Natasha will never sound believable or even remotely interesting when translated into an Anglo-Saxon dialog. The Russian language has sounds irreproducible in any other language, particularly Teutonic ones.

KLC: How about some Nabokov?

Her death saved me from insanity. Plain human grief filled my life so completely that there was no room left for any other emotion. But time flows, and her image within me becomes ever more perfect, ever more lifeless. The details of the past, the live little memories, fade imperceptibly, go out one by one, or in twos and threes, the way lights go out, now here now there, in the windows of a house where people are falling asleep. And I know that my brain is doomed, that the terror I experienced once, the helpless fear of existing, will sometimes overtake me again, and that then there will be no salvation.

—Vladimir Nabokov, *The Terror*

Comments?

AP: Nabokov came later in my life. I came to appreciate his subtle cynicism and caustic voice when older and over-exposed

323

to life's irony and society's paradoxes.

KLC: How about one more? This quote is inspired by your passage:

> He suspects reality to be like a boring novel—an obsolete, archaic novel filled with dull details no one cares about.

Would you say *Moby-Dick* is the quintessential example of what you were thinking of?

> Be it said, that though I had felt such a strong repugnance to his smoking in the bed the night before, yet see how elastic our stiff prejudices grow when love once comes to bend them. For now I liked nothing better than to have Queequeg smoking by me, even in bed, because he seemed to be full of such serene household joy then.
> —Herman Melville, *Moby-Dick*

AP: Absolutely. *Boredom*, like its evil twin *excitement* is truly relative. They can't exist without contrast with each other. What's riveting to one bores others to tears.

KLC: You don't draw extra attention to your prettiest and most eloquent descriptions. Are you expecting the reader to stop to savor these passages or are you hoping they will slip unnoticed into the subconscious and build a general and delicate esthetic effect?

> In cold morning air and trampled silence, the rattletrap world wakes and chases away the dream

world.

Then he found himself at a bar where women with soft bodies and hard hearts palmed his money and laughed at his quips.

He felt ragged and half-alive with blood as dry as chalk dust.

AP: I consider these perfectly self-indulgent examples of selfishness in my writing. I enjoy poetic flourishes like these so much that I can't think about anything else. I become a literary narcissistic monster. My own words carry me into a drunken stupor.

KLC: You have a nonlinear style that keeps the reader on his or her toes. Do you ever worry about asking too much of the reader?

AP: There are times when I am smitten with my own words and I ignore anything external. It's hard enough to please myself; I can't worry so much about the beloved reader. I need them and love them, but if they are satisfied with simple, linear stories, they can gorge themselves on the disposable work of others. There's plenty of it out there for them to consume.

KLC: This story contains more graphic gynecological anatomy than any other of your stories. We have mutual friends who write erotic fiction and apparently they sell a lot of it. I'm not sure who reads this stuff—lonely, neglected housewives, I suppose. Clearly you could, if you wished, write steamy, kinky stories to appeal to this audience. Can we expect you to move into this genre real soon now?

AP: No, not intentionally. I let myself be driven by the moment. I could write erotica—pages filled with genitalia in various combinations, but that's not my calling.

KLC: My sense of Karl is that he's an inept and hopeless poet. Did you mean to imply he has some skill?

AP: No, I envisioned Karl as a weak link—the literary equivalent of a premature ejaculator—powerless to please any ladies.

KLC: Perhaps I'm simply an oddball, but I know how stories are gestated and built and there is at least one novel embedded in this story—the theme I'm thinking of relates to the gray, ghostly women who live in the poet's walls. What do you think?

AP: Absolutely. Secretly, I dream big. Perhaps I *will* grab the reins of this story and drive it further into the night.
 Someday.

Open Season on Tubby
Ken Coffman

HUGH GRAYSON HAD a keen eye for the way they moved. He wasn't seriously on a hunt, but believed in being ready in case opportunity smiled. At the corner of Broadway and 27th on Capitol Hill, he caught a glimpse of a massive something slipping between a cargo van and a newspaper stand. He unslung his 30-06 rifle and peered though the 10X scope. They were supposed to wear a black armband on their right arm if they had a doctor's pass or were in a government-approved weight-reduction program. Hugh looked carefully—he needed to be sure.

No armband.

Now the question was: would this tub of lard weigh in at more than three-hundred pounds? It could be a two-hundred-and-eighty pounder dressed against the misty cold in thick layers of clothing, and that would be murder. Then, another sob-story about mistaken prey—followed by endless court appearances, public outrage, crusading reporters and civil liberties lawyers, newspaper stories, a spike in talk-radio ratings followed by fines, penalties and jail time. Not to mention discredit brought on the hunters.

It was necessary to err on the side of caution.

On the other hand, the chubs were often driven to slip in and out of convenience stores and fast food joints to feed their

327

relentless hunger. They had to eat. A lot. So, sometimes they took chances.

He decided. The game was fair. While keeping the prey in his sights, Hugh slipped around parked Subarus and Priuses until the shot was clear. Knowing they sometimes wore body armor, he took his time and waited for a clean headshot. The rifle's crack echoed down the city streets.

The body fell to the sidewalk with a rubbery thud. Hugh ran to the body—wary in case tubby was not quite dead. From hard-earned experience, he knew wounded desperates could be very dangerous. However, from the way blood and brain matter sprayed across the concrete, there was no question about it...this one was fully and wholly deceased.

Hugh clicked the safety on the rifle, leaned it against the brick wall and waited. In minutes, sirens approached. Hugh kept his hands out of his pockets and tried to look unthreatening. The first cop on the scene wore a nametag that said Smith. He took in the scene.

"You sure this one is a triple-pounder?"

"We'll see, won't we?" Hugh said.

He already had his ID and hunting permit out. Smith took them and looked them over carefully. He looked at Hugh's face and compared it to the license photograph.

"You seem familiar," Smith said.

"Maybe from the news. I bagged the first one in Seattle."

"How many so far?"

"Three. This one will make four."

"This one looks a little light to me."

"I ain't been wrong yet."

"Okay, we'll see. Hang loose for a while."

Smith strode up the sidewalk and pushed back onlookers.

"Give us some room, will ya?" he said.

The meat wagon pulled up and backed to the body. The

driver was short and husky with three-days of dark beard and yellow teeth clenched on a dead cigar. He uncoiled cable and wrapped it around a foot. Once winched, the body pendulumed. Blood pooled on the sidewalk.

"Hurry up. I don't want it to weigh-in light."

The driver frowned. "Don't get your titties in a twist. We make allowances for bleeding out," he said.

Officer Smith came back. "Where we at?" he said.

The driver tapped the scale and peered near-sightedly at the dial.

"No problem. Three-ten after a pound or two of loss. Legal kill."

Hugh held out the tag. "Can I get you to sign off?"

Smith sighed. "Do I have a choice?"

Hugh shrugged. "The law is the law," he said.

"Right," Smith said. He scribbled on the tag. He turned to the driver. "How long until rendering gets here?"

"Few minutes. They like to collect 'em fresh."

Smith sighed. He turned back to Hugh.

"This is an ugly business. My mom is a big-boned woman—packs a few extra pounds. You gonna shoot her too?"

"Tell her to lay off the mashed potatoes and we won't have to worry over it, will we?"

"I don't like what we've turned into."

"Long as *you* do your job, *we* don't have a problem."

Hugh looked at the game tag to make sure it was signed properly, and then picked up his rifle and walked up the sidewalk. A large man stepped out and moved to block Hugh's way when he tried to slip by. Hugh sized him up.

Two-fifty, maybe two-sixty.

"Get out of the way, citizen," Hugh said.

"I don't care what the law says, you're a stinkin' murderer. A filthy, disgusting lowlife bounty hunter. I hate you guys. I should…"

"Should what?" Hugh said. He turned back to address the Officer Smith. "The beefer is blocking my path," he said.

"Move along," Smith called out.

The large man slowly moved aside.

"Don't think we're done yet, hunter."

Hugh looked the man over from head to toe.

"That's right," he said. "You keep eating and I'll see you again real soon."

He threw the rifle strap over his shoulder and eased through the crowd.

As it often happens in Seattle, mist gave way to drizzle which gave way to a light rain. Hugh adjusted his collar as he trudged along Broadway.

It was a cold, bitter and nasty day.

Notes on *Open Season on Tubby*

AP: My first impulse after reading *Open Season on Tubby* was to get on the scale and weigh myself. The story has the gripping quality of crossing the line between fiction and a morbid reality—the reader is caught in its sinister web. Where did the inspiration for the theme come from?

KLC: A lot of my stories come from thinking about current events and considering the effect public policy has on our lives. Most people believe health care should be a government service, but they don't consider what comes along with that idea. Once your neighbors pay for your healthcare, they have a vested interest in your health habits—whether you smoke, drink, eat too much, ride a skateboard, or a bicycle or motorcycle.

As examples, society can order you to wear a helmet or

ban smoking, even in private places in some cases. What gives the government the right? Once public health is a government service, they can make rules and laws about things which contribute to public health.

AP: Mechanically, the writing style is solid—not at all soft or fuzzy. In spite of that, you create a cinematic flow—like something Orson Wells might have done. Did you visualize the whole scene while writing it?

KLC: When the writing is going well, I visualize the characters interacting with their environment and simply transcribe what I see. The concreteness of the setting is something that comes natural to me. The more absurd the theme, the more I like to give the story a gritty, down-to-earth reality. It's a way to glide around a reader's defenses and slip into the subconscious. If I do my job properly, the setting is common and vivid and makes you more-readily buy into the world of the bizarre, surreal story.

AP: What is the meaning behind this macabre subject? What did you have in mind? Is this a linear message related to only the obvious obesity issue or did you have something more in mind—something more political?

KLC: The idea of hunting and killing citizens is silly, of course. But, there is a cynical strategy that works well: demonizing your enemies.

I don't smoke (well, a cigar now and then) and I hate second-hand smoke, but I'm impressed with how the activists demonized smokers. I remember, not so long ago in Arizona, how shocked I was to see a hardware store employee smoking a cigarette in the aisle of the store. To me, it was unthinkable.

How did this happen to me? I like to think of myself as a thoughtful, analytical person, so this is a great victory for the activists. How did I allow them to affect my thinking so fundamentally?

How far will activists go when creating demons out of thin air? Are large people unhealthy? Do they consume more than their share of resources? Are they next on our list of evil doers?

AP: Hugh Grayson carries a distinguished name; he is not your average Joe. Is there more behind his identity?

KLC: When I pick a name, I'm generally trying to achieve something. For example, in my Glen Wilson series of novels, Glen is such an extreme character—so, for contrast, I wanted him to have a very vanilla, inconspicuous name. The same goes in this story. Hugh Grayson is a distinguished, cultured sort of name in a contrast to his character as a cold-blooded killer.

AP: You use sarcastic humor in your stories—and there is an obvious literary smirk in this one. What can you say about that?

KLC: We spend our precious time on earth doing trivial things like watching sports on television, playing computer games or writing short stories. With pseudo-serious, self-absorbed points-of-view, I think it's important to keep perspective and maintain a sense of humor about things. It is simply my nature to put a spotlight on silliness we take so seriously.

I like to harass my kids for spending their time playing video games, but I like rock music and I play my guitar. From my father's point of view, these activities were equally wasteful. And they are. If I spend an hour playing chords or picking out patterns on the guitar, what difference does that make in the grand scale of things? How does it affect the cosmos?

Humor is an important tool for the writer. The logical conclusion of a policy can look funny when you jump right to it, but appear reasonable and rational in small, incremental steps.

Some people don't have the money to properly take care of themselves. They have poor medical care. We should create a government program to take care of them.

Off the Boat
Adina Pelle

TOGETHER, SETH AND Finch walked off their ship and entered the first bar they found. Four weeks of hard labor had exhausted them. Finch vowed he would never work on a fishing boat again. With a pocketful of money for now, he cared nothing about the future.

The bar was called Bittersweet. It rested between a railway and the shoreline. Waves washed up the beach; then the white foam slowly retreated. Occasionally, bigger waves came in and swept away the foam, along with drunkard's vomit, plastic trash and cigarette butts. The odor from Bittersweet was strong—redolent with cheap tobacco, rank beer and working-man's sweat.

A rusty car covered with obscene graffiti scrawled in yellow paint was parked in front of the bar.

"For your health, Finch," said Seth while topping off a glass.

The absinthe was diluted with tap water, but, to them, it still tasted good because it was nowhere near as bad as the galley-brewed bilge they drank on the ship—their only weapon against freezing in cold, stormy weather.

A sailor's life was hard. When a tempest overtook them, they faced death. Slippery decks. Cables that writhed like snakes. Machinery with wide, hungry maws like sea monsters.

It was a job from hell, but it paid in cash. Money hung heavy in each of their pockets. They felt rich that day.

"We did good," mumbled Seth. "With this money we can live like kings for at least two months."

"You are a wise man, Seth. A very smart fella', you know? You're the smartest guy I know. You should be president or something like that."

"And you, Finch, are as dumb as a dog."

While teasing each other, they tilted their heads back and laughed. In their slobbery mouths, yellow, cavity-filled teeth gleamed and flashed in the intermittent bar light.

Finch proposed they order supper. With a wave, he gestured for the waitress to come closer. She was very young with blonde hair and a nice smile. She wore a short yellow dress with a white apron. Around her neck was a white scarf decorated with black spots.

"Que voulez-vous boire?" she said.

"What'd she say?" Seth asked.

"She wondered what we want to order."

"Tell her she is a very nice girl and we have money. She should give us whatever we want."

They both looked at her and smiled.

She smiled back.

Seth sipped his absinthe and belched.

She turned and walked from table to table—the men admired her long, beautiful legs exposed by her very-short dress.

"Let's go," Seth announced abruptly.

"But we feel so good here, Seth," Finch whined.

Seth replied quickly.

"Let's take the bottle go somewhere better," he said.

Finch was irritated.

"Go where?" Finch argued. "No. Here, it's quiet. I have no

desire to move from this chair. Besides, that blonde waitress has nice legs. She likes us and when she bends over to lift the dirty plates from the tables, I can see her underwear—red with black dots. What would I give for a kiss from her? I'd give up all the whores in the world for a night with a girl like that."

"Are you nuts? You're hopeless. You fall in love with all the waitresses. I've seen this a thousand times."

"And you, Seth? You're not sentimental at all, mate. But I love you anyway."

"Go to hell, you filthy, impotent pig," Seth responded—half-joking and half throwing angry looks in Finch's direction.

They continued to drink. After a while, the absinthe turned bitter. The waitress—with a spray of freckles across her milky cheeks—passed by several times. Finch smiled at her. He was smitten.

All the tables in the bar were occupied—all seats were taken. People lined up to take vacant places at the counter. The noise was intolerable. Under his breath, Seth cursed a few times before lapsing into silence. He thought about the blonde waitress and the dirty things he would like to do to her.

The heat from the absinthe burned their guts; it was a feeling Finch recognized as an old friend. The freckled waitress passed by their table several times. Her smile was like the warm morning sun on a quiet sea.

Finally, they got a fresh bottle of absinthe, paid their tab and left the bar.

It was dusk when they stepped out. The restless ocean heaved and hissed under the darkening sky. They walked by the quay while passing the bottle back and forth. Down the dusky beach, umbrellas appeared in the mist like misshapen bodies; like lonely sentinels, they stretched along the beach mixing with clinging shadows as the last glow of the sun slowly evaporated. They left the umbrellas behind; soon they were only vague shapes in the distance.

"Come, my friend, let's find a whore," Seth proposed. He grinned—revealing filmy umber teeth.

"Okay," Finch said.

He took a swig from the bottle of absinthe. His throat burned. By the time they reached the red light district, the bottle was nearly empty.

They found a woman on the roadside. She sat on the dirty curb with her legs crossed—wearing a miniskirt that exposed more than it covered. Her shoulders were slumped; she looked tired. Her long, red-tinted hair was pulled back in an unruly ponytail. It looked like a wig. Her lips were painted a garish red. Thick makeup on her face could not hide the dark circles under her eyes and the landscape of deep wrinkles on her cheeks.

"Bonjour," Finch said.

She struggled to her feet and tottered on absurdly high heels. She studied their faces, then told them the fee. When they hesitated, she offered to couple with both for the same price as one.

Finch thought it sounded like a good deal.

Seth agreed.

They stepped closer to exchange the cash. Seth put his hand on her butt and winked at the grinning Finch.

"Hubba-hubba." he said. "That's all woman."

She led the way emanating the odors of cheap perfume and working-girl sweat. There was nothing elegant in her movements; she was like a puppet controlled by a clumsy master.

Finch felt a visceral attraction. She encompassed all the women who lived in his memory—traces of former wives, girlfriends and casual lovers. His flesh trembled with desire and vibrated with freshly awakened memories. He wanted to hold this woman the whole long night, just hold her in his arms and sleep.

Yes, that's what he wanted.

The house they approached was on a narrow, dirty street. It had a small wooden terrace with all sorts of discarded objects scattered across it.

Broken toys.

They climbed a stairway where sheets of wallpaper hung from the walls like old skin.

In the hallway, the woman smiled at them while searching her purse for the key. Her smile was awkward and held a hint of shyness, like a little kid.

Seth—with a friendly grin on his face—touched Finch's shoulder. Gallantly, he motioned for Finch to go first. The woman opened the door and waited for Finch to slip by. She closed the door slowly, trying not to wake the rusty hinges.

After entering, Finch looked around. The room was dark—black curtains covered the window. The only pieces of furniture were a metal bed with a lumpy mattress and a wardrobe in the corner. The room smelled of mold, sweat and urine. She put her purse on the bed and spoke.

"How do you like it, handsome?"

She lay on the bed and pulled off her wig. Short, dark spiky hair jumped out like springs.

Finch liked that.

She worked off her blouse.

Her small breasts were decorated with pink nipples—she looked like a child. He sat next to her and touched her belly with shy fingertips. He wanted to collect and savor each pleasure. He took her in his arms and rubbed his chest against her breasts—he kissed her lips and neck, but she remained indifferent—as rigid as a porcelain doll. She did not respond to his touch.

"You are beautiful," he said.

She pointed at a box of condoms on the nightstand and turned her eyes to a remote corner while he rolled the rubber over his semi-firm manhood.

He lay back on the bed and closed his eyes. Then, there they were—all the women he'd ever sexed with, just as he remembered them. The first woman, a big girl with brown eyes. The second with blonde-dyed hair, rosy-lips and small breasts with nipples that tasted like olives. White skin. Dark skin. Yellow skin. He thought about all the women and tried to remember their names.

The whore giggled.

"Not a man. Impotent."

Finch opened his eyes and examined her distorted face. She looked like a demon. He pushed her back, slapped her with the back of his hand and punched her in the stomach. Seething with anger, he looked at her while pulling on his pants. She crouched on the bed, trembling in pain and moaning softly.

"Stinking, nasty slut," he said. "Give my money back."

"No," she cried. "I'm sorry. You are a man. I know what to do. I must have the money." She crawled toward him and begged through steaming tears. "I'm sorry. I must have the money."

Teary-eyed, she told him about her infant son and how she must pay for his hospitalization. Then she explained about her parents locked in a mental institution. She didn't want to be a prostitute, but she needed money.

"Stinking whore," Finch said.

He glanced at the money, but left it when he walked from the room.

Seth was in the hallway—passed out and snoring. He held the empty bottle against his chest. Sweat drained from his forehead. There was a puddle on the floor.

Urine.

Seth was his only friend and here he was sleeping in filth like a pig. Finch bent over and worked Seth's wallet from his sodden back pocket. He worked his hands into Seth's front pockets and removed the damp bills and change.

Then, he left without an ounce of remorse.

He didn't want any friends.

Notes on *Off the Boat*

KLC: A lot of your stories are light-hearted and cheerful, but this one is not. It seems to come from a very dark place. Do you find the writing of stories like this to be psychotherapeutic?

AP: Yes. When I'm under the clouds of an approaching storm and have no umbrella, I run for cover under my words.

It's a good reminder of where I was mentally when I wrote the story. Like a doctor's file if you want.

KLC: Another thing different about this story is the vividness of the external setting. Most of your stories explore an internal landscape. This one has poetic imagery and fine-pitched details.

...drunkard's vomit, plastic trash and cigarette butts...

...cables that writhed like snakes. Machinery with wide, hungry maws like sea monsters...

...umbrellas appeared in the mist like misshapen bodies...

Why does this story earn this fine attention to detail when others do not?

AP: I had in mind a desolate place—a sordid one under the surface of our affluent society, one I know exists.

I grew up in big cities as a middle class child only remotely exposed to the misery of alcohol, poverty and menial work. And when I say remotely, I mean I heard my parents talk about the poor or saw for myself wretches drunk in ditches without anyone acknowledging their existence. My characters in this story are drunks, but just stating that fact was not enough—I had to make the landscape spin in a daze too.

KLC: The three main characters deserve no compassion. They are unredeemed losers. Do you feel any sympathy for their lot in life?

AP: Absolutely, yes, I do! I understand them, with their sad failures and little hope for the future. This kind of morose writing acts as a buffer between my life and the merciless forces at work in the lives of others.

KLC: I want to bother you about the only names in this story: Seth and Finch. Is there a literary reference I'm missing? The only 'Finch' I can think of is Atticus Finch from *To Kill a Mockingbird*, but that doesn't resonate. In this case, are you giving throw-way names to throw-away characters?

AP: Seth carries a biblical weight, almost like a fate he cannot run away from, but Finch is a light and pleasant soul despite his hard and brutal life.

KLC: In most of your stories you deliver thought-provoking entertainment for your reading audience. To me, this story seems more inward-looking. How can I put it? This story is no

341

Mesh

extrovert. It's more withdrawn. Am I capturing an accurate sense of it?

AP: Yes, you captured my intent.

KLC: This could be a stretch, but there is a lot of animal imagery in this tale. Sea monsters. Pigs. Dogs. Are you creating soulless characters who act like animals and trying to warn us against something important?

AP: Yes, I had Pieter Bruegel landscapes in mind—visceral and disturbing when examined closely.

KLC: We should be used to this by now, but you tease the reader without mercy. These characters *almost* come to life—we almost see beyond their dysfunction to glimpse their underlying humanity. But then the veil falls. Wouldn't it be easier to write characterizations without nuance?

AP: No, not really. I like to leave room for anything which might change the course of the story.

KLC: You might not want to give away your thinking this easily, but the last line seems to convey a message. What I take away is that Finch does not want or need any friends. However, I do and I value them very much. I come away feeling very glad I am not a man like Finch.

AP: Friends come in different shapes and sizes. I find it hard to believe you would tolerate the kind of friend a man like Finch would make.

342

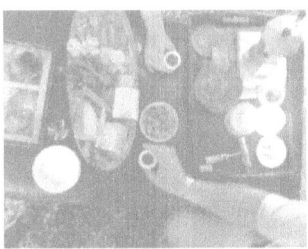

Invasion from the Planet Tampon
Ken Coffman

PENELOPE LAKE SMILED sweetly, a bad signal of her mood. Sitting at the head of a walnut conference table, she watched the other ladies enter the room in groups of two or three. She sampled the snippets of conversation.

"Did you see that dress?"

"Was it designed as a color blindness test?"

"Oooh, I could have scratched her eyes out, tinted contact lenses and all."

"And then she said she was thirty-three, but that bitch is at least forty."

Penney (which only her slumber party friends got away with calling her) tapped ruby-painted fingernails on the table and waited for the girls to settle down. Soon the room was still except for the rustling of silken underclothes and the snap of compacts being closed and returned to the eel skin handbags which were the rage this season.

"Ladies, if I can have your attention, we have important items to discuss. Alice, would you please read the minutes from the last meeting?"

Alice sashayed to the podium with high heels click-clicking on the floor. She smoothed her paisley chambray dress before beginning to speak. Her voice was nasally and whiny.

"Thank you, Penelope. Item One. We voted and approved

343

Springtime Doily Week for the second week of April." She adjusted her reading glasses and peered at the ladies. "A lovely idea to follow Daffodil Week, I think. My sister, Clara, makes the most beautiful crochet pot holders with satin borders and little cerulean forget-me-nots accenting the corners..."

Penelope interrupted. "Could you simply carry on with the minutes please, Alice?"

Alice sniffed and continued.

"Well, we're snippy today, aren't we? Item Two. As of the eleventh of October, which was yesterday, ladies, the waist size for 'petit' has been relaxed by one inch. Item 3. We discussed the evaporation of our atmosphere and the coming destruction of all life here on Venus."

"Thank you, Alice," Penelope said. "We'll continue our discussion of planetary annihilation with a presentation from Marta."

Alice snorted and walked back to her chair. In passing Marta she rolled her eyes and plugged her nose. Several ladies tittered furtively.

Marta was blowsy. Ragged around the edges, the paint on her nails was chipped and her hair had not been dyed and permed for two months so it showed dingy yellow roots and stood up like she was stuck in a windstorm built for one. Her nerves were ragged and she chain-smoked long cigarettes in an ivory holder. She wasted no time getting to the point.

"We have two years before we get microwaved and there isn't a damned thing we can do about it. The destruction of the ozone layer is nearly complete and thus far, no method of reversing this phenomena has been discovered."

Her next comment raised a quiet gasp from the more tanned ladies.

"Incidences of skin cancer are up by twenty-seven-percent in the last three years and we can expect continued, exponential growth as time goes on."

Alice raised her hand. "What does exponential mean? You use words like that just to make the rest of us feel stupid, don't you?"

Several ladies nodded in agreement.

"In answer to your first question Alice, exponential means the numbers get real big real fast. In regard to your second question, I really don't think you need my help to appear ignorant."

Penelope slapped her hand on the table to halt the impending brawl.

"Get on with the presentation, Marta."

"Millions of pounds of fluorocarbons poured into the air as propellants for our hairspray and deodorants ate the protective ozone layer of our atmosphere, so we are exposed to higher doses of ultraviolet radiation from the sun every day. Within about fifteen years our beautiful planet Venus will be an arid desert and all life will be destroyed. Thank you, ladies, for your attention."

As Marta walked back to her seat she stuck her tongue out at Alice who was whispering scandalous rumors to her neighbor.

Penelope sat quietly for a moment looking at the crowd around the table. A few of the women were ashen; these were the ones who understood the end was near. The rest touched up lipstick using small mirrors. Penelope shook her head with hopelessness.

"We're seeing more and more evidence that what Marta has said is true and we're in serious trouble, girls. I've asked Valerie Bogle to give us a report on the nearest habitable planet."

The ladies began murmuring. Penelope heard comments like "I'd rather die first," or "How gross."

"Please come up, Valerie," Penelope said.

Valerie was pretty—with a pageboy haircut and shiny red high heels that matched her nails and lipstick. She spoke with a high-pitched voice that made it hard for anyone to take her seriously.

"As you know, I've been studying the planet Earth for most of my life. Earth is habitable for us. My specialty is the inhabitants of Earth, those we call Men. I admit the Men of Earth are disgusting. After all, they live in simple houses made of hewn plants and wear rudimentary clothing made of plant fibers. However, it is an error to judge these crude creatures based on their appearance and lifestyle. Many think Men are dull creatures, but they have high basic intelligence, simply not directed properly. Their society is based on primitive rituals. They spend their non-working time observing bizarre ball games and drinking an icky alcoholic preparation called beer. They bath irregularly, freely belch and do their toilet in unprivate places without the neuroses we associate with high intelligence. By night, they engage in ruthless, violent physical battles for unknown reasons but are always friends in the morning. All in all, a very puzzling race."

Alice interrupted.

"I've heard quite enough of this nonsense. How can you say these beasts are intelligent? They wallow in their own stink, waste their time watching sports on television sets and drink disgusting brews until they can't even stand up. And speaking of standing up, they urinate on bushes."

Several of the ladies nodded their heads. "I say we wipe out these grotesque things and take that planet for ourselves. Let's turn it into something beautiful."

Penelope fumed. "Shut up, Alice. Let Valerie continue."

Valerie smiled meekly at Penelope and riffled through her notes. "I'm through anyway, but I thank you, dear Penelope.

These Earth Men are backward and uncivilized but are just a little less evolved than us, that's all. I find their incomprehensible behavior fascinating. Thank you for your time."

"Can we have a break now? I need to powder my nose," Alice said with urgency.

Penelope nodded and watched as the women gathered into groups of two and three and headed toward the toilets surrounding the conference room. A maid walked around the table filling tea cups and distributing butter cookies from a silver plate shaped like a flower. Penelope nibbled a cookie and checked to make sure her hairclips were in place. She stared out the window at trees turning yellow under the harsh sun blazing in the sky. The planet was turning from the damp green she remembered from her childhood to arid yellows and dusty browns.

At least these colors are from complementary color groups.

Still, she felt sadness for the demise of her planet. The women began to stroll back into the room. Penelope stood to address them.

"I know some of you don't understand what is happening. The fact is, our planet is dying and we do not have a way to reverse the process. Somewhere between two and fifteen years is all we have left. For this reason I ordered a study done by Marcia Kamen. Marcia is a brilliant woman. Her credentials in genetics and cellular physics are unequaled. Please give her your fullest attention. Marcia, please come up."

Marcia wore a black wool dress that ended north of her knees—with a simple strand of cultured pearls around her neck and matching earrings. She stood at the podium and took a sheaf of papers from her briefcase.

"Thank you, Penelope, for the kind introduction. For those that don't know me, I've been a professor at Willifred and Mary University for many years and have done a lot of work in cellular biology. Penelope asked me to look into how we might be able to live with the Men of planet Earth. This has been an interesting problem—with not only scientific, but moral and philosophical aspects. As you know, the atmosphere of Earth is compatible with ours and the native flora and fauna could provide us with sustenance. The main concern is whether we could coexist with the Men because their society is so far removed from ours. They are a happy-go-lucky race, but they create weapons that we can't even dream of. They have guns that shoot hundreds of rounds per second and pierce steel plate. Even if we could get them to accept us they would put up with us only in places we would find undesirable. We could never motivate them to help us build new homes, to feed us or to even carry out our garbage. Though we could offer much in cleaning technology to spruce up their planet, make them eat better food and develop healthier habits, I don't think they would tolerate it. I don't see an answer."

Penelope raised her hand.

"You've done research on controlled mutation?"

"Yes."

"And this research shows promise?"

"Yes, very much so."

"I want you to think very carefully about this next question. Would it be possible to alter the Men's genetic structure so they *require* our race to survive? Perhaps to prevent them from reproducing among themselves and have our race be the bearers of their young?"

Marcia sputtered. "We don't have the right to play Goddesses. What you are suggesting would be immoral, unethical and nasty. I don't care how good it would be for them in the long run, we don't have the right to interfere with their society, such as it is, and in their lives."

Many of the women around the table understood and were lost in thought or shaking their heads in wonder.

"Regardless of what you think of the idea, could it be done?"

"Yes, with more research and a few years to put a program into place, it could be done," Marcia replied. "But it wouldn't be right."

An hour later, after heated discussion, the resolution to invade Earth was voted upon and the motion carried. The project was christened 'Project Eve' and was a great success for the race of women.

Notes on *Invasion from the Planet Tampon*

AP: This is a cool piece. It reminds me of something similar I wrote, but from the completely opposite end of the spectrum. Women perish and men find life challenging without feminine craziness, kookiness and healing touch.

And I am not even talking about sex.

What do you think of this scenario?

KLC: We all have a natural, self-serving point of view which I toy with in this story.

AP: I almost feel the cat fight looming in the background. How did you get such a perspective in the land-mined territory d'estrogen?

KLC: From hanging out with women and observing them like laboratory specimens. I have lots of female friends and they are, each and every one of them, odd, alien creatures.

Including you, my friend—no offense intended.

AP: How do you perceive women? Don't hold back!

KLC: When have you known me to hold anything back? I pour it all out.
    Women mix beautiful, irresistible sweetness with cruelty, brutality and earthy, messy, disgusting coarseness.

AP: Do you embrace the stereotype that boys will be boys and women talk too much?

KLC: Don't most stereotypes hold elements of truth? If they didn't, they'd be called lies. That said, my wife is not gabby. Generally, she doesn't speak at all unless she has something important to say. My daughter, on the other hand—she loves a good chat. So, each woman is different—beautiful and flawed in her own way.

AP: Again, you touch on a subject that seeps throughout your work. Energy, pollution, etc. How much does that subject control your thinking? I ask because I never think of these topics.

KLC: You want to talk about politics? Are you sure? It endlessly irritates me how the left claims ownership of environmental issues—as if you can only be a curator and protector of the environment if you embrace the whole package of collectivist, politically correct nonsense.
    All thinking people want to protect and conserve—and waste nothing.

AP: The ladies you dressed up so coquettishly (stiletto red hills, ruby nails) remind me of an episode of the Real

Housewives of—fill in the blank. On behalf of cerebral women, please don't do that.

KLC: You're funny, Adina. I've never dressed a woman in my life and my attempts were dismal failures. Ask my wife about the practical saddle shoes I bought her when we were teenagers.

I report what I observe. Complain to the next woman you see who is all dolled-up.

Hard-to-get Stella
Adina Pelle

NICHOLAS WATCHED WITH trepidation as the girls in his class changed overnight from asexual little girls into untouchable beings—bearing hidden land mines that might detonate with the telekinetic power of a boy's random stare.

At the same time, the new English teacher joined the quivering, sexually unstable passion play Nicholas and the other boys lived in. Stella was her name. This sultry young lady who tortured the English teacher bore breasts and hips from the fantasy world of sexually frustrated men and boys.

When she bent to look over Nicholas' notebook, plucking at obvious mistakes as if removing lice from a mutt, he gasped for air and jumped from his seat—the way he panicked while swimming and sprang from the water—deathly afraid of drowning. When he leapt, he accidentally touched a breast and stammered random words he could barely articulate.

"Will, what, can I—excused, please?"

While looking straight in his eyes with a witchcrafty awareness, she quizzed him.

"What's the matter—you need fresh air, boy?"

It was clear she understood the boiling turmoil before her eyes.

After the lesson was over, Nicholas saw Stella in the schoolyard standing near a wall embroidered with graffiti. He

352

gathered his courage and wandered near. Stella examined him like a specimen before speaking

"What? Are you worried? I'll show them to you."

Without looking at him, Stella removed specks of imaginary pollen from her pulsating bosom. Nicolas was filled with hopeless trepidation. She continued.

"But first you need to amaze me," she said.

She walked away—expecting Nicholas to follow.

He had no idea where she was headed. Following her on crowded sidewalks, he ignored the questions his mind produced. She walked fast and slipped around idlers. They turned on Main Street—all the while, he was scared of losing sight of her.

He felt more calm after two minutes of chasing her—staring with fiery retinas at the flirty hem of her short skirt. He knew exactly what he wanted from her.

Everything.

Over her shoulder, she spoke with a sly, wicked tone.

"Look at the intersection. Do you see the pedestrian crossing—how the cars fly over the white stripes? I will cross and you will wait."

Nicolas understood what was being asked of him. When the traffic light turned green—Stella sauntered to the other side of the boulevard.

He remained behind and waited for the crossing light to turn red—waiting for her gesture. When the traffic came up to speed, he took a deep breath and dashed toward the other side—causing the drivers to slam on their brakes to avoid hitting him.

On the opposite sidewalk, Stella's eyes gleamed with invitation. He ran through a hellish cacophony of screaming brakes and bellowing horns—with tires screeching like nails on a chalkboard.

Drivers poked their heads out of their car windows and screamed as pedestrians on Main Street watched the student scamper among cars with his backpack flopping on his back. He succeeded in not getting hit while cars slammed furiously into each other.

Nicholas plummeted to the curbside and fell at Stella's feet. She made no gesture to help him up. When the inevitable cop showed up, she disappeared. Nicholas suspected she'd fooled him, but, thank God, in the park near an alley that led to the Saint Anne's Cathedral, Stella waited for him—standing by an old woman taking sunflower seeds one-by-one from a greasy sack and feeding them to squirrels.

"Well done," Stella said. "You earned the show. But wait—let's find a suitable place."

She led him to a narrow alley, complaining loudly about the retirees taking all the private benches in the park. Nicholas realized his happiness depended on finding a suitable bench— and he found one. The bench was not hidden; on the contrary, was in the open. He took it as a blessing. They sat and his thoughts galloped.

I have to see this—how she takes her sweater off right in front of the shiny cross of the Saint Anne's Cathedral.

Stella leaned toward him—pressing his chest with her breasts while releasing his backpack. Then she whispered.

"Lie down on the bench."

She took his head onto her lap. Nicholas saw her sweater lifting out to swallow his face, eyes, and gaping, astonished mouth.

She lifted her white bra, letting his breath tickle the trembling pink-white skin of her breasts. They surprised him—when freed from their dual cotton cages they were more expansive and upright than he imagined. And he never forgot his instinctive reaction. He opened his lips and stretched out his tongue to touch the pink flesh.

As soon as he touched the silky flesh, she smacked him on the forehead and snarled.

"Not so fast. Our city has wider streets, with lots of fast traffic. I know a place. If you cross it and live I am yours from the waist up for five minutes."

He smiled and sent his words toward her naked breasts.

"Yes, and after that, if I cross the most dangerous intersection in the world, what will you do then?"

She pushed his head away and rearranged her sweater and undergarment.

"We'll cross that bridge when we get to it," she said.

Notes on *Hard-to-get Stella*

KLC: Perhaps I'm an out-of-touch old man, but it seems that the purpose of birth control, abortion, the collapse of traditional morality and the relentless stream of media messages is for one reason—to create an endless supply of young women who willingly give exploiters an infinitely valuable commodity—their virginity and chasteness. From a woman's lifetime perspective, how wrong am I?

AP: Birth control reduced the "barefoot and pregnant" cycle but I have a hard time associating it with lost morality. I am not one that burned her bras back when Gloria Steinem was marching on the streets.

KLC: As your story illustrates, the woman's body is an amazing weapon that can be used against men. Stella is very conscious of this. I've never seen a girl's locker room or been behind the scenes where they talk. Are most young women as knowing as Stella?

AP: Yes, without a doubt. Women, starting as girls, know the exact value of their inventory. Ultimately, I guess it's a good and important part of the evolutionary puzzle of the survival of the species. As a matter of fact, there was a study done which pretty much concluded women tend to expose more skin the closer they are to their fertile cycle.

KLC: This is a horrible cliché at this point, but again Nabokov's *Lolita* comes to mind.

> There is nothing more atrociously cruel than an adored child.
> —Vladimir Nabokov, *Lolita*

It seems to me that Stella tries out the power of her sexuality like a warrior might test a shiny new sword...weighing it by slashing it through the air. Is that a fair analogy?

AP: Absolutely. Stella is the ultimate prize men ran after for ages—starting wars, losing fortunes, sending careers into the toilet, destroying social status, etc.

KLC: Take us back to those turbulent days. How cruel were you?

AP: There is no doubt I carried the genetic message Eve passed along and I clearly remember times when the catharsis generated within my being was unmistakably coming from the awesome power I understood I had. But overall, I was a pretty naïve teenager...

KLC: It's a sad reality, but most of our lessons are learned by fumbling through things and making mistakes. As a parent, it seems like the best we can hope is that the mistakes aren't too self-destructive or linger into permanence. Does it surprise you how many people seem to lack any self-awareness at all?

AP: Yes, it does surprises me sometimes—though it is so commonly observed that we get used to it. What causes the problem? Poor education? Bad role models from pop culture? The moral void a lot of us grow up in—or grow up in but rebel against? There are endless reasons and excuses for the mistakes we make.

KLC: Is it your sense that Nicolas will survive the tests and get to the Promised Land?

AP: Yes. Nicolas is a fool just like Paris vis-à-vis Helen of Troy. He'll earn his trophy but lose his soul.

The Lady and her Hero
Ken Coffman

JOHN HELD UP a hand. Erika stopped.

"Did you hear that?" John said.

Dew glistened on scattered stones and wind rustled the leaves of towering maple trees. A sliver of moon peeked from behind a ragged cloud. John raised his torch, but the light was feeble and did nothing to dispel the gloomy, stygian darkness.

"I heard a dog, perhaps," Erika said, "or a catamount or a rogue. I'm not sure we should have come this way on the night of lost souls, John."

John put his hand on the handle of his sword.

"Silence, woman. I think we're being followed."

"With you to protect me, John, I will be unafraid," she said.

She wore a long dress and a cape with a furry hood tied tightly around her thin face. The dress's lacy hem was wet from the tall, damp grass around the stones. Her boots, leather-laced up her shins, were flecked with clumps of grass and mud.

John pointed the torch at a disused path between leaning stones.

"This way," he said.

"Are you sure? Maybe we should go back. There are wolves and bears and worse in these woods. Robbers and

358

murderers and men with evil living in their hearts."

John lifted his cape and gestured to the sword hanging in its scabbard.

"No one will dare to taste the fury of Blood Blade in the hands of John of the hill clan Smith—not even on the All Hallows Eve. Stay near, woman."

Nervously clutching her rucksack of booty, Lady Erika looked to the left and right and stayed close on John's heels as he led the way. Two figures dressed in black stepped from behind a stone monument.

"What have we here?" the tallest said.

"Stand aside and let us pass in peace," John said.

The tall figure laughed. "Bold words from such a small person."

"And outnumbered, too," the shorter, more stocky scoundrel said. He drew a dagger from his belt. "We'll have your sack, peasant."

John straightened and slowly pulled Blood from the scabbard. Its blade gleamed in the faint moonlight.

"Begone before my patience expires and Blood spills blood."

The shorter thief stepped back, but the taller stood his ground. John raised the sword and placed it on the taller thief's neck.

"Hear my words, ruffian. I'll open your neck and let the earth drink the black fluid of your heart. Challenge me if you dare."

"Very well," the taller hooligan said. "On this night, as I feel an unusual kindness toward lost strangers, we shall allow you to pass. However, the next time our paths cross, the result will be much different."

"We'll leave the consequence of that meeting to the gods of fate and destiny."

The two dark figures turned and disappeared into the misty gloom. When they were fully gone, John returned the sword to its place on his belt and turned. He placed his hands on Erika's shoulders.

"You're very brave," she said.

Maybe, he thought.

His heart pounded in his chest. Hoping his boldness would be rewarded, he leaned forward an inch. She raised her head and closed the gap. Their lips touched—just for an instant. Their first kiss. John's heart soared and he felt a hundred and ten feet tall.

He looked deeply into her hazel eyes.

"We'd better find our way home," she said.

"Yes," John said. "I know the way."

With his soul singing, he took her hand and led her on the trail between the stones.

I earned her kiss, he thought. The first of many, I hope.

They skirted a weeping willow and came out on Oak Street by the Church of the Nazarene. It was late, but there were still clumps of Halloween revelers clutching paper bags of loot and strolling on the sidewalk under the street lights. He felt a weak wave of regret. He'd promised his brother all the Milky Way and Snickers candy bars in his bag and there were at least a dozen. However, with Erika's kiss still on his tingling lips, he knew his brother's deal was a bargain.

They walked to the gate outside Erika's house.

They shared a kiss, so maybe he could ask. He summoned remnants of courage.

"Can I meet you tomorrow and walk you to school?" he asked with his eleven-year-old heart in his throat.

With her hand resting on the gate latch, she turned.

"Yes," she said. "That would be nice."

Notes on *The Lady and her Hero*

AP: How sweet. I had a very nice warm, fuzzy feeling after the story was over.

I also liked the twist. I did not think about kids dressed up for Halloween and trick or treating. I expected some classic scary Halloween story. You guided the reader with a steady hand.

KLC: A lot of these stories are experiments to see what I can do. Writing mechanics are one thing, but can we make the reader feel something? Can we create characters with soul? Can we tease and amuse the reader? That's where the writing morphs into art.

AP: This is an innocent take on first love: the first kiss. In movies and TV, we are inundated by explicit, visceral sexuality. The innocence of a first kiss or hand-holding gets lost in a sordid mess when adults make pressure children to act like grownups...do you agree?

KLC: I think kids *are* pushed to grow up too fast. This may be the only time in their lives where things are magical and unpolluted by death, drama and despair. Why not slow down and let innocence die later in life?

AP: I remember my first kiss—a stolen peck on the cheek that made me dream for days. Do you remember yours?

KLC: Hmmm. My memory of childhood is very poor. That would be a sad thing to forget, but I really don't remember. As a kid, I was shy and insecure. I had nearly no experience with women until late into my teen years. You'd think I'd remember, but I don't. I was probably terrified.

AP: You raised a boy and a girl…what are the differences compared to your own childhood?

KLC: With my mother's passing, there are pictures that take me back. My formative years were dismal and sad. I was a hopeless kid from a rural backwater. Deep inside, that's still what I am.

AP: Men like to be needed and I guess that starts at a very young age, from birth. Did you have any words of wisdom for your son?

KLC: I spewed endless words of wisdom[16] mixed with terrible nonsense. I hope some of my ideas about art and living a full, uncompromising life will linger, but who knows?

You're right that every man wants to be a hero and savior and protector. How constructive is modern society when it breaks down this urge and replaces it with hedonism and exploitation?

---

[16] As reported by my daughter, these include the following:
If you make a mess, clean it up.
If you don't know why you're doing something, then don't do it.
When my kids would point out a situation was 'unfair', I would say:
Thank you for pointing that out.

The Serpent
Adina Pelle

"YOU'RE NOT GOING anywhere," he mumbled to himself, but his inner voice was doubtful, like the weather on a September afternoon. "If only I could forget her," he sighed.

The thought scared him more than the pain that came with it.

How could I forget her?

He could not, did not want to lose her image. It was tattooed on his corneas and that was certainly the way he wanted it.

What would days and years mean without her?

Not being able to eat or sleep meant nothing to him, nor did patching the deep cuts she carved in his heart. She was always someone else's lover, never his. It would be impossible to go back now. The crowd pushed forward for a glimpse—the stage was close. The mob made him think of a giant boiling caldron with each hot and sweaty body pushing for the surface. Thrusting upwards. Twisting.

He fought to enter without being trampled. Being experienced in the turmoil, he succeeded.

She did not appear until the crowd chanted her name, screaming hysterically. When she finally emerged on stage with the snake magically coiled around her neck like a scarf, the uproar stilled.

Stepping close to the edge and emerging from a veil of artificial fog, her figure slid slowly toward the reflectors. In hanging silence, the woman floated in the light with the snake on her shoulders—a true queen of the jungle. At every turn, her black, shining hair drew arcs and coils in the dark night air. From the dim room, the thousands watching were subjugated.

The serpent slowly descended along her arms and hugged her belly—sending a wave of voluptuous dizziness through the viewers. It slid up to her breast, its head approaching and smelling. A single bite would be fatal.

A snap of her fingers was followed by a bewildering silence. The reptile descended to the floor and slithered around her, lascivious but obedient. The same snapping fingers could have the room kneeling at her feet.

Strangely, most remembered only the danger that hung in the air, followed quickly by desire, fear and insanity. Exhaustion. Incomplete and mixed feelings brought on a state of delirium.

Leaning over, her red lips touched the reptile's head and kissed it.

After the show, men crowded, as usual, in front of her changing room. Amid the hundreds of faces around him, the scrawny man, bearing a large bouquet of red roses, targeted the door to her room. He eagerly desired the same private experience as everyone else.

Using his elbows to advance the short distance, he looked over the heads of the others, full of emotion, remembering his first time. If it were possible to make one wish...only one, only once, he would not want anything but a night with the serpent woman.

But what could I offer a woman who had everything? How could I convince her we belong together? There must be a way.

She took the flowers and kissed his cheek. His knees changed their structure and molecular constitution, turning into quivering jelly.

With a soft voice, she told him to stop looking for her. With her green eyes, a perfect continuation of the snake skin lingering on her shoulders and through never-ending batting lashes she looked at him with pity.

"Understand there's no use. I will never choose you and there will never be anything between us."

He saw her red lips moving, but did not hear a thing. Her scent made him delirious.

He wanted to say something nice, words that would pierce her armor of ice, but it was difficult to articulate a sentence in her vicinity.

Though the snake hissed a few times, *she* was silent.

Tonight's chosen man was tall and well built.

Watching in puzzlement as they walked away, his mind tried to decipher the good luck that hit other men but mysteriously eluded him. When she left on the arm of another man, his heart bled and the nightmare was endless. She never seemed to satisfy her hunger for other men.

A sudden lightning and rain staggered the two in their path. Happy as a child because he had his umbrella, he ran up and held it up above her, ignoring his rival. She stopped and uttered the words he always hoped to hear:

"Come…"

Abandoned in the rain, the other man looked dead, like a chair forgotten on a porch.

She seemed absent for a while. There were no words to articulate. The snake broke the silence by hissing.

She caressed it and laughed.

"Did you know he does not work unless fed?"

"I know nothing," he admitted.

"I feed him only after the show. As a reward, right?"

He understood only that he was closer he had ever been to her and that was all it mattered.

The creature's scaled head moved—sniffing him. He resisted an involuntary reflex to pull back.

She spoke—amused by the situation. "It only attacks when starving. The rest of the time it's pretty predictable. If you're afraid, you can go."

He strenuously denied the accusation. He'd go nowhere, no matter what happened.

She smiled devilishly and continued talking, mostly about former lovers. He no longer cared. They were together.

She saw him suffering, but did not stop talking. He could bear anything and endure the merciless details of those who passed through her bed, because tonight he was chosen.

She was cold to the touch; it made him shudder. In the hotel room, she switched on the light and the tension in the air, a certain pressure or strain, puzzled him. He wondered what was coming.

"Kiss me," she said.

He obeyed and felt drunk with ecstasy. He forgot about the creepy snake lingering between them.

She seemed so small, so cold, and the man felt the need to protect her...but she asked him to lie down instead. He immediately obeyed, his whole body shivering.

Pleased to see him outstretched, she quickly removed her clothes. Her naked body was unreal. She moved with hypnotic grace. Eyes sparkling. He tried to warm her by caressing her breasts, wanting her desperately, but she didn't let him move, concentrating on his pupils, wrapping herself around his body with unexpected slithering force, squeezing like a vise. She leaned over and unfolded her hair, sniffing, smelling his neck, moving toward his belly until his overwhelmed manhood disappeared in her hands.

He felt something wrap around his foot. An unusual numbness crept up his body; an ascending coldness. His breathing became heavy; he trembled. She hugged him and dispelled his fear. The serpent's head moved forward on his belly, wet and fluid. She kissed his neck, face and eyes as the snake climbed. She ran her tongue over his belly, stooped and twisted her spine like a reptile in ways impossible to describe. He closed his eyes and became a train about to derail.

Was it her tongue, or the serpent's?

No woman made him feel this way. There was no another woman. The world no longer existed. This odd and overwhelming fusion *became* the world. She gathered herself on his chest with her upper lip trembling. He heard her moaning and somewhere the hissing serpent made its presence known. He felt a sting and his eyelids struggled, shaking spasmodically. Warmth pervaded his bones. He could not move. Who was encasing him, the woman or the snake? A whiff of blood in the air.

Whose blood?

He parted his swollen eyelids to see her hair change into writhing snakes. He was unafraid and regretted nothing.

Then, at last, the rain washed everything away.

Notes on *The Serpent*

KLC: You probably think I'll immediately reach for the Holy Bible…

AP: I hope so. The Judeo-Christian biblical account of man and woman is what ignited my thoughts; not necessarily the biblical sin as much as the misogynist events from that time. It always rubbed me the wrong way that women never asked for a rib and yet God found no other way of delighting the lonely and desperate creature but by taking part of him, twisting it in a million knots and giving it back to alleviate boredom and loneliness. Of course Eve was flummoxed and befriended the serpent...

KLC: Well, you're right, we go right to the Book of Genesis:

> *003:001 Now the serpent was more subtle than any animal of the field which Yahweh God had made. He said to the woman, "Has God really said, 'You shall not eat of any tree of the garden?'"*
> *003:002 The woman said to the serpent, "Of the fruit of the trees of the garden we may eat,*
> *003:003 but of the fruit of the tree which is in the middle of the garden, God has said, 'You shall not eat of it, neither shall you touch it, lest you die.'"*
> *003:004 The serpent said to the woman, "You won't surely die,*
> *003:005 for God knows that in the day you eat it, your eyes will be opened, and you will be like God, knowing good and evil."*[17]

For a slightly different slant, we can go to The Book of Mormon...

2 Nephi 2:18 And because he had fallen from heaven, and had become miserable forever, he sought also the misery of all mankind. Wherefore, he said unto Eve, yea, even that old serpent, who is the devil, who is the father of all lies, wherefore he said: Partake of the forbidden fruit, and ye shall

---

[17] Translation from the World English Bible

not die, but ye shall be as God, knowing good and evil.

I don't want to quiz you on the obvious biblical aspect of your story. Have I asked this before? In what language did you first read the Bible?

AP: I actually first read the Bible in Romanian. My grandparents (my mother's parents) hid their Semitic roots for years after the war and well into their Communist existence. Greek Orthodoxy was the stamp of normalcy so they played that game. Ultimately no one in my family took solace in organized religion.

KLC: I will confess that my first thought was not directly about the Bible. I thought of my favorite movie: Blade Runner.

> *Announcer: Ladies and Gentlemen. Taffy Lewis presents Miss Salomé and the snake. Watch her take the pleasures from the serpent that once corrupted man.*

Of course, this too is a not-very-oblique reference to the biblical legend.

AP: That's exactly what I was going to say. I never saw Blade Runner but the quote makes it clear where the idea came from.

KLC: I could probably find a hundred cultural references to the serpent from the Garden of Eden. What was on your mind when you took this theme from its dusty shelf?

AP: My first and foremost thought was to revolt; no one asked you men for a rib, so why the misogyny? Everyone knows there is no spirituality, no sanctity, no truth without the female.

But men? Because of this biblical detail, they live in a perpetual fantasy world. Women came from men. Nonsense! God must have a sick, twisted sense of humor.

KLC: Suppose I suggested the legend of Eve and the serpent is the world's oldest penis joke? What would you say?

AP: I'd say all penis jokes are the same. If you heard one you heard them all.

KLC: What if I brought my imaginary pet snake over to your house for you to admire?

AP: In the words of Indiana Jones: "I hate snakes." I could have changed the course of humanity—I would not talk to a serpent if I were around in biblical times.

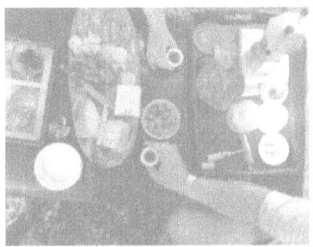

Penelope Waits
Adina Pelle and Ken Coffman

SOMETIMES HE HAD an irresistible impulse to shout her name.

Pea-Nell-Oh-Pea.

If she was Greek, that's how her name would sound. Since meeting her, the name took on a life of its own—as if it was not a name but something physical that could be stored in a cupboard or hung on a barren wall.

She never protested his cruelty; instead, her typical attitude was shy, amused detachment. Underneath, she was perpetually insecure and nervous—as manifested by a shy rosiness that spread across her cheekbones.

Penelope.

If he had not pissed in the hallway on his way home—while on a drunken outing with PJ—he might never have met her.

Their first year together had already passed. The year was okay, but unmemorable. He cheated on her ten times. Only ten times? He could not remember. The other women were necessary, since Penelope's coital dance was no longer fresh.

He looked at her while slowly inhaling from his cigarette. Black hair stirred by an evening breeze. Narrow eyes, brown skin and small, naughty breasts glimpsed through loose-button gaps in her white dress.

371

The air between them was magical, mysterious, warm and humid—redolent with an exotic, musky aroma. He could not stop now; her taste and smell went through his body like the tobacco—spicy and making his pulsating blood flush. Glands did what glands do.

Penelope.

If the girl passing while he and PJ pissed in the hallway had not accepted their spontaneous party invitation, he would not have met her.

He ordered her a glass of wine.

She almost never drank.

Who knows why?

He did not remember seeing her more than slightly tipsy. For him, alcohol was necessary to blur his eyes like a fog holding back storm clouds gathering on the ridge of the hill. Alcohol was a curtain insulating him from reality—needed to dull his sharpened thoughts. Otherwise, he'd be like a disturbed psychopath obsessed with giving himself a blowjob.

A second glass of wine.

Penelope became more talkative and blabbered all sorts of things he normally never listened to. This time however, he was alert to all the details—the inflections of her voice and the way the wind moved the hair on her forehead—the way her breasts swelled with every breath—the way her monologue was interrupted by a smile or the wine glass reaching her lips.

Like a dying man in the desert, he craved every drop of Cabernet tickling his throat. The draughts made him think of a powerful ejaculation. His heart beat like kettle drums announcing a powerful orchestral climax.

Penelope.

If the sad girl passing while he and PJ pissed in the hallway had not stopped and turned back, he would never have met her. She must have been lonely.

What other woman would accept an invitation from a man pissing in a hallway?

Dusk brought a shiver—a welcome coolness in the atmosphere. The wind blew in a certain direction as if created by a thousand unseen birds flying and moving columns of air with invisible wings. He finished the wine and thought about drinking more but decided it was better to quit now. He was sure there was a full bottle back home.

She touched his hand—squeezing his fingers against her dainty palm. In moments like this he felt as if her spirit flowed between them—directly absorbed by his skin and streaming through his veins straight into his heart.

While paying the check, he threw an illegal stare at the undulating ass of the waitress. His mood changed. Later, when he kissed Penelope, he felt like an innocent prisoner sentenced to death in a horrible miscarriage of justice.

The night descended like a black dress on the city's fat body. The stars above resembled an expensive, imaginary necklace, like ones admired in London behind Harrods' window.

They stopped several times to look at the sky and kiss. He did not choose it, but his hungry pores, like suckers on an octopus, absorbed her essence. He swallowed every breath and kiss as if they were the only things keeping him alive. His skin tingled and made him feel as if he was no longer in control of his body.

Penelope.

If the girl passing while he and PJ pissed had not pretended not to notice the crude, animal act they performed in the darkened hallway, he would have never met her.

In his room there was no bed, just a mattress he'd paid a fortune for laying directly on the floor. A collection of shelves stretched across the wall around the television set, which was used only to watch a movie now and then. In the corner, there was a chair and a writing desk. The remaining space was occupied by a huge mess—one that men claim as a sign of bohemian creativity. Most women do not believe this, but it is said a man should not trust anything women say because their minds are like the IP address on a router—changing every ten seconds.

At home, he opened the wine and poured two glasses. He gulped half a glass with greed. Penelope stood close and threw her arms around his neck and hopped into his arms. He quivered under her weight, but pulled her to his chest— seeking her mouth as if it were an oxygen mask. He parted her lips, penetrating her toothy defenses with his tongue while his body shook like a tall building in an earthquake, crumbling from the top floor all the way to the ground. He reached a hand below. Between her legs, he felt as if his saliva had already reached her vagina.

Penelope.

If he went out for coffee and waited for her to leave instead of shaking his bed so the girl in it fell into his arms— this wet morning would never have come.

Keeping her on top, he waddled back to the mattress and fell on his back. Slipping fingers through her hair, he kissed her and sought her mouth as a cave hidden in the mountains, a cool, wholesome place where he could hide from the heat. Hot air warmed his lungs—descending below his belt and igniting his insides like the light reflected in a water glass left on the kitchen table beside the window.

Penelope.

If PJ and his hookup did not leave the party to go to the chick's place—leaving him to entertain Penelope alone, the glass by the window would have never been so full of light.

The coils of his orgasm found warm release, but then, as

always, their shared fluids cooled.

Suddenly, he had a vision. They were husband and wife and had been married for years. No children, though she desperately wanted them. There was an unbridgeable gulf between them; both were bored with their nonexistent sex life. Their relationship was a crime neither were guilty of committing. Sooner or later, out of need for affection or the self-destructive desire for a change, they would do the other wrong.

While immersed in this thought, he lit a cigarette and sipped tepid wine.

When he looked at her, her smile changed—hanging on the upper corners of her mouth like shadows—as if she read his thoughts and morphed into a witch. After finishing his cigarette, the tension in his body returned. He wanted to be somewhere far away.

Alienation will settle between us like a cobweb. Let us cleanse our hearts now and purify them through another fire with another love and more life—stronger and better.

The force behind his thoughts flabbergasted him.

She carefully sewed together the pieces of their relationship with fine silver thread. In reply to the words he did not speak, she whispered like a breeze through trees.

"There is nothing old that cannot be renewed."

A more pleasant image filled his mind: the clench and release of muscles in the waitresses' ass.

"It's too early to sleep," he said. "I'm going out."

Penelope.

Had he not spoken to the lonely girl passing as he and PJ pissed in the hallway…he could barely remember what he'd said.

But, she remembered.

"You are the most beautiful woman in the world."

In that dim hallway, she stopped and turned with hope written on her face.

"Me?" she said. "Me?"

Penelope.

Notes on *Penelope Waits*

KLC: This is probably due to a criminal lack of imagination, but if a character is named Penelope, then I will automatically think of the Homeric legend.

> *The wife of Odysseus in classical mythology. Penelope remained true to her husband for the ten years he spent fighting in the Trojan War and for the ten years it took him to return from Troy, even though she was harassed by men who wanted to marry her. She promised to choose a suitor after she had finished weaving a shroud for her father-in-law, but every night she unraveled what she had woven during the day. After three years, her trick was discovered, but she still managed to put her suitors off until Odysseus returned and killed them.*[18]

The legend of Penelope is symbolic of patience and faithfulness. Do you think patience and loyalty like this is ever rewarded in real life?

AP: Rewarded? No. I don't think our society looks at the old model of matrimony with the slightest sympathy. Women are taught to be tough and equal to men. A docile wife weaving

---

[18] From *The American Heritage New Dictionary of Cultural Literacy*, Third Edition, 2005, Houghton Mifflin Company.

her weight in textile would be perceived as a bore, and frankly, if you came home after years at sea would you feel excitement to be back to square one?

I reread the legend and I'm uneasy about it. Old Penelope speaks through the ages about honor, peace, the sanctity of a promise and the absolute value of love. But I know the world we live in. How many modern Ulysses would tie themselves to a ship's mast to avoid beautiful naked and willing sirens?

KLC: Uh, none? I think our modern morality is defined by pop culture. The Stephen Stills song comes to mind:

> Well, there's a rose in the fisted glove
> And the eagle flies—with the dove
> And if you can't be with the one you love, honey
> Love the one you're with...[19]

AP: I refuse to function on that premise.

Call me naïve, idealistic, stupid—call me anything you want, but love in its true, ideal form needs to survive.

> *There is always some madness in love. But there is also always some reason in madness.*
> —Friedrich Nietzsche

Can I respond to the quote of the great philosopher Stills with another from Nietzsche?

> *What else is love but understanding and rejoicing in the fact that another person lives, acts, and experiences otherwise than we do...?*

---

[19] Stephen Stills, Sony/ATV Music Publishing LLC

KLC: This story shows two authors. What can you say about the contributions we made to this tale? Did you ever want to scream and slap me for molesting your work?

AP: Molest my work? Is that a joke? An engineer compresses the words into exactness—that's why I don't worry about sharing my ideas. We're trying something different. We'll ram them into the readers' heads together.

I admire Oscar Wilde and often find myself smirking at his words and cynical thoughts.

> *A man can be happy with any woman as long as he does not love her.*
> —Oscar Wilde

What do you think?

KLC: Can I be a cynic and a hopeless romantic at the same time? Much of the time, it seems impossible for men and women to coexist—then my wife hands me a cup of hot coffee and the world seems to be in perfect harmony.

We're absurd animals so it does not pay to take ourselves too seriously. On the other hand, what else do we have? We exist. We are. I refuse to give in to self-loathing and nihilism.

One thing I like about this story is the evolution of our understanding of the origin of the couple's relationship. By the end, we understand why sad Penelope is attracted to a pathetic drunk pissing in the hallway. There is poetic repetition and a slow unveiling of the whole story. This seems like a delicate thing; something hard to conceive and nurture. Do you feel a deep satisfaction when a story transcends the words and...works?

AP: Here's a simple answer: yes. Transcending the unconventional is what I had in mind with Penelope. Like you said, we are ridiculous animals. We fall in love for reasons hard to understand by anybody else, even ourselves.

> Never pretend to a love which you do not actually
> feel, for love is not ours to command.
> —Alan Watts

How honest can we be with ourselves—or with anyone else?

> A little sincerity is a dangerous thing, and a great
> deal of it is absolutely fatal.
> —Oscar Wilde

Penelope does not express her thoughts clearly, but her manipulative lover sees through her—and takes advantage.